Madge moved close, rested her warm hand on Judd's forearm.

The touch seared his nerves, stung his thoughts and made him waver. But God's justice took too long. His mother shouldn't have to wait.

"Judd. I like that name. Suits you so much better than Justin."

He covered her hand with his. "I like it better, too." Especially the way she said it.

"Judd, I don't want to see you hurt by taking on the role of avenger."

Caught in her steady gaze, he couldn't argue.

But he couldn't agree either.

"I'll not do anything wrong."

She lowered her eyes, leaving him floundering for determination about his course of action.

"I pray you will learn God's way is best."

He squeezed her fingers. "I appreciate that."

Neither of them moved. She kept her head down. He let himself explore the feel of her hand beneath his— strong from hard work and yet soft. Just like Madge herself.

Linda Ford

The Cowboy Tutor
&
The Cowboy
Comes Home

LOVE INSPIRED
INSPIRATIONAL ROMANCE

LOVE INSPIRED®
INSPIRATIONAL ROMANCE

Recycling programs for this product may not exist in your area.

ISBN-13: 978-1-335-47441-4

The Cowboy Tutor & The Cowboy Comes Home

Copyright © 2020 by Harlequin Books S.A.

The Cowboy Tutor
First published in 2012. This edition published in 2020.
Copyright © 2012 by Linda Ford

The Cowboy Comes Home
First published in 2012. This edition published in 2020.
Copyright © 2012 by Linda Ford

This edition published by arrangement with Harlequin Books S.A.

For questions and comments about the quality of this book, please contact us at CustomerService@Harlequin.com.

Love Inspired
22 Adelaide St. West, 40th Floor
Toronto, Ontario M5H 4E3, Canada
www.Harlequin.com

Printed in U.S.A.

CONTENTS

Linda Ford lives on a ranch in Alberta, Canada, near enough to the Rocky Mountains that she can enjoy them on a daily basis. She and her husband raised fourteen children—four homemade, ten adopted. She currently shares her home and life with her husband, a grown son, a live-in paraplegic client, and a continual (and welcome) stream of kids, kids-in-law, grandkids, and assorted friends and relatives.

Books by Linda Ford

Love Inspired Historical

Big Sky Country

Montana Cowboy Daddy
Montana Cowboy Family
Montana Cowboy's Baby
Montana Bride by Christmas
Montana Groom of Convenience
Montana Lawman Rescuer

Montana Cowboys

The Cowboy's Ready-Made Family
The Cowboy's Baby Bond
The Cowboy's City Girl

Visit the Author Profile page
at Harlequin.com for more titles.

THE COWBOY TUTOR

What doth the Lord require of thee, but to do justly, and to love mercy, and to walk humbly with thy God?
—*Micah* 6:8

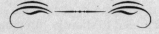

This book is in special memory of my mother, who faced many challenges, including the Great Depression, tuberculosis and being mother to a blended family. As I read her journals and the articles she wrote, I see a woman who was hurt time and again by events and by the people she loved, and yet she determined to show nothing but kindness. Seeing her life through her eyes has given me a deep appreciation for her spirit.

May her children arise and call her blessed.

Chapter One

Golden Prairie, Alberta, Canada
Summer, 1932

Madge Morgan groaned as steam billowed from the hood of the old clunker that served as car, truck and general chore vehicle. "Why couldn't you save your cantankerous behavior for two more blocks?" So close to her destination, yet so far. And she was late. Mrs. Crebs, her best and most demanding customer, had already warned Madge she wouldn't pay to have her laundry done unless it was delivered spotless and on time.

Madge glanced about. She could either trudge back to the center of town and the public pump for water for the radiator and get to the Crebses' late, or trundle down the street with the bundle of laundry. And still be late.

Her heavy sigh lifted her unruly bangs and provided a welcome breeze to her brow.

Better late than never. She only hoped Mrs. Crebs would agree. At least she couldn't complain about the condition of her clothing and household articles. They were crisp and spotless.

She grabbed the bundle, staggering under the weight of six sets of sheets, all nicely pressed and folded, and an amazing collection of table linens, trousers and starched shirts, all done exactly as Mrs. Crebs desired. She draped the girls' fresh dresses over her arm and plowed toward the imposing Crebs house. The stack blocked her view, but the path was straight and level right up to the front steps. Of course, she would dutifully take her armload around to the back door.

The wind pushed her dress about her legs and fought for ownership of the pile of laundry. A pair of sheets slithered sideways. Madge struggled to keep everything together. She should have tied the bundle with twine, but she hadn't expected to trundle it down the street. She hurried on her way.

And hit a wall, staggered back and lost control of her load. "No!" Her wail was far from ladylike, but she was past caring as the laundry landed in the dirt, little clouds of dust greeting its arrival.

"No. No." She swallowed back the scream tearing at her throat. No sense in announcing her problems to the neighborhood.

She saved her fury and frustration for the source of her problem—the wall shuddering her to a halt—a living, breathing wall that grunted at her impact. "Look what you've done."

Black eyes snapped. She was certain he saw more than an ordinary man, and she almost quivered. Almost.

She knew she'd never forget their intensity…nor the surprise in his voice giving it such deep tones.

"Me? You personally own this sidewalk or something?" He picked up his battered cowboy hat and slapped it against his leg before cramming it on his head, restricting his dark, overlong hair to a thick fringe around the brim. He had a square forehead and a firm mouth.

She suddenly remembered his question. "I own my share. What are you doing in the middle of the way?"

"Standing here. Minding my own business. Is that a criminal offense? First I heard of it."

"Not criminal. Just…dumb." The accident wasn't his fault, and this whole conversation bordered on the absurd. "These things are as dirty as mud." Mrs. Crebs was going to have a kitten. Probably a whole batch of them, squalling and demanding attention. Nothing to do but pick up the items and try to explain what happened. She reached for the scattered articles, now tossed into disarray by the relentless wind.

Seems the man had a similar notion and bent at exactly the same moment. They cracked heads.

"Ow." She straightened and rubbed her brow.

"Ouch." He grabbed after his hat, getting away in the incessant breeze.

The wind increased, picked up gritty dirt and pelted them. They turned their backs into the attack and waited for it to pass.

She scooped up flapping laundry. The starched-and-ironed tablecloth was no longer gleaming white. Mrs. Crebs would be offended, especially when she heard the whole thing had been witnessed in amusement by a couple of men on the sidewalk and several ladies peeking from their windows.

The man responsible for her predicament reached for a starched and now crumpled shirt. She snatched it from him.

"Only trying to help," he murmured, sounding faintly amused.

"You've already done enough." How was she going to explain this?

Despite her protests, he helped gather up garments and piled them in her arms. Fabric draped and flapped over her shoulders. She hesitated, annoyance and worry warring with good manners.

"You're welcome," the man said, grinning widely.

It wasn't his fault. Yet whom else could she blame?

The foolishness of trying to place responsibility for this whole situation on anyone or anything was as silly as trying to attribute the drought, the depressed prices and life in general to someone. Her life, her future, was in God's hands. Not man's. Amusement smoothed her annoyance and relaxed her eyes.

He must have seen the change in her. His grin deepened.

She assessed this stranger. Handsome. Holding himself with strength and confidence. She'd already noted his dark eyes and how they probed. Realizing she stared, she looked away. "Sorry," she gulped and slowly brought her gaze back to his. His wide grin erased the last flickers of annoyance, and she chuckled. "I don't always run full force into strangers. Nor do I usually take out my frustrations on unsuspecting visitors. It's just been that kind of day. I apologize."

He touched the brim of his hat. "Not a problem. We all have our share of troubles these days."

"Far too true." If she didn't take care of Mrs. Crebs, her difficulties would multiply several times. She tore her gaze away from the stranger and paused. "Are you staying in town?" Heat stung her eyes at the boldness of her question. Quickly, she added, "If so, welcome." She fled with her embarrassment. Now the man would think her both cranky and a dolt.

Her feet slowed as the Crebses' house came into view. *Lord, help me be gracious. Help Mrs. Crebs be charitable and give me another chance.* She sucked in a deep breath that did little to calm her nerves, and knocked on the back door.

Mrs. Crebs yanked it open as if she'd been waiting for Madge. Madge knew she would have been staring at the big clock hanging on the wall and clacking her fingernails against the table as she waited. "You're late again. It's inexcusable." Then she saw her laundry and shrieked.

Madge grimaced at the shrill sound, then hurried to explain. "I had an accident. I'm sorry. I'll take everything home and do it over. I promise it will be spotless."

Mrs. Crebs snatched articles from Madge. "You've ruined my best tablecloth."

"I'll fix it." She would fall on her knees and beg for another chance if it would do any good.

"Don't bother. I've given you more than enough chances. I'll find someone else. Someone I can trust.

I've never heard of the Chinaman dumping laundry in the dirt."

The door slammed in Madge's face. Mrs. Crebs, with her five children, had been Madge's best customer. Without the few dollars she made doing the Crebses' washing, Madge would never scrape together enough for the upcoming mortgage payment.

The future looked bleak.

However, she would not entertain defeat. Somehow, with hard work and perseverance, she would earn the money. *Lord, open up another opportunity for me. Please.*

With no reason to hurry, she didn't dash back to the car. Instead, she went out the back gate and headed for the church to pray. She desperately needed God's help.

Judd Kirk watched the woman rush down the street. That had been an interesting encounter. The first thing he'd noticed about her—aside from the alarm on her face as the stack of linens had tumbled to the ground—had been the mass of wavy brown hair tugged by the wind. Her brown eyes had flashed as if driven by an inner urgency. He recognized the feeling…he'd personally dealt with his own inner force for the past year. She hurried down the street as if chasing after something beyond her reach.

He shifted his stance to study the reason he stood here. The silent house. Obviously still empty. For how long? He'd searched for the man since he'd returned home, as soon as his brother had informed him of the details. This was the closest he'd come to locating him—a house he understood had been rented by the one he sought.

He glanced around. Someone stood at a front gate and called across to a fellow sauntering down the sidewalk. Called him by name. They both watched Judd—noting the stranger in their midst. Golden Prairie was small enough that a fellow hanging about for no apparent reason would attract attention. And speculation. Notice would make him conspicuous and likely alert his prey to his presence.

Not something he needed or wanted. But he intended to stay until he completed his business. Best, however, if he blended into the surroundings.

What he needed was a job allowing him to hang around without raising questions.

Turning, he headed back toward the main street. The storekeeper would know what work was available, preferably out of town yet close enough to allow him to watch this place.

He clumped along the wooden sidewalk and stepped into the store. Dust hung in the air. The scent of leather and coal stung his nostrils. The shelves carried a good array of canned and dry goods. But the whole place held an air of defeat—much like the land around him. And its occupants. "Afternoon."

"Uh-huh." The bespectacled man nodded and gave him a long, unblinking study. "You another of Mrs. Morgan's prospects?"

Judd had no idea what the man meant, but it seemed a trail that might lead somewhere. He would follow it and see. "Could be."

"Well, you ain't the first. In fact—" He tipped his head and seemed to count something on the inside of his eyelids. "Lesse, a young fella went out just a bit ago. He was number four. I guess that makes you number five."

"Seems a lot." But he didn't know what they were talking about, so he had no idea if it was or not. Perhaps, with a little leading, the storekeeper would spare the information.

"Mrs. Morgan is a mite particular, especially concerning her eldest daughter, Miss Louisa. Frail she is. Not like Miss Madge. There she goes now." He nodded toward the window at a vehicle chugging along, coughing and complaining.

In the car sat the young woman who, a short while ago, had steamed into Judd. Madge, the man said. Madge Morgan. Somehow the name suited her. Determined despite disagreeable odds.

The storekeeper languidly continued. "Now, there's a hard worker. Ain't nothing goin' to stop her. No, siree. That gal has been fighting for a decent livelihood since Mr. Morgan died. Doin' mighty fine, too."

Judd followed the car's erratic passage past the store. A fighter. And pretty, too. He brought his attention back to the information the storekeeper had hinted at. "What's Mrs. Morgan looking for in particular?"

"Just what it says in the advertisement. Here it is if you need to refresh your memory." He pointed to a newspaper clipping tacked by the cash register. "Don't think she wanted us to know what she was up to but my brother found the ad in the city paper and sent me a copy."

Judd leaned over to read:

WANTED: A GOOD MAN TO TEACH IN-
VALID LADY FINER ASPECTS OF LAN-
GUAGES AND ARTS. ROOM AND BOARD
IN EXCHANGE FOR LESSONS. MUST BE A
TRUE GENTLEMAN.

"A tutor?" Never expected that.

"Miss Louisa's interested in learning."

"How old is Miss Louisa?"

"Well, lessee. I think Miss Madge must be eighteen
now, though she has more smarts than many twice her
age. I guess that would make Miss Louisa nineteen.
The three girls are pretty close in age."

"Three?"

"Yup. There's Sally, too. Guessin' she's seventeen.
Miss Louisa's the prettiest, but in my opinion, Miss
Madge, now she's the one a man should consider. Why,
if I was twenty years younger…"

Judd stared as the man's voice trailed off and red
crept up his neck before he cleared his throat and shifted
away.

"You say there's been plenty of interest in the job."

"Mrs. Morgan is particular. Hey, lookee, there's number four now. Maybe ask him how it went."

"I guess I might." In private. He left the store, strode
toward the approaching car and signaled the man to
stop. "Hear you were out to the Morgan place."

"Indeed I was. A most promising situation. I didn't
meet Miss Morgan, but I understand she is frail but

eager with a goodly desire to learn. I believe her inter-ests lean toward art history and literature, though I'm certain with a little guidance she will develop an equal keenness for science and Latin." He rubbed his hands together in anticipation. "The mother is overprotec-tive, which might pose a handicap, but I believe I could have success in overcoming that." He sat up straighter, though he was small, so his effort to look important lacked impact.

"Well, good luck to you." Judd stepped back and as-sessed the information as the man drove away. His years in university might prove productive after all, even if he hadn't pursued being a teacher.

Yes, indeed, this job would serve his purposes very well.

A week later Madge sang as she hung another batch of laundry. Father had had no idea how the big room upstairs would be used, strung now with row after row of lines, providing a place to dry things away from the invading dust carried by the relentless winds buffeting the house and all God's creatures.

It was her number one selling point in her offer to do laundry for others—the promise of sparkling white linens. The only way she could guarantee that was by hanging them indoors, out of the dust-laden wind.

She finished pegging the sheet on the line, removed the earlier items, now dry, and started ironing. Her pet cat, Macat, who kept her company as she worked, set-tled on the nearby stool and began a grooming ritual.

Doing laundry day after day was hard, relentless

work, but it was satisfying to produce stacks of fresh sheets and crisp shirts she delivered in town to those people who still had money to pay for her services. Thank God for the few who seemed unaffected by the Depression. The coins she earned slowly collected in the old coffee can downstairs.

Through the open window she watched Sally dump the bucket of kitchen scraps to the chickens, then pause to look around. Her younger sister was quiet and content. Louisa, her older sister, seemed satisfied with her life, as well. Madge was the one with a restless drive to get things done. Without Madge's constant prodding and working, the others might be lulled into complacency until the house was taken from them, never letting the specter of being homeless cross their minds. Even Mother's concern didn't match Madge's determination that the family not end up in such a state.

Madge had managed to persuade one more lady to let her do part of her laundry—only the sheets and table linens, which she hesitated to hang out in the dust. Madge appreciated the job but it didn't make up for the loss of wages her work for Mrs. Crebs had brought in.

As she folded items, she muttered to Macat, who watched her every move. "It's going to be close." In fact, too close for comfort after having been forced to buy a new tire for the car. She clattered down the stairs, Macat meowing at her heels. She ignored the cat's demands, paused on her way through the kitchen to say hello to Sally, who sat surrounded by the mending, and Louisa in her lounge chair reading, with her little dog, Mouse, curled on her lap.

Madge hurried to the front room and Father's desk. She opened the drop lid, scooped up the coffee can, sat down and slowly counted the change and few bills. Her cheeks grew taut, and she felt the heat seep from them. "It's not all here." She couldn't believe it. Who would steal from their savings?

She scooped up Macat and held her close, comforting herself in the silky fur.

Mother paused at the doorway. "Madge?"

Madge struggled to form a thought. A word. "The money. Missing. Stolen."

Mother slipped into the room and closed the door behind her. She patted Madge's shoulder. "It's okay. I took it. I meant to tell you but I—"

"Took it? Why?"

Mother glanced around to make sure they were alone, then whispered. "For Louisa."

"More medicine?" Madge wouldn't resent the expense. Louisa had had pneumonia a number of times. The disease left her lungs weak and required all of them to guard her health. Sometimes it seemed, no matter how hard Madge worked, Louisa's illness ate up way too much of the money. Or the car bit into their savings—though she had figured out how to fix tires on her own, how to adjust the throttle and choke and how to wire things together in hopes they would limp through a few more days. She wished they still had a horse so she could resort to using a wagon. Mentally, she put it on the list. Perhaps someone would trade a horse for her labors. Then she'd need to figure out a way to get enough hay for another animal. She kept her attention on scratch-

ing Macat behind the ears, afraid Mother would see her
worry and frustration if she lifted her head.

"Not medicine, dear."

"Then what?" Medicine she understood. What else
could there be? Though Mother had a habit of under-
estimating the expenses and the limited resources for
earning money. Father had always protected Mother
from the harsh realities of life, so even in these hard
times, Mother remained optimistic, always believing
things would somehow, as if by magic, fix themselves.

"I want to help Louisa find a husband."

"You bought a man?" Madge couldn't decide if she
was more intrigued or shocked. How did one go about
purchasing a man? How much did it cost? Did you get
to select size, color, style? Her thoughts flitted unexpectedly to the man she had bumped into in town. She
blinked away the memory of black eyes and dark hair
and returned to considering Mother's announcement.

If one bought a man, was there a money-back guarantee?

Mother pulled a clipping from her pocket and hesitated. "You must promise not to say anything."

"Certainly." Her curiosity grew to overwhelming
proportions.

Mother unfolded the scrap of paper and handed it to
her. "I placed this ad in a paper."

Madge read the notice. Then she read it again.
Mother had advertised for a teacher for Louisa. "It says
nothing about marriage."

Mother sat in Father's chair—a sure sign of her mental state. Madge watched her closely. Was she hiding something?

"You know there are no eligible young men around. Most of them are in relief camps."

Madge nodded. The government had created camps for the unemployed young men where they built roads, cut trees and did a number of labor jobs. The idea of work camps was fine. Give young men a place to sleep, food to eat and a job. Get them off the streets. But to her thinking, it only hid the problem. She bit her tongue to keep from saying what she thought of many of the prime minister's political moves. Surely a smart man, a man from their own province even, could do something to stop this horrible decline.

Mother continued. "The rest are riding the rails, hoping to find a job somewhere or trying to avoid the relief camps." She sighed long and hard. "I simply can't stand by and let Louisa turn into an old maid, having to depend on her sisters to take care of her as she gets older."

"Ma, she's only nineteen." She smiled as Macat jerked her head up and meowed as if agreeing with her.

"I was married and had her by that age."

"I know." Those were different times. Mother knew as well as anyone. No point in reminding her. "So the money...?"

"I used it to buy the ad for a tutor."

"You actually found someone?"

"I did. A very nice man who starts today."

Madge opened her mouth. Shut it with an audible click. Tried again. "You did all this behind my back?"

Mother smiled gently. "I felt I had to do something. I

know we need the money for the payment, but I thought the wages from Mrs. Crebs and the other jobs you've picked up would be enough." She paused a beat. "On my part, I can cut down on expenses. We don't need meat as often as we've been eating it. We'll trust God to provide and do our best to live wisely." Her look begged Madge to understand.

None of them had expected Mrs. Crebs to be so miffed.

She squeezed Mother's hands. "And this man you hired?"

"He seems ideal for Louisa—gentle, well-educated.... I know I can count on you to do everything you can to help me in this. But please don't say anything to Louisa about my ulterior motives. You know how offended she'd be."

Madge nodded, even though she felt as if she had hung her sister from a tree to be plucked like ripe fruit. "You're sure he's a good gentleman?"

"If he's not, I will personally run him off the place with a hot poker."

Madge chuckled at the sudden spurt of spunk her mother revealed. Sometimes she suspected she and Mother were more alike than Mother cared to confess. "I'll do what I can to help the cause, but if I suspect he's not suitable, I will be right at your side with another hot poker."

The two of them laughed. Mother patted Madge's hand. "I can always count on you." Her expression faltered. "However, I didn't expect my decision would come at such a bad time."

Madge couldn't bear to have her mother worried. "I'm sure things will work out." She wouldn't burden her mother with the fear rippling up her spine.

Mother nodded, accepting Madge's reassurance. "Now I best get back to the kitchen before the girls wonder what we're up to. By the way, the gentleman arrives this afternoon."

Madge waited for her departure, then studied the funds in the can. How was she to pay the mortgage? She'd have to find another job, earn more money, perhaps speak to the banker about a few days' grace. She rubbed the back of her neck. Where was she going to find someone willing and able to pay for any kind of work?

Lord, I can't help but worry. The idea of the four of us being out on the street is enough to cause me concern. Lord, it's beyond me to see how to fix this. However, I know You are in control. Please send an answer my way before we lose our house.

Maybe this tutor, poor unsuspecting man, might offer a future for Louisa. Madge giggled, picturing him. No doubt gray-haired and asthmatic. But Louisa would never pay a mind to such things so long as he was attentive and educated. She paused to pray he was everything Mother expected before she returned the can to the desk and closed the drop lid. Time to return to washing and ironing. She sat Macat on the floor and headed back upstairs with her pet purring at her heels.

A while later, dinner over, she hung about waiting for the arrival of the expected man.

Louisa had primped and put on her best.dress. She had gathered up her favorite books. "I'm going to ask him if he's read these. That way I'll know what we can talk about."

Madge never quite understood Louisa's fascination with books and ideas. Since she was small, Madge preferred to be outdoors. It turned out to be a good thing she'd followed her father relentlessly, begging to help. After his death three years ago, she stepped into his role and took care of the chores and so much more. They'd had to let most of the land go, but Madge had insisted they must keep enough for a milk cow and her calf. Again, she wished she'd kept a horse, as well. But looking back was useless.

Sally shoved aside the stockings she had been carefully darning. "I'm going to the garden to see if I can find any greens left after that last blow."

Mother stopped her. "Sally, I want you to meet this man first."

Sally sat back down with a soft sigh. Madge wanted to make her face life squarely. Why was Sally so shy? Seemed Madge had gotten too much boldness and Sally none.

"Very well, Mother," Sally murmured, twisting her hands and looking so miserable Madge had to quell her frustration. At least Mother didn't relent and let her go, as she often did.

Mother pulled aside the curtain. "He's coming." She sat down and feigned disinterest.

Not prepared to pretend she wasn't filled with curiosity, Madge planted herself in front of the window.

Macat climbed to the ledge to join her. "He's driving a Mercedes Roadster. About a 1929 model, if I'm not mistaken. Makes our old Model A look as pathetic as it is. He must have washed his car before he left town."

"Madge, get away from the window. He'll think we're spying."

"Mother, I am spying. And if he thinks we shouldn't be interested, well… He's getting out now." She laughed aloud. "And he's wiping the dust from the fenders. If he figures to keep his pretty car dust free he'll have a full-time job."

Louisa hissed. "Madge, stop staring. He'll think we have no manners."

"No. He'll think I have no manners. You'd never give him reason to think it of you."

Louisa giggled.

Madge didn't have to look to know her pretty sister had blushed becomingly. Everything Louisa did was pretty and becoming.

"I couldn't stand to work with a man who wasn't clean and tidy," Louisa said.

"Well, this one is downright fastidious. And he's headed this way." Madge turned from the window. But only to move toward the door to invite the man in. And give him a good once-over before she allowed him to spend time with her older sister.

She waited for the knock, then pulled the door open. The man before her sported a beard. His hair was short and tamed. His dusty suit hung on his body as if he'd recently lost weight. His subdued coloring supported the idea. He seemed faintly familiar. As she stared, he turned away and coughed.

"Excuse me, ma'am. I'm here to tutor Miss Louisa."

"Have we met before?"

He shook his head. "I don't think so."

"Didn't I run into you on the sidewalk a week ago? Literally."

"Ma'am. I'm sure I would recall such a thing."

She stared into dark eyes. They no longer probed, but she would never forget them. Yet no flicker of recognition echoed in the man's face.

Could she be mistaken? She tried to recall every detail of the encounter. Certainly this man looked tidier, wore schoolteacher clothes, and slouched—but the eyes. How could she be confused about them?

She hesitated, not yet inviting him in. What reason would he have for pretending she hadn't seen him before? And why did her heart feel shipwrecked at the idea of Mother choosing this man for Louisa?

Madge sucked in bracing air, straightened her shoulders and stepped back. She was not one to entertain fanciful ideas. Not Madge Morgan, who was practical to the core.

"Please, come in." Whoever he was, whatever he hid, she'd watch him so keenly he'd never succeed in doing anything but what he was meant to do—tutor Louisa.

Chapter Two

Judd knew she recognized him, but it was imperative he remain incognito. He'd grown his beard, cut his hair and changed his appearance as much as possible. He'd even found a suit coat that hung on him, hoping to persuade anyone who cared to notice that he'd lost a lot of weight. Of necessity he would give a false name, for if his prey heard his real one, he might suspect something. He did not want the man warned and cautious.

Mrs. Morgan joined her daughter. "Madge, this is the man I told you is to tutor Louisa. Justin Bellamy. Please come in, Mr. Bellamy."

Judd limped into the room. He figured a lame leg and poor lungs would complete his disguise.

He immediately saw the young woman who would be his pupil. A chinalike beauty in a pale pink dress sat beside a table laden with textbooks and sketch paper. A small white dog with black spots sat on her lap, studying Judd with interest. He figured Louisa's hands on the dog's back persuaded the animal not to go into attack mode. Though the dog would offer little threat.

"My daughter, Louisa."

Judd bowed. "Ma'am, I understand you're interested in furthering your education."

Louisa smiled—sweet and gentle—a marked contrast to the decisive study from Madge, who followed him across the room like a cat watching a pigeon, waiting for the right time to pounce.

He sucked in air and remembered to slouch as if it hurt to walk. She could play guard cat all she wanted. He refused to have his feathers ruffled.

As if to reinforce Judd's feeling of being stalked, a big gray cat jumped from the window ledge and sauntered over to examine the toes of his boots.

Louisa spoke, drawing his attention back to her. "I'd love to go to university. Unfortunately…" She trailed off, but he understood the many things she didn't say. It was too costly. Her health wouldn't allow it. It simply wasn't practical. But she was fortunate her mother cared enough about her thirst for knowledge to hire a tutor. He would do what he could to satisfy her.

"It's a stimulating environment. I'll do my best to share some of what I learned."

She leaned forward, eagerness pouring from her in waves. "I especially want to learn the history of the great artists. And if you would be so good as to…" Her voice fell to a whisper. "Tell me what it's like to be surrounded by so much learning, so much knowledge." As if uncomfortable with her burst of enthusiasm, she

ducked her head, but not before he'd seen the flood of
pink staining her cheeks.

"I'll do my very best."

To his left he could feel Madge building up a boiler
full of steam.

Mrs. Morgan saved them both from the explosion he
feared would sear the skin off him. "This is my youngest daughter, Sally."

Judd turned, noticed for the first time the younger
girl shrinking back against her chair at the far side of
the table.

Her gaze darted to him and away. Then she lifted
her head and gave him a sweet smile. "Welcome, Mr.
Bellamy."

"Justin, please." He'd never remember he was Mr.
Bellamy, but at least Justin started the same as Judd,
which is why he'd chosen the name. He remembered
to cough as he glanced around the circle of women.
Madge's gaze waited, hot and demanding. He gave his
most innocuous look, rounding his eyes in faux innocence.

"I'll show you to your quarters," Madge said, her
voice full of warning. "Then you can get to work."

"Yes, ma'am."

She pulled her lips into a terse expression, and her
eyes narrowed before she spun around.

He followed her swift stride outside, his own pace
slow and measured, though he fought an urge to march to
her side and match her step for step. As the wind blasted
him in the face, he gave a cough for good measure.

She waited by his car. "Get your things and follow me. It's just across the yard."

Mrs. Morgan had said he'd have his own private quarters when he spoke to her in town, having arranged an interview there. Another reason to convince him he wanted this job. He would be able to slip in and out unnoticed as he tracked his foe.

He followed her to a tiny house—one small window, a narrow door and a low roof. She opened the door and stepped inside with him at her heels. Only the wall facing the yard was boards. The others were sod. "It's a—"

"A soddie. Yes. The original house. I hope you'll be comfortable." The tone of her voice suggested she wished anything but. "The bed's made up. There're shelves for your belongings."

She'd been waving at things as she talked but now spun on him. Her gaze raked him. "I know you're the man I saw before. If you're up to no good, I'll soon enough find out."

"Miss Madge, you must be mistake—"

"Don't Miss Madge me, Justin Bellamy. Whatever your scheme, I'll not let you harm my family." She marched for the door—all of three steps away. "You'll be taking meals with us. Supper is at six, which gives you time to earn your keep by teaching Louisa something she wants to learn."

Judd watched her until she slammed into the house. Her suspicions were going to make his stay complicated, but he'd simply have to be extra cautious. He hated being dishonest, but he didn't have much choice.

He recalled Madge's anger when she'd plowed into

him on the sidewalk. Remembered how she'd relented and chuckled. Too bad she couldn't find humor in this situation. He'd love to hear her laugh again, see her eyes flash with amusement.

He flung his bag on the bed. He was not here to let pretty brown eyes confuse him. On the surface he was here to teach Louisa history and other subjects.

His real reason, however, would never take second place to his job. And if he felt any tug of regret that his dishonesty made an enemy out of Madge, he firmly ignored it.

Madge returned to the house. She'd been churning out clean sheets all morning and hauling them upstairs to hang and dry. She still had two more tubs to do, but she welcomed the chance to stomp up and down the stairs, huffing and puffing. Macat, sensing her mistress's mood, climbed to her perch on the stool and observed with narrowed eyes.

"I'll keep this to myself," she muttered to the cat. "No need to worry Mother or Sally or frighten Louisa, but that man is hiding something."

But what? And why did it make her so cross?

She hated herself for denying the truth and even more for admitting it, but since she'd bumped into him a week ago, she'd thought of him once or twice—dark, intense eyes full of honesty. Or so she'd believed. She snorted. "Honest, indeed. That man is lying through his teeth."

But then, so was she. Thought of him once or twice?

Ha. But she did not want to admit the truth… He came to her mind almost constantly.

She pretended she didn't notice him return from the cabin with two books under his arm. Instead, she rushed upstairs with the last load of wet laundry, and muttered protests as she hung the sheets.

Only when she was certain he would be ensconced in the front room with Louisa did she clatter down the stairs, rushing past the doorway without allowing herself to glance in. Macat followed at a leisurely pace, protesting Madge's haste.

Madge's emotions gave strength to her muscles, and she carried the wash water, two buckets at a time, to the garden where she rationed a drink to the few surviving plants. Whatever they raised was essential for providing adequate food, so she'd constructed wooden windbreaks around the plants in the hopes of nursing them through the dust storms and drought. Still, they didn't promise more than a bit of cabbage or a few scrawny potatoes.

She drove off the grasshoppers, only to watch hordes more replace them.

She paused from her labors to glance toward the heavens. *God, You see our situation and that of so many people. Please send relief. And make it possible for me to find more paying work or some source of income.*

Trusting God was difficult when the circumstances offered nothing but failure. But as long as she could remember, she'd made it a practice to trust Him. She never doubted His love. It was as solid as the Rock of Gibraltar—as Father had always said. His love surely meant He would meet their needs. Having a home seemed pretty essential to her, especially given that they had no male protection and Louisa was frail.

She drew in a deep breath and settled her assurance on God's provision before she returned to the washtubs and turned them over to dry. Until tomorrow, when she would begin another stack of laundry.

Finished with that part of the task, she stepped inside and paused to watch Louisa and Justin bent over a book. Harrumph. She knew he was hiding something.

Louisa glanced up, a glitter of pleasure in her eyes.

Instantly, guilt flooded Madge's lungs. Mother had approved this man. Decided he was an appropriate candidate for Louisa. Seeing Louisa's enjoyment after an hour shamed Madge. She had no reason to be so distrustful or so—

Lord, help me. Not only am I suspicious, but I am annoyed because I saw him first. Unless he has a stronger twin.

She could always hope.

By the time Madge had finished ironing and taken care of a few outdoor chores, Sally announced supper. Madge had decided to give Justin the benefit of the doubt until she had something more solid than a chance encounter on the street to base her suspicions on.

Mother and Sally had the meal almost ready, but Madge helped place the serving dishes on the table. She noted with a mixture of gratitude and annoyance that the extra plate had been placed besides Louisa's, which put Justin across from her. Not that it mattered where he sat, but perhaps this was the best place for him. From this position she could steal glances at him, perhaps catch something in his eyes he couldn't hide.

Besides the dark intensity she recalled.

Mother announced the meal was served, and they sat around the table, Justin taking the indicated spot. Knowing her expression would give away things she didn't want known—like interest and regret—she kept her head lowered until Mother said the blessing.

For a few minutes they were busy passing food. Somehow Mother and Sally managed to make their meager supplies stretch to satisfying meals. Tonight the hunk of meat she'd received in lieu of wages from one of her customers had been ground and mysterious ingredients added until it looked generous and succulent. The aroma had teased her taste buds for the past hour. Sally had managed to scrounge enough lamb's quarters for rich greens and had stolen new potatoes from under the plants in the garden. Two small, tasty nuggets each. Now, with a man sharing meals, they would have to make food go further. Justin Bellamy had better prove his worth.

Madge had almost balked at accepting the meat instead of getting the cash she needed, but tonight she was grateful for good food.

"This is wonderful," Justin said. "I haven't eaten this well in months."

"You can credit Sally with her inventiveness," Mother said.

Justin turned to Sally. "Thank you, Miss Sally."

Sally ducked her head. Always so painfully shy.

Madge supposed it came from being the youngest. Then she flashed Justin a bright smile. "You're welcome."

Madge studied Justin, assessing his reaction to Sally's gratitude. But he only gave a slight smile and a quick nod. Then, before she could look away, his gaze shot to her. "You have a very nice home."

She nodded. "No need to sound surprised."

"Madge!" Mother scolded.

But Justin laughed. "I'm not at all surprised."

Did she detect a hint of acknowledgement? As if admitting they'd met earlier?

"Tell me more about yourselves." He held Madge's gaze a moment longer, then shifted to include the others. "How long have you lived here?"

Madge held her tongue for almost a second, but she burst with insistent curiosity and the words poured forth. "Surely you and Louisa have discussed this." After all, they had sat almost head to head, undisturbed, all afternoon. A little sting of jealousy shocked her. She couldn't resent the time he spent with Louisa. That's why he was here.

"No. It's been strictly business."

Louisa blushed. "He told me of the first day in college when there are get-acquainted parties. He says within a few days it's easy to tell those who want to learn from those who only want to have fun. Or freedom from parental control." She drew in a rough breath. "I can't imagine wasting such an opportunity." Her sigh was long and shaky.

Madge stuffed back any remnants of resentment. She'd always been able to do what she wanted—work, run, play, ride—whereas Louisa's activities had been shaped by her weak lungs. She must not resent any scraps of happiness her sister found.

Not even if they involved a man like Justin—a man about whom she held suspicions and a lurking sense of something else, which would remain nameless and denied.

Mother took on the job of telling Justin about the family. "We moved here from the city of Edmonton six years ago. My husband wanted to farm. We bought this place and built a new house." She sighed. "In hindsight, perhaps we should have been satisfied with something much smaller, but at the time the economy was so bright. My husband died unexpectedly three years ago—just before the crash. At least he was spared that."

Somehow Madge didn't think Father would be as glad as Mother seemed to think. He'd surely have wanted to shepherd them through this crisis, see they were safe and sheltered. They needed him now like never before. But obviously the Lord thought otherwise.

"I'm sorry for your loss. I'm sure it's been tough to manage."

Justin sounded as if Mother's loss really mattered to him. Did he understand how hard life was? Truly, without assurance that God would take care of them, there were times Madge wondered how they would make it through another month.

"The situation is difficult for everyone. We are perhaps more fortunate than some," Mother said.

"How's that?"

Madge continued to study him, drawn inexorably by

the gentle concern in his voice. Their gazes touched, and he held the look for a moment before sliding away, leaving her feeling washed and exposed. She must guard her thoughts better, lest he guess at her confusion of interest and caution.

Mother spoke her name, and Madge shifted her attention to hear her words. "Madge has kept us all afloat."

Madge revealed nothing in her expression. None of the agony some of her decisions had caused as Mother explained how she'd negotiated a deal to give the bulk of their land to the bank in exchange for keeping the house and a mortgage they could manage. She might soon be forced to admit it was too much if God didn't provide an answer to her prayer for another job, another source of income.

After a few minutes she interrupted the discussion. "It's your turn. Tell us about your family and where you're from."

Judd hauled his thoughts to a halt. He didn't want the conversation focused on him. He'd tried to plan what he could reveal and what he must hide. Figured he had it worked out satisfactorily, but still he didn't like the thought of having to tell half-truths in order to keep his identity a secret. Besides, he'd enjoyed hearing how Madge managed to save their home. And not just save the home to live like paupers. These people ate decently and were together. Not everyone could claim such success.

His jaw tightened. His own mother could testify to

that, but it wasn't her fault things had turned out as they had.

Four pairs of eyes silently urged him to share. One pair, especially, challenged him. He'd tried to divide his attention equally among those at the table, but again and again, his gaze left the others to watch Madge. She wore a practical brown dress. Her glistening brown hair tumbled about as if it had a mind of its own.

Aware they waited for his answer, he pulled his thoughts back from concentrating on Madge. "My mother is a widow, too. She's had a difficult time because of the reversal of her fortunes."

Mrs. Morgan sighed. "The crash hit so many people. Now the drought is touching even those who had no money to lose in the first place. On top of that, the low prices for our products…why, wheat is down to twenty-eight cents a bushel. How can farmers hope to survive?"

They all shook their heads. He let them think his mother had lost everything in the collapse of the financial markets. Only in her case, it was a scoundrel who'd brought about her personal crash.

Mrs. Morgan continued. "At least she has you to help."

"And three more sons."

"Four boys?" Mrs. Morgan perked up.

He wondered if she regretted having only daughters.

"I expect your mother is well taken care of."

"She is now." Shoot. He shouldn't have said "now." Four pairs of eyebrows shot upwards, and four pairs of eyes demanded an explanation. Aware of an especially intense gaze from across the table, he turned to Mrs.

Morgan, afraid his emotions might reveal themselves despite his best intentions. Could he explain without giving away more than was safe? "We didn't realize how badly she needed help. She had too much pride to confess it. Somehow she managed to hide it even from Levi, who is still living at home."

"Tell us about your brothers. Is Levi the youngest?"

"Yes. He's seventeen. Redford is the next one. He's teaching. Has been for…well, he's twenty-three, so I guess he's been teaching four years now. Then Carson is a lawyer. He's a year younger than I am."

"How old would that make him?" Madge demanded.

Judd tucked away a smile. Curious about him, was she? Even though she watched him with as much concentration as did Louisa's small dog. "Carson is twenty-five."

They studied each other across the table, measuring, assessing. He wished he didn't have to conceal the truth about who he was. But he did. Determination stiffened his muscles, making his mouth tighten.

Her eyes narrowed. "How did you hurt your leg?"

"Madge!" Mrs. Morgan sounded as if she couldn't believe her daughter, though whether because her question was so bold or because of the hint of mockery in her voice.

"I got thrown from a wild horse." At least that part was true.

Louisa gasped. "A wild horse? Why would you be riding such a creature?"

"My job was to break him. I decided to do it the fast way. Only it proved to be the slow way for me. Someone else had to finish the job while I lay around recuperating." Again, that part was true.

Madge squinted at him. "I thought you were a teacher. Isn't that why you went to university?"

He chuckled, pleased he confounded her with the truth. "After a year of teaching I realized I didn't really like the job, so I let Redford apply for the position and I headed to the foothills. That's where I was when my mother lost her home." If he'd been around, he might have seen what was happening. Perhaps been able to stop it.

Instead, he'd been away, unaware of events, but he aimed to right things as best he could now. The man responsible for his mother's loss would not escape without somehow paying. Judd didn't much care how, so long as he paid. He'd watch the man, see what he planned, who he picked for his next victim, then confront him, expose him to one and all, make him own the truth and then turn him over to the law. He wondered if the courts would make him repay his victims. Sometimes he considered taking the law into his own hands but so far had listened to the voice of reason—or moderation, perhaps—drilled into him by his mother.

"Where is your mother living now?"

Mrs. Morgan's question pulled him back to the watchful interest of Madge and the quiet curiosity of her sisters. "Mother and Levi found a good home with Carson in Regina, Saskatchewan."

"I'm glad. It must be a relief for her."

"And me."

Mrs. Morgan's gaze softened. "Your mother is blessed to have sons who care about her."

"She's doubly blessed. Her faith has never faltered. She's certain God will take care of her no matter what." She'd repeated the words over and over as she tried to make Judd understand the man who stole her money shouldn't be hunted down and tied to a fence to dry. "'God,' she'd said, 'is in control. He will see to justice.'"

"As do I," Mrs. Morgan said. "Girls, I want to assure you I interviewed Justin at length about his faith, and he convinced me he is a strong believer."

At her faith in him, guilt burned up Judd's throat. He certainly believed in God, had become a Christian when he was only eight, but he wasn't willing to sit back and wait for God to take care of things that were in his power to deal with. Like the man who stole his mother's life savings.

"Where were you when you broke your leg?" Madge sounded like Carson with his best lawyer voice. Her question was more than a question; it was a demand for an explanation.

"On a ranch in the foothills of Alberta."

"A cowboy." She sounded as if that explained everything.

His heart fell as he realized his words verified her suspicions about meeting him on the street a week ago when he'd been dressed as a cowboy rather than a teacher. In hindsight, it might have been better to disguise that fact. But it was too late now. Somehow he had to convince her—all of them—he was no longer a cowboy. He shrugged and remembered to cough. "It seemed like a good idea at the time, but it's not as romantic and adventuresome as one might think. It's mostly hard, unrelenting work that wears many a man down to the bone." He spoke the truth—a relief to his burning conscience, though it wasn't an opinion he shared.

"Wouldn't the fresh air be good for your lungs?" Madge asked, her voice signaling a touch of disbelief.

"Madge, I'm sure Justin doesn't care to have his health problems as part of our conversation."

Madge gave her mother an apologetic smile, then fixed Judd with an uncompromising look. He didn't claim any special powers at reading a woman's mind, but he got her loud and clear. She silently warned him she would be challenging everything he said and did.

He would have to guard his words and steps carefully.

She pulled her gaze away and pushed back from the table. "It's getting late. I've lingered too long. Sally, Mother, do you mind if I don't assist with dishes tonight? I still have to get the cow and calf home and milk the cow. I have laundry to deliver to two customers as well as pickup for tomorrow's customers."

"I'll help you." Judd pushed back, then remembered his frail health and struggled with getting his breath. He'd watched her pack heavy baskets of wet laundry up the stairs. Fought an urge to assist as she'd emptied the tubs.

"No need."

Louisa released a sigh, causing Judd to think she'd been holding her breath for a long time. "I wondered if we could do more lessons tonight."

"Louisa, I don't want you overtaxed," Mrs. Morgan said. "Besides, I told Justin he would have the evenings to do as he wished."

"Of course, Mother."

Judd already realized how hungry Louisa was to learn. If the students he'd had in school had been half as eager, he might have found teaching a little more rewarding. But even then it wouldn't have satisfied his love of wide-open spaces. Ranching had called to him. It was still in his blood. As soon as he finished with this other business, he'd head west again and perhaps find a place where he could start his own little ranch.

"I don't need help." Madge interrupted his thoughts. "But you're welcome to accompany me. I could show you around a bit."

The warning in her eyes let him know she had more in mind than friendly welcome. His lungs twisted with anticipation.

Mental dueling with Miss Madge might prove to be a lot of fun.

Chapter Three

"Where are we going?" Justin asked as he limped along beside her.

Her first thought had been to stride as fast as usual, leaving him to catch up as best he could, but she'd invited him to accompany her for a specific reason—to try to discover who he really was—the cowboy she'd seen on the street or this weak, namby-pamby man who seemed to prefer books to cows and horses. She'd glimpsed eagerness as he'd talked about ranching. Unintentional, she was certain. But it made her more curious. More convinced he hid something. More confused on how she felt about him.

"I'm forced to take the pair wherever I can find something for them to eat, even if it's only weeds, which make the milk taste awful. Louisa needs the nourishment."

"How do you plan to feed them through the winter?"

The question was continually on her mind. "I've kept the calf for butcher." Feeding another animal strained her resources, but if she could provide adequate food for the family… "I hope I can trade some of the meat for winter fodder."

"Though if no one has any feed…"

She knew as well as he how scarce hay would be. "Perhaps we can get some shipped in."

"Or might be a farmer is giving up and ready to part with what he's scraped together."

"In exchange for cash, which is as hard to find as hay."

They fell into a contemplative silence. Suddenly she realized how easy it had been to talk to him about her problems, how comfortable they'd fit into each other's strides, even with his limp, and how she ached to tell him everything crowding her brain. But she didn't trust him, she didn't want to be attracted to him, and even though she'd seen him first, he was Mother's pick for Louisa. Her protests chased through her thoughts like runaway children. "I must hurry. The cow will be begging to be milked by now." She lengthened her stride, forcing him to step, hop and limp to keep up. She slowed and chuckled.

He caught up to her and coughed a little, though she noted he wasn't out of breath.

"Something funny?" he asked.

"Yes. Us. Look at me. My chin stuck out, rushing across the prairie like I'm trying to outrun a fire, while you hop along like a rabbit with a broken foot. Anyone seeing us would surely shake their head in disbelief." She laughed again, then realized how he might interpret her comments and clamped a hand to her mouth. "I'm so sorry. I didn't mean to mock your limp."

He only laughed, his eyes flashing with amusement. His dark gaze held hers as she gave another nervous laugh. She wasn't sure if she should be embarrassed more by her ill-considered comment, her continuing suspicion or the way her heart lurched as his look invited her into exciting territory full of adventure, excitement and something she couldn't…wouldn't…try to identify—a sense of connection.

She tore her gaze away and forced her steps toward the little slough where she'd found some dried grass for the cow. The cow's desperate lowing reached her, followed by the bleating of the calf. They directed her thoughts sharply back to her responsibilities. She'd tethered them so the calf couldn't suck the cow and steal the precious milk. "The cow needs milking. The calf needs feeding."

"Sounds like a song." He repeated the words, setting them to a rousing camp tune. "And the wind keeps blowing till my mind is numb." He added several more verses, each more mournful than the first, yet comical, and she laughed.

"I see you missed your calling. You should be in the entertainment world."

He grinned, a look so teasing and inviting her mouth went dry. "I don't have a hankering for being pelted with rotten tomatoes when I jest about how hard times are."

She lifted one shoulder in resignation and acknowledgement. "Might as well laugh as cry, I say."

"Amen."

She allowed one brief glance at him. Remnants of his amusement remained, and something more that she recognized as determination—an echo of her own heart. "And do what one can to make things better."

"Exactly."

Her brief glance had gone on longer than she should have allowed. Thankfully they reached the struggling trees at the almost dry slough, and she hurried to release the cow. When she turned to do the same for the calf, Justin already held the rope. Together they headed for home. Usually she had her hands full keeping the calf away from the cow, but with Justin helping it was a lot easier, and they reached the barn in short order.

She turned the cow into the stall. "Do you mind putting the calf in that pen over there? There's a bit of grain for it."

He did as she asked, then lounged against a post, watching as she milked. Usually she found the time relaxing, but not under his study. "You don't need to stay here."

"See no reason to leave. Unless you want me to."

Did she? Of course she did. Even if she didn't suspect him of something dishonest, even if he was the spotless character Mother seemed to think he was, he held no interest for her. Mother hoped he'd be a match for Louisa.

So why then did she shake her head? "Of course not. Thanks for your help." She returned to the soothing rhythm of milking, as aware of Justin's presence as if he shouted and yodeled rather than waited quietly.

She finished, poured some milk into a trough for the

calf and headed for the house to strain the rest for the family. Sally took the pail as she stepped inside.

"I'll take care of this. You go deliver the laundry."

"Thanks."

A few minutes later, Madge sat behind the wheel of their reluctant automobile and tried not to envy Justin his better car. Justin had continued to follow her and, without seeking permission, climbed in beside her. Obviously he meant to accompany her. She couldn't find the strength to suggest otherwise. Besides—she clung to her excuse—she might discover something about him he didn't mean for her to find.

The clean laundry, smelling of soap and hot irons, sat in neat piles behind them, covered with an old sheet to protect it from the dust.

When they arrived at her first delivery point, he got out and grabbed a basket.

"I can manage. I do all the time."

"Yeah. I guessed that." He led the way up the side-walk. "You remind me of my mother."

"Should I be insulted to be compared to an older woman or flattered it's your mother?"

He chuckled. "I meant you are independent just like her. She could have let us know she was in trouble, but she didn't. Even when we found out, we practically had to force her to tell us the truth. When the bank fore-closed on her house, she insisted she and Levi could find a place somewhere. It took all of us talking fast and hard to convince her to move in with Carson."

"She sounds like a strong woman." Even as she spoke, Madge shuddered. "I intend to see we don't lose our house. I think Mother and I could manage, but Louisa would suffer ill health from the upset. Who knows what Sally would do? At times she seems ready to conquer any challenge, yet at other times I fear a harsh word will destroy her." Why she was telling him all this left her as puzzled as Sally often did in her reactions to life.

They reached the door, so conversation came to a halt. Madge handed over the clean items and received a few coins. She tucked the money into her deep pocket to add to the coffee can when she got home. The payment was due next week, and she knew without counting she would never make it.

"I need something special to happen," she muttered, then wondered if she'd lost her mind to utter the words aloud.

"What do you mean?"

"Never mind." She eased the automobile down the street to her next delivery. Again, Justin insisted on carrying the basket to the door. Thankfully, the distance was short, making conversation impossible.

She drove three blocks and picked up another batch of laundry.

"Seems to me you're working hard, finding ways to cope. What is it you're worried about?"

She snorted. "We're in a depression. No jobs. No money. Drought. Poor prices. What isn't there to worry about?"

"I hear ya. But not all those things touch each of us personally. For instance, you have work. You have a source of food and your house."

"For now," she muttered, immediately wanting to

smack herself for revealing more than she intended. This wasn't his problem. She didn't even trust him, for goodness' sake. Why would she want to share her problems with him?

"Your house is still mortgaged?"

She grunted. Let him take it for agreement or not. Whatever he wanted. She didn't intend to discuss this with him.

"Are you in danger of losing it?" His quiet words flushed through her, leaving a trickle of anger and determination.

"Not if I have anything to say about it." She took the corner too fast and skidded. Let him think about that instead of talking about losing the house. She couldn't contemplate the possibility. Her anger fled as quickly as it came. "I'm not worried. God has promised to take care of us. I simply have to believe He will." Though it would require divine intervention within the next few days.

"There again, you sound like my mother."

She glanced at him and gave a tight smile that did not budge the determination tightening the skin around her eyes. "She must be a good woman."

He grinned. "I think so." His gaze lingered. Did he think the same of her?

And what difference did it make if he did?

She tried to think of all the reasons it didn't matter, but for a moment, for the space of a heartbeat—for the time it took to blink away from his gaze—she let herself imagine he had complimented her, and she allowed herself to enjoy the thought.

She headed out of town toward the farm. Her journey took her past the Mayerses' place. Young Kenny stood at the end of the garden, a few feet from the edge of the road. She squinted at him. "What's he doing?"

"Best I can guess is he's taking the chickens for a walk."

She sputtered in surprise. "Never heard of walking chickens." But indeed the boy had half a dozen hens tethered by a foot and marched them up and down the end of the garden.

Madge crawled to a halt and leaned out her window. "Kenny, what are you doing?"

"Ma says the chickens have to eat the grasshoppers before they get to the plants." He sounded as mournful as the distant train whistle. "Says I have to keep them here until dark."

"Sounds like a chore."

"It's boring. Stupid chickens wouldn't stay here, so I roped 'em. Now they got nothing to do but chase hoppers." One chicken tore after a hopper to Kenny's right. Two others squawked at the disturbance and flapped in the opposite direction. Kenny had his hands full keeping everything sorted out.

"Well, have fun," Madge called as she drove away. She didn't dare look at Justin until they were well out of Kenny's hearing, then she saw him struggling as much as she was to contain amusement.

They started to laugh. Madge laughed until her stomach felt emptied and her heart refreshed. She gasped for air and dried her eyes. "Never seen that before."

Justin shook his head. "Thought I'd seen every kind

of critter that could be led. 'Course, the chickens weren't exactly cooperating, were they? I think poor Kenny is going to end up trussed by his feathered herd."

They burst into fresh gales of laugher as she turned into the yard. The laughter died as they approached the house. She slid a worried look at him. Would he think her silly? But his eyes brimmed with amusement and something as warm as fresh milk, as sweet as clover honey and as forbidden as taking candy from a baby. Yet she couldn't deny the way his glance sought and found a place deep inside where it seemed to fit perfectly.

She tore her gaze away and delivered a firm lecture to herself. Everything about this man was wrong, wrong, wrong. For starters, she knew he was hiding something. Plus, he had been handpicked as a suitable mate for Louisa. What kind of woman would entertain thoughts for a man intended for her sister?

She bolted from the car and reached for the laundry baskets, now full of tumbled, smelly items. But Justin beat her and held them in his arms.

"Where do you want me to put them?"

She nodded toward the coal shed she used as a laundry room. "In there would be fine." She hesitated as he disappeared into the dark interior, then slowly followed, wondering if she didn't step into danger as she crossed the threshold. She grabbed the pull chain, and a bare bulb lit the interior. "On the bench."

He deposited the baskets and looked about, sneezing at the smell of coal dust. "Pretty dingy in here."

"That's why I move everything outdoors unless it's too dusty. Or rainy."

"Rain would be a welcome reason."

"Indeed." The shed was small, and she looked everywhere but at Justin. His closeness pressed at her senses, making her skin warm, filling her lungs with tightness, causing her eyes to sting with embarrassment and pleasure at their recent amusement.

"I enjoyed our little outing."

The softness in his voice pulled her gaze inexorably toward him. His eyes were dark, bottomless, echoing the blackness in the corners of the room. Something about his expression caught at her, held her, joined them in a common thought.

"Especially meeting Kenny and his herd."

A grin started in one corner of her mouth and worked its way across her face. "If it keeps the grasshoppers out of the garden, he will surely be in high demand all over the county."

Justin chuckled. "The price of chickens will skyrocket."

"No one will be able to afford to eat a hen."

"Might put an end to this financial crisis."

They both laughed heartily at their foolishness, but something happened in that shared moment, something Madge would not admit. She could not, would not feel a union of souls beyond anything she had before experienced.

She jerked away. "Thanks for your help and have a good night."

He followed her outside and paused, as if waiting for her to turn and face him. She would not.

"Good night to you, too." He limped toward his quarters.

She headed for the house. Just before she stepped inside, she turned. He paused at his own doorway and glanced back. Her heart jerked in response. He lifted one hand in a little wave. She did the same, struggling to keep her breathing normal, and then ducked inside and quietly closed the door.

"Did you have a good time?" Louisa sat in her lounge chair. Her voice was soft but her eyes hard.

Madge knew her sister didn't care for Justin accompanying her. Not that she had invited him. Or welcomed him. Or so she tried to convince herself. "I delivered laundry and picked up more. Not exactly a fun occupation."

"What did you talk about?"

She couldn't remember anything except their shared laughter and didn't want to tell Louisa about that. "Huh? Pardon? Who talked about what?"

"You and Justin. You must have said something. After all, you went to town and back. You spent the better part of an hour together."

"I didn't know you would object. Where are Mother and Sally?"

Louisa sighed. "I want to have all his attention. Is that so wrong? He's a good teacher and might turn into a good friend. They're in the living room unraveling an old sweater of Father's."

Guilt clawed at Madge's throat. "I'm sure he'll find you very interesting. You'll soon be the best of friends." He wouldn't be interested in someone like Madge. She was only an old workhorse. Louisa was a graceful swan. "Just be careful. We know very little about him."

Louisa looked ready to argue, then sighed. "It's not like I expect anything but a few lessons from him."

Madge knew Louisa wanted more. And who could blame her? Louisa missed out on a lot of fun because of her health problems, but they had shared confidences all their lives. Louisa dreamed of all the things Madge did—home, love, security. "Do you want help preparing for bed?"

"I can manage." Louisa put Mouse down, and he rushed to the bottom of the stairs where Macat waited. Louisa pushed to her feet.

Madge wrapped her arm about Louisa's waist and held her close. Louisa had been ill so many times. Madge would do anything to protect her. "You mustn't overtire yourself. You'll end up sick. Then you wouldn't be able to study with Justin." She injected a teasing note into her voice and pretended she didn't feel the tiniest ache in her thoughts…her lungs…her heart.

She paused at the front-room door. "Mother, Louisa and I are headed upstairs. Good night."

"We'll finish this before we go up." She spared a brief smile, then turned back to winding yarn as Sally carefully pulled out row after row.

Upstairs, Madge offered again to help, but Louisa insisted she was quite capable of getting to bed on her own. Madge smiled a little at Louisa's faint determination, then retired to her own quarters. Thankfully Father had built the house large enough for the three girls to have their own small rooms. The big room where she hung sheets to dry had been intended as an upstairs parlor for the women when they had company. Mother's room was downstairs off the front room. Madge savored her solitude. She could think and pray and struggle with her wayward thoughts—as she did tonight—without the others knowing.

Louisa had carefully, guardedly, expressed her interest in Justin. And rightfully so. He was perfect for her, as Mother had already seen. At least, if he turned out to be honest he would be. Madge had no right to think of him as anything but Louisa's tutor and, perhaps in the future, Louisa's husband. And her own brother-in-law.

That settled, Madge opened her Bible. She had established a habit of daily reading as a youngster when Father had carefully instructed all of them in the value of such a practice. All three had promised Father they would read at least a few verses every day. Mother continued to remind them of their promise and the value of keeping it. Sometimes Madge mentally excused herself as being too tired, but she'd discovered she found incredible strength and guidance in the Word and comfort in prayer.

She read the chapter where her marker indicated she had quit the night before. The passage was Micah, chapter six. She began to read, got as far as verse eight and stalled. "What doth the Lord require of thee, but to do justly and to love mercy and to walk humbly with thy God?"

Her thoughts smote her, and she bent forward until her hair fell to the page. Macat thought she wanted to pet her and pushed under her arm, but Madge ignored her. *Oh, Lord, I have forgotten to be humble. I have forgotten mercy and justice. I've been so caught up with fighting my attraction to Justin and in fretting over how I'll pay the mortgage that I've forgotten who You are. I trust You to help me be true and faithful in everything.* Both in her concerns over the needed money and her wayward, unwarranted thoughts about a man who filled her with such nagging doubts. *Lord, show me, reveal to me any secrets he is hiding that might harm us.*

A few minutes later she crawled into bed, her mind at rest, her heart at peace. She would trust God and keep her distance from Justin.

Over the next few days Madge did her best to live up to her decision. Justin kept busy with Louisa. The little bit she saw of them together reinforced her resolve. Louisa's cheeks took on a healthy color. She showed more enthusiasm than she had in a long time. Several times Madge heard her laughter ring out like bells. The sound both seared and cheered her, reminding her of the laughter she'd shared with Justin and, at the same time, reaffirming how perfect he was for Louisa. She caught bits and pieces of conversation between the two as she hurried up and down the stairs. Justin was always so kind and patient with Louisa. In fact, Madge told herself, a perfect match for her. She was happy for Louisa.

If only it was anyone but Justin.

Judd watched Madge hustle up the steps and clenched his teeth. She worked far too hard, packing heavy baskets, carrying buckets of water, delivering the laundry and caring for the cow. Why, he'd even seen her with her head in the bonnet of their old car, adjusting things so it ran.

He wished he could help her, but his job was to teach Louisa, who devoured every bit of information he relayed to her. He'd had to send back home for several more books.

The evening he and Madge had spent together had been enjoyable, but she had pointedly avoided him since. He couldn't help but wonder why. Had he offended her in some way? He intended to find out.

His opportunity came when she began to empty the washtubs. She grabbed her back and stretched as if she hurt. And well she might. The endless work was heavy. "I think I'll help Madge carry away the wash water. She looks tired."

"But—" Louisa ducked her head and swallowed loudly, then her gaze sought her sister and her expression softened. "Of course. To my shame I confess I often take her strength for granted. Yet if something were to happen to her we would all pay an awful price. Go and help her."

"You have this book to study. You're a good student. I feel a fraud trying to teach you. Really, all you need are the books and you could manage on your own."

Bright color stained her cheeks. "How kind of you to say so." She stroked Mouse's back. "But it's because you explain things so well."

He chuckled. "So long as you're happy."

The color in her cheeks deepened. Was she so susceptible to a few kind words? The poor girl needed to get out more, mingle with people. Learn to fight her own battles. Like Madge.

Madge—who seemed set on making it impossible for him to spend time with her.

He hurried out and caught up the pails while her back was turned.

She spun around. Surprise filled her eyes and then, what he hoped was pleasure. The look disappeared so quickly he wondered if he imagined it simply because he wanted it.

"What are you doing?"

"I'll carry the water to the garden."

She faced him, her stance challenging, her expression wary. "Why?"

"You're opposed to a little help?"

"Yes." She hesitated. "No. I just want to know why."

"Hate to see you doing all this hard work by yourself." He dipped the pails into the tub and, ignoring the splashing water, headed for the garden, remembering in time about his limp and cough. He gave two coughs for good measure.

"You're not exactly robust."

He didn't miss the skepticism in her tone and knew she still held suspicions as to who he was—Justin, the crippled teacher, or Judd, the strong cowboy she'd blasted into on the path in town. Not that she'd ever heard his name. Nor had anyone around here. All to his benefit.

Madge found a third bucket, filled it and traipsed after him as if she had to prove she didn't need him.

He paused, caught the glimpse of pain before she

hid it. "Your back hurts. If you don't rest, it will only get worse."

She scowled at him, which so delighted him that he laughed and earned himself an even deeper frown. She stomped past him, making sure to slop water on his oxfords.

He laughed again. Madge haughty and annoyed was much better than the Madge who ignored him. His grin remained firmly in place as he followed her. Seeing how she measured out the water to each plant, he did the same. "You should borrow Kenny's trained hens to eat the grasshoppers." He eased his gaze toward her, pleased as could be when her eyes widened and she laughed.

"I'll tell Sally about Kenny. Maybe I can convince her to train her chickens to do the same job."

He emptied the second bucket, and they returned for more water. Questions plagued him, but he waited until they trekked back to the garden to voice them. "Why have you been avoiding me?"

She snorted. "What makes you think I am?"

"Oh, little things. Like waiting until I'm not around to drive off with your deliveries or ducking out of sight when you see me crossing the yard. Or how about the way you race up the steps if I so much as look your direction? I thought after that first evening we might be friends."

"Friends?"

"Is that so hard to picture?" Her reaction stung. Why, lots of young women would be pleased to be friends with him. "Is it because of this?" He slapped his "crippled" leg. "Or this?" He pressed his palm to his chest and coughed. "Am I not good enough for you?"

She stood tall and proud, her expression shocked. "What an awful thing to say. As if I'd judge a person by such standards."

"Exactly what standards would you use?"

"I expect a man to be honest, upright, noble. Have a sense of humor." Her eyes brightened as if she remembered the laughs they'd shared, then she lowered her head. "But right now all I'm interested in is making sure we have food to eat and a roof over our heads."

He understood that drive. Seeing his mother get justice excluded all else in his thoughts. Or it had until recently, when interest in Madge also took root. "You work far too hard. There must be some other way to get enough to pay your mortgage."

She sniffed. "If you know of something, be sure and let me know. I have three days before my payment is due."

"Will you make it?"

"I'm still waiting for heavenly intervention. If you're concerned, you could pray for me."

He hesitated. She wanted him to pray for her? Did he believe God could provide a stay of execution? He didn't know. For too long he'd depended on his own strength and abilities. It hadn't seemed necessary to call on God for anything.

She headed back for the last of the water. "Sorry I asked."

"No, don't be sorry." He hurried after her, almost forgetting to limp. "I was just trying to think of the last time anyone asked me to pray for them. It's been a while. But it will be an honor to ask God to help you."

She faced him. "Ask and believe."

Slowly he nodded. "I will. I do." Her insistence made it impossible to do otherwise. A strong woman with a strong faith. His respect for her grew.

Her brown eyes flashed. Her brown wavy hair, damp from her hard labor under the glaring sun, was a becoming tangle. Her arms were bare and tanned. In fact, she glowed with health. Even more, her glow revealed an inner beauty of determination and faith.

He forced resistance into his thoughts. He dare not be distracted by her attributes, no matter how appealing she was. He was here under false pretences, living under an assumed name. She would despise him if she discovered the truth.

He didn't intend she should. There was too much at stake for his real identity to be revealed. Yet it stung to know how she would react if she found out.

Chapter Four

Madge counted the coins again. Still not enough, despite Justin's promise to pray. Perhaps it had been only empty words.

Or maybe she was trusting his prayers more than her God.

Yet neither had produced the necessary help.

She turned to Macat, who sat on the nearby chair, totally disinterested in Madge's problems. "I'll simply have to speak to the banker. He'll surely understand and allow me more time."

She slipped to her room, changed into her best dress, brushed her hair into tidiness and donned a hat she normally saved for church. Intent on looking her best, she powdered her nose. "I look like a farmer with my brown skin."

Macat watched from the comfort of the bed. If cats thought about the actions of humans—and Madge was certain this one did—they must wonder at all this fuss in the middle of the day. Madge had hurried to get the laundry done earlier than usual. It was ready to deliver while she was in town. "There." She checked her reflection in the mirror. "That's the best I can do. Wish me well." She grabbed her white gloves to pull on before she stepped into the bank.

Macat had nothing to offer but a puzzled meow.

Sucking in air that seemed thin, Madge admitted her nerves danced in trepidation. She fell to her knees. *Lord God, You see our need. I'm short on the payment. Mr. Johnson is likely a decent man but he's still a businessman. Help him see my intentions are good and honorable. Help him be open to allowing me more time.* She remained on her knees several minutes until she felt calmer. God was just and righteous. He would tend to her needs.

Pushing back little tremors of doubt and nervousness, Madge marched down the stairs. "Mother, I'm on my way to town to take care of things."

Mother nodded. She knew the mortgage was due today, though Madge had spared her the truth and let her assume Madge had earned enough for the payment. She shot a look at Justin and Louisa in the living room bent over a book, too engrossed in each other to even notice her. Resentment tore at her throat. The money she needed had gone to advertise for Justin. So Louisa could be amused.

She choked back her…it wasn't jealousy. She wouldn't admit it. But she'd conveniently forgotten the other unexpected expenses that had sucked at the coins in the can. Momentarily, she closed her eyes. She was only overwrought because of her worries. She would trust God. He was sufficient.

She slipped outside without a backward look. Thankfully the vehicle started on the first try, saving her from having to crawl under the hood.

A few minutes later she parked in front of the bank, pulled on her gloves, took a deep breath and climbed the stone steps. The big doors creaked as she pushed them open. The interior had always seemed to be almost funereal, every sound subdued, the lighting muted, the atmosphere somber.

Madge had come on honest business. She had no reason to shiver. She sucked in the stale air and straightened her shoulders before she approached the teller. Mr. August, a thin, bespectacled man, was a deacon at the church. The way he squinted through his glasses always made her feel as if he examined her under a magnifying glass.

"Mr. August, I'd like to speak to Mr. Johnson, if I may." Her voice came out strong and clear, revealing none of her nervousness.

Mr. August tipped his head up and down as if trying to bring her into focus. Then he nodded. "I'll see if he's available." He shuffled into the far room, the banker's sanctum. No one ventured into the room without being invited. Madge had been there only once before—with Mother, when they'd informed him they wanted to sell the farmland but keep the house. Mr. Johnson had been most agreeable about conducting the business that left them with a mortgaged house but unencumbered by the debt on the land. Madge wasn't unaware the deal had turned out nicely for Mr. Johnson. He had sold the land to a newcomer just before the crash. She supposed the new owner owed money to the banker, too. The crops wouldn't produce enough for feed and seed for the farmer, let alone earn enough for a mortgage payment.

She pressed her lips together. She would not lose her house to a bank that already owned half the town, due to the misfortunes of those who had to cope with the financial difficulties of the day.

Mr. August returned. "He'll see you shortly. Just wait over there." He jabbed his finger toward the three chairs parked against one wall.

Madge sat and waited. She and Mother had done the same last time. No doubt this was part of the way bankers dealt with customers, as if needing to prove they were in control. Her resolve mounted. He might control the money but not her fight. And she would fight to keep the house.

Finally she was called and shepherded into the office with enough pomp and respect, she might have expected to be presented to King George.

Mr. Johnson half rose and indicated the chair across from his very wide desk. He waited until Madge seated herself and adjusted her hands in her lap.

"How may I help you?"

"I've brought the mortgage payment." She dug the heavy envelope from her purse and handed it to Mr. Johnson.

His lips curled as if the package was noxious, and he put it on the edge of the desk as far from him as possible. "You could have given this to one of the tellers to count."

She nodded. "I realize that, but there is a small problem." *Please, God. Help him agree.* "I'm a bit short."

The way he blinked and drew himself tall, she knew he wasn't seeing this as a small thing.

"I'll pay the full amount. But I need a little more time."

"Where do you propose to get the money? Everyone in the country is in the same position."

"I have some paying customers. I'll find more. You know I'm honest."

He didn't answer. After a long pause, he sighed.

She wished she could let out her breath, too, but her future—and the future of her mother and sisters—hung on what he decided.

"Here's what I'll do."

Her heart ticked with fear and dread. He opened a drawer and rattled through the contents. If he didn't soon tell her his plan, she was going to pass out from nerves.

"I've let out the Sterling house to some shirttail relative of my wife's." He palmed a pair of keys and considered them. "I keep getting possession of houses I can't sell. Neither can I rent them. No one can afford to pay. It's a losing business."

Madge couldn't find it in her heart to feel sorry for his predicament.

"I guess I have to be content with having someone occupy a house and keep up with repairs. Anyway, this nephew of a nephew, or whoever he is, is a bachelor.

He's asked me to find someone to clean the house and prepare it for occupancy. Could be, with hard work, you might earn enough to pay what you owe me. His name is George Gratton. He's arriving sometime in the next week or ten days." He handed her the keys. "Can you manage to have the house ready in time?"

"Certainly." If she had to work day and night she would do this job and earn the money to take care of the remainder of the mortgage payment.

She rose and held out her gloved hand. "Thank you, sir. You won't be sorry."

Mr. Johnson's handshake was perfunctory. He already had his attention on the papers before him.

Madge didn't care. She practically skipped from the bank and out to her car. *Thank You, Lord. Forgive my doubts and fears.* She would have to hurry through the work she already had. But if she got done before supper, she'd be able to work at the house in the evening... after she'd taken care of the cow and calf and delivered laundry.

How much should she tell the others? Would they be concerned she'd taken on too much? But it had to be done. Plain and simple, she didn't have any choice. None of them did.

So after supper, she donned her oldest clothes, put buckets and rags in the car and headed for town. No one had expressed any concern when she'd announced her plans. Justin had taken to disappearing after the evening meal. She refused to admit she might have welcomed his company. Only twice more had he gone with her to bring the cow and calf home. She told herself she didn't enjoy his presence more than she should, didn't find his comments amusing, didn't find comfort in being able to talk to him about the farm, the garden and, yes, even feed for the cow.

She'd begin work on the house then visit Joanie, seeing she was nearby. She missed her best friend. They'd shared secrets and dreams since Madge and her family moved to the area, but lately Madge was too busy to spend time with her. Of course, she couldn't tell Joanie the whole truth of how she felt about Justin, but still, she could enjoy her friend's company, which would cheer her up.

Judd had to force himself to walk away from the farm each evening. He'd discovered how much fun it was to spend a few pleasant hours with Madge after a day of slaving over books with Louisa. Although Louisa enjoyed it a great deal, Judd grew increasingly aware of why he'd abandoned teaching in the first place. He longed for activity, fresh air and open spaces. As he watched Madge work, he itched to help her. Shucks. He ached to do anything physical instead of being the lame, cough-ridden Justin Bellamy.

His only reprieve had been the few hours he'd spent helping Madge. They seemed to find a hundred things to laugh about the few times she'd allowed him to accompany her. He found her an intelligent conversationalist with strong opinions on how the country was being run.

"Run into the ground," she insisted, last time he'd gone with her to bring the calf home.

"And how would you fix things?"

She chuckled. "I don't suppose I could. But it seems to me there is too much being taken from the poor only to benefit the rich. And shepherding all those single men into camps…why, that's just wrong."

"Some of them are happy enough to have a place to sleep, a meal to eat and work to do."

"I have a friend whose brother is in one of those places. He gets twenty cents a day for backbreaking work. What an insult."

He half agreed but wanted to see her get fired up with passion. "For some, it's better than what they had."

"Pity the man who finds that sort of life a blessing."

He chuckled. "What would you do with them?"

"Treat them with dignity. Don't let the banks take away their land. Do something about the low commodity prices. Seems to me that wouldn't cost the government any more than sending them to camps." She sniffed. "Though from what I hear, the camps aren't costing them much. I don't know how the men will survive winter in the poor quarters." She stopped to stare at him as if he had something to do with the conditions. "Everyone deserves to be treated fairly, honestly and with dignity, don't you think?"

"Yes, ma'am. I certainly do. And let it be known I fully agree with you. That's part of the reason I took this job." He paused to think momentarily of the future. "I'll head back west to the ranching country when the time is right."

She considered him for a long hard moment, searching deep into his thoughts.

He'd done his best to appear open and honest. But there were things he must hide, even though it pained him to do so.

"When will the time be right?"

"I can't say, but I'll know." When he had dealt with the man who stole his mother's savings and robbed her of her home.

"I don't expect you can be a cowboy, though, with your leg and all."

He hadn't thought of that. "More like cook's helper. But, like you said, the fresh air is good for my lungs."

He pulled his thoughts back to the present and reminded himself why he had really taken the job. He set his will firmly to watching for the man, even though it required he give up evening pleasures with Madge. Tired of being crippled, tired of being confined indoors so many hours, after supper he slipped into his comfortable trousers and boots and donned his worn cowboy hat. The soddie was at right angles to the house, and he discovered if he ducked out the door and pressed to the wall until he reached the cover of the barn, he couldn't see the house. He assumed they, likewise, couldn't see him.

Once a safe distance from the farm, he sucked in cleansing air, glad he didn't have to slouch and cough, and he stalked across the prairie with long, hungry strides.

He could have taken his auto, and had several times, but the walk loosened his joints, cleansed his brain and renewed his determination to complete his task.

As usual he tried to be invisible as he headed toward

the house where that man would be living. He'd begun to wonder if his information was incorrect. But this evening, his waiting and watching seemed about to be rewarded. Someone had been there. Rugs hung over the railing. The porch had been swept. But the place now looked closed. No lights came from any of the windows, though he viewed it from all four sides just to be certain. He must have missed the man. Perhaps he'd gone for supper or to visit someone. Maybe his newest mark.

He lingered for some time, hoping the object of his interest would return, but as dusk descended he temporarily abandoned his task and turned his footsteps toward home. It was too dark to cross the prairie safely, so he followed the road.

The sound of an automobile reached him, and he jumped into the ditch and hunkered in the shadows.

The car neared. It was Madge. She'd been in town all this time? Had she seen him?

He remained in his position until the car putted away. She often delivered laundry in the evenings but never this late.

He straightened and returned to the road. He'd have to be more careful in the future and somehow find out why she'd been in town so late so he could avoid her.

Discovering the reason for Madge's late outing proved easier than he imagined. The next morning he simply mentioned to Louisa, "Did I see your sister coming in late last night?"

Louisa didn't answer for a moment, then sighed. "I

guess she got another job cleaning a house. I wish she didn't have to work so hard, but I'm glad she can."

This must have been the intervention Madge had wanted—a job enabling her to earn enough money to pay the mortgage. "I expect you're grateful she'll manage to keep your home safe."

Louisa lowered her gaze and seemed to consider Mouse, who never left her lap for more than food and time outside. "I'm grateful. Truly, I am."

"Then why do you sound so doubtful?" Could she resent Madge for managing so well? He frequently compared the two girls in his mind. And Sally, who was so quiet and yet always made sure her sisters and mother were taken care of. Madge, though, was the one to note. She had drive and purpose.

"I'm not doubtful. Not really."

He remembered he had asked Louisa a question.

"It's just— I feel guilty that I can't help."

"I'm sure she understands."

"Of course. Though…"

Over the days they had spent studying, Judd had unwittingly learned many of Louisa's secrets and sensed he was about to learn another.

"Sometimes I don't understand," she whispered. "Why must I be content to remain indoors doing practically nothing while Madge does the work of two women?"

Judd laughed. "You call memorizing dates, learning Greek and reading copious amounts nothing? It's hard work in its own way." Yet he wondered as well if life had been fair in giving Madge so much work, though he supposed he meant God rather than life, and he knew he had no right to question his heavenly Father. Nor did Madge seem to mind. She appeared to thrive on hard work.

"It's fun."

"Maybe Madge finds her work fun, too."

Louisa tipped her head. "Are you saying God has made us uniquely suited to our roles in life?"

"I suppose I am." Though it hadn't entered his conscious thoughts. But perhaps God had, likewise, equipped him to do for his mother what his brothers hadn't or wouldn't. When he'd hinted at his plan to Carson, the man had turned all lawyerlike and insisted if a law had been broken, he would have dealt with it.

Where was the justice in that? But because no law had been broken, Carson said there was nothing they could do.

Judd had other ideas.

As Madge hung laundry the next day, she thought of the previous evening. She hadn't been able to get the visit with Joanie she'd hoped for. Not with all Joanie's family hanging about asking questions.

"Who is the young man out at your place?"

"How is your mother?"

"Did you hear the Hendricks up and moved away? I never saw them but heard they had the truck loaded to the gunwales." This from Joanie's father, Mr. Sharp. "Not the first to walk away from his land. 'Spect he won't be the last, either. Times are getting downright tough for everyone."

"Except the bankers who are snapping up the abandoned land and throwing people out of their houses," Madge added.

"Yup. But owning worthless houses no one wants isn't terribly profitable, I'd venture to say."

Madge remembered Mr. Johnson saying something similar. But it elicited no pity in her heart. "Then why don't they just let the people stay?"

Mr. Sharp shrugged. "'Spect it goes against their nature. Bankers are a different breed. I thank the good Lord my business is paid for lock, stock and barrel." Mr. Sharp owned the general store. She knew from her own experience much of the trade was by the barter system. In exchange for necessary supplies, she'd promised part of her butchering when the time came.

Madge noticed the glance Joanie and her mother exchanged. She intended to ask Joanie what they worried about first chance she got.

When she prepared to leave, Joanie pulled her aside. "I'm so glad to see you. It's been ages. But this was an unsatisfactory visit. Let's meet somewhere soon."

Madge agreed. "But I don't know when we can arrange something. I'm cleaning the Sterling house. I'll be busy there every evening for a while."

"Perfect. I'll come and keep you company."

The next night, Madge had barely arrived at the Sterling home before Joanie came skipping down the lane. Madge grinned at her friend and handed her a mop and bucket. "I don't expect you to work, but you can carry this in for me."

"I don't mind helping. It's just so nice to have a chance to visit." Joanie sounded cheery. Perhaps a bit too much, as if she didn't want to reveal a worry. But Madge knew her friend. The worry could be real or so small it hardly mattered, but Joanie would soon enough share it and end up laughing before she finished relaying her tale of woe.

Madge had done some basic preparation in the front room—hauled out the carpets ready to beat and crowded the furniture into the hallway. Now she and Joanie started a fire in the stove, heated water and tackled a major scrubbing. They visited as they worked.

"Tell me about Louisa's tutor. What did you say his name was?"

"Justin Bellamy, he says."

Joanie giggled. "Do I get the feeling you don't believe him? Why would a man lie about such a simple thing?"

"Maybe not his name but—" She told Joanie about running into a man earlier in town. "I'm certain it's the same man, but Justin isn't anything like him."

"Oh. A mystery. Maybe he's a wanted man." Joanie intended to sound teasing and mysterious.

Madge paused to look out the window. "Wanted? Maybe. But not by the law. I don't see him as that kind of person." But she could see him wanted by a woman. Maybe he was hiding from a soured relationship. Why did the thought both sting and cheer her? It really didn't make any difference, except she needed to know Louisa wasn't getting into something messy. She'd seen the growing fondness in her sister's eyes. Mother must be very happy.

Madge should be, too.

But she couldn't shed her little suspicions about Justin. Nor could she quite dismiss a fledgling jealousy she loathed.

Joanie edged around to plant herself in front of Madge. She grabbed Madge's chin and stared hard at her.

There was no point in avoiding her gaze. Joanie could be quite persistent, so she tried to look mysterious.

Joanie chortled. "You like this man. I can see it in your eyes."

Not even to her best friend would she confess such a thing. Any more than she would tell her why Mother had hired Justin. Not simply to tutor Louisa, but for something far more lasting, if Mother's plans worked out. Madge had no intention of interfering with those plans. "He's not my sort."

"Don't try and pull the wool over my eyes. I've known you far too long."

Madge returned to scrubbing walls and hoped Joanie would do the same or at least drop the subject.

But she didn't. "I remember our little secrets. I know you want to get married and have a family of your own some day."

"That was before Father died and the country fell into a depression. Who has time to think about such things now?"

"I do." At the sad note in Joanie's voice, Madge forgot scrubbing the walls and turned to her friend.

"Your time will come. Some day."

"I don't see how. Seems all the single men have disappeared. Those still around are needed by their families."

"You mean Connie?"

"His name is Conrad. But he's not the only one."

"Joanie, things will work out."

"How can you be sure? People often have to live with disappointment." She squeezed the water out of a rag and returned to scrubbing.

Madge did the same, but she wasn't prepared to leave the subject just yet. "God provides. Like this job for me. I need more money for the mortgage. I prayed. And even though I didn't trust God wholly, He answered."

"Here I am worried about not having a boyfriend while you struggle to keep your house. I'm sorry."

Madge again heard a note of worry. She faced her friend. "What else is bothering you?"

"I guess we're all in the same boat. Father gets lots of goods for trade, but that doesn't pay the bills."

Guilt struck Madge, and she vowed to buy no more than absolutely necessary unless she could pay cash. Right now that meant she'd buy nothing. Every penny she made would go to the banker. "I wish things would turn around soon. In the meantime, what can we do but the best we can?"

"I know, and I don't mean to complain."

They worked in silence for a bit.

Madge's thoughts went to Justin. It was only reasonable he had his own interests to pursue in the evenings, but despite her vow to pretend she didn't care, she half hoped he'd join her when she went to get the cow. Nor would she object to his company while she cleaned this house. Not that she didn't appreciate Joanie's presence.

"Hello? Are you there?"

She realized Joanie stared at her, amusement drawing her eyes upward.

"I was concentrating."

"Lost in a dream world. Didn't even hear my question."

"Sorry. What?"

"He must be quite the charmer."

"Who?" As if she didn't know. Her cheeks burned with guilty heat.

"Ho, ho. So if it isn't Justin, than who?" Joanie ceased work to squint and consider. "Nope. Can't think of anyone but Justin who might make you get all flustered."

"I am not flustered." Madge determinedly asked after mutual friends. When had Joanie seen them, and how were they? From the look on her friend's face, she knew Joanie understood her intention and played along out of the goodness of her heart.

They finished the room. "It's a bigger job than I thought it would be," Madge said as she stretched her back to ease an ache between her shoulders. "I'm not sure when this man—George Gratton—is coming." Nor how much he was paying. Hopefully more than twenty cents a day.

"What do you know about Mr. Gratton?"

"Not a thing, except he's some distant relative of Mrs. Johnson's and is unmarried."

Joanie frowned. "How is it that you get two unmarried men in your life and I get none?"

Madge laughed, not fooled by her friend's pretend annoyance. "You've had eyes for no one but Connie since you were fourteen years old and he fell out of the tree into your lap. I think you secretly branded him right then and there."

"Conrad. And I did not. Besides, what difference does it make? He has his family to care for."

"Things will work out."

Joanie tossed her head. "So you say. Sometimes I think you simply refuse to admit anything you can't control."

The words stung. "I do not."

"Sure you do. How often have you pretended you didn't want something if you knew you couldn't have it? Like the time Louisa got the dress fabric you wanted. All of a sudden you didn't care."

"That was five years ago. I was still a child. I hope I've outgrown being jealous of my sister."

"Have you?"

She wished she could assure her friend she had. She didn't like the little resentment burning a hole in her heart that it was Louisa who had Justin by her side all day, his attention focused on her. "He's not my sort." As soon as the words were out, she knew she had given away her secret.

But Joanie didn't laugh or tease. "Things will work out. Didn't you just say so?"

Madge refused to answer. It was one thing to ask God to help her when she needed something good and noble and right. When it was selfish and involved hurting her sister, she had no right to ask.

Joanie chuckled. "What a pair of worrying old maids we've become." Only her eyes didn't laugh.

Madge knew why. Could they both end up alone for the rest of their lives? It was a dreadful thought, but a real possibility.

She would not think of Justin Bellamy. Even if he proved to be noble and honest and all the things she admired in a man because, whether he knew it or not, he would belong to Louisa.

God, help me not to be a jealous sister.

But even prayer did not erase the forbidden longing.

Chapter Five

Judd watched the house as Madge and her friend cleaned. So this was the job she'd gotten. He leaned back in the shadows, fighting anger and a protectiveness that curled his fists. Surely George wasn't making Madge his next mark. But no, that didn't make sense. Madge didn't have anything to give the man. Did she? He carefully reviewed everything she'd told him, things Louisa had said, even things he'd overheard in conversations among the women. Nothing indicated they had anything but debt.

The girls in the house laughed as they worked. He grinned, finding enjoyment in seeing Madge having fun.

A long, silent ache slid down his throat and wrapped around his heart. He wished he could join them. If only he didn't have to hide the truth about who he was and what he intended.

His insides boiled with nameless yearning. He must deal with his restlessness before it boiled over and he did something he'd regret. Like storm into the house and demand to know why she was aiding his foe. Not that she knew.

A deeper truth couldn't be ignored. He wanted to push inside and confess everything. He ached to be honest with Madge.

Glad he'd shed the Justin Bellamy disguise, he turned on his heel and strode down the back lane, thankful for the shadows to hide him. His gait ate up block after block until he reached the edge of town. He stood and stared out at the prairie, dotted here and there with dark shapes of houses, little fireflies of lights coming on in scattered windows. He sucked in air until his edginess settled. Then he examined his feelings.

He hated being dishonest with Madge. He wanted to tell her every fear and anger and frustration he felt. Yet what choice did he have but to continue his deception?

Slowly, a cunning idea grew. Perhaps this was for the best. Madge had access to the comings and goings of George Gratton. Judd could use the information to his advantage.

For several minutes, he warred with himself. How could he think he cared for Madge yet be prepared to use her as an unknowing spy? But surely she'd understand if she found out. After all, she was a fighter, prepared to do what she had to to keep a roof over their heads. Yet he knew her stubborn struggle to keep her family safe wasn't the same as his quest.

However, he hoped she would never discover his duplicity until he saw the man punished—see justice carried out—for what he'd done to Judd's mother.

He'd tell Madge the truth when the time was right.

His mind set on a course; his jaw tight, his insides tense, he strode back into town.

It felt good to stretch his legs. He concentrated on the way his muscles released pent-up energy to avoid the guilt jabbing at his thoughts.

The house was again in front of him. He stopped to stare. Too late, he realized Madge had come to the lane to empty her bucket and had likely watched him for several seconds.

"Why, if it isn't Justin Bellamy, his limp all gone. And what, Mr. Bellamy, brought about this sudden healing?"

Caught. All because he had been carrying on a little battle with himself. He had no choice but to explain—but how honest must he be?

Madge hadn't believed him from the beginning. Anything he said now would be met with double doubts.

Even in the low evening light, her gaze was direct, demanding.

He couldn't tell the whole truth. "You're right. I am the man you ran into that day."

"I knew it. Why the pretense?"

"I have to hide my true identity."

"Have to?" Her tone was hard.

"Let me explain."

"Oh, please do. I'm dying to hear your story."

Yes, she was going to find it hard to accept any explanation he gave. "Justin Bellamy isn't my real name." He sorely wanted her to know him as Judd, but how much dare he risk?

"Do you intend to tell me who you really are?"

"First, I must have your promise not to tell anyone my true name."

She busied herself with the mop and bucket before she answered. "How can I promise when I don't know the reason?"

Ah. He understood her concern. Should he be a culprit, she'd feel honor bound to turn him over to the law. But how could she consider it possible of him? "Madge." He spoke softly. "Do you think I would have a dishonest reason for doing this?"

She chuckled—more a regretful than merry sound. "You're asking me to trust your honesty when you just admitted you're living a lie?"

"I'll try to explain, but surely you know I wouldn't be doing something morally or legally wrong." It stung that she would doubt him, but what could he expect? He had deceived her. He would tell her his story and hope it made her more forgiving. "I told you my mother lost her savings."

"Not unlike many people."

"No. Only she lost hers to a con man."

She nodded, still unbelieving but waiting for more.

"He pretended to love her to gain her confidence. He promised he'd marry her. She believed him. When he said he had an investment opportunity that would double her money, she believed that, too. Only once he got his hands on the funds, he disappeared. It almost destroyed my mother. Cost her her house and savings."

Still Madge waited, though as she faced the house, he believed he saw a flicker of sympathy in her eyes.

Perhaps it'd only been a flare from the light coming from inside, because when she turned back to him, her expression was hard. "I'm sorry, but I fail to see what this has to do with me or my family."

"I searched for him for several months. Learned he—" If he said the man was about to move into the community, she would no doubt put the facts together with her task of cleaning this house. He didn't want her alerted. "I learned he had moved into this community to play his con game again."

Madge studied him. "Most men are moving out of the area."

"Must be a few moving in."

Reluctantly she nodded. "I guess."

"I aim to find him and stop him from doing to another woman what he did to my mother."

Her expression revealed a struggle with doubt and sympathy.

He caught her shoulder and looked hard into her dark, steady eyes. "If he hears my name, he'll figure out who I am. How long do you think it will take him to guess why I'm here? Warned, he'll likely move on but perhaps with someone's savings in his pocket."

She held his gaze, steady, demanding and something more—something that caught at his heart and tugged it gently in her direction.

"What's your name?" Her low question almost broke through the barriers he must keep firmly in place. He forced resolve into his thoughts.

"You vow you won't tell anyone?"

She nodded, her look full of so much promise he struggled to find his voice.

"Judd. Judd Kirk."

"Judd." His name on her lips was sweet as a kiss.

He looked deep into her eyes, his world shifting to higher, rarer air.

"You haven't found the man yet?" Her words sent his thoughts back to his plan.

"No, but I'm close."

She nodded, not releasing her dark-eyed hold on him for even a heartbeat. "And when you do?"

"I'll make him pay." He'd force the man to give back the funds. He'd somehow make him suffer as much as his mother had. But if he hadn't been so trapped by Madge's intensity, he might have guarded his words more carefully. He wished he had when her expression hardened.

"You're talking revenge."

"No. I'm talking justice."

"What about the law?"

"There's nothing they can do."

She considered him a moment. "But isn't God the righteous judge?"

Her words were soft but challenging, striking at a place between his faith and his life that held nothing of substance, only waiting silence. His sole defense was to point out things widening the breach. "Can you look around at how this world is going and say God is treating us fairly? Why doesn't He do something to stop this drought and everything else tearing this country apart?"

She shook her head back and forth. "I don't know

why bad things happen, but I believe we can trust God to take care of us."

"Could you say that if you lost your house?"

She grew fierce. "I'm not going to let that happen."

Fierceness grew in his heart, too, and edged his words. "My mother didn't expect to lose hers, either. She trusted a man. I intend to see her get some recompense." Hoping to make his actions more acceptable, he added, "And make sure that man doesn't repeat his game." He hadn't realized until this conversation how much he wanted more than justice. He'd always soothed his conscience by telling himself he only wanted to stop the man from cheating another woman.

"Judgment is in God's hands. If you are determined to exact vengeance, you will surely be twice bitten."

He crossed his arms over his chest. "I don't know what you mean." Wasn't sure he wanted to. He would make that man pay for stealing his mother's house and savings. Nothing she said would change his mind.

"Not only are you stricken with bitterness at what happened to your mother, but if you take things into your own hands you will be touched by the evil of vengeance." She moved closer, rested her warm hand on his forearm.

The touch seared his nerves, stung his thoughts and made him waver. But God's justice took too long. His mother shouldn't have to wait until eternity to see it.

"Judd. I like that name. Suits you so much better than Justin."

He covered her hand with his. "I like it better, too." Especially the way she said it.

"Judd, I don't want to see you hurt by taking on the role of avenger."

Caught in her steady gaze, he couldn't argue.

But he couldn't agree, either.

"I'll not do anything wrong."

She lowered her eyes, leaving him floundering for determination about his course of action.

"I pray you will learn that God's way is best."

He squeezed her fingers. "I appreciate your concern."

Neither of them moved. She kept her head down. He let himself explore the feel of her hand beneath his— strong from hard work and yet soft. Just like Madge herself.

She sighed. "I've been trying to guess who this man you want to find is, but I can't think of anyone. It would be awful if it was someone I know."

"Not too likely. He's only an obscure relative of one of the families." He hoped she wouldn't take that bit of information any further. "I don't expect he's making himself too visible." Entirely true at this point. "Now enough of this. Can I help with anything?"

Slowly she eased her hand away and grabbed the mop and bucket. "I'm done for the day. Mr. Johnson left a note on the door saying the occupant would be here in two days' time. I'll have everything ready by then. Mrs. Johnson sent over a stack of bedding, so I'm to make up the beds. Though I have no idea if I should make them all or—" She shrugged.

Judd followed her to the house and scooped up the rest of her cleaning supplies. "Mind if I catch a ride back home with you? I walked to town."

"Leg doesn't hurt much now?" He heard the teasing tone in her voice.

"Not when I'm Judd Kirk. Though I did hurt my leg just as I told you."

"I expect your cough is better when you're Judd Kirk, too."

Ah, would he ever hear his name from her mouth without it strumming his heart like a harp? "Lots better, thank you."

She grinned at him and they both laughed.

Judd. She liked the name. Just as she'd liked the cowboy she'd bumped into weeks ago. Since that day, she'd allowed her fancy to build a solid picture of him in her imagination. She'd envisioned long, thrilling rides clinging to his waist as a black horse galloped across the land. She'd ignored her suspicions that Justin and Judd—the name sang through her brain—might well be the same person. Instead, she'd given him a double. Now her foolish, childish pretendings had taken form and substance.

She shifted and gripped the steering wheel as they headed toward home. His presence filled far more of the space beside Madge than the bulk of his body.

His plans for revenge crowded her thoughts, and as she focused on what he'd said, she was able to push her embarrassment and discomfort to the back of her mind. She had never considered getting revenge on anyone, but somehow she suspected it truly had a scorpion tail of regret. She must convince him his chosen course of action might destroy him.

For Louisa's sake, of course. She didn't want to see her sister dealing with the aftermath.

She shuddered as she thought how, if he persisted, Judd could be hurt, or get himself into trouble with the law.

"I know it's not my business, but I really think there must be another way to deal with this man you mention without stooping to revenge."

Judd chuckled. "I'll not do anything illegal or sinful, if that's what worries you." He sounded mighty pleased at her concern.

"I just don't want my family, Louisa especially, involved, even by association, with something that could bring hurt or harm." There, she'd said it rather well. No reason for him to read more than normal caution in her words.

"I fail to see how what I do will in any way affect your family. And why Louisa especially?"

Because Mother plans for Louisa to become your wife. But she could hardly tell him the truth any more than she would allow herself to acknowledge how the thought stung. "I suppose I'm being overly cautious, but we've all done what we can to protect Louisa. Her health has always been a bit delicate."

"She doesn't strike me as particularly frail."

Did she detect a note of impatience in his voice? But no, she'd observed them together often enough to know he treated Louisa with nothing but patience and gentleness. It would be wise to change the topic of conversation before she revealed more than she should. "You're not really planning to go back to the ranch as cook's helper, are you?"

His laughter rang out, filled the small space and raced through her heart like fresh water in a summer-drenched stream.

She gritted her teeth. It was going to be hard to remember Louisa's claim on this man. *God, give me grace. Help me be concerned only with protecting Louisa and helping Judd.*

The next evening, Judd helped her carry the clean laundry to the automobile and climbed in beside her. "I'll ride along with you and help with the deliveries."

"You're still Justin." He hunched inside the baggy clothes of his tutor role. She longed to see him in his jeans and the cotton shirt that fit across his shoulders, allowing her to admire his strength.

"I must keep my secret from your sisters and mother."

"I still think you're wrong." She'd thought of little else all day, praying for wisdom to say something to make him change his mind. "It says in the Bible that vengeance belongs to God alone, who will recompense."

He drew in air until she wondered if his lungs would explode. "I can see this is going to be a problem for you. So let's deal with it and be done. I told you I won't do anything wrong, so can we stop calling it revenge? I only want to see justice done."

Justice and revenge were too closely related for Madge's peace of mind, but she didn't want to spend their few precious hours together arguing. "Fine. I'll let it go."

"Great."

"So what else should we talk about?"

He chuckled. "I'm dying to know what you were like as a little girl."

"A bit of a tomboy, I suppose. I liked to follow my father around and help him. I must have been a dreadful nuisance, but he never seemed to mind. When Mother objected I was not as ladylike as she wished, Father always said, 'Leave her be. You never know when it might come in handy to know how to do these things.'"

"Seems he was right." He shifted so he could see her face.

She darted a look at him, saw his gentle smile, sucked in a sharp breath and jerked her attention back to the road, trying to ignore how his look made her feel—not that she could even find a word to describe it. Special. That was the closest she came. His smile made her feel special.

"You manage very well. I've admired you as you work so hard. Fact is, many times I've had to remind myself I'm Justin, a teacher, not as strong as I want to be, when all the time I've wanted to be Judd and haul those heavy baskets up the stairs for you."

Her gaze edged sideways. Her heart beat a frenzied rhythm against her ribs as she stared into his dark intensity. His smile filled his eyes.

"You did?" Oh, but her voice sounded squeaky and surprised.

"Sure did." He reached out, caught a strand of hair trailing across her cheek and pushed it into place. "You work too hard."

The car had drifted almost to a standstill. She tore her gaze from his and back to the road, trying to assess his words. Did he care about her? Her heart sang a secret song, but she stilled it. He was not for her. Mother had picked him for Louisa.

Or had she? She'd picked Justin Bellamy for Louisa. There was no such person. Judd Kirk was a strong cowboy. An outdoor man. A—

She slammed the door on her thoughts. She would not look for excuses. God saw her inner being. No amount of mental wrangling would make her envy pleasing to Him.

They reached town. He insisted on carrying the baskets of laundry to the door for her, limping up the path at her side.

"Others need to believe I'm Justin Bellamy. I can't afford to let that man guess my real identity," he said when she mentioned it.

She wanted to protest further but feared it would bring a wedge between them, so she let it go. For now.

After she'd collected the next day's work from her various customers, she headed for the Sterling house. Judd helped her carry in supplies. "I need to scout around. I'll be back in—what? An hour? Two?"

"Better make it two. I want to have everything ready tonight. Mr. Gratton arrives tomorrow."

"Two hours, then." He touched the brim of his hat.

She hated watching him leave and wanted to say something more about his intention, but she only nodded, then headed indoors.

* * *

Judd strode away as if his mission required it, but George Gratton was the man he sought. He had no reason to look further. He simply had to observe the man and wait for the right time and situation.

Madge's convictions about revenge had seared his conscience. But he could not walk away from his goal. Mr. Gratton must be stopped. Justice must be served.

Madge did not know she worked in the house of his enemy, and he didn't intend to tell her.

He had two hours to pass and nothing to do. He wandered to the edge of town and stared out across the prairie. A man could settle down here and be content. Why had he thought he wanted to go back to the foothills and ranching? The idea no longer fit. A bit of land of his own, a nice little house, a wife—

A chuckle sprang to his lips. His land and house were just wisps in his mind but "wife" had shape and form. Madge. He reflected on the idea. She'd make a very nice wife—hardworking, cheerful, determined.

Buoyed by thoughts of Madge, he moseyed back to the center of town and parked on a bench outside the store to wait. He listened to conversations around him, hoping to hear something about George Gratton.

A man sauntered by and paused to study Judd. "You waiting for something?"

Judd explained he was tutor to Miss Louisa. "Her sister is cleaning the Sterling house."

"I heard someone was moving in."

Judd risked asking more. "Anyone you know?"

"Heard it was a relative of the banker's wife."

Judd already knew that. He wanted to know why. "What do you suppose brought him here?"

The man leaned on the wall and picked his teeth with a straw. "Heard he was going to work at the bank. Suppose he'll be helping the banker take people's homes from them." He chomped down on the straw and then spat it out.

Judd expected Mr. Gratton's methods would serve the banker well. He could see how Gratton could use this to his advantage, too. With access to personal financial information, he'd learn who he should befriend. His situation would enable him to steal from someone else. Judd clenched down on his back teeth. He would see that another helpless woman or vulnerable family wasn't hurt by this man.

Two hours later he returned to the house. Madge stowed cleaning supplies in the car and looked up at his approach.

"Any success?"

He drew back, at a loss over her question.

"Locating this man you seek?"

"Oh. Yes. I'm certain I've located him."

She quirked an eyebrow and waited. When he didn't offer any more information, she prodded. "Someone I know?"

"Can't say. Doesn't matter. I'll watch him and when the time is right—" He pressed his lips into a grimace.

She edged closer and touched his arm. "Judd, please reconsider. I fear there is a fine line between justice and anger."

She cared. The knowledge almost made him willing

to give up his plan. Almost. But he couldn't shake the burden of guilt pressing against his heart. "If I'd been home, I would have stopped him before he stole Mother's money. Now the best I can do is—"

"Can you get her money back?"

"Maybe."

"Can you get her house back?"

"Depends on whether the bank has sold it already." Mother said she didn't care about the house, but Judd was certain she only wanted her sons to feel better.

"Have you prayed about this?"

Her words tore at his conscience, warring with his faith. But he didn't see how he could trust God to fix this problem.

He hadn't told Mother his plans. He'd guessed her reaction would be much like Madge's. "This is something I have to do."

They got into the automobile, but if Judd thought Madge had forgotten the subject, she proved him wrong.

"Judd, you can't undo the past. Even if you feel you failed your mother by not being there, this is not going to change anything."

"I did fail her. As the oldest, I should have protected her."

"What about Carson? He's a lawyer. Why didn't he stop the man?"

He'd posed the same question to his brother. Carson had insisted Mother had not told anyone her plans, had not consulted anyone. None of them had known what she'd done until she'd informed them she would be moving out of the house. Only after much prodding had Carson managed to squeeze the truth from her.

"I intend to stop the man."

Madge made a sound of distress. "I fear for you."

"You do?" The idea tasted like honey. She had both hands on the steering wheel, and he reached over and squeezed one. "I'm glad you care."

A jolt ran through her arm to his. "Of course I do. My family could be hurt by anything you do."

He removed his hand and stared out the window. He didn't want her to care for her family's sake. He wanted her to care for his sake. Though either way, it would make no difference. He had his mind set on this course. The man had to pay, had to be stopped. Judd must somehow make up for failing his mother.

Chapter Six

Madge dropped Justin at the soddie, refusing his help to unload the baskets of laundry. She needed the time to sort out her feelings before she went indoors.

Judd had accused her of caring. She hadn't denied it. She couldn't. But the knowledge left her shaken and struggling for mental balance. Her only defense was the argument she'd given him—what he did had the potential to impact her family, especially Louisa.

Louisa had not yet gone to her room when Madge entered the house. She sat in an upright chair, Mouse in her lap.

Madge stiffened her spine, knowing something was amiss. "You should be in bed by now. You'll overtire yourself with all this studying and staying up late."

Louisa gently stroked Mouse, then lifted her head and gave Madge a look fit to cause her heart to stall. "Mother told me about Justin."

Madge quirked an eyebrow. "I'm sorry. Is that supposed to mean something?"

"She didn't hire him just to be my tutor. She picked him as my future husband."

Madge sat down.

"She said you knew."

Madge could do no more than nod. In a secret corner of her thoughts, she'd clutched the idea that neither Judd nor Louisa knew of Mother's plan, so she wasn't really stealing from her sister. Now she could no longer deceive herself. She resisted an urge to say she'd seen him first.

"And yet you spend every evening in his company." Louisa's voice rang with accusation. It was an exaggeration. They'd spent only a few evenings together.

"You have him all day. Besides, I don't invite him along. He has business in town so he finds it convenient to catch a ride."

"He has his own auto which, I'm sure I don't need to point out, is in much better shape than ours. Besides, what's this business he has?"

Madge tried to ignore the little surge of pleasure that she knew Judd's secret and Louisa did not. A flood of guilt followed—hard. How petty to feel in competition with her sister. "Ask him yourself. After all, you two should be getting to know one another better."

They smiled at each other, but Madge wasn't fooled. Behind Louisa's smile lay a scowl, just as one lay behind her own.

"I'm tired. I'm going to bed. Do you want help?"

"No, thank you."

Good, because I don't feel like helping you.

But a few minutes later, in her room, her uncharitable

attitude haunted her. *Lord, forgive me. I've known from the beginning what Mother's plans were. I knew better than to think about Judd in a romantic way.* She had no one to blame but herself that her heart had betrayed her. She'd let her imagination take her so far off course.

Holding her Bible on her lap, she bowed over it and prayed for wisdom to deal with this situation and strength to do what was right. Paying no attention to where her bookmark lay, she let the pages fall open and skimmed over the words before her. She'd marked the last two verses of a psalm. "Search me, O God, and know my heart; try me, and know my thoughts; and see if there be any wicked way in me, and lead me in the way everlasting."

Oh God, give me the strength to keep my face toward what is right. Judd cannot belong to me. Not without hurting Louisa, and I couldn't live with myself if I stole him from her.

Even as she murmured the words, she wondered if Judd might have something to say about the arrangement. No. She would not keep allowing herself excuses and loopholes.

Judd had accompanied them to church each Sunday. Today was no different. The five of them crowded into the car. Judd offered to drive, so Madge made sure Louisa sat beside him. She crawled in the back with Mother and Sally and pretended she didn't see his look of surprise.

When they got to church she lingered behind, waiting for Judd to follow the family into a pew. He hesitated, glancing at her. She smiled and nodded as if everything was fine when, inside, sharp talons scraped at her heart. Why must he be all she'd ever dreamed of in a man? Not as Justin, but as Judd. Strong, adventuresome, determined—her eyes stung with worry. Though he'd said nothing about how he planned to make the man he sought pay, she feared his determination would end in disaster.

He waited a moment, and when she made no move toward joining the family, he sat—but not before she'd seen his mouth draw down in resignation.

She spotted Joanie and went to sit with her.

Pastor Jones had a good sermon. At least she suspected he did because of the way others in the congregation nodded agreement and murmured, "Amen." She couldn't concentrate, as her gaze insisted on sliding toward Judd, sitting calmly beside Louisa. Anyone watching would think he listened intently. She wondered if he did. From the little she heard of the sermon, she understood the pastor exhorted them to trust God in these hard times.

"He is the answer to our suffering and sorrow. He is the One who offers hope, justice and everything we need for godliness and contentment."

Throughout the service, Joanie shifted and glanced around. Something bothered her.

As soon as the final "Amen" had been said and people began to move about, Joanie turned to her. "Conrad isn't here. None of his family is. Something's wrong. I know it."

It was unusual, but perhaps not a cause for worry.

"I'm going out to see for myself."

"How will you get there?" The Burnses' farm was ten miles from town, and Joanie's family didn't own a car. Nor even a horse and buggy.

"Can you take me?"

"Certainly." She welcomed the chance to do something away from home, away from Judd and Louisa and the knowledge of her forbidden attraction. "I'll take the others home first."

"Hurry. I'm terribly worried."

Madge squeezed Joanie's arm. "You're disappointed because you hoped to see him."

Joanie's eyes crinkled in amusement and embarrassment. "True. But then, it's not as if I see him any other time."

Madge gathered up her family and hurried them to the car, explaining she'd promised to take Joanie to the Burnses'. "She's worried because none of them showed up today."

Mother tsked. "I do hope they aren't sick."

"They should give up and move on," Louisa said.

Sally gasped. "Louisa, how can you suggest such a thing? What will they have if they leave?"

Louisa sighed. "Surely there are better places with more opportunity. I can't think it's as bad all over the country as right here."

Madge kept her opinion to herself. From what she'd heard, people were worse off in many other places. "Hurry up, girls. Joanie is waiting for me."

"Where's Justin?" Louisa demanded. "We can't leave him behind."

The thought crossed Madge's mind to do exactly that. She knew he often walked to town in the dusk. But the others only knew him as Justin, with a bum leg and poor lungs.

"There he is." Louisa waved, indicating they were ready to leave.

Justin limped over and crawled in the passenger side. That left Madge to drive and share the front seat with him.

She didn't care. She ignored him for the few minutes required to reach home. But it took a great deal of effort to concentrate on the conversation in the back and on her driving.

The trip seemed longer than usual. She put it down to her need to hurry for Joanie's sake—not her acute awareness of Judd so close, nor his probing glances. If they'd been alone, he would have surely demanded an explanation for her strange behavior. He couldn't miss the fact she'd gone out of her way to avoid him. Thankfully Mother and her two sisters shared the car, preventing him from making a comment.

She pulled up to the house and waited for everyone to get out. Mother and her sisters hurried inside. Judd gave no indication he meant to get out.

"Any objection to me going along?"

She wanted to argue, but try as she might, she couldn't dredge up a single word of protest.

"I'll switch to the back when you pick up your friend."

Still, she could do no more than stare at him.

"Who knows what you'll find at the farm? Might be a wreck and you'll be grateful for my company."

"Fine." As she drove from the yard, she glimpsed Louisa at the window and instantly regretted her decision. But it was too late, and she didn't want to waste the day arguing with him. But then, she also didn't want to confront the questions she expected he wanted to ask. So she began talking about Conrad's family.

"Conrad's father died several years ago. He's the eldest and has been running the place since. He has four younger siblings. Mary is…well, she must be fourteen by now. Then there's Quint—he's a couple years younger than Mary but a big boy. I expect he's a lot of help to Connie now. The two little girls are six and seven. Rosie and Pearl."

"Uh-huh."

"They live on a farm. But you know how farming is right now. The drought, the dust, the grasshoppers." Her voice trailed off. These were all things he was well aware of.

He nodded, his gaze fixed on her as if realizing why she poured out all this information.

She rushed on so he wouldn't get a chance to probe. "Connie's mother has been sick a lot lately. I expect she's under the weather again, and Connie didn't feel like he should leave her to attend church."

"Perhaps we should stop by and ask the doctor to visit."

"Conrad's mother refuses to see the doctor. Says she can't afford to pay. Besides, I don't think it's up to me to make such a decision."

"I suppose not, though I would expect you'd do what you had to do, with or without permission."

He sounded as if he thought doing so was admirable, and she allowed herself a quick glance. And instantly regretted it. His dark gaze filled with questions, demands, regrets....

She swallowed hard and forced her attention back to the road.

A regretful sigh whistled past his teeth. "Just as I'd expect honesty from you if I have somehow upset you."

"Honesty from me?" Her voice squeaked a protest. "Now, that's ironic from a man pretending to be something he isn't."

"You know my reasons, and I've been honest enough with you about them."

"Perhaps because I found you out?"

"Maybe I wanted you to."

At the gentleness in his tone, she couldn't stop herself from glancing at him again. At the teasing smile on his lips, she understood he was trying to correct whatever had made her avoid him so pointedly all day. Thankfully they had reached town, and she was saved from trying to explain.

Joanie stood on the front step waiting. She ran to the car as Judd stepped out. "Oh, excuse me." She ducked to peer at Madge.

"Joanie, this is Justin Bellamy."

"The tutor?" She eyed him up and down, winked at Madge, then, before Madge could do or say anything, climbed in. "Let's be on our way."

Madge hoped no one would detect any hint of the

heat flooding her cheeks. Joanie was wrong. There was no romance. Nothing to make her nudge Madge and giggle as Judd closed the door after her.

"I didn't invite him along," she whispered before Judd climbed into the back.

Joanie took the conversation no further. Instead she amused them with tales of adventures she and Conrad had been on. Madge knew it was her friend's way of keeping her worries at bay. By the time they arrived at the farm, Madge was almost as worried as Joanie. It was unusual for none of them to attend church. Mary often brought the younger children if her mother was ill. And Connie made an effort to come, if only to see his favorite gal—Joanie.

They turned down the trail toward the house. The two little Burns girls sat dejectedly on the step as Madge pulled the car to a halt. The wheels hadn't ceased rolling before Joanie bolted from the car and rushed to them.

"What's wrong? Where is everyone?"

"They's inside with Momma," Rosie said.

"Momma is very sick." Pearl shuddered.

Joanie hugged them both, but her glance sought out the mysteries of the house.

"I'll take care of them," Madge murmured. "You go see what's going on." She pulled the two trembling girls to her side.

Judd held the door open for Joanie. "Can I help?"

Joanie shivered. "I don't know." She slipped inside.

Madge edged the girls away from the step, into the sunshine. She wanted to ask them how long their momma had been sick, but it was plain as jam on toast that the children were near to breaking down. Instead she sat on the empty water trough and pulled them to her side.

Judd had not followed. She told herself she wasn't disappointed as she watched him walk around the house. A few minutes later, he appeared with two half-grown kittens and handed one to each of the girls. "Found some lonely kitties just begging for attention."

The girls buried their faces in the soft fur and murmured affectionately to their pets.

Madge's eyes stung with appreciation at his gesture. "Thank you," she mouthed.

He nodded and sat by Rosie. As with Madge, the closed door to the house seemed to have an unusual pull on his gaze.

Her heart lifted with relief when Mary came out and stood motionless. Then she saw the girl wasn't motionless at all. Her shoulders shook.

"I'll stay here. You go talk to her," Judd whispered.

She left him with the younger girls and hurried over to pull Mary into a hug. But Mary resisted.

"What's wrong?"

"Momma."

"How is she?"

Mary rocked back and forth and sobbed gently.

Madge did not like the way Mary acted. As if… What should she do? She shot a desperate glance at Judd.

He eased away from the little girls, making sure they remained with their attention on the cats, and came to her side. "What's the matter?"

"I'm not sure."

"Wait here," he said to Mary and, taking Madge's hand, pulled her into the house. She knew the way and led him to Mrs. Burns's bedroom where she lay abed, Conrad at her side, his hair tousled, his eyes shadowed as if he hadn't slept in days.

Joanie pressed to his side, rubbing his shoulder. Tears streaked her face.

Judd stepped forward and touched his fingers to Mrs. Burns's throat. "She's gone."

Conrad nodded. "I know," he choked out.

"How long?" Judd asked.

"This morning. But I couldn't bring myself to admit it. Mary only just realized when Joanie came." He shuddered, then reached up and claimed one of Joanie's hands.

Judd looked around, then murmured to Madge, "Didn't you say there was a younger boy?"

"Quint."

"Where is he?"

Conrad glanced about, as if only now aware of his brother's absence. "Likely gone to the barn."

Judd stood. "You need to inform the pastor. Let the neighbors know." But no one moved.

"Can you do it?" Joanie murmured.

"Of course." He captured Madge's hand and pulled her from the room with him. "Get Mary doing something. I'll find Quint and send him to the neighbors to ask them to go for the pastor."

She didn't move. The shock of seeing Mrs. Burns

lying there dead and cold, of seeing Conrad so shaken, left her stunned.

"Madge, they need our help."

Suddenly her fears and concerns exploded. "How will they manage? Their father is already dead. The girls are so young. Mary only fourteen, and now she'll have to be the mother. I can't even think."

He grabbed her shoulders and turned her to face him.

She clung to his dark gaze, searching for and finding strength, encouragement and something she knew she must deny, but at the moment needed so badly she couldn't move.

"Madge, don't try and solve all their problems at once."

She nodded. And shuddered. She wanted to collapse in his arms and pretend none of the past few minutes were real.

He squeezed her shoulders. She sucked in a strengthening gasp.

"You'll be fine." He seemed to know she was now ready to face the difficult task ahead and dropped his hands from her shoulders before going to find Quint. For two quick breaths she felt rudderless, lost, then she hurried outside and found Mary shivering against the corner of the house. "Let's make tea for everyone." Mary allowed Madge to lead her indoors. Over the girl's shoulder she saw Judd talking to Quint, and then the boy raced across the field to the nearest neighbor. He smiled encouragement as he strode over to join her.

Together they managed to get Mary busy in the kitchen and persuade the little girls to have sandwiches.

Joanie drew Conrad from the bedroom and convinced him to eat something.

By then the neighbors had arrived. Quint tried to escape to the barn again, but Judd gently urged him to join the family in the kitchen.

Shortly afterwards the pastor drove in, accompanied by his sweet wife. But the girls clung to Madge, Conrad to Joanie, and Judd looked to Quint, who watched for signals as to what he should do. Just as Madge watched Judd for smiles of encouragement and nods of approval. He seemed to know exactly what to do and took care of a hundred details no one else had the heart to deal with—like the scrawny cow bellowing to be milked and the eggs waiting to be gathered. He filled the water pails from the well and replenished the coal bucket so they could keep the kettle boiling as neighbors continued to arrive and offer help. According to the custom of the area, the body would lie in the house, with neighbors and family keeping constant vigil until the funeral service.

He must have also sent a message to Madge's family, as Sally arrived bearing a chocolate cake. She rushed over to hug Madge. "Are you okay?"

Madge clung to her sister. "I can't stop wondering how they'll survive. The children are much younger than we are, and yet I wonder how we'd manage if Mother left us."

"Pray to God we won't have to find out. Now let's see what needs to be done." She glanced around. "Seems pretty organized already." Surprise filled her voice.

"Judd—Justin got things going."

"Very good." Sally practically rubbed her hands together as she headed for the kitchen to add her help.

Madge stood in the yard watching neighbors slip in and out of the house, clustering in knots to discuss the loss. Then the conversations shifted to other things. It all felt impossible. Like a dream from which she would awaken and thank God it wasn't real. Only it was. It had left her shaken to the core. She looked about. Judd talked to a couple of the men, Quint at his side.

Not giving herself a chance to consider her actions, Madge made her way to him. She longed to press close, feel the comfort of his arms around her. But such comfort did not belong to her. She would allow herself only the strength of his presence.

Chapter Seven

Judd glanced around the gathering crowd. He aimed to help the family cope, but most of all, he wanted to take the look of shock and sorrow from Madge's eyes.

He'd found Quint in the hayloft huddled to the wall, a cat nuzzled against him. The boy had understood his mother had died but didn't know how to react. He'd been grateful for something to do when Judd sent him to notify the neighbors.

Joanie seemed incapable of doing anything but clinging to Conrad, whose eyes were wide and unfocused.

Madge opened her arms and her heart to the younger girls and shepherded them through the day. She managed very well once she'd shaken her initial shock.

Watching her kindness convinced him his feelings for her were growing ripe, ready to mature. Was it love? Whatever it was, he couldn't let it distract him from his reason for being here—George Gratton.

Madge crossed the yard and stood close to him. Sensing her need for reassurance and comfort, he squeezed her shoulders. She stiffened momentarily, then sighed and leaned closer. They broke apart in a heartbeat rather than cause gossip among the neighbors, but Judd hugged her shape and memory to him even though she now stood a circumspect twelve inches away. Seemed he needed her as much as he hoped she needed him.

More people arrived, and Madge moved off to welcome them. One of the neighbor men beckoned to Judd to ask him about the chores.

For the next two days their lives were like that—passing silently as they went from one task to another. Only the daily ride back to the Morgan place provided them with a chance to be alone, and then the conversation dealt with details of the Burns family.

As soon as they reached home, Madge hurriedly changed into her chore clothes—overalls and an old cotton shirt that must have been her father's. She rolled the sleeves up to her elbows and set to work. Despite her protests, he insisted on helping.

"I'll get the cow and calf."

She hesitated only a moment. "Thanks. I'll start the washing." Several women held back on their regular orders, understanding Madge had her hands full helping the Burns family, but a couple insisted they must have clean laundry.

He brought home the cow and calf and did the milking. Not the sort of job a cowboy often did, but he discovered it surprisingly soothing to lean against the cow's flank as warm streams of milk filled the bucket. Sally took the pail when he carried it to the house.

Louisa sat at the table where they usually did their

studies. "Justin, I wonder if you could help me with this lesson?"

He glanced over his shoulder. Madge had already put in a long day at the Burnses', serving neighbors, managing to do some laundry so the children would have clean clothes for the funeral tomorrow and helping Joanie and Mary keep the children occupied and the confusion organized. She must be worn out. He wanted to help her, but of course, Louisa was feeling neglected. So he buried his sigh. "Certainly. We can work until you're tired."

"I won't get tired very early. I napped all afternoon so I could do lessons this evening."

Yes, she napped while her sister slaved. Not that he had any right to resent the fact. Louisa wasn't strong like Madge. Strong and kind and helpful and independent—

He struggled to keep his thoughts on Louisa's lessons as Madge carted baskets of wet sheets upstairs to hang. If only he could stop pretending to be Justin, the schoolteacher, and be Judd, the rugged cowboy. Then he would have no qualms about refusing Louisa's request and helping Madge.

The funeral was the next day. Everyone hurried through morning work so they could be ready to go to the church right after lunch.

The building was crowded, the yard full of those who couldn't fit inside. Room had been reserved for the Morgans in the church but Judd remained outdoors.

The family followed the simple casket in, Joanie at

Conrad's side, practically holding him up. Quint and Mary each held the hands of one of the younger girls.

Judd ducked his head at the sight of such grief and confusion.

Following the service and interment in the nearby graveyard, the ladies of the church set up a lunch. People filed by the family and offered condolences.

Quint slipped away, unnoticed by the others. Judd followed him to where the buggies were hitched. He dropped his arm across the boy's shoulders but said nothing. Simply was there for him.

Quint shuddered. "Why did God have to take my momma?"

"Son, I really don't know." Why did God allow such awful things to happen?

"She used to say plants need deep roots to survive. Said roots grew deep when the plants had to fight wind and drought and other bad stuff."

"Guess that's so." But plants didn't have hearts, feelings. They couldn't wonder why or resent the elements.

"Momma told me I'd be a better man for having to deal with hard things. Said God would help me through them."

"Your momma sounds like a wise woman."

"She was." He sucked in air. "But I don't like hard things."

Judd nodded. "Don't guess any of us do." He tried not to think of his own circumstances. Nor how God hadn't seemed concerned enough to help his mother.

"Momma would be disappointed in me if I didn't

stand up like a man." The boy straightened and Judd's arm fell to his side.

"All of you have a heavy load to carry now."

Quint's shoulders sank. "I know." He pulled himself tall again. "But I aim to make Momma proud." He glanced toward the crowd around his older brother and sister. Saw the younger ones playing, unconcerned about the future. For a moment his gaze lingered on the little ones. Judd sensed he struggled with wanting to stay young and carefree like them, a child, then he looked back to Conrad and Mary. "I better go." His stride faltering only once, he returned to their side and faced the greetings of the neighbors.

Judd glanced about for Madge, found her surrounded by a knot of women. She seemed to be in a heated discussion. He slipped to her side.

She shot him a grateful glance as she continued to speak to one of the women. "I think it's up to Conrad and Mary to decide what happens to the younger girls."

Judd jerked his attention to the circle of ladies. "What's going on here?"

Only Madge seemed inclined to answer. "Some think Pearl and Rosie should be taken away."

"They need to be in a proper family," one of the women murmured. "Or the orphanage where they will be cared for."

Judd cleared his throat and gained their attention. "Aren't you forgetting they have a family? Would you deprive them of that after they've had the misfortune of losing their parents?"

Some women shuffled about, but the speaker wasn't

convinced. "The older children are way too young to be parents."

"Conrad is eighteen. I venture to say many of you were married and had a baby by then."

"That's so," several acknowledged.

"But Mary is only fourteen."

Madge shook her head. "I can't believe we're having this conversation with the grave over there not even filled in."

Judd took her elbow, hoping to calm her. "My grandmother was but fourteen when she moved west as a newlywed. She didn't have a home to go to. She and her new husband had to build one with their own hands. They faced challenges most of us have forgotten about. Mary and Conrad, Quint and the little girls have each other. They have a warm home and a farm—"

"Farm is more of a burden than anything."

Judd went on as if he hadn't been interrupted. "They have a cow and chickens and a garden Mary has been responsible for for the past two years. They are family. They love Rosie and Pearl. They'd never consider them a burden or extra mouths to feed. I think if we are concerned about them we should do what we can to assist them."

One by one the women nodded agreement and moved off, except for the most vocal one who lingered a moment, then marched away.

"I hope she won't make trouble for them," Madge said, still clinging to his arm.

"I doubt she will if she doesn't have the support of anyone else."

She faced him. "You handled that very well. Thank you." Their gazes held and said so many things they had never confessed. Judd allowed himself to believe her lingering look echoed his own thoughts. Something special and real was developing between them.

"Madge." Mrs. Morgan quietly took her daughter's arm. "I need you."

Madge jerked her head to one side, avoiding Judd's eyes. "Of course, Mother."

As they edged away, Judd wondered what Mrs. Morgan said to cause Madge to nod and look regretful.

Over the next few days they all struggled to get back to their normal routines, but Judd found himself more and more restless—a feeling he could not explain. It was as if some inner, unidentified purpose drove him. He tried to force that nameless feeling into the shape of George Gratton but found it impossible. He scolded himself. He could not let sweet thoughts of Madge steal away his resolve to deal with the scoundrel. He'd bring Gratton to justice, then his heart and thoughts could seek after Madge.

Evenings he often accompanied her to town, but more and more, he waited and slipped away as Judd Kirk. George had moved in before Mrs. Burns's funeral. Judd watched the house, seeing the man cooking his own meal, sitting at the chair reading or sometimes standing on the porch enjoying the air.

Judd wondered whom he intended to take advantage of in this town. Whomever and whatever Gratton had in mind, Judd planned to find out and reveal it before anyone was duped. It would require patient observation for the right timing. Judd would have to wait for the man to reveal his hand enough that he could be proven the shyster he was.

Over supper that night, Madge barely waited for them to all be served before she spilled her news. "I met Mr. Gratton today. You know, the man I cleaned the Sterling house for. He asked if I would be willing to work two afternoons a week for him."

"Of course, you agreed to," Louisa said. "Seems you are always looking for more work."

Louisa's voice was gentle, but Judd sensed an unkind dig. From the hurt flitting across Madge's eyes, he knew she felt it, too.

"I'm only trying to earn enough to pay some bills."

He wondered why she didn't lay the truth before them—if not for her hard work, they might lose their home. He supposed she wanted to protect them from worry.

"Anyway, what I really wanted to tell you was what a nice man he is."

Judd's heart twisted so hard he clenched his fists to keep from protesting.

"He thanked me for doing such a good job of cleaning the house, then asked me if I could make a meal or two a week for him. I told him I wasn't as good a cook as my sister, Sally, but he said he was willing to give it a try. Then he asked if I thought the small parlor could be made into a bedroom. He's planning to move his mother in with him, and she's apparently not well enough to be going up and down stairs. I said I thought it would suit very well, so he wants me to prepare it for her."

"How good God is to provide you with another job," Mrs. Morgan said. "Perhaps you can give up some of your laundry customers now."

"I don't think so, Mother."

"I can help with the laundry," Sally offered.

The sisters studied each other for several seconds. Judd guessed Madge had grown used to seeing her sisters as frail and unsuitable for heavy work. Madge needed to see Sally was no longer a little sister needing protection. He sensed Louisa was also far stronger than any of them were willing to believe.

Finally Madge nodded. "I'd appreciate your help."

Judd was pleased for Madge's sake. At the same time, he wanted to grab her and warn her not to take George Gratton at face value. Was the man figuring to gain something from his contact with Madge? Perhaps to be introduced to Mrs. Morgan? But the woman had nothing to steal. Of course, Mr. Gratton didn't know that. Or perhaps this woman he planned to bring to the house was not truly his mother. Maybe she was part of some scheme he had cooked up.

Judd simply couldn't believe the man wasn't working some angle.

Having Madge at the Sterling house two afternoons a week forced Judd to be a lot more careful about watching the place. She often stayed to clean up the evening meal, forcing Judd to stay out of sight until she left for home.

He was caught between avoiding her and wanting to spend every moment with her.

The next day, Sally handed Madge a covered dish hot from the oven. "Would you take this to the Burns family? And see if they need anything."

Madge hesitated. "The laundry."

"There's only some sheets to iron. I'll look after that. They know you better than me. They'd rather see you."

Madge nodded. "I'll go. I've been wondering about them." She headed out to the car.

Judd rose. "I'll come along, if you don't mind."

Madge stopped midstride. She turned slowly. He followed her glance around the room. Why did Louisa purse her lips and Mrs. Morgan send some kind of silent warning to Madge? Had they taken note of his evening absences and wondered if he conducted some shameful business? He wished he could assure them such was not the case, but he couldn't. Not without revealing far too much of his true identity. "I'd like to see how Quint is doing and the rest of the family, too, of course."

Another silent message passed between Madge and her mother, then Madge nodded. "Of course you must reassure yourself as to how they're doing."

So a few minutes later he sat beside her in the car, the succulent aroma of the hot dish filling the interior. Even though he'd already eaten, his taste buds were tempted.

He wanted to say things from his heart, but Madge quickly began to fill in the silence. After a few minutes of listening to her chatter, he decided she was purposely making it impossible for him to speak of anything important, and he settled back to listen. He would get a chance. He'd see to it. He had it on his mind to tell her how his affection for her was developing. Hopefully she would admit similar feelings.

His teeth stung as she talked of her growing regard for Mr. Gratton. She'd be shocked and dismayed to learn he was the man Judd wanted to bring to justice, but she'd understand when Gratton revealed his true colors. Meanwhile, he needed to concentrate on what she said.

"Joanie hoped Conrad would see this was a good time to ask her to marry him. They've been together since they were fourteen. But no, he says it wouldn't be honoring his mother's memory if he tried to replace her so soon. Pshaw. Mrs. Burns would be the first to agree Connie has waited long enough. The whole family would benefit from having Connie married. 'Twould stop the old ladies in town from grumbling about the two little girls needing a proper home."

"They're still at that? I thought they'd have let it drop by now."

She laughed. "You mean after you set them straight at the funeral?"

"I figured I made my point very clear."

"Oh, you did, indeed." She sobered much too quickly. "Some people aren't happy unless they are stirring up trouble."

"Does Conrad know about this?"

"Joanie told him. Thought it would persuade him to reconsider, but he said it wouldn't be fair to expect her to take over so much responsibility. Said they would manage as they were and no one would be taking his little sisters."

"No reason they should." The idea of someone trying made him as angry as hearing Gratton had stolen his mother's savings. "Where is the justice in this world?"

She slowed the car to look at him. "Judd, you showed justice when you defended the family and when you stood by them after their mother's death. We see glimpses of justice every day. Or maybe, more importantly, we see evidence of mercy. God's mercy."

"How is that evident in the drought?"

"Even in the drought He has not forsaken us. I believe the fact I am able to find feed for the cow and her calf, or earn enough money to pay the mortgage, is surely evidence of God's continuing care."

"I suppose I don't have your kind of faith."

"What kind do you have?" She held his gaze, demanding, searching.

He wanted to look away but found he couldn't. He wanted to throw all his doubts out the window and believe as he once had—before he'd drifted so far away, before he'd decided he would see Gratton pay for his deeds.

For a moment he wrestled with the promise of peace in trusting everything to God versus the need to exact his own form of justice. But he could not let the man get away with what he'd done. Somehow Gratton must pay and, above all, be prevented from repeating his sly tricks.

They approached the Burnses' farm, providing him an excuse to deflect her question. "We're here."

She flicked him a disappointed look but let the subject go as she drove up the lane to the house. Two little girls burst from the door and rushed to the car to hug Madge and give Judd shy smiles. Mary came to the doorway. "Welcome. Come in." She looked much better than when he'd seen her at the funeral. In fact, she was a pretty little thing. He suspected Conrad would not have her as surrogate mother for many years. Long enough perhaps to see the little ones able to cope on their own— or perhaps Conrad would come to his senses and marry Joanie.

"Is Quint about?"

"He's out with Connie trying to put up some hay."

"Thanks." He wondered where they would find enough grass to provide hay for the winter. He found them in a low spot behind the barn, cutting Russian thistle and packing it into a stack. The thistle was thorny and difficult to work with. Even though they wore leather guards on their legs and arms, both were scratched and bleeding.

If Madge saw this, she would surely change her mind about justice and mercy.

Seeing him, they eagerly abandoned the job. "We'll finish later," Conrad said to Quint. "It's a wonder we found this patch before it dried up and blew away. It will go a long ways toward feeding the milk cow over the winter."

Thorny thistles hardly qualified as a blessing in Judd's opinion, which he decided he'd keep to himself.

Quint seemed to have grown several inches. Judd realized it was because the boy stood straight and tall.

"You're looking better, apart from all the scratches," Judd said.

"Feeling better, thanks. I forgot for a little while that God will not abandon us. Connie told me the last thing Momma asked him to do was read a Bible verse. We're all going to memorize it and remember it when we get discouraged."

"That's great." Madge would be so glad to hear it. He wished again his faith were so clear and strong.

"I don't know if I've got it a hundred percent right, but this is it, Psalm sixty-eight, verse five, 'A father of the fatherless, and a judge of the widows, is God in His holy habitation.'"

Conrad squeezed Quint's shoulder. "God will take care of our every need. Isn't that what Momma always taught us?"

Quint nodded, his eyes filled with trust. "Yes, she did. And I don't aim to forget."

Both of them shed their leather guards and torn shirts. Conrad noticed Judd's curiosity. "We don't want to upset the girls." They put on fresh shirts.

They trooped to the house for tea and cookies. Madge and Mary laughed at something as Judd and the boys stepped into the kitchen. Then Madge gave the girl a quick hug. She glanced over Mary's shoulder, saw Judd, and her eyes seemed to smile deeper, happier, as if she were glad to see him.

His steps faltered. He saw her more clearly than ever before. She had an incredible capacity to love, to believe the best in people, to encourage others and to fight for what was right.

It made her see George Gratton as the man wanted to be seen—a good man with noble purposes.

Judd counted on her sense of justice to make her see the man for what he truly was when Judd revealed the truth.

Madge broke away from the intensity of their locked gaze and waved toward the table.

As soon as everyone was seated, Conrad cleared his throat. "Let's say grace over our blessings." He reached his hand toward Mary on one side and Quint on the other. Quint reached for Judd's hand. Judd had no choice but to reach for Madge's.

Their gazes met and held in an electric burst that consumed the distance separating them and erased awareness of the others. For an eternal moment all that existed was each other and raw honest feelings between them, then she bowed her head.

His head bowed, he struggled to find solid ground for his thoughts and feelings.

Conrad prayed a simple prayer. Judd opened his eyes, uncertain where to look. His feelings were too strong to let the others guess at them. Looking at Madge would certainly make them more difficult to control. But he couldn't stop himself from a quick peek in her direction. Had she felt the same shuddering, overwhelming sensation?

But as her glance touched him, then went on to Mary without a spark of anything out of the ordinary, he sucked back disappointment. Seemed he was the only one who had felt the zing between them.

She turned her attention to the tea and cookies, and a short time later, Madge and Judd left, promising to visit again soon.

"They're doing okay, I think," Madge said. "Better than I thought they would." Such ordinary words. Had she really been unaware of the sparks between them that almost seared his skin?

"They'll do just fine if it depends on them. However, so much depends on crops, rain, prices and a thousand things they have no control over."

"But God is in control. I asked you earlier what kind of faith you have. You didn't answer."

He should have known she wouldn't forget. He considered his words carefully. "Madge, I once had a simple faith. Childlike. Then life got complicated."

"In what way?"

"I'm not sure I can explain."

"Try. I truly want to understand."

Because she cared and because he wanted her acceptance, he tried to shape his vague thoughts into some sort of sense. "I left teaching because I found it boring and headed west to ranching country. Out there a man lives or dies, fails or succeeds, by his own strength. He counts on only his own wits. I never saw any need of God's help. Then my mother lost everything, despite her unfaltering faith. All I could think to do was what I'd learned in the west country—take care of the business myself."

"But where did faith enter the picture?"

"You mean did I consult God? I didn't. Seems His hands are more than full with trying to fix the problems of the world."

"You're suggesting He's falling down on the job?"

He hadn't meant for his tone to reveal his doubts, but

her words pretty much explained how he felt. "When I see how the Burns family is coping, I am amazed. It almost makes me wish I had their simple faith."

"Their 'simple faith,' as you call it, has been birthed through loss and disappointment, and thrived and strengthened through more adversity."

"Quint told me about trees…plants…needing wind and storms to grow deep roots."

"That sounds like something Mrs. Burns would say."

Judd stared out the window. His self-sufficiency sounded rootless and weak when compared to the Burnses'. But he didn't know how to change. He'd lived life on his own terms too long. Perhaps Madge realized that and despised it. But he couldn't change who he was. Wouldn't even consider it until George Gratton received proper justice.

A sign, weather-beaten and almost buried in drifted soil, caught his attention. "Does that say For Sale?"

"Yes. The old Cotton place."

"What's it like?"

"Nice enough, though it's been empty almost two years. Do you want to see it?"

"I'd like to."

She jerked to a halt and reversed to the turnoff. "I hope we can get through." Soil had blown over the trail in many places, but she managed to plow through it until they reached the farmyard.

"Let's look around." Something inside him quickened at the stately two-story house, the hip-roofed barn, the row of smaller outbuildings. "Buildings appear solid."

"Mr. Cotton spared no expense. Borrowed heavily. Now he's gone."

They stepped around dirt drifts to the house. He tried the door. It opened with a grating squeal. "They even left some furniture."

"They took only what they could carry with them. The bank claimed the rest."

He stepped into the room that had served as kitchen. "A good size." One door led to a pantry, another to a generous-size room complete with table, chairs and sideboard. The third door—with double-wide sliding panels—led to the front room and off that was a bedroom or parlor or whatever need it suited. "This is fantastic. Why isn't someone living here?"

"Who can afford to buy it?"

"Let's go upstairs." Four bedrooms and a roomy closet opened off the hallway. He couldn't get over the beautiful house standing vacant.

They returned outside and explored the rest of the buildings. Struggling trees stood behind the house.

A restless yearning grew in Judd's heart. "I could see myself living here."

She watched him. "No money in farming."

He caught her chin and gazed deep into her eyes, seeing the willingness and promises he ached for and feared he would not see. "I could do something else until the economy turned around."

A flare of interest crossed her face. "I thought you wanted to go back to ranching."

"I've never had a reason to consider anything else." His fingers rested on her chin. She made no move to put distance between them. For days he'd ached for a chance to be alone with her, share the truth of his growing fondness for her. "Now staying here seems pretty alluring."

Tiny smile lines creased the edges of her eyes as she correctly interpreted his words to mean the allure was to more than an empty farm.

"I could see myself putting down roots in this place, especially with someone special to share it with."

She swallowed hard. Her eyelids flickered downward, then jerked up to reveal deep longings.

He caught his breath. "Madge." Slowly, anticipating each second of preparation, he lowered his head, tipping her chin a little so their lips touched gently, clung briefly. He wanted more. Everything. All of her forever. He wanted to share his life, his heart, his dreams, his all. Longing made his kiss grow more urgent.

"No." She pushed back, shoulders heaving in frantic gasps. "No. I can't do this." She spun around and raced away.

"Madge. What on earth?" He caught her in three strides and pulled her to a halt. She fought him, batting at his hands, rolling her head back and forth. He would not release her. Not without an explanation.

"What's wrong? It was just a little kiss."

She broke free again and backed away, her eyes wide, her lips pressed tight. She looked ready to cry.

His heart cracked with concern, and he reached for her. "Madge, whatever it is, I'm sure we can fix it."

She kept a safe distance between them. "No, we can't. You. Me." She shook her head. "No. Louisa—"

She broke off and clamped her lips tight. Stubbornness hardened her eyes.

"What about Louisa?"

"Nothing. Only that you are supposed to be her tutor."

"I am her tutor. What does that have to do with you and me? You aren't making sense."

She headed for the car. "Doesn't matter. You and I just can't be."

He grabbed her arm again. "I deserve more than that." At least he liked to think he did.

Her eyes suggested she wanted to explain. But she said, "I simply can't tell you more." She left him standing ankle-deep in a brown drift.

What secret could she be hiding to make love between them impossible?

A niggling doubt made its way to the surface of his thoughts. Was her rejection because of his duplicity in continuing to pose as Justin Bellamy? Did her strong morals make him an undeserving suitor because of his continued quest for justice?

If so, he must somehow convince her he was correct in his stand. The best way would be to prove Gratton's evilness as soon as possible.

Madge waited for him at the car.

"Go ahead. I'll walk the rest of the way. I need time to think."

She closed her eyes and sucked in air.

His heart seemed to beat thick syrup. Whatever her

reasons, he was not mistaken in thinking her decision hurt her as much as it did him.

He would find an answer to this unnamed problem before it tore them both apart.

Chapter Eight

Madge forced her heavy limbs into the car and grabbed the steering wheel. She sat for a moment, unable to think what she meant to do. *Start the car.* She did. *Head for home.* She aimed the car down the trail.

By the time she reached the main road, her shock gave way to weeping, and she pulled to the side and pressed her face to the back of her hands, letting tears drip over the spokes of the steering wheel.

His kiss had been the sweetest thing in the world, making her forget everything but his arms about her, his presence in her heart and the way her whole being wanted to belong to him.

What was she going to do? She pulled her head up. Perhaps if she spoke to Mother, explained how she felt...

She must try. She couldn't live with this war of longing and guilt inside. Nor could she let herself care for Judd without Mother's approval.

She lifted her head and snorted. As if she could hope to keep herself from caring. She thought of him with every breath, dreamed of him in every dream. Touring the old Cotton place, she'd thought of sharing each room with him, filling it with their love and hard work.

She'd speak to Mother as soon as she got back home, and if she gave the answer Madge hoped for, she would explain everything to Judd when he returned.

Louisa watched at the window as Madge slid from the car. She could tell Louisa wasn't pleased. The tight set of her lips made Madge's blood scrape through her veins.

Perhaps, before the next hour was out, Louisa would be reconciled to Judd caring for Madge.

Wasn't she always telling Judd to trust God to do what was right? Now was the time to practice what she preached. *Lord God, please make things work out*. She relaxed marginally.

"Hello, Louisa," she said cheerfully as she stepped into the room.

"What have you done with Justin?"

Madge pressed her lips together. Was it so obvious they had kissed?

"Why didn't he come back with you?"

Oh. Only that. "I left him a mile or two down the road. He decided he wanted to walk."

Louisa perked up. "Have you two had a spat?"

"No. Where's Mother?"

"In the other room. Why?" Louisa's voice demanded answers.

"I just want to speak to her." She headed for the front room. When Louisa started to follow, Madge said, "It's private."

Pretty Louisa marred her looks with a scowl fit for a banker about to lose his last penny. "You're up to something. And I think it involves Justin. Which means it involves me."

"If it does I'll be sure to notify you." She crossed the threshold and pulled the door closed after her.

Mother sat before the radio listening to a program. She glanced at Madge, then reached over to turn the knob off. "What is it?"

She sat by her mother and sought for the words to explain. "Mother, what do you think about Justin?"

"He seems a fine young man. He and Louisa have a lot in common. And hasn't Louisa's health improved with his attention?"

"Louisa appears fond of him, doesn't she?" She knew the answer but hoped—prayed—mother would have seen it differently.

"I'm happy with how their relationship is progressing. Why do you ask?"

"I just wonder—" Wanting the man chosen for her sister was downright selfish. "Does Justin know your ultimate goal concerning him?"

"I haven't said anything yet. It seemed premature."

"Don't you think he should? Besides, what do you really know about him?"

"Having him here every day gives us a good chance to assess his character."

Madge didn't respond. Justin wasn't even real, yet Mother and Louisa thought he was the right man for the eldest sister. "I think you should ask him about his past, his plans for the future. Maybe it's time to see what his interest in Louisa is."

Louisa burst through the door. "You're trying to steal him from me. Isn't it enough that you have good health while mine is poor? Or that you get to do the things you want? Seems you just can't stand to see me get anything before you do, even though I'm older."

Madge stared at her. Sweet Louisa revealing such venom? Hardly seemed possible. "I'm not trying to steal anything from you." She hoped her guilty secret of a stolen kiss didn't send telltale pink to her cheeks.

"Then where is he? Why do you take him with you, then leave him to find his own way home?" She turned to Mother. "She left him to walk. Poor Justin with his bad leg. He'll be coughing all night after this."

It was all Madge could do not to snort in disbelief. "He'll be fine."

"Well, I'm concerned." The look she gave Madge told of a care beyond thinking of him walking a mile or two.

Madge smiled gently. "You have no reason to worry." She would not be guilty of taking what her sister wanted and deserved. She glanced at Mother, wanting to say more, wanting to urge her to question Justin more closely, assess his interest.

Mother watched Madge and Louisa with wise knowing.

Madge shifted her attention to the far corner of the room. She did not want Mother to guess at her heart's yearning. If only Mother would question Judd, ascertain the truth, then perhaps both she and Louisa would change their minds about the man.

But until that happened, Madge would avoid him.

She bid them good-night and hurried up the stairs to crumple on her bed. Somehow she'd expected this to turn out differently. Didn't God see her heart? Know her affection for Judd? But Louisa cared about him, too. No, she cared about Justin. If this deception continued, Louisa was going to be hurt badly when she discovered Justin wasn't real. Or maybe Judd wasn't real.

She touched her lips, remembering their recent kiss, and smiled. Oh, Judd was real enough. And the way she'd felt holding his hand at the Burnses' place was further proof.

What was she to do? Could she persuade Judd to tell the truth? Or encourage Mother to probe and discover it herself?

She flipped to her back and stared at the ceiling. Shouldn't she trust God to order things rightly? But what if she left the situation in God's hands and Louisa and Justin—or would he be Judd?—married? Could she still trust God?

Sometimes it was so very difficult not to take things into her own hands.

Madge was beginning to really welcome the afternoons spent at the Gratton house. Mr. Gratton usually came home before she left. They often worked together before she served his supper and headed home.

He had a narrow bed moved into the room they were converting for his mother. At her suggestion, he put in a chiffonier and a wardrobe. Madge hung pictures, made up the bed and draped a colorful quilt over the foot.

"It looks welcoming," George—as he'd instructed Madge to call him—said. "Thank you for making it so."

"It was fun." Even more importantly, working here got her away from home and provided an escape from Judd. When she left each afternoon, he still sat with Louisa. She hoped his instruction was confined to Greek and art and didn't include lessons on romance.

He'd glanced up more than once as she crossed the yard carrying a basket of clean articles but couldn't offer to help her with the laundry deliveries, as he'd still been with Louisa. That had been her intention.

She shifted her attention back to George. "What's your mother like?"

"She's not as strong as she used to be, though she'd never admit it. Wait, I'll get a picture." He thumped up the stairs and returned with a small likeness of a lady with silver hair and a direct look. There was a strong family resemblance.

"She looks sweet," Madge commented.

He chuckled. "Sweet and determined. Tell me about your family."

She told of her sisters and described their life in quick detail.

"No beau?"

She hesitated. Wished she could deny it. But she couldn't admit it, either. "No," she said.

"I sense there's more to it."

"I care about a man, but he's not for me."

"Who is he for, then?"

"For another. One more worthy and deserving." She

tried to believe it, but a stubborn bit of defensiveness argued Judd would find Louisa far too soft and needy.

"My dear, any man who would think that isn't worthy of you."

His kind words brought a sting to her eyes. She wished she could explain Judd hadn't suggested such a thing.

George wisely dropped the subject. "I have a few family mementos to put out. Would you help me?" He brought in a box. They set out family pictures and hung some paintings—only copies but still lovely. Then he pulled out a crystal bowl. The light struck it, sending flickers of color across the room.

Madge caught her breath. "It's beautiful." She could picture it full of truffles or Christmas oranges. Or sitting on a crocheted doily. She put it in the center of the table—she'd find a doily later. Would the table abandoned at the Cotton farm clean up as nicely as this one had? She rubbed the polished surface. Not that she had anything like this crystal bowl to put on it. The floors at the farm looked as if a good cleaning would fix them, but the old wallpaper would have to come down.

She closed her eyes, pushing away such useless dreams. George moved to her side, staring at the bowl.

"It's all I have left of my former life. Alas, like many, I over invested in the market. Got too bold and, I suppose, too greedy. Lost everything. To my sorrow, I lost more than my own."

"I'm sorry."

"It taught me a lesson…don't trust in things that can be so easily lost."

Trust. She'd never found it as difficult to trust God as she did now. Would He make it possible for her to love Judd, or…she could barely breathe…would He provide the strength for her to watch Louisa marry him?

"Sometimes—" her voice was a mere whisper "—it's hard to rest in God."

"True, my dear. But easier than taking matters into our own hands and having to deal with watching things crumble before our eyes."

She sensed personal, raw experience behind his words, but they were wise comfort. She'd trust God to work things out.

It was late when she finally headed home. Truth was, home no longer felt like a place of safety and shelter. She feared she would encounter Judd at every turn and had come to dread Louisa's dark glances. If George had invited her to stay and share his meal she would have done so gladly, but he seemed to expect she'd want to hurry back to her family.

She'd purposely delayed her return until she was certain supper would be over when she arrived. Sally had left food in the oven for her. Although she wasn't hungry, she pulled the plate out and sat down to eat. Mother came from the front room to join her.

"Where's Louisa and Sally?" Madge asked.

"Sally has gone to visit friends. Louisa is in bed."

"In bed?" That was three days in a row she'd retired early. "Is she sick?" Or pointedly avoiding Madge?

Mother's hands moved restlessly across the table. "She's begged for an afternoon nap the last two days."

That wasn't a good sign. "I thought—" She assumed

once Madge backed off, Louisa would grow closer to Justin. Actually, she'd hoped Justin would tell her the truth about who he was, and Louisa would—what? Did Madge really think Louisa would see Judd as less attractive than Justin? "Has she argued with Justin?"

"Not to my knowledge."

"Do you think we should ask the doctor to call?" To her shame, she mentally counted the pennies the visit would cost.

"I don't know. It isn't like she has a fever or complains of any pain. Let's wait a few more days."

The next day Madge pushed aside her desire to avoid Judd in order to observe Louisa. She paused going up the stairs with laundry to watch the pair. Judd read from a textbook. Louisa stared out the window, her mind certainly not on the studies. That alone was more than enough evidence Louisa was sick.

A few minutes later Madge returned, and when she glanced in the room, she saw Louisa with her head back and her eyes closed. Either she was ill or had overtaxed herself with too much studying.

Madge made sure she was at the table for supper, even though it took every scrap of self-control to keep her gaze away from Judd. Not that she needed to look his way to note his ink-stained hands reach for a bowl of potatoes. Hadn't he said he hated teaching? Her nerves crackled in response to the tension emanating from him. Was he resenting the time he spent tutoring Louisa? Had Louisa guessed? Perhaps that explained the way she picked at her food.

Whatever the cause, Madge determined to get to the bottom of it. As soon as Judd left for the evening, she would speak to Louisa.

Judd didn't linger. Madge tried to convince herself she didn't regret the fact, but part of her followed him across the yard. Would he change into Judd clothes and go to town? Would she see him there?

She curtly cut off such thoughts and headed to the front room where Louisa lay on the sofa, her head on a pillow, a blanket wrapped around her. Madge edged a chair close and sat down. "Louisa, what's wrong with you?"

Louisa's eyes flew open, and Madge blinked before the anger she saw. "Besides never having any energy and always having to take whatever scraps people toss my way? Why, nothing, dear sister. Nothing."

The accusations burned a hole in Madge's heart. "Louisa, that's not fair. I don't do that. I've always helped you as best I could."

Louisa looked ready to cry. "I know you do. I'm sorry. I'm just feeling such a burden to everyone."

Madge knelt beside the couch and pulled Louisa into her arms. "You're my sister. You could never be a burden."

Louisa shivered. "Even if I took the man you love?"

Madge stiffened. Were her feelings so obvious? She'd tried her best to hide them. She forced a little laugh. "Can you see us falling in love with the same man? I can't. You'd want someone kind and gentle and interested in studies." Like Justin. "I'd want someone bold, adventuresome, hardworking." Like Judd. Oh, what a muddle.

"No one will ever love me. I'm too much bother."

That brought a genuine laugh from Madge. "You need to clean your mirror so you see the beautiful girl there next time you look in it."

"You think I am?"

Madge pushed away to grin at her sister. "Louisa, I'm the workhorse and you're the beauty. If you weren't my beloved sister, I'd be jealous."

Louisa laughed. "And if you weren't my sister, I'd be jealous of how hard you work."

"Don't ever wish to trade places with me."

"Sometimes I do."

"Oh, no, dear sister, never." How could she harbor selfish thoughts when Louisa was so generous?

Louisa sat up and faced Madge. "I could not bear if something came between us. Especially if it was my fault."

"That will never happen." Madge vowed not to be guilty of creating a rift between them. If Louisa loved Judd and he learned to love her…and why wouldn't he? As she said, Louisa was the beautiful one.

They talked sister stuff for a few minutes, then Madge left to make her deliveries, more convinced than ever not to interfere with Mother's plans for Louisa and Justin.

She dropped off laundry at two places, picked up more to wash at two other places and decided to drive past the Gratton house before she headed home. Maybe George would be on the porch and she could stop for a visit. She found a great deal of comfort from his wise words.

But he wasn't outside. The only light was in the front room. She glimpsed him sitting in an armchair reading. She had no right to disturb him.

A shadow separated from the fence, and she stared as it turned into Judd. Was he waiting for her? Hoping to catch a ride home?

She could not bear the thought of being sequestered with him in the tiny space of the car, filled as it was with so many memories, so she pretended not to notice him and sped on by.

Madge hoped her little talk with Louisa would make her feel better. She purposely avoided Judd as much as possible, thinking Louisa would take heart. It stung more than Madge cared to admit to snub him, especially when she caught a flash of confusion on his face. She didn't know what else to do. Seemed every choice she made hurt someone. She prayed long and hard, but her prayers yielded no change—not in her heart nor in the situation between Louisa and Justin.

Despite all she did to help her sister, Louisa grew more and more morose. Finally, Mother called a family meeting. "Louisa, I've consulted both Sally and Madge and have their full agreement. We don't like to see you going downhill this way. I've decided to ask the doctor to visit. Perhaps he can suggest a tonic or something." The worry in Mother's voice spoke for all of them.

Louisa bolted upright in her chair. "No, Mother. It's

not necessary. My ailment isn't something the doctor can give me a prescription for."

"You can't go on this way."

Louisa seemed to fight an internal battle, then she nodded. "You are quite right. It's time I fixed things." She pushed from the table. "I need to be alone to work things out and then I'll take the action I need." As regal as a queen, she left the room.

Mother, Sally and Madge stared after her.

"What on earth?" Mother asked. "What is she talking about?"

"I don't know," Madge said. Sally echoed her words.

But they didn't have to wait long to find out. Louisa returned an hour later with a quiet determination in her expression.

"Are you okay, dear?" Mother asked.

"I'm fine." Louisa's voice was firm, and she sat down and opened a book.

Madge waited until Mother went outside to help Sally in the garden to approach her sister. "Louisa, what's going on?"

Louisa smiled. "I've been guilty of feeling sorry for myself and worse, but I've repented and I intend to correct my behavior."

Madge opened her mouth twice—once to protest, but no words would form, and a second time to demand specifics.

"That's between myself and God," Louisa said—and she would say nothing more.

Finally, in frustration, Madge gave up prodding her sister. "I have no idea what you think you've done, but so long as you've dealt with it and can stop moping about...all I want is for you to be happy."

Louisa nodded, her expression serious. "I want the same for you."

Madge nodded. She'd never questioned Louisa's love, just as she hoped Louisa would never have cause to question hers.

Chapter Nine

Judd sat beside Louisa in their customary place. He struggled to keep his thoughts on the lesson he'd prepared, but it proved a challenge, especially when Louisa looked for her usual keen attention. "I've heard good things about the play, *Deacon Dubbs,* that the community of Bowwell is putting on." Louisa mentioned a town almost an hour's drive away.

Judd murmured a noncommittal sound. Louisa had made her interest in him quite plain. He'd done his best to make it equally as clear that his interest lay elsewhere—on her sister.

"Madge has mentioned she'd like to see it."

Judd grunted. He had no idea what Louisa meant.

"She might go if you invited her."

"What?" He stared at innocent-looking eyes. "I hardly think so. She finds it impossible to even be in the same room as me." The way she jumped up and escaped if he entered the kitchen hurt like pouring kerosene on an open wound—one of his grandfather's favorite medical treatments. Once he'd thought she seemed as eager to spend time together as he was.

Until he'd kissed her.

"I can't see how it would hurt to ask her." Louisa studied him with demanding eyes. "Unless you object to a little outing with her."

Object? Not in this lifetime. Did Louisa mean to encourage him in Madge's direction after the way she had hinted at her own interest? "Let me see if I understand you correctly. You're suggesting I ask Madge to accompany me to this play?"

"Just a thought," Louisa murmured.

Louisa's encouragement convinced him he should try again with Madge.

But finding a chance and constructing the right words proved a challenge as she continued to avoid him.

Finally, he decided to combine two things. He would study the Gratton house as he did most evenings, only this time he planned to show up when Madge prepared to leave, providing him a chance to talk to her.

That evening he waited, leaning against the car door, and watched her approach as she left the house. She didn't see him at first. When she did, she faltered and glanced over her shoulder as if planning to seek refuge inside the Gratton house.

"You've been avoiding me. Why?"

She shook her head. "I'm not." As if to prove him wrong, she took two steps closer.

"You're sure of that?" He kept his arms crossed and continued to lounge against the car, although every nerve in his body ached to reach for her, pull her against his chest and breathe in her sweetness.

"Sure, I'm sure."

"Care to prove it?"

She backed up so fast he feared she'd fall.

He realized she'd interpreted his words as a challenge to a kiss. He hadn't meant them that way, though he had no objection to it. He quickly pulled his thoughts back to reality. "If you don't object to my company, then come with me to the play in Bowwell."

"A play?"

Did she sound disappointed? "I heard *Deacon Duff* is playing. Supposed to be a good play."

"Deacon Duff?"

Why did she seem so confused? He'd wanted to allow her a chance to say no, but now he couldn't bear the thought. "Let's make a day of it. We'll go in time to have supper. I think you'd enjoy the play. What do you think?" *Say yes.*

"I really can't."

"Why? Are you afraid to take time away from work?" At the stubborn denial on her face, he pressed his point. "Shouldn't trusting God mean a person can relax once in a while?"

"Of course I can relax."

"Then you'll come with me?"

"Fine. I'll go." She sounded as if he'd forced her into a corner and her agreement was out of necessity.

He wished he could see her better, but dusk had fallen and her face was shadowed. He moved closer, searching her expression. When he saw her tiny smile, he relaxed. She didn't seem to mind the idea at all.

They picked Friday as the night they would go.

He held the car door for Madge and bent over to the open window as he closed it. "I'll see you later."

"You could ride home with me." She smiled, then ducked her head, as if she didn't want him to see her expression.

He fought the urge to catch her chin, tip her face and assure himself he'd seen a flash of eager welcome. Judd considered accepting a ride with her, but he still hoped Gratton would reveal his hand. Perhaps tonight someone would come calling under cover of darkness, or Gratton might now set out to meet someone—most likely a lonesome widow woman with a secret stash of cash. "I'll be along later."

He stepped back so she could drive away. And he started counting the hours until they headed to Bowwell.

Friday finally arrived. He wished he'd asked her to leave right after lunch, but she would likely have demurred, claiming she had work to do. He watched her scurry around in order to do the laundry before it was time to go.

Louisa noticed his distraction. "Seems she could use some help if she's to take most of the afternoon away from her work. Which is a great idea, as far as I'm concerned. She works far too hard."

"Yes, she does." He tried to force his attention back

to Greek conjugations. Somehow the whole language was clear as mud.

"Someone should help her," Louisa said.

"Uh-huh."

Louisa stared hard at him.

"Me?"

"I doubt I'd be of much use."

He tried to guess if Louisa had some ulterior motive, for her suggestion but her eyes were guileless. A small smile tugged at the corners of her mouth. He stared at her. She met his study without blinking. But her suggestion confused him. A few days ago she would have clung to him, fretting she'd never learn all she wanted without his help. She seemed to resent any time he spent pursuing other activities, especially if they involved Madge. Now if he didn't know better, he would suspect her of playing matchmaker.

Not that he was about to object.

"You're sure you don't mind?"

"I wouldn't suggest it if I did."

He slammed the book shut, apologized for the sharp noise and then hurried away without giving her a chance to say anything. Her laughter followed him out the door.

Madge had finished rinsing the sheets. He grabbed the basket.

"What are you doing?"

"I'll carry this up the stairs for you." Before she could open her mouth or dream up a protest, he clattered up the steps.

At first Madge didn't move, then she raced up after him. "Aren't you supposed to be teaching Louisa?"

"She kindly gave me the rest of the afternoon off."

Madge squinted at him. "She did, did she? Now, why would she do that?"

"'Cause she's afraid you won't get your work done in time to get ready, maybe?"

"She is?" She turned and grabbed a wet sheet and pegged it in place.

He ducked under the line so he could face her. "You seem surprised." No more than he had been.

"It seems odd to think of Louisa passing up a moment of lesson time."

"Do you question every kindness?"

She wrinkled her nose, but before she could voice an argument he let the sheet fall between them. He didn't intend to analyze Louisa's generous offer. The afternoon ahead promised all sorts of fun and delights that had nothing to do with the play they planned to see.

He returned outside to empty the wash water, carefully applying it to the growing plants. Despite the damage inflicted by the grasshoppers, there would be potatoes and carrots, beets, onions and even some chard, which he had developed a fondness for since coming to the Morgan household. As he headed back for the rest of the water, he glanced up and caught Madge watching him. He grinned and nodded. She blushed as bright as the combs on the chickens pecking in the yard and ducked out of sight.

Yes, it promised to be a fine day.

He hung the tubs to dry, then hurried to get ready. He wanted to go as Judd but wasn't sure how he could accomplish it without giving away his disguise. Only one way to do it. He waited for Madge to come down with the baskets ready to deliver. "Put them in my automobile. We'll take it."

Her eyes widened in surprise and—dare he think—delight.

"I'll drive up to the door of my shack and wait for you in the car."

As she realized what he intended, a becoming pink filled her cheeks. Just like a summer rose. "You're going as Judd," she murmured.

"Can't imagine enjoying the day any other way." He could never think of himself as Justin when he was with her.

He drove his car close to the soddie, then hurried into clothes that fit and boots that made him feel real. He only wished he could shave off the beard, but not yet. Instead, he trimmed it well, then, carrying his hat under his arm, he slipped into the car, hoping no one would take note of the difference in his appearance. He had only a moment to wait before Madge rushed across the yard wearing a dark blue dress with a white collar that made her eyes look as brown as pure chocolate. She'd brushed her hair back and held it in place with shiny combs.

His tongue grew thick at her beauty. Keeping his thoughts and emotions under control might well turn the afternoon into delightful torture.

He wanted to spring out and open the door for her, but, afraid her sisters and mother would be watching from the house, he sat as she climbed in. "Sorry for not being a gentleman," he murmured.

She chuckled. "Guess that's what happens when you live a double life."

A tiny argument sprang to his thoughts, but he dismissed it. He wouldn't ruin the day by referring to his reasons for being Justin Bellamy.

The sun shone with usual brightness but seemed to hold less bite and more kiss. The wind blew, but gently. Or so it seemed to Judd. The sky had a diamond-like brilliance as they delivered the clean laundry then headed down the dusty road toward Bowwell.

"Have you been to the town before?" Madge asked.

"No. You'll have to provide directions as to where we should eat and where the play is held."

"There's also a park in the center of town, though I wonder how it's fared with the drought and all."

"We'll have to check it out." He hoped there'd be lots of sheltered coves where he might admire her beauty and perhaps steal a kiss. Remembering how she'd reacted last time he kissed her, he decided to avoid the pleasing occupation until he could be certain she'd welcome such attention.

The hour-long drive passed quickly and pleasantly as they discussed how the Burns family was doing.

"Conrad still hasn't changed his mind about marrying Joanie?"

"No. He's a stubborn man. I'm afraid he's going to break her heart."

She shifted the discussion to Gratton. "His mother is due to arrive soon. The place is fixed up nicely for her."

He didn't want to ruin the day by talking of that man,

but he couldn't resist one little question. "Are you sure the woman is his mother?"

She sucked in air nosily. "Of course she is. He showed me her picture. Who else do you think she might be?"

"I don't know. Maybe a woman he doesn't want to confess to having no legitimate relationship to."

She studied him intently. He fixed his gaze firmly on the road ahead. He should have kept his doubts to himself.

Finally, when he thought he would suffocate from trying to keep his thoughts under control and his face turned forward, she spoke. "I hope you don't let what happened to your mother make you bitter and mistrusting."

Her words sliced through his conscience. Knowing Madge's concern, he almost threw his plans out the window. Almost—but not quite. "I don't intend to let it. I have one goal in mind—see a certain man brought to justice. That's all."

She turned to watch the passing dusty fields. "I'm looking forward to the play. Everyone says it's hilarious."

He gratefully accepted her attempt to avoid conflict between them. "I'm looking forward to it, too." Only it wasn't thoughts of the play filling him with eager anticipation. It was the pleasure of her company.

Soon they came to the main street of Bowwell. Unlike most prairie towns that had one long road running either perpendicular or at right angles to the railway tracks, the streets in this town formed a T. One corner was a square filled with poplar and maple trees with benches along the perimeter and pathways leading inward to the heart.

"That's the park I mentioned. It looks better than I expected, though there is usually an abundance of flowers in the planters."

He parked at the side of the street. "We have lots of time. Shall we wander through it?"

"I'd like that."

He rushed around and opened the door. As she stepped to the sidewalk, he held his arm out for her. She tucked her arm through his and smiled up shyly. He pulled his elbow close, pressing her hand to his ribs.

The park, although struggling against drought and grasshoppers, was still a pleasant place. Big trees sheltered Judd and Madge from view as they walked along the path. More benches were placed sporadically, inviting them to sit and talk. But they sauntered on. Only one woman hurried through, shepherding three children ahead of her. Muted sounds reached them from the busy streets, but other than that, they might have been alone.

Something nagged at his thoughts and demanded an answer. "What made you change your mind?"

Only the slight twitch of her arm at his side gave any indication that she knew what he referred to.

"About what?"

"Being in my company. I'd begun to think I carried the plague the way you avoided me."

"I didn't avoid you."

"You did." He pulled her around to face him. "Maybe someday you'll feel you can tell the truth about why."

Madge stared at a spot past his shoulder. "Because... we thought... Mother planned..." She drew in a deep breath and looked directly at him. "I'll tell you what. I'll tell you the reason when you tell the others the truth about who you are."

He searched her eyes a long time, and what he saw filled him with hope and longing. He wanted to be completely honest with her, let her see into every corner of his heart, open every thought to her. He nodded. "It's a deal, but not just yet."

Disappointment flashed across her face, and she lowered her head.

He wanted to lift her chin and kiss away every doubt, but how could he when he hid the truth from her? "You keep your secret and I'll keep mine." It should have made him feel justified, but instead, it built an invisible wall between them.

No reason to let it. He had told her all she needed to know. She would only be hurt if she learned Gratton was the man he sought to bring to justice. And whatever *her* secret, it did not stop him from caring about her and hoping there could be something special and lasting between them.

He pulled her to his side again. "Let's see the rest of the park." But too soon, they reached the end and had to retrace their steps.

They returned to the heart of town. "Where do you suggest we eat?"

She appeared to ponder the question. "I've only eaten in one place with a very special person."

Jealousy ground through his insides. He kept his

voice low. "Yeah. Who?" Somehow, despite his intentions, his words sounded like gravel under the wheels of the car.

She noticed and laughed. "My father."

He chuckled, as pleased as she. "Would you like to go there?"

"Yes, I would." She still held his arm and pulled him to the right. "It's the Silver Star dining room down at the end of the block."

He'd have let her take him anywhere, but she only led him to a low building with a row of windows facing the street, through which he saw white tablecloths, points hanging neatly from each side. They stepped inside, and a young woman in a black dress and tiny white apron led them to a table next to the window, partially hidden by a branching fern.

The girl slipped away, leaving them to study the menus. Judd didn't care what they ate, but he wanted the evening to be special, memorable for Madge.

"The beef tenderloin sounds good."

"It does."

He ordered fresh lemonade to accompany the meal and sat back to study Madge as they waited for their food. Aware of his scrutiny, she darted little glances at him and fiddled with her fork. Realizing he made her nervous, he shifted to look out the window. "Why did your father bring you here?"

She chuckled. "Because I insisted I should accompany him when he came to inspect a piece of machinery. I wanted to see him conduct business." A faraway look filled her eyes. "He was a canny businessman. He managed to walk away from most deals pleased with his negotiations while the other party took his money and considered themselves fortunate to have made such a good bargain. I learned a lot from him."

He could see her doing the same—getting the deal she wanted, yet leaving the other person thinking he had gotten what he wanted. "Your father sounds like a good man."

"He was a great man. He never compromised, yet he never accepted a bad deal, either. I miss him." She sighed. "I wonder if he would be disappointed in me for persuading Mother to let the farmland go."

Her sadness tore at Judd's insides, and he reached across the table and captured her restless hands. "If he was the astute businessman you say he was, he would know and approve that you did what you must to salvage your home."

The smile she favored him with slid through his thoughts like warm honey, sweet and healing. He held her gaze, drinking deeply of the way she openly met his look, silently baring her heart to him. "Madge, I—"

"Your meals." The interruption ended the opportunity to say how he felt.

He swallowed back the urge to tell the woman he didn't care if he ate or not. But Madge smiled her thanks.

They waited until the server moved off. Madge gave him an expectant look. He realized she waited for him to offer the blessing. For an uncomfortable moment, Judd wasn't sure what to do. He wasn't much for praying out loud in public. Yet his conscience wouldn't allow him to partake of such a lovely meal with Madge across from him without thanking God. Madge smiled sweetly and his nervousness disappeared.

"I'll say the grace," he said.

She reached for his hands and bowed her head. For a frantic heartbeat he couldn't move. Couldn't think. Her gesture was so full of simple faith in him, it made his lungs stall. He vowed he would never do anything to make her trust falter. Then he bowed his head and, from a heart overflowing with gratitude, he offered a sincere prayer of thanks.

For a few minutes, they ate in silence. The food was as good as it smelled.

She paused. "What was it like growing up with three brothers?"

He thought of Louisa, who didn't have the energy to do anything vigorous, and Sally, who was so quiet and shy she almost disappeared into the woodwork. Amusement filled him. "I expect a lot different than growing up with two sisters."

She chuckled. "I would think so. I want to know about it. Were you mischievous?"

"We were a handful. It's a wonder we didn't drive my mother crazy."

"Why? What did you do?"

He tipped his head and pretended to study her seriously. "If I tell you, you might decide you want nothing more to do with me."

Her eyes sparkled. "Maybe. Maybe not. Why not take a chance and see?"

"Okay. First, let me say that Levi managed to stay out

of trouble better than the rest of us. Being the youngest by a few years, Mother managed to keep him closer to home. But the three of us—me, Carson and Redford—we ran wild. Nothing bad, of course."

"Of course not." She looked suitably doubtful. "But details, sir. I'm waiting for details."

He could not refuse the interest flashing in her eyes. "We used to tie ropes to trees and see how far we could swing from one to the other. When we were much younger, you understand."

"Of course," she murmured.

"Sounds innocent enough, but we kept getting bolder, making the distance between ropes longer. One day we made it to our greatest challenge. I was the biggest and I made it safely." He chuckled. "I really had to reach and guessed Carson, who was close in size, might make it. He did. By then we both knew Redford was too small, but we nudged each other and didn't say anything. You see, he was always insistent he could do anything we could. So we let him try."

"Tsk. How badly was he hurt?"

"Would you believe he broke both arms?"

She gasped. "He did? How awful. And to think you could have stopped him. I hope you were suitably punished."

He roared with laughter. "He didn't break anything, though we had a hard time explaining away the bruises all over his body."

She stared in disbelief. Then her eyes narrowed. "You tricked me."

He nodded, his heart brimming with amusement.

She laughed—a rich, full-throated sound. "I pity your poor mother. I expect you made her life…interesting. Challenging."

"Mother was always a good sport. She understood the difference between innocent, boyish fun and maliciousness. Beats me how she could have been sucked in by that shyster."

She sobered and looked ready to tell him again how he should leave things in God's hands.

He did not want to hear it. "We gave the teacher a heart attack one day. Carson had a pet mouse he carried around. I didn't want to be outdone by my brother, so I tamed one, too, though I have to say mice aren't easy to tame and even harder to keep in one place. We decided to take them to school one day."

Her expression flared with surprise and shock.

"Don't ask why. It seemed like a reasonable thing at the time. We put them in our overalls." He patted his chest to indicate the breast pocket. "They both wiggled loose while we were standing saying the Lord's Prayer and ran up to the front. Mrs. Porter opened her eyes to see the little guys scurry across her feet. Boy, did she scream."

Madge shuddered. "I'm beginning to think I was fortunate to have sisters."

"Our punishment was to memorize three chapters in the Bible. And we didn't get to choose them. I can still say them. 'In the beginning was the Word, and the Word was with God—' You want to hear it all?"

Her laughter again tugged at his heart. "I'll pass." She grew more serious. "When did you become a Christian?"

"That teacher who made us memorize Bible passages?"

She nodded.

"She also told us she forgave us and went on to explain how some things aren't only silly tricks. They are sins and only God can forgive them. We'd heard it before, both at home and at church, but when Mrs. Porter told us, it made sense and both Carson and I knelt at our desks and asked Jesus to forgive us."

"That's sweet. But Jesus is so much more than a means of forgiveness."

"I know what you're going to say. Let's leave it for now."

"I just wish you would see how God can be trusted to take care of justice."

"As the oldest son, I have a duty to protect my mother."

Her eyes grew dark and troubled, but she only shook her head.

Knowing one sure way to divert her from the topic that created dissent between them, he said, "Tell me how you became a Christian."

"My father taught us well about God's love and care. He always came to our rooms and said our evening prayers. One night he simply asked if I had yet decided to be part of God's family. I said I'd like to be."

"You did it to please your father?"

"In part, but I truly believed the things I had learned and I was ready. He did the same for Louisa and Sally. We could never figure out how he knew when each of us was ready."

"Sounds like he knew his girls. Just like Mother knew her boys. You know, we could never fool her. She always was aware of when we'd done something we shouldn't have."

"What about your father? You never speak of him."

"He died when I was young—shortly after Levi was born. I can barely remember him. Mostly I remember being the man of the family, making sure Mother and the younger boys were taken care of." He'd failed in his responsibilities more than once, but never to the degree he had in letting Gratton steal Mother's home.

Madge watched him closely, and he realized his regret and bitterness likely showed on his face. He didn't want to hear any more about letting God manage without his help.

"I believe it's time to go to the play." He paid the bill, and they left the restaurant.

"It's in the town hall." Again she rested her hand in the crook of his elbow.

Again, he pressed her arm close.

"Thank you for the lovely meal and for telling me more about yourself."

"You're welcome. I enjoyed learning more about you, too." He would never get tired of listening to her, hearing of her childhood. He would never get tired of her company. Perhaps today was the start of them becoming more than mere friends.

Chapter Ten

Madge made no objection when Judd pressed her arm to his side. Why would she? She loved it. She wanted this evening to last forever. Too soon she'd have to return home to reality, to face Mother's faintly chiding glance and Louisa's…only, something about her sister had changed. Maybe putting aside self-pity, as she'd confessed, had made her more generous. She'd shown unusual kindness by seeing Madge got her chores done in time to attend the play. But it seemed more than that. Why hadn't she protested when Madge had said she and Justin were going to the play? Was she that certain of his interest? Or was she pretending a generosity she didn't feel? But she'd never known Louisa to be deceitful, so she had to believe her actions were genuinely kind. But what did it mean?

Determined not to deal with it before she had to, she pushed the questions aside. For now she would accept the pleasure of the evening and face the consequences when she must.

She enjoyed her time with Judd, seeing him as a man who wanted to protect his loved ones. The idea thrilled her to the core. Yet she feared for him. Feared his path would lead him into danger. At the very least, would cause him to disobey God. But she had said all she could. She'd pressed him to trust God. She must do the same in this situation.

A crowd gathered at the hall doorway, everyone jostling good-naturedly to be admitted first. Judd dropped his arm across her shoulders and pulled her close to shield her from some young man who got a little too enthusiastic with his pushing.

Her heart swelled with pleasure at his gesture. She breathed deeply of his scent. A warm sense of well-being filled her limbs with a delightful melting sensation.

They edged into the hall, paused at the ticket booth to purchase admission, and then he led her down the aisle to a place where they would see and hear well.

They settled in, and he reached for her hand, pulled it back into the bend of his arm, then rested his palm over her fingers.

She ducked her head to hide the pleasure she suspected would be all too evident in her face. Tried to tell herself it was only because he felt responsible to protect those under his care.

He leaned close to whisper, "I haven't offended you, have I?"

Swallowing back a strange tightness in her throat, she looked into his dark eyes, not inches away. He seemed uncertain, and she suddenly cared not if he saw how much she enjoyed this closeness, but her voice refused to work. She could only shake her head.

"Good." With a wide grin he settled back, though she didn't miss the fact that he leaned closer.

The lights dimmed and the play began. It was funny and touching. The audience laughed and clapped and cheered. For Madge, the magic was multiplied each time she glanced at Judd and met his eyes, sharing the moment with him. More than once, their eyes locked, and for an instant they were alone in the room, unaware of the others, their interest in the entertainment forgotten.

Thankfully, the audience would make a noise reminding her they were not alone, forcing her to turn and concentrate on the activity on the stage.

It ended to a standing ovation and several curtain calls.

Judd stepped into the aisle and waited for her to move in front of him. Everyone pushed toward the exit. He cupped her shoulder with his big, warm hand and guided her toward the door. She was protected, sheltered by his body.

She would have gladly stood in the crowd forever, pressed to him, guarded by him. But all too soon they broke into fresh air. With no more excuse to stand so close, Madge moved a step away.

Judd caught her hand and pulled her to his side. Their pathway led them past the park, and at his suggestion she gladly accompanied him down the shadowed lanes.

"Did you enjoy the play?" he murmured.

"It was fun." She'd enjoyed his company even more.

"I sure laughed when they went to the garden and

he tried to tell her he still loved her, but when he sat on the wheelbarrow it broke."

Everyone had laughed. "They seemed to be plagued with nothing but disasters."

"Yet they did manage to admit their love."

"But one thing bothers me. Why did they waste so many years?" The main characters had been childhood sweethearts, but the man had wandered away and married another. The play took place seventeen years later when he returned, after his wife died, to find the leading lady an old maid owner of a huge ranch. "Besides, didn't it look like he had suddenly found out she had this big ranch? As if he was interested in her riches." As soon as she spoke the words, she wished she could pull them back. The last thing she wanted was to remind him of his mother and his quest to see the gold digger man brought to justice. Quickly she rushed on before he realized what she'd said. "I know if I loved someone, I would tell them. I wouldn't want to waste seventeen years."

He reached for her hand and squeezed it. "Me, neither." Then he stopped and pulled her into his arms, looking down into her face.

Her heart rapped so hard, she was sure he would feel it.

"In fact, it's time I said I think I might be falling in love with you."

"But…" *You are supposed to fall in love with Louisa.* Madge had done all she could to stay out of the way so it would happen. Hadn't she? What would Mother say? Louisa?

But the arguments fell to the ground like last year's leaves.

She had just vowed she would tell someone if she loved them, but her mouth refused to work. All she could do was bury her face against his chest, smiling as she felt his heartbeat beneath her cheek.

He seemed to understand her unspoken message and wrapped her more tightly to him, their hearts beating as one. Then he shifted and caught her chin with his strong fingers, tipping her face upward.

Even in the dim light, she saw the eager question in his eyes. For answer she stood on tiptoe and lifted her head. He read her intention and quickly claimed her lips. This time she had nothing to fear, nothing to hide, nothing to hold her back, and she put her whole heart and all her love into the kiss. He gave equally as much back, carrying her upward on the wings of love and joy.

He broke away with a sigh. "I think we better go home."

She snuggled to his side. She was in no hurry, but Mother would worry if they were too late. She hated the thought of facing Mother, though, so she clung to his arm and pressed her cheek to his shoulder as they returned to the car.

He held his door open and retained hold of her hand as she slipped in, preventing her from sliding across the seat to the window. He started the car and negotiated his way out of town, then used only one hand to drive—the other pulling Madge closer.

She didn't object in the least. A whole hour together

to enjoy his company. She let her head rest on his shoulder.

Their conversation often fell silent on the drive. She was content simply to be with him. He hadn't exactly said he loved her, but she knew he meant it. She didn't understand her hesitation to confess her love, then smiled as she recalled something her father had said. "Never tell a man right off you love him. Wait until he commits himself." His advice made her decide to wait. Once spoken, the words became a vow.

When he started talking about how he'd like to buy the Cotton place and fix it up, she knew it was only a matter of time until Judd would make the commitment.

He gave a mocking laugh. "'Course, I could never afford to buy it from the bank."

Madge said nothing. Many young couples were putting off marriage because of financial difficulties. She did not want to be another. All she could do was ask God to provide a way for their love to thrive and come to completion in marriage.

She chuckled. Here she was thinking marriage, and he had only said he might be falling in love. It was because she had already fallen solidly, irrevocably in love. It was such a sweet, overpowering feeling it couldn't be dimmed, even by the idea of facing Mother and confessing her feelings.

"What's so funny?"

"Nothing. It's just been a great night. I will never forget it."

His arm tightened around her. "Me, neither."

All too soon they arrived at home. The yard lay in

darkness, allowing him to step out and pull her after him without fear of anyone seeing him as Judd.

He leaned his hands against the car, one arm on either side of her, preventing her from hurrying away, though she had no intention of doing so.

She would gladly remain here sheltered by his arms, feeling his breath on her cheek, loving him so much it made her shiver.

He lowered his head.

She met him halfway, clutching at his shirtfront. He kissed her thoroughly. After a satisfying moment, he lifted his head, breaking the contact. She sucked in air.

"Thank you for a nice evening." His voice was thick, and she buried the sweetness of the sound in her heart.

"You're welcome."

He kissed her again, quickly, then backed away. "Good night."

She hesitated. But he was right. Time to head indoors. She brushed his chin lightly, delighting in the feel of his thick beard that had tickled her as they'd kissed. What would his face feel like shaven? She recalled a strong jaw and chiseled chin from their first encounter. Remembering that incident, she chuckled.

"What's amusing you now?"

"I was remembering how I almost bowled you off your feet the first time I saw you."

He cupped her head between his palms. "You certainly left an unforgettable impression. Now go to bed."

With a smile on her face and a song in her heart, she crossed the yard. And came to a decision. She would keep her love a secret from the others for now. Until

Judd revealed his true identity and Mother realized there was no Justin for Louisa to marry.

Madge's work seemed lighter over the next few days. She sang as she hung sheets, and she ran up the stairs as if the baskets she carried were empty. Every time she passed the living room, Judd glanced up and smiled at her.

She tried to be restrained, for she didn't want Mother or her sisters to notice. But they must have wondered when they looked outside and observed her staring into space, a smile on her lips and her work forgotten.

Today was her afternoon to work at Gratton's. His mother was due to arrive, and George had asked her to come by and help her settle in.

Alone in the car with no one to hear and wonder, she sang. If this was how being in love felt, they ought to capture the feeling and sell it to sick people, who would recover instantly and begin dancing.

She laughed at her silliness and sobered as she parked in front of the Gratton house. She looked forward to meeting Mrs. Gratton.

She smoothed her hair as best she could, stepped out and brushed her skirt, then marched to the house and knocked.

"Come in," a gentle voice called.

She stepped inside. A silver-haired woman she recognized from George's picture sat in a high-backed chair watching the door as if she'd been there for hours.

"You must be Madge. I've been waiting for you. I'm George's mother. I suppose you think you should call me Mrs. Gratton, but I don't want you to. I much prefer my given name, so call me Grace."

Madge giggled. George was right. His mother's body might be somewhat frail, but her spirit was obviously not.

"George made me promise on the Bible—really. On the Bible, if you can imagine. As if he couldn't trust his own mother's word any other way. What a naughty child. I should have spanked him more when he was young." Her twinkling eyes informed Madge she thought nothing of the sort. "Oh, yes. I started to say he made me promise not to unpack a thing but to wait for you. So here you are, and now we can unpack." She pushed to her feet a little slowly, as if her joints hurt, but she picked up pace as she headed for her bedroom.

"He fixed up this room downstairs. When I asked what was wrong with the bedrooms upstairs, the impudent boy said nothing except they were upstairs, and I wasn't to set so much as one foot on the steps. Can you imagine him thinking he could boss me around like that?" She turned, caught the way Madge grinned and smiled back. "I let him think he can so he feels better."

The woman was amazing. She kept up an amusing prattle while she perched on the edge of the bed—in obedience to George's orders, she said—and supervised Madge unpacking her stuff.

Two hours later, Grace declared she was satisfied with the work. "Now we must have tea. You'll make it, of course."

"Certainly." She enjoyed Grace's company. They

laughed together over tea, and then Grace kept her amused as Madge prepared supper for them.

"Would you stay and eat with us?" Grace asked.

There was a time she would have welcomed the invitation, but now she couldn't wait to get home and see Judd and share the news of what a delightful woman Grace Gratton was. The others would love hearing of her spark as much as Madge had enjoyed it. She'd get double the pleasure—the firsthand experience and the joy of sharing it with the family and seeing their spirits lift.

Over the following days, Madge and Judd managed to steal some time together every evening. Sometimes it was to deliver laundry. Other times it was to simply sit outside in the shade and talk, usually with Mother or one of her sisters joining them, but occasionally they were left alone. Madge wondered that Louisa didn't spend every minute possible with them, but she cherished those times alone too much to beg trouble, so she didn't say anything.

She'd discovered Judd was a great storyteller and a tease. As he recounted tales from his time working as a cowboy, she laughed. But she learned something more. Once Judd set his mind on some action, he didn't let it go, whether it was riding a horse, bringing a cow in or…bringing to justice the man he blamed for his mother's financial difficulties. Although the trait was admirable, she couldn't help but worry how his plan would end. And she prayed he would find peace. Yet when she questioned him, he said he still sought the man.

"Perhaps he isn't here." She hoped Judd was mistaken and would drop his quest.

"No. He's here. I just have to watch." He would say no more.

Judd also asked about her childhood and her work. His interest made her open up and share things she had almost forgotten—dreams, hopes, failures, disappointments....

She had never felt so safe with anyone before.

The afternoons she worked at Gratton's were enjoyable, even though they meant she would not see Judd again until after supper.

Her mind drifted from the meal she was preparing for the Grattons, and she stared out the window. She heard the door open as George came in. Grace had gone to her bedroom to rest, and he paused to look in on her.

Madge sighed and pulled her mind back to her task. But just as she started to turn from the window, a movement caught her eye. A man clung to the boards of the fence across the lane. She squinted. It was Judd. Her heart danced for joy. He'd come to wait for her. She hurried through the rest of her work and refused Grace's invitation to join them.

Outside she waited at her car, but Judd did not appear.

How odd. She delayed her departure until she knew it was useless to linger.

Had she been mistaken? Or had he rushed home to wait for her there?

Her heart bubbled with joy, and she hurried down the road. The family had moved suppertime back so she could eat with them. Mother and the girls sat at the table as she stepped into the room. But Judd was absent. Where was he? If he hadn't waited for her in town, why wasn't he here?

Mother provided the information. "Justin said he had things to attend to and wouldn't be here." A trickle of suspicion crowded the corners of her mind. What was he doing watching the Gratton place? That would make George…no! It couldn't be George. Perhaps Judd only hoped for a chance to speak to her.

Madge gave her attention to the food and hoped no one would notice her confusion.

The next day, Judd didn't mention his absence the evening before, and she would not. It was enough to have him at her side, enjoying the quiet of the evening. Yet he said good-night early, and later, she thought she detected him leaving the soddie. No doubt off to find the man he sought. Again, the uneasy suspicion. Was he watching the Grattons?

It wasn't possible.

Two days later, she put the finishing touches on supper for Grace and George. Again she stared out the window, and as George came home, she saw Judd lingering in the shadows.

He watched the house. No doubt about it.

Horror filled her thoughts. It made cruel sense. The questions he asked, his interest in what she did at the Gratton house.

Her insides sucked flat as she realized why he was so keen to spend time with her. A cry filled her lungs and remained there, trapped by the awful truth.

"I have to go," she murmured to Grace and George. They must have wondered at her hasty retreat and the fact that she raced out the back door instead of leaving from the front as she always did.

Judd jerked away from the shadows as she dashed into the yard. He looked about, as if hoping for escape, and then tucked in his chin and spun on his heel.

"Judd, wait!" She would not let him leave without an explanation.

He stopped. She didn't slow her steps until she stood close enough to see the way his eyelids flickered. Breathing hard, as much from the way her insides twisted as from exertion, she faced him. She knew her expression likely revealed something of what she felt—hurt, anger and a thousand things that defied explanation.

"Why are you watching this house?"

"'Spect you've figured it out already."

"You're wrong. George is not a bad man like you think."

He crossed his arms over his chest and looked unimpressed. "If he were obviously evil, he wouldn't be fooling helpless women, would he?"

"You're wrong," she repeated. "But too stubborn to admit it."

"I'd be glad to admit it if I thought it was true."

She leaned back, almost drowning in a confusion of protests and realizations. "You used me to spy on them."

"How do you get that?"

"Maybe everything you said was only to make it easy for you to get information on them." Anger built like a balloon, ready to burst. "Was that all I was? A way to find out about the Grattons?" The truth of her words burned away her anger. Left her empty. So empty all she could hear was the echo of her silent screaming pain. "From now on you'll have to do your own dirty work." She spun around and marched to her car.

"Madge, you know that's not true. My feelings for you have nothing to do with the Grattons." He grabbed her arm to force her to stop and listen.

She jerked back. "Your behavior is despicable. How can I believe anything you say?"

His hand fell off and he let her go.

She stifled a cry as she hurried away. Thankfully she had heeded Father's advice and refrained from telling Judd she loved him. But it didn't change the fact that she did.

She'd loved foolishly and too eagerly.

Her hand shook as she started the car and drove homeward. How would she put him from her mind? Especially as he would be in the house tutoring Louisa.

She considered speaking to Mother, but why should anyone else pay for Madge's stupidity?

By the time she reached home, she had come to a decision. She would avoid Judd at all costs and somehow convince her family nothing had happened. Keep busy. Work. That would be her excuse.

Stubbornness had its value, but it could not erase the pain claiming every cell of her body and catching at every breath.

Chapter Eleven

Somehow Madge managed to drive home without crashing into anything or hitting the ditch, though her mind had not been on handling the car. She parked by habit and stumbled to her room without anyone questioning her.

Numb from head to toe, she lay on her bed, pulled Macat into her arms and stared at the ceiling. How could she have been so easily fooled? Anger burned through her. Judd's actions were every bit as despicable as those he accused George of—deceiving a woman for his own gain. And he was wrong about George. She knew he was. But then, maybe she was a simpleton when it came to detecting falseness in men. Seems her trust of Judd proved that well enough.

How was she going to see him day after day? It wasn't like she could walk away. Without her efforts, the family would lose their home.

Oh, God, what am I going to do?

But God did not send an answer.

She sat up and pushed the cat to one side. God didn't do for a person what they could do for themselves. Comfort and guidance were to be found where she always found them—in God's word. She pulled her Bible close and read page after page, seeking solace and something more—a way to cope.

Someone came to the house. She recognized Judd's voice as he spoke to Mother. Despite herself and all her resolve, her heart lurched against her chest like Mouse at the door when he heard Louisa on the other side.

Her feet hit the floor before she realized how foolish it would be to give him another chance, knowing he'd used her to get information on George.

She sank down on the bed, caught Macat in her arms again and buried her face in the warm fur. At least animals were loyal and true. They didn't pretend one thing while planning another. They simply loved you and let you love them back.

The voices stopped murmuring and the door closed. She tiptoed to the window and peeked out to see Justin limp across to the soddie and duck inside. Justin indeed! Everything about him was false—from his name to his limp to his reasons for pretending interest in her.

He didn't so much as look over his shoulder to see if she might be at the window.

She knew her annoyance at his failure to do so made no sense, but it robbed her of the last faint hope that he truly might care.

Louisa came up and went to her room. Sally followed. She listened to the girls preparing for bed, heard

Mother making rounds to check the house before she retired to her room. Then all was quiet.

All except Madge's mind. It refused to rest.

She scolded herself for being a fool. A moment later she congratulated herself for never telling him she loved him, though—her cheeks burned at the thought—she'd certainly been free enough with cuddles and kisses. Then sorrow, pain and despair filled her. How would she manage?

Only with God's help. Trusting Him had never been so challenging. Or so necessary.

She fell asleep praying.

Groggy, she stirred as she heard a car motor in the yard. Then she sighed, rolled over and fell back into a deep slumber.

Sally shook her awake. "Madge, wake up."

She struggled from a troubled sleep. There was some reason she must speak to Judd, something she had to say, but he kept dancing in and out of reach, leaving her frantic. It took her a moment to realize her thoughts were but a dream and Sally stood over her talking.

"Are you okay? You don't ever sleep in like this, especially when you have so much laundry. I've filled the tubs but…"

"What time is it?"

"It's gone past seven."

Madge leaped from the bed. "You should have wakened me before." She hurried into her work clothes and raced down the stairs and outside to start the laundry. She'd never get it all done today.

Sally followed. "We haven't had breakfast yet. We waited for you."

She would have refused, but she couldn't stop eating in order to avoid Judd. Girding a protective shell around her, she marched indoors.

The table was set for four.

Mother noticed her interest. "Justin told me last night he had family things to attend to and wouldn't be returning."

Relief scoured through her insides, followed by painful regret. Would she never see him again?

She held her chin high, determined not to reveal any hint of her pain and confusion.

Somehow she ate, did the laundry, packed heavy baskets up and down the stairs. The work was endless. She barely finished in time for supper, then had to make the deliveries.

In town, she passed the Gratton place, slowing to a crawl and checking out the back lane where she'd seen Judd.

She didn't see him. She didn't care. She never wanted to see him again. And if he hurt Grace or George...

But the pain clawing at her insides could not be denied.

The next day she was due to work at the Grattons'. Grace noted her mood immediately.

"Why the sad countenance? Some man done you wrong?"

Grace's touch of resignation made Madge smile for

the first time since she'd discovered Judd's deceit. "Why must it be a man?"

"Because you are a woman. And until today the trials of the current situation in the country have not bothered you. I'm not so old I don't remember what it was like to be young and in love. Why, I fell in love with George's father when I was fourteen. Even told him so. He laughed and said I was too young to know what I was talking about." She sniffed. "Little did he know that I intended to marry him one day. And I did. He didn't stand a chance from the beginning."

Madge's smile widened. Grace would never take no for an answer, although she might let a person think she had.

"My advice is, if you love a man and he's worthy of it, hang on and pray for him to turn around."

Madge sobered. She didn't know if Judd was worthy of her love. Through her mind ran flashes of the times they had spent together—the trip to Bowwell, the evenings they'd sat and discussed things close to their hearts. She'd felt so connected. Felt his heart to be true and honest. Even in his disguise as Justin, he'd been candid with her.

Except for the fact he intended to get even with George. It was not something she could overlook.

Grace watched her. "Ah. You have doubts. Then, my dear, listen to your head, but don't ignore your heart. Things are not always as they seem."

Though she tried, Madge couldn't see how to excuse Judd. She turned her attention to her work, glancing out the window many times but not seeing Judd. She denied any disappointment. Why would she want to see him out there spying? What would she do if she did? She certainly couldn't allow him to continue to spy on her friends.

Feeling as if she had worked three days without sleep, she made her way home and dragged herself upstairs to her room as soon as she could escape without raising questions.

Macat lay on the bed, and Madge curled around the warm body and fell asleep.

She dreamed of laundry. Piles and piles of it. The more she washed, the higher it grew until it blocked the sun. Her heart filled with wrenching terror, and she fought her way through the stacks, fighting against sheets wrapping about her. Finally she broke through to where the house stood. Only it was gone. In its place fluttered a piece of paper with the bank's name in large black letters.

She bolted upright. The mortgage payment was due at the end of the week. Thinking about Judd had pushed the thought to the back of her mind.

The panicked feeling of the dream clung to her. She sucked in air in a vain attempt to calm herself, with reminders the mortgage payment would be ready on time. She had only to wait for George to pay her.

The fear and restlessness of her dream would not leave. She got to her feet and walked to the window to stare at the dark soddie. Judd was gone. She missed him with an ache as big as the piles of laundry in her nightmare.

But did she miss Judd or the man he pretended to be—the man she wanted him to be?

Judd dusted off one of the chairs and pulled it toward the table. He'd tried camping outside, but the wind blew his stuff around. The dust invaded everything, including his eyes and his food, and he couldn't start a fire for fear of it racing away.

So he'd moved into the Cotton house, sure no one would object to him parking there for a while.

He sank his elbows to the table. He missed Madge. Had no one to blame but himself that she'd discovered his secret. Maybe he'd even wanted her to. He sure didn't like hiding the truth from her. Plus, he wanted her to be wary around George. Any man who would steal from a helpless woman needed to be watched.

But she hadn't understood. Had not tried to see the situation from his side. He couldn't face her day in, day out and pretend his heart hadn't shattered at her reaction. Besides, it was time to get on with the task bringing him here—stopping George Gratton, seeing he got his just deserts.

He dug into the beans he'd warmed at the stove. He'd walked around the farm several times and poked through every room in the house. With every step, he saw more and more possibilities for the place.

If Madge would ever forgive him… Perhaps once she understood George truly was a despicable man, she might.

He scraped the plate clean, pushed it away and hurried to town, crossing the dusty fields in swift strides.

No more reason to pretend to be Justin, except he had no desire for George to learn his true identity. Not until he could discover what the man was up to in Golden Prairie. But he assured himself anyone seeing him would dismiss him as one of many homeless men who wandered the countryside.

He moseyed along the tracks as if he had nothing in mind but the next train, then angled toward the Gratton house in a circuitous route.

He knew what time George got home from work. He knew when George's mother went to bed. So far he'd been unable to spot any unusual movement around the place after that, but then he'd spent far too much time waiting for Madge and paying scant attention to other activity around the house.

All that was about to change. He would watch continually until he learned what was going on.

The first night, he went back to the Cotton place after he was certain George had retired to bed, thinking perhaps that was part of the ruse. Maybe he only wanted people to think he'd gone to bed.

So the next night he stayed until George left for work in the morning. Exhausted, he made his way back to the farm and threw himself on a cot and slept for eight hours without stirring.

Five nights in a row it was the same. The only break from the monotonous routine was Madge's arrival. Those days, he wandered down the lane to the back of the Gratton house earlier, telling himself he only wanted to be sure Madge was safe.

He caught glimpses of her through the window and

as she stepped outside to sweep the step. He backed away, determined to stay out of sight, though his heart begged otherwise. If only he could make his presence known and think she would welcome him. But it wasn't possible with his task still ahead of him. He could not abandon it. Not with a clear conscience.

He stayed out of sight until she returned indoors, then relaxed marginally and continued his vigil.

George arrived home. Judd watched Madge serve the meal, then leave.

Though his heart followed after her, he forced himself to stay hidden—waiting, watching, sure that eventually he would learn what he needed.

Two nights later, his vigil was rewarded. After Mrs. Gratton retired to her room and turned out the light, a man entered by way of the front door. Judd, at the back, couldn't make out who it was, so he slipped closer until he could get a wider view through the windows. The visitor turned.

Judd saw him clearly. He stared a moment and then retreated out of sight.

The pastor.

What dealings did a man of God have with a scoundrel like Gratton? Could he be involved in a scheme?

This situation might be more complicated than he anticipated.

Madge slowed at the turn off for the Cotton farm. She eased to the side of the road and looked at the tracks in the dust. The last two times she'd passed, she'd thought she'd seen something that shouldn't have been there.

Faint depressions in the dirt, grass bent as if tramped on. Now she knew she hadn't been mistaken. Someone was going in and out of the place. She sat back and stared out the window, her hands gripping the steering wheel hard. Who could it be, and what business did they have there? She hadn't heard it had sold, and news of such would have traveled like wildfire through the town's gossip chain.

It could be harmless. Some hobos looking for shelter. Likely nothing to be concerned about.

But still, someone should investigate.

She contemplated her options. The lane was right there before her. If she was careful...

She turned the car and, with as much stealth as a banging motor allowed, headed toward the buildings.

The sunlight caught on something metallic. She found the cause and gasped. Judd's car was parked against the barn, as far out of sight as possible.

Her heart jumped with joy. He hadn't left.

Sanity pushed doubts into her thoughts, cooled her heart. There was only one reason he would still be here. To get to George.

She glanced about. Saw no sign of him. No doubt he was in town watching the Gratton house. Anger twisted through her. Anger at his duplicity, the fact he would stay for revenge but not for her.

There was only one way she could imagine putting an end to this plan of his.

Madge prepared tea for Grace—beautiful teacups with matching teapot, creamer and sugar dish. "I lost most of my nice things when the financial markets took a hit," she had several times explained. "George blames himself. As if he had the power to control the ups and downs of business. I told him we let greed get us into this situation, and now we have no one to blame but our own greedy natures. Why, I think God must look down from heaven and wonder if He didn't make a mistake in giving us free will. It's not like we've used it especially wisely, is it? Why, when I think of the Great War…" She shuddered. "If I could, I would march all the naughty boys—and it's always men who start wars, isn't it? I would march them—oh, I don't know where." She pressed her fingertips together and considered the problem.

Madge smiled. She liked the way Grace's conversations dashed from one thing to another, often finishing the first thought down a long convoluted conversation trail.

Grace dropped her fingers and beamed. "I know what I'd do with them. I'd give them all the orphaned babies in the world to look after. Why, by the time they changed all the nappies, washed all the little garments, fed the poor little ones and cleaned the house, they would be much too tired to think of going to war."

Madge chuckled at the solution. "Too bad they don't think to let women rule the world."

Grace sighed delicately. "But God is ultimately in control. I know He can do a better job than I, even if I don't understand why He lets things go on in such a shameful way. I guess if I've learned one fact in my long life—" She added a dramatic sigh for good measure. "It's that things have a way of working out in ways that surprise us. I cling to a verse in Romans, 'And we know that all things work together for good to them that love God, to them who are called according to His purpose.' Chapter eight—one of my favorite chapters. I recall memorizing it in school."

Madge wondered if it was one of the chapters Judd had memorized for his teacher. Her glance went to the window. Was he out there? She filled the fine teapot and set out some sugar cookies she'd made.

Grace presided over the table with a regal bearing. "I used to have ladies drop in at teatime."

"You will again, once you get to know a few. The ladies will be thrilled to visit with you." Tea was a great time to entertain guests, and Madge knew exactly who Grace should entertain—Judd Kirk.

She had to be patient. Two days ago she'd been certain she'd seen his shadow lean out from the protection of the shed in the backyard. Today she was ready. "Excuse me a moment."

She slipped out the front door and edged around the side of the house, knowing if Judd was leaning against the wall, she could approach from his blind side. Quietly, she moved along. As she neared the last corner, she paused, caught her breath and listened.

Did she hear him breathing?

Certain she did, she gathered up her muscles and burst around the corner. He was there, and she grabbed his arm. "I thought I might find you here."

She feared he would try to escape at her touch, but

once he saw who it was, he settled back. "What are you doing?"

"I think it's time you came out of hiding."

"Are you crazy?" He tried to shake her off, but she held on tightly, causing him to stare at her hand as if checking that it truly belonged to her. "You promised you wouldn't give away my true identity."

"I did. Of course, at the time I didn't realize you were set on dishing out vengeance to people I happen to care for."

He grabbed her shoulder. "You can't take back your word."

"I don't intend to." She hoped and prayed he would do so himself. "I keep hoping you'll admit you are mistaken about George."

"When will you accept I'm not?" His eyes bored into her, pleading with her to agree with him.

She saw his longing. Suspected her expression conveyed the emptiness and loneliness she'd experienced since he'd left. "Judd." Her voice fell to a pleading whisper. "Give it up."

A shadow crossed his face, and anything she thought she'd seen disappeared in hardness. "I can't."

She pushed aside the emotions clogging her thoughts—how she missed him, wanted him—and returned to her original plan. "I was afraid you'd be stubborn. So I'm inviting you to tea." She pulled her arm through his elbow, firmly leading him up the sidewalk.

"Tea?" Poor man sounded bemused and suspicious at the same time.

She'd counted on a measure of surprise to give her

a moment's advantage. They made it three feet before he realized she led him toward the back door of the Gratton house.

He stopped. "I'm not going in there."

She urged him forward a step. "Why not? You might discover something to your advantage."

He dug in his heels.

"Unless you're afraid of a sweet little old lady."

"Of course I'm not." He allowed her to steer him ahead, then stopped again. "You must promise you won't tell my real name."

"Justin Bellamy it is. For now."

Without further urging, although she kept a firm hold on his arm just in case, he walked toward the door.

"Grace," Madge called. "I've brought company for tea." She led Judd into the dining room.

Grace looked up and smiled gently, though her eyes twinkled. "Why, where did you find this fine gentleman?"

Madge jabbed her elbow into Judd's side to make sure he understood the irony of Grace's words. "He was outside. Grace, allow me to introduce Justin Bellamy. He's my sister Louisa's tutor. Well versed in Greek and the arts, I understand."

Judd nudged her in the ribs to warn her not to get carried away.

Grace waved to a chair. "How nice to have a gentleman join us for tea. Bellamy, you say? I knew some Bellamys back in Toronto. Geoffrey and Janet Bellamy. Any relation of yours?"

Judd sank to the chair. "I don't think so, ma'am."

Grace poured tea and handed out sugar and cream. She passed the cookies. "Madge made these for me. They're delicious. But then, everything Madge does, she does well. I suppose you know that already, young man."

Madge groaned. But Judd grinned. "From what I've seen, she's a veritable dynamo."

Madge spared him a glower before she turned to Grace. "He's not interested in my—"

"Graces?" Grace provided. "I've always enjoyed using that word. I find it hard to believe the man isn't interested, unless his eyesight is faltering." She fixed Judd with an innocent pair of eyes that Madge knew were hiding a spark of mischief fit to start a raging fire. "How about it, Mr. Bellamy? Do you have something wrong with your eyes?"

"Not a thing, ma'am."

He sounded far too pleased for Madge's peace of mind. She prayed God would use this opportunity to show Judd that Grace was a sweet lady, adored and spoiled by her son. Then he'd realize George could not possibly hurt anyone, especially a woman.

"Now tell me where you got your expertise in Greek and the arts."

The two of them were soon sparring good-naturedly about the virtues of one university over another and which artists could be considered worthy. They disagreed vigorously about which artists were the best and why.

"I used to have an original by a fairly modern painter who is gaining a bit of renown," Grace said. "I lost it, along with most of my treasures. As I told Madge, greed caused our misfortune. I have regrets over losing most of my beautiful things, but now I see how God is working it out for my good. I have this lovely young woman to keep me company several days a week, and now I've met a gentleman with a sharp mind, if rather questionable taste when it comes to the great artists." She laughed.

Judd pushed his chair back. "I really must be leaving."

Madge watched harshness cross his expression, followed swiftly by a genuine grin.

"It's been a delight meeting you and trying to convince you of your error in artistic choices."

Grace chuckled. "It's been my pleasure. See the young man out, Madge."

"Of course." She led the way out of the room.

"No need to hurry back," Grace called.

Madge's cheeks grew uncomfortably warm.

Judd laughed and murmured, "She appreciates me."

Madge opened the door. "She doesn't know the truth, does she? What would she think if she knew you were trying to destroy her son?"

Judd's jaw clenched. "By the sounds of it, he's gambled away her things, too. She might just thank me."

"You know she wouldn't. Think about what you plan. Think about Grace and what your actions would do to her."

Judd walked from the house with long strides. Not once did he glance back at her.

Chapter Twelve

As Judd walked away, he realized he should never have allowed Madge to force him into the house. But he'd been so startled by her appearance and her touch, he'd been too befuddled to refuse.

"Shoot," he muttered to the wind. No matter what he did, where he went, he could not get her out of his mind. He snorted. More like he couldn't get her from under his skin. His frustration stirred anger in his soul. What right did she have to sneak up and scare the liver from him? For a moment he'd wondered if his thoughts had led to her turning up. It was downright scary.

He curled his fists and mentally banged them against his forehead. He reached the rail tracks before he realized how far he'd gone and ground to a halt.

This was not where he should be. No, George would be home shortly, and he needed to watch the man.

What was the pastor doing visiting him? Certainly he might be there for spiritual guidance, but Judd sim-

ply couldn't accept that possibility. Not without proof.
He knew what George had done to his mother. Feared it
would happen again, though he'd yet to find evidence.
But working in the bank gave George opportunity to
learn people's finances, learn the value of different
properties. It was only a matter of time until Gratton
picked a mark.

When he did, Judd intended to be ready.

He sank in the dusty yellow grass and wrapped his
arms about his knees, pulling them to his chest as if he
could protect himself from the war of emotions raging
through him.

Calm down. Think rationally.

Someone had to stop George. Bring him to justice.
That was Judd's chosen task and solemn responsibility.

But whatever he did to George would directly affect
Grace, and he'd liked the woman. No doubt, exactly
Madge's intention.

George had to pay. But making him pay would hurt
a sweet innocent lady. Just as George had hurt Judd's
mother.

Would Judd's actions be any more or less despicable
than George's in the end?

He pressed his face to his knees. *God in heaven, I
don't know what to do.* Could he trust God to take care
of providing justice? He hadn't seen any evidence of it.
Could he hope to regain what his mother had lost? Only,
he admitted, if he could either get Gratton to admit he
had the money squirreled away somewhere or could intimidate him into offering some kind of compensation.
It was the best he could hope for. Yet the idea didn't

sit as comfortably with him as he'd pretended in front of Madge. After meeting Grace, the whole thing made him feel a bit of a bully.

But what else could he do?

He stared out at the drifting soil, driven endlessly by the wind. The sun shone with unrelenting heat. The sky was brittle. Too bright for his eyes, and he squinted.

How could he trust God when things were so bad? It was more than George. It was the economy, the weather, everything.

Surely if God was loving and fair, He would put an end to this.

Bits and pieces of scripture he had memorized so long ago blasted through his mind, as if driven by the wind: 'The world was made by Him and the world knew Him not.' 'Every branch that beareth not fruit, He taketh away; and every branch that beareth fruit, He purgeth it, that it may bring forth more fruit.'

Could it be all this hardship had an eternal purpose? Was an eternal purpose enough reason for suffering? Could he wait until eternity to see his mother's suffering addressed?

It simply didn't feel right.

He bolted to his feet and strode back the way he had come. But halfway there, he changed his mind and headed for the Cotton place.

Madge watched for Judd to return, but when it was time to leave she'd seen no further sign of him. Had he changed his mind? She prayed meeting Grace had convinced him to do so.

Yet her thoughts troubled her as she drove down the road. She wouldn't be satisfied until she heard from Judd's own lips that he'd dropped the whole idea of revenge.

She slowed as she passed the Cotton place. If he was there, she could speak to him.

Her face warmed at the conversation that had followed his departure. Grace was convinced Judd was the man of Madge's choice and had sung his praises.

Not that Madge needed to hear them. She needed no convincing. But he was living a double life, and he planned something that would hurt Grace and George.

"Life is not always as easy as one, two, three," she'd murmured in protest of Grace's continued chatter.

At the sadness in her eyes, Madge wished she'd kept silent.

"My dear," the older woman had said. "Life will always be complicated. But we must not let it steal the sweetness waiting for us every day. Even when everything seems dark and forbidding, God is there offering light."

Madge nodded. "I know that." But she found it harder to believe and trust than she had when she was young and carefree.

She sighed and put her foot down on the gas pedal. Until Judd changed his mind about the Grattons, she would struggle to find the sunshine in her life.

The mortgage payment was due in three days. Madge needed her wages from George. She hated to ask, but she didn't have a choice. She brought it up when he came in for supper.

"I've been meaning to talk to you about that."

She heard the apology in his voice, and her lungs tightened.

"I'm afraid I can't pay you cash. By the time I paid the grocery bill and rent on this house, I had nothing left."

He'd tricked her. Led her to believe he'd pay her. Was Judd right about this man? Was George nothing but a fake and a cheat?

"But I need the money."

He held up a hand in a conciliatory gesture. "I do have a suggestion. Mother has a car parked in Calgary. It's a fine vehicle. Much better than the one you drive. I propose I give it to you in lieu of wages. If you don't want it, you can sell it."

What good was a car? She needed money. Her chances of selling the vehicle were even more remote than his. Surely he knew it.

Sadly it seemed Judd was right. George used people to his own advantage.

"I'm sorry," George murmured. "I had expected to sell our belongings and have a little cash left over. It simply hasn't worked that way. I've made a mess of things for so many people. It seems I can add you to the list."

He sounded so contrite, she almost changed her mind. But no. He had cheated her.

Madge mumbled something completely unintelligible and staggered from the house. She climbed into her car and headed home. The mortgage payment was still due. She had to figure out a way to make up the deficit. If only she could talk this over with someone. But she didn't want to worry Mother. And Judd…well, Judd still hung about watching the house. He'd likely only point out that this confirmed his opinion of George.

She wished she could believe it didn't.

She pulled to the side of the road a short way from town and leaned over the steering wheel. *Lord God, why is this happening? Don't You care that we could lose our house?*

She recalled Grace's gentle voice. *All things work together for good.*

She didn't see how it was possible this time.

Lifting her head, she looked about and saw she had stopped within feet of the Cotton lane. Would Judd be there? She longed to be pulled into his arms and cradled against his chest, knowing her worries would diminish in his embrace.

Torn by her loyalty to and fondness of Grace, her disappointment and uncertainty about George and her hungry love for Judd, she couldn't think straight.

Before she could consider her actions or change her mind, she turned into the side road and drove toward the Cotton place.

Judd sat on the front step contemplating his choices— to continue with his quest to bring George to justice, and in so doing hurt another defenseless woman, or let it go, and in effect say what happened to his mother was of no consequence. Then there was the possibility that, unchecked, George would persist in his evil ways, and another innocent woman would end up hurt.

He buried his head in his hands. His plan had seemed simple and straightforward to start with. Now it had become tangled until he couldn't think straight.

At the sound of an approaching vehicle, he jerked to his feet. Someone might take objection to his trespassing. He jumped from the step and headed for the barn, where he might hope to remain hidden, though his car stood beside the shed and his belongings lay scattered about the kitchen.

He ducked out of sight before the vehicle reached the yard and pressed to the wall, straining to hear. The car drew to a halt. The motor died and quiet rang in his ears. Then footsteps sounded, and the door squeaked open. He held his breath, waiting for what would come next.

"Judd, are you here?"

Madge. His breath whooshed out at the sound of the familiar voice, and then his lungs refused to work. Madge. If he could just pull her into his arms and explain everything, he would feel a thousand times better.

He burst from the barn. "Madge, I'm here."

She raced straight toward him. He saw the eager longing on her face and broke into a jog, meeting her halfway across the yard. He opened his arms and she came into them, just like a horse headed for the open doors of a familiar barn. He pressed her close, her hot breath against his chest.

She shuddered.

"Madge, what's wrong?"

"Everything," she mumbled, clinging to him in a

way that made him want to keep her forever close to his heart. "Nothing."

He chuckled. "'Nothing' doesn't make you shake like a leaf."

She lifted her head, her eyes hot with protest. "I'm not." But she shuddered again and laughed. "I am."

He pulled her close. Whatever had upset her, he would fix it. Slowly, so as not to make her leave his arms, he edged them toward the doorstep and sat down, turning her so she remained in his embrace. A grin caught his mouth and softened his eyes when she clung to him. "Now tell me what's wrong."

She rubbed her cheek against the fabric of his shirt, like Macat looking for attention.

He would gladly accommodate her need for comfort, and he stroked her hair.

She sighed. "Our mortgage payment is due tomorrow, and I don't have enough money. I'm not sure what to do."

"Is the banker apt to be lenient?"

"I expect he'll decide to foreclose."

Put them out of their home? Where would they go? Judd had to fight to contain his anger at the injustice of the situation.

"I tried to get the banker to give us the house mortgage free when he sold the land, but he wouldn't."

Of course not. Bankers had to squeeze the last penny from defenseless widows and single young women. "How much do you still owe?"

"A lot." She named a sum that in better days would

have been laughable but in the current situation was an impossible fortune.

"The house is worth much more than that, isn't it?"

"I expect the banker hopes so." She sighed against his chest.

He tightened his arm around her. He wanted to hold her safe and secure from every danger and threat. But he couldn't. Life contained too many unknowns, too many uncertainties. Slowly, words formed in his mind—a blend of what she'd said and what he'd learned in the past, though he hadn't been able to apply it to his life. He hoped she would find comfort in what he said. "I remember you telling me God was in control. He would do what was right and just."

She snorted. "How naive I was. Advice is easy for others. It's not so easy when I'm faced with an insurmountable barrier." She turned to look deep into his eyes. "I apologize for thinking I had solutions for your life because I clearly don't."

He couldn't bear the look of defeat in her gaze. "You didn't suggest you had the answers. You told me God did. That's a whole different thing."

She searched his eyes, looking past every defense he normally kept in place, delving into his secret hopes and dreams and, yes, beliefs. He hadn't applied the promise of God's care to his own situation, but he desperately wanted her to apply it to hers.

A slow, pleased smile caught the corners of her mouth and filled her eyes, and with a sigh of contentment, she again pressed her cheek close to his heart.

"Besides, what would the bank want with another house no one can afford to buy or even rent?"

A jolt shook her body. "Exactly."

They sat without speaking for a few minutes. He would have gladly stayed there until dark, holding her, feeling her trust. One thing nagged at his mind, though. "I thought you'd have money for this payment with the laundry you do and the work at Gratton's."

She seemed to hold her breath.

When she didn't answer, alarm snaked through his veins. "Did something happen?" He didn't trust George, but surely he wouldn't take advantage of Madge. If he had... Judd's fists curled. The size of his vengeance would not be measured.

She snorted. "Not like you're thinking. George is a good man. I'm a hundred percent convinced of it."

He lifted her from his chest to study her face. "Then why the doubtful tone?"

She wouldn't meet his gaze.

He caught her chin and for a moment considered kissing her rather than getting to the truth. He pushed the idea away—though not too far. He'd pursue that desire after he got the facts.

Slowly, reluctantly, she raised her eyelids and looked directly at him, regret filling her gaze. "He can't afford to pay me what he owes me."

He made an explosive sound. "The scoundrel."

She pressed warm fingers to his lips to quiet him. "Instead, he offered me a new car."

"Which won't pay the mortgage."

"No. It won't."

"I tried to warn you. That man must be stopped."

"Didn't you just assure me God is in control? Was it only idle words meant to soothe me?" She pushed from his arms. "Judd, I don't know what you believe. I don't think you do, either. I fear talk comes too easy for you." She stood, putting a cold six inches between them.

He reached for her, but she avoided his touch. He swallowed back an empty feeling that dried his insides as if they'd been blasted by the hot prairie wind. He didn't want to lose her. Not even for a moment or a few inches. "Madge, it isn't just words." But was it? Where did the words end and the believing begin? Did believing mean he walked away from George and what he did? "Don't I have a duty to stop George from doing further wrong?"

Her stubbornness faltered a moment. "Is it responsibility you seek, or is it a way to ease your guilt over not protecting your mother as you thought you should, whether or not she needed or wanted it? Seems to me if it's the former. You would be seeking the truth, not bullheadedly waiting for a way to exact your personal form of justice. There's a verse in the Bible that says, 'What doth the Lord require of thee, but to do justly and to love mercy and to walk humbly with thy God?'"

"Exactly. I'm seeking justice. That's what God requires of me."

"Only He asks us to combine it with mercy and humility. I think that would require you to investigate both sides of the picture."

He had all the facts he needed from his mother, though she'd been reluctant to admit them. Again, he reached for Madge, managed to catch her hand and draw her close. She let him pull her forward but stopped with a breath between them. She lowered her head so he saw nothing but the tangle of her dark curls. If that was all he could have, he meant to enjoy it and pressed his face into her hair, breathing in the sweetness of her.

He knew she wanted closeness as much as he did when she sighed. His insides flooded with love.

But then she slipped away and faced him.

"I am never certain who you are—Judd or Justin?"

He started to protest, but she held up her hand.

"And do you believe in trusting God? Or are you set on being in control?" She waited, but he had no answers.

Regret and resignation filled her eyes, and she nodded. "Until you know the answers to those questions, it is impossible for me to trust you." She turned on her heel and strode toward her car.

He reached for her but dropped his empty hand. She was right. Until he knew what he truly wanted and who he was, until he either took care of this business with George or...

He could think of no alterative and stood helpless as Madge drove away.

Madge's insides rolled and rebelled. She had gone for comfort and instead ended up more upset. Why was Judd so set on dealing with George? If he truly felt George was doing unethical things, then he should report him and let the law take care of it. But he seemed to want more than justice. Judd was discontent with how God handled things. It had come down to a trust issue. Could he trust God or not?

She sighed. And what about her? Did she believe God was to be trusted, no matter what? A few hours ago, she would have known the answer without hesitation. Of course she could trust God. So could Judd. Everyone could. But, with the threat of being evicted chomping at her heels, it was more difficult than Madge had ever suspected possible.

She managed to hide her worries from Mother and her sisters. That night she stood in her dark bedroom, staring out toward the Cotton place. From her window she saw the top of the barn. Nothing more. But she'd seen Judd's things in the house and imagined him there. She'd found comfort in his arms. Her heart longed to be with him, held close. She relived every word, every gesture of their embrace. But then reality had forced her to break away, had stolen the joy his arms had given.

Something he said triggered an idea: What did the bank want with another house they couldn't sell or rent?

She considered her options. It just might work.

Lord, I don't know what Mrs. Gratton's car is like. It may not serve the purpose at all. But—she fought a lingering, resistant moment of doubt—*I ask You to work things out. I trust Your love and care.*

Chapter Thirteen

Sally chatted next morning as they did laundry together. Madge appreciated her younger sister's help and conversation, but today her insides were too knotted with anticipation—or worry, if she were to admit it—to listen to Sally, and she let the words roll over her without any notice. Until a certain name entered the exchange.

"Are you still pining for Justin?" Sally demanded as they hung sheets.

"I'm not pining." Besides, Justin didn't even exist.

"I'm certain I saw him in town the other day. Is he still around?"

"I think he is." She was glad the sheets hid her face so Sally wouldn't see the heat rushing up her cheeks as she remembered how close he was and the precious few moments they'd shared. If only life didn't throw up such big roadblocks.

"Why doesn't he come calling? I thought he was a friend." Sally's voice gave a telltale quiver.

Madge sighed. Her little sister had always been too tender, too easily hurt. Madge vowed she'd do her best to avoid causing Sally pain. Losing the house would shake her to the core. Madge's heart turned to prayer. She needed God's divine intervention to carry out her plan.

She realized Sally waited for an answer to her question. "Justin is a friend, but perhaps right now he has other things to take care of." Until he did, he would be wise to stay away. Madge did not want her family in any way—even by association—involved with Judd's plans.

"I'm going to town early," she said after lunch. "George asked me to stop by today." Thankfully, neither Mother nor her sisters seemed to think it unusual. She turned to Sally. "Do you mind ironing the sheets for me?"

"Of course not. Macat and I will do it."

Madge's cat meowed from her perch in the window.

Content everyone would be happy in her absence, Madge drove from the yard. She automatically slowed as she passed the Cotton place. Every ounce of her heart cried out for her to stop and see if Judd was there. Perhaps try yet again to convince him to leave justice in God's hands. Not that she believed George needed justice.

If only there were some way she could mend the situation. But she couldn't without revealing Judd's secret—and she wouldn't go back on her word.

There was one thing she could do. Pray. It was enough. Her faith rested in God. She was about to challenge her trust and see if she could rely on it.

She chuckled at her convoluted reasoning. She was beginning to sound like Grace.

She slowed in front of the Gratton house but didn't stop. She intended to see George at the bank.

She went to the wicket and boldly informed Mr. August that she'd like to speak to Mr. Gratton.

George came out immediately. She followed him into a tiny office with a desk barely big enough for a sheet of paper and pen and ink.

"Madge, I want to say how sorry I am." He looked uncomfortable. "The banker informed me your mortgage payment is due tomorrow. I had no idea. I tried to persuade him to extend your credit…."

"Never mind that. I've reconsidered. I'll take the car in lieu of wages."

"I'll send for it tonight. Stop by tomorrow and you can take delivery of it. I vow I'll make it up to you at the first opportunity."

She left the bank without a backward look and didn't draw a satisfying breath until she sat in her car. *Lord, please grant success to my plan.*

She moved woodenly through the next twenty-four hours, not daring to think what the future might hold, yet determined she would trust God as she faced it.

After lunch the next day, she drove to the Gratton house and went inside. Grace sat waiting for her. She held out a key.

"I think this is yours."

Madge faltered. "I understand it was your car. You don't mind giving it up?"

"Pshaw. George won't let me drive anymore, so what

good is a car to me? He's afraid I might have one of my spells. Can you imagine? As if I would. They only come on when I'm overtired. Sometimes he treats me like a baby. I remind him I fed him bread and milk when he was small. Why, I could tell you things he did when he was a youngster that would make you see him in an entirely different light."

Madge held her palms toward Grace. "No, thanks." She had too many opposing views of the man already.

"I'm glad you're the one to get my car. Come on. I'll show it to you. It's out back."

Madge followed her. With a flair for drama, Grace opened the door, bowed and waved her through. Madge gasped. "This isn't a car. It's a…it's a luxury."

"A DeSoto. Best of its class."

"It's wonderful." She raced down the steps to circle the car. "I heard about these but never expected to see one." A sleek beauty and much faster than her old Ford. The DeSoto had six cylinders, plus spoke wheels that gave it an extra classy feel, a split bumper and rumble seat. It would never be big enough for the family, but it would serve her purpose very well. In fact, it was beyond her dreams or expectations. *Thank You, God.* And to think she'd harbored doubts when she left the house this morning.

Grace handed her the key. "It's yours. Take it for a drive."

"I will." She climbed in, grinning so widely it hurt her face. She smoothed her hands over the soft seat and back and forth over the steering wheel. A lovely car. One to be proud of. She could almost imagine keeping

it for herself. She sighed. That would defeat her purpose entirely, but before she went to the bank she'd take
Joanie for a drive.

She parked in front of the Sharp home and sat behind the wheel, as proud as a princess at her coronation.
The car handled like a charm, and the big motor purred
with absolute confidence. Her grin did not flatten a bit
as she went to the door and knocked.

Joanie answered and squealed. "It's about time you
came to see me." She hugged Madge.

Madge knew the moment Joanie saw the automobile.
Her squeal shifted to a sound of awe.

"Where did that car come from?"

"It's mine. Care to go for a drive?"

"Whoopie! In that thing? I guess I do." She called
to tell her mother she was going out and raced toward
the street. By the time Madge reached the driver's side,
Joanie had squirmed into the new leather seat. "This
is so nice." She shifted and faced Madge. "Spill it all.
What did you do to get this fancy machine?"

"I worked for Mrs. Gratton. This will pay my wages,
plus several more months of work." They drove through
town, drawing more than one set of admiring eyes as
Madge explained the deal. She hoped the banker would
hear of the car in the next few minutes. "I'm not keeping it."

"Why not? It's beautiful."

"Not big enough for the family, though. And can you
see me hauling laundry around in it?"

"A girl driving this kind of car shouldn't be doing
laundry."

They both laughed at the way reality and fancy clashed in this automobile.

"How are Connie and his family doing?"

"Conrad," she corrected automatically. "They're doing fine so far as I can tell, though to talk to Conrad you'd think it was all they can manage to get the little ones dressed every day."

"I suppose they're missing their mother."

"Of course. I didn't mean that. It's just, he refuses to see how I could help. He says it's too much to ask of me. Perhaps when the little girls are grown up, he says." She made a disgusted sound. "As if I intend to sit at home waiting ten or twelve years. No, siree. Not me."

"Maybe you'll find someone else." She knew Joanie would never entertain such an idea.

"Maybe I will."

"Joanie." Her voice revealed her shock. "I can't believe you said that."

Joanie sighed. "I guess I don't mean it, but I've got to do something."

It was such a familiar feeling. Seemed to have infected all those her age—her, Judd, Joanie—and she suspected others who had not said it aloud in her presence.

They left town, and Madge pulled to a stop at the side of the road so she could face Joanie and talk. She told of her worries about paying the mortgage and how she trusted God to take care of her in her need. "I believe this car is an answer I didn't imagine could be possible."

"This car? I don't understand."

"Banker Johnson won't be able to stand knowing

someone else has the best car in town. I'm prepared to trade it for the mortgage. Though when I came up with the plan, I had no idea I would be getting such a nice car. I only knew I needed a bargaining chip in order to present any sort of option to the banker. I prayed God would make him willing to negotiate. But look. God has supplied far beyond what I could ask or imagine."

"Isn't that a Bible verse?"

"It is. My point is to ask God for an answer and trust Him to work it out."

Joanie looked doubtful. "I can trust God for me, but this is Conrad. He's so stubborn." She bounced around to stare out the front window. "It makes me want to march out there with the pastor and demand Conrad marry me on the spot."

Madge had a good laugh at the picture she imagined. Joanie, all fight and prickly, Connie, casting about for some place to hide and the preacher wondering what was going on. "You think it would work?"

Joanie's shoulders slumped. "Conrad would just get angry."

"Then you have no choice but to trust God to change Conrad's mind."

Joanie turned and studied Madge hard—hard enough to make Madge squirm. "I saw you with a man the other day. Who is this mysterious cowboy no one has ever seen?"

Madge struggled to hide her surprise. Judd seldom came to town as himself. "Where did you see us?"

"In Bowwell, at the play."

"You did? Why didn't you come over and say hello?"

Joanie laughed. "You seemed rather interested in the man. To the exclusion of glancing about with any concern at who else might be present." She giggled. "I could see stars in your eyes from across the room."

Madge groaned. She should have known someone would spot her. "You're sure you haven't seen the man before or since?"

"I think I would have noticed." The way she quirked her eyebrows and batted her eyes made Madge laugh.

"You have seen him. Promise you won't tell." Joanie nodded. Madge knew she could trust her friend without reservation. "He's Justin."

"Louisa's tutor? Oh, no. I would have recognized him."

"He's not teaching Louisa anymore. And it truly is him."

"You're sure?"

"Very sure."

"I get it. He really is the cowboy you plowed into. But why was he hiding it? Where is he now? What is he doing?" Joanie almost burst with curiosity.

Madge picked one question to answer. "He has business to attend to."

Joanie studied her long and hard. "Aha. I see."

"What, pray tell, do you see?"

"You're in love with the man."

Madge snorted. "You just want everyone to be in love."

"Right. I want everyone to be as miserable as I am."

Madge would not confess she shared the emotion.

Instead she started the car. "I have to get to the bank before it closes."

A few minutes later Madge drove to the front of the bank, feeling better than she had in some time. She paused behind the wheel to pray. *God, please let Mr. Johnson see this car and want it so bad he'll agree to my deal.* As she stepped to the sidewalk, she saw Mr. Johnson peeking out the window. She ducked her head to hide a grin. Seemed he'd heard about the car and had to see if the reports were true.

A few minutes later she left the bank with a valued piece of paper in her hands and the keys to the car in banker Johnson's. The man had been very eager to agree to her suggestion.

"Thank You, God," she murmured as she walked toward the Gratton place to retrieve the old, half-reliable car she was to own and repair for goodness knew how long into the future. She'd seen a few people reduced to pulling the motors out of their cars and hitching the chassis to a horse. They mockingly called them Bennett buggies after their Prime Minister, who seemed unable to do anything to stop the decline of the country. The Morgans could well come to the same situation. Only they didn't have a horse. But unable to find feed, farmers were abandoning them all over the country, letting them forage for themselves. Perhaps she would be able to get one really cheap, maybe even find a wandering one. She sighed. Then she would be faced with trying to find enough feed for a third animal. Her concerns were common; so many people suffered even worse fates as they had to sell their animals for mere pennies. Silently she beseeched God to end the drought.

As she neared the turnoff to the Cotton place, she slowed. Should she stop and tell Judd the success of her afternoon or leave him alone until he finished with this Gratton business? If only she could persuade him to let go of this ugly nonsense before he destroyed George and hurt Grace. Not physically, but emotionally. She had a responsibility to try again to get him to change his mind. She could speak from experience this time when she told him how God would take care of things.

She'd faced the same choice he must—trust God or do it herself. God had answered beyond her expectations with the mortgage. She would trust Him to work in Judd's life, too.

God, keep him from hurting himself or another. Let him learn to depend on You to deal out justice.

For a moment she struggled with the desire to help God by speaking to Judd. She yearned to go to him and press her cheek against his chest, find sweet comfort and rest. She shook her head. Knowing he wanted to hurt, perhaps even destroy George, which would ultimately hurt Grace, made it impossible to give Judd her heart completely and wholly.

She continued homeward, propelled by the good news to share with her family.

Judd stared out across the dust-drifted yard. He ached all over, as if he'd shoveled a wagon full of grain in record time. However, the ache was not physical. It came from his heart. As if his blood had turned thick and struggled to flow through his veins. This strange malaise had started yesterday when he'd let Madge drive away. Not that he could have prevented her. She'd made that plain enough.

She'd wanted assurances he would let this go. Wanted him to leave this for God to handle. He had no doubt God would handle it. But that didn't prevent the man from doing more evil in the meantime. Nor did it give Judd a chance to get some sort of justice for his mother.

As the eldest, he should have been there to protect his mother. Instead, he'd been off pursuing his own adventures.

He jerked his head up. Madge had accused him of hunting George in order to ease his conscience.

No. It was more than that. Justice. Mercy. Humility. Madge had suggested he needed all three to justify his actions.

His insides rebelled at the idea. Justice he understood. The other two made him feel like a whiner. More fitting for Justin than Judd.

Takes a big man to admit he's wrong. Mother had said the words often as she tried to teach four boys to temper their adventures with gentleness. What would she think of his actions? He didn't have to think hard to know she'd side with Madge. He could see the pair of them standing shoulder to shoulder, their arms crossed over their chests, their eyes blazing.

"Good thing she isn't here." He had his hands full with Madge. He didn't relish the idea of a second fighter confronting him.

But right now he wished he had his arms full of

Madge, her cheek pressed to his chest, her breath warm and sweet.

It was hard to contemplate mercy. He wasn't even sure what it meant, except he was certain it required more than looking for retribution.

Humility was even harder. He had nothing to apologize for. But a huge dose of humility would be required to follow through on the idea just now forming in his mind with such stubbornness it could well be one of those settlers who dug in their heels and vowed they would not leave, come drought or high winds.

He didn't know if he could do it. Certainly went against his nature. But if the idea had come from God…

God, Madge is always talking about trust. I guess I need to trust You. I'm going to do this and see how things work out. It sounded like a qualified yes, and perhaps it was. But it was also a step of obedience.

He went inside and cleaned up. He studied himself in the mirror. Soon he'd shed the beard, but not now. He had something more important to take care of.

A glance at his clock revealed it was time. He crossed the yard to his car and drove to town, where he motored down the streets to the front of the Gratton house.

George would he home by now. Judd strode up the steps and knocked. When George opened the door, Judd said, "Can we talk? I have something you need to hear."

Chapter Fourteen

George's mother saw him. "Why, it's that nice Justin Bellamy I was telling you about. He came when Madge was here."

Judd stepped into the room. "Ma'am, I have a little confession to make. I'm really not Justin." He watched George. "My name is Judd Kirk."

George fell back a step. "Edna's son." His color faded like a white blind pulled over his face.

"That's right."

"What are you doing here? How is—" He swallowed hard. "How is your mother?"

"I guess as well as one could expect, considering." He would not speak of the matter in Grace's presence. "I'd prefer to talk to you in private."

George struggled to pull himself together, then nodded. "Come into the front room."

Grace sighed. "Obviously this business is much too profound for a woman. I will wait in the kitchen." Sniffing, she marched regally into the far room.

Judd followed George and chose a straight-backed chair while George perched on the edge of the maroon sofa.

George cleared his throat. "What can I do for you?"

Judd thought he'd sorted it out, but now anger combined with pain at how much his mother had lost. "You stole my mother's savings and left her to face the consequences. She lost her house. While you—" He pointedly looked around the nice home the Grattons lived in. "You seem to have done well."

"I didn't steal her money. She gave it to me to invest. I promised she'd make a good return. But then the crash came and I lost it all."

How convenient to blame the crash. "Left her penniless." He curled his fists, warring a desire to plow them into the man's nose. "Never spoke to her after you did so."

"How could I face her?"

"Like a man."

"Her money is gone. My mother's money is gone. I foolishly thought I could make a fortune in the stock market. Instead, I lost it all. I ruined my mother as well as yours."

"How do you intend to repay it?" His voice was brittle, unforgiving, but he would not accept any petty excuses.

"I can't." George's face wrinkled as if he fought back tears. "At least not now. But I will repay every penny if it takes the rest of my life."

"Noble words, but is she supposed to sit in abject poverty clinging to someday?"

George's face whitened even more, something Judd would have thought impossible. "Is she?"

"She lost every penny. What was she to do? It's only because she has three grown sons she isn't begging on the corner of a street, sleeping in alleyways." It was an exaggeration. Mother insisted she and Levi would manage quite fine. She would find work, maybe as a seamstress, and Levi was old enough to earn money, though they knew there were forty able-bodied men for every job. Nevertheless, she said they would be happy enough in a tiny house a friend had offered her.

George leaned over his knees, cradled his head in his hands. "I wanted to take care of her. We met at a church supper and became friends. I was so impressed with her. She had such eagerness for life. When she learned I worked in a bank and did investments, she asked me to invest her savings. She trusted me." He moaned. "I've ruined so many lives."

From this position, Judd saw a broken man. Pity stirred within his chest. Mercy? Was that what it was? Madge had suggested he seek the truth. He had to know. "What exactly did you do?"

George told a story of an opportunity presented to him by an acquaintance, a chance to double his money in a matter of weeks. "Fail proof," he said. "How could I be so gullible? So greedy?" Turned out the venture had disappeared into a bottomless pit like so many in the 1929 crash.

"Why didn't you tell my mother the truth?"

George closed his eyes and struggled for control.

"You have to understand, I love her. But instead of caring for her, I ruined her. I couldn't face her."

Loved her? He hadn't considered that possibility and wasn't ready to accept it.

George gave Judd a demanding look. "Is she okay?"

"She's living with my brother."

"Please, don't tell her you've seen me. I want her to forget she's ever heard the name George Gratton."

"I can't give such a promise." He didn't know if he would have done his duty unless he informed his mother he'd seen George. Nor was he satisfied there was justice while George lived in this big house. He glanced about, noted with surprise the sparse furnishings.

George observed his interest. "This house is not mine. I'm here by the generosity of Mr. Johnson, who is related to my mother's cousin. We lost our house, most of our fine belongings, too. Everything except a few things Mother refused to part with. Like I said, I ruined my mother as well as yours. To my sorrow and shame."

He pushed to his feet and held out his hand. "You have my word that I will spend the rest of my life repaying my debt."

Judd refused the hand. "I've dealt with sneaky salesmen before. Words come easy, appear sincere, but beneath is a scheme. What's yours?"

George dropped his arm to his side and staggered back as if Judd had struck him. "I have no scheme. I have nothing but regrets."

"I've seen people coming and going late at night." Only one man, but maybe George would admit to more.

"There's been no one but Pastor Jones, who has come to offer me spiritual comfort."

Judd rose and stared out the window. It all sounded reasonable. But was it only smooth talk? How could he trust the man?

In his mind he pictured Madge, leaning forward, pleading as she told him to trust God to handle things. Was God asking the same thing? Yes, he knew he could trust God, but he was reluctant to trust men—one man in particular. But he was tired of sneaking around, pretending to be Justin Bellamy, forcing every thought to the task of watching George Gratton.

A smile pulled at his mouth. He might have tried to force every thought in that direction, but the vast majority of them headed down quite a different path to a pretty, intense, high-minded young woman and the way she fit so neatly in his arms and smelled of laundry soap and fresh air.

With a start he realized how foolish he looked, grinning as he stared out the window at nothing. He sobered and faced the man.

"I don't know if I buy your story or not. Be warned. I intend to remain in the area, and if you try cheating any other women out of their savings…"

George nodded. "You're welcome to keep an eye on me because I assure you I have nothing in mind but working hard so I can return your mother's money."

"Be that as it may." He headed for the door. As he reached for the handle, he paused. Seemed he was treating George in a way he wouldn't want his father treated if he were still alive. He slowly turned. "I hope you prove to be honest." He left without giving George time to reply. Far as he could tell, the man had said all he needed to. The proof lay in what he did from now on.

He drove to the store for a few supplies. The weekly paper, *Golden Prairie Plaindealer,* lay on the counter. He dropped his pennies on the dark wood and took a copy, then headed home.

The first thing he did was lather up his face and shave off the beard. No more Justin Bellamy. Then he sat down and read the news.

One item in particular caught his attention. He folded the paper to leave it on top, and he let himself dream and plan.

A knock sounded on the door as Madge and Sally cleaned the kitchen. Louisa and Mother had moved to the living room to write letters to the cousins and aunts back east.

Madge's heart clamored up her throat and clung there. Perhaps Judd had come calling.

"Who could that be?" Sally asked.

But Madge rushed to answer the knock, paused to calm her expression, then threw open the door. "Judd," she whispered. He was Judd. He wore the cowboy hat she remembered, his hair a dark fringe around the crown. He wore the shirt and pants she'd seen him in at their first encounter. And his beard was gone. She stared. Yes, strong chin and jawline, just as she remembered.

Sally had followed. "Justin? You look so different."

Judd jerked off his hat. "May I come in?"

Sally nudged Madge aside. "Don't worry about her. She's just surprised to see you without your beard." She hissed at Madge, "Stop staring."

Madge jerked her gaze to the window but in truth saw nothing through it. She felt Judd in every pore. Breathed in a scent of shaving soap and prairie wool. What was he doing here? Why had he come as Judd?

"Sally, your sister seems to have forgotten her manners." Judd's voice rang with amusement.

Madge tried to pull herself together. It didn't do for him to see how much he surprised her. Practically tipped her off her feet, in fact.

"Invite me in. I'll explain everything to the whole family."

"Come along. Mother and Louisa are in the front room." Sally led the way.

Judd hesitated, waiting for Madge. She pulled herself together and followed Sally.

"This ought to be good," she whispered before they entered the room.

Louisa and Mother glanced up from their letter writing and gasped.

"Why, look at you," Mother said. "You look so strong and…"

"Tall," Madge said, suddenly enjoying the discomfort in Judd's face and the confusion in Louisa's.

"I have a confession to make."

"Not only is his beard gone, but his cough and limp are all better, too."

Judd sent a pleading look in her direction. "You aren't helping."

She giggled as joy began to paint her insides sunshine bright. Could this mean what she hoped it did? That he had settled his problems with George without wreaking havoc?

At his demanding nod, she sat down and folded her hands demurely.

"First, I must apologize for leading you to believe I was Justin Bellamy. My real name is—"

Madge couldn't stop staring at him and at the way he gave her quick, darting glances. She wondered if she made him nervous. The idea provided a great deal of pleasure.

He explained who he was and why he had felt he had to hide his true identity. "I confronted Mr. Gratton tonight."

Madge jerked forward so hard her neck protested. "You did?"

He nodded. "After much prayer, it seemed the right thing to do."

Their gazes locked as they exchanged silent messages of acknowledgement. He'd listened to her. Her heart could barely contain her joy.

Mother cleared her throat.

Madge slid her gaze away, knowing her cheeks were as red as they felt. Sally's giggle confirmed it.

"He said all the right things. How he hadn't meant to lose Mother's money and was too ashamed to tell her face-to-face. He said he'd lost his mother's money, as well."

"Do you believe him?" Mother asked.

"I don't know. I'm not prepared to dismiss all my doubts."

Mother nodded. "Sometimes caution is wise."

"And what are your plans now, Justin?" Louisa giggled. "Whoops. I mean Judd."

"I'm not certain. I used to think I wanted to go back to being a cowboy, but it no longer feels right."

Mother smiled. "I'm sure you'll find what works for you." Her smile touched Judd, then angled toward Madge.

Madge lowered her eyes, lest Mother see how much she wanted to be part of his plans for the future.

"Can we offer you tea?" Mother asked, signaling to Sally to prepare it.

"Not today, though I'll gladly join you another time if I'm welcome."

"Of course you are. Anytime." Sally and Louisa murmured agreement.

Judd got to his feet. Madge stared at him. So tall. So handsome. All cowboy.

He faced Mother. "I'd like to take Madge for a drive, if that's okay with you."

"Why, it's just fine with me."

"Madge?" Judd reached for her hand.

She put her fingers in his firm palm and let him lead her from the room, wondering if her feet actually touched the floor.

He settled her in his car and drove from the yard.

"Where are we going?" She asked the question only in the hope he might believe she was thinking straight. In reality she didn't care where they went.

"To the Cotton place. There's something I want to show you."

"What?"

"You'll have to wait and see."

She turned to look out the side window, hiding her smile from him as memories of previous visits to the Cotton place danced through her mind. She had high hopes this visit would be even better.

A few moments later they stopped in front of the house. Judd raced around and opened the door for her, took her hand, pulled it around his elbow and pressed it to his forearm.

A thrill of expectation rippled through Madge. She longed to turn immediately into his embrace, but Judd had something else in mind and led her toward the house. "I'm so pleased to hear you resolved things with George."

Judd squeezed her fingers. "At first I only wanted to please you so you would spend time with me. But then I really felt I had to trust God. I intend to keep an eye on George." He chuckled. "It's not like God needs my help. Maybe I'm still learning exactly what trust means."

"Oh. I haven't told you how God answered my prayer." They reached the house, but rather than go inside, they sat on the step, much as they had done not very long ago. She gladly snuggled close to his chest, reveling in his nearness. "Something you said gave me an idea."

"I don't recall saying anything profound."

"I guess it just comes naturally for you." She giggled and nuzzled her cheek against his shoulder.

He squeezed her tight. "Maybe you are too easily impressed. Exactly what did I say?"

"You asked what the banker would want with another house he couldn't sell or rent."

"I did? Must have slipped out unnoticed. If I remember correctly, I was somewhat distracted by a certain pretty miss."

She sat up, breaking from his arms, and pretended shock and hurt. "You've been seeing someone else?"

He blinked, startled by her question, then he grabbed her in mock fierceness. "I have eyes for no one but you." He sobered as he looked deep into her soul.

She grew still. Searched his gaze, and found love and belonging in his heart. With a sigh that came from the depths of her being, she leaned toward him.

His eyes darkened to midnight, and he caught her mouth in a gentle kiss.

Several intense heartbeats later she snuggled against his chest. "I was about to tell you how God answered my problem before you interrupted me."

His chuckle rumbled below her ear. "Some delays are worth it."

"Umm." For a moment she didn't speak, so content she was loath to move.

"About the mortgage?" he prompted.

"Oh. Yes." She sat up and faced him so she could keep her thoughts in order, though at the look in his eyes and the way his gaze kept dropping to her mouth, her mind seemed full of peanut butter.

"The mortgage?"

"I told you George had offered me a car in exchange

for the work I did. Even though I had no idea what sort of car it would be, I hoped it would prove a bargaining chip with the banker. I wanted to offer him a trade for two or three months' payments."

Judd nodded. "Good idea."

"You should have seen the car." She laughed, then described it. "Banker Johnson saw me drive up and was already drooling by the time I got to his office. I explained I didn't have enough money for the whole payment. He kept looking outside to the car. When I casually suggested I might be able to trade something, he almost jumped from his chair." She savored the feeling of victory for another moment. "In the end I walked out with the mortgage in my hand—free and clear—and he got the car he drooled over." She shivered playfully. "Isn't that great news?"

He pulled her to his chest and held her so close they breathed as one. "It's the best news."

She wondered at the way his voice caught, then forgot everything but the sweetness of his embrace.

With a deep sigh he eased her back. "Come inside. I want to show you something." He pulled her to her feet and kept his arm about her as they went into the kitchen.

He'd tidied since she'd been here last. Dust no longer layered every surface. The table gleamed, and the floor—she gasped. "It's clean enough to eat on."

"I pulled up the old linoleum and found a very nice wooden floor beneath. You like it?"

"It's beautiful. But why are you going to all this work on someone else's house?"

He led her to the table and held a chair for her. She

sat, though she wondered at his delay. What did he have to show her that required she sit? Tension trickled across her shoulders.

"Look at the paper."

She pulled the newspaper toward her. A page of notices and advertisements. Nothing to hint at the cause of Judd's barely concealed excitement. "Exactly what am I supposed to notice?"

He tapped one ad. "Read it."

She read aloud: "'Property to be sold for back taxes. Farm with house and barn. Excellent property. Taxes to be paid by cash or service to the municipality. For more information or to take possession please contact...'" She glanced at Judd. "I don't understand. Notices like this appear all the time."

"Not like this. Finish reading the ad."

"'Property formerly owned by Jacob Cotton.' It's this place."

"Yes. I'm getting it." He pulled her to her feet. They stood in each other's arms, yet with inches between them. He searched her face as if desperate for her reaction.

"You'll be living here? So close?" Her joy began as a tiny bud and blossomed to a full-blown wildflower. She knew her feeling was evident in her eyes. She didn't know how to keep it under control and buried her face into his shirtfront to hide it.

His arms tightened around her. "I hoped you'd like the idea."

She did. Oh, how she did. To have him so close she had only to run across the fields to visit him. He could do the same to see her. They'd be able to attend church together, go on outings.

He eased back to look in her face. "Madge, I love you. I want to marry you and share my life and this place with you."

Her joy caught in her throat. Tears stung her eyes.

Judd's expression grew uncertain. "Surely you guessed how I feel. Shoot. I should have waited."

She found her voice. "No need to wait. I love you, too."

"You'll marry me?"

Reality hit with the suddenness of a clap of thunder, shuddering through her. She pressed her lips tight to stifle a cry. Sniffing back tears, she shook her head. "Judd, how can I? Who will take care of my family?" And what about Louisa? Yet it hurt like mad to refuse him.

His smile turned to stone. "You said the mortgage was paid."

"But we still have to eat. Pay for gasoline. They count on me to earn the cash." And what about Louisa? The question again thundered through her head.

He dropped his arms and stepped away.

"Judd." Her voice protested even as her heart ripped like torn paper. "We'll be close."

He strode to the window and stared out, his shoulders heaving as if he'd run ten miles.

Madge pressed her knuckles to her mouth. Had she lost him? Agony like a deep cut filled her. *Lord, help him understand.*

Slowly he turned. She expected anger, hurt, disappointment. Instead he smiled—a look of such patience and hope she couldn't believe her eyes.

He crossed the room and held out his arms.

Without hesitation she let him pull her to his chest. She shuddered as she thought how close she'd come to losing him.

"I'm sorry. I shouldn't have reacted like that."

She clung to him. How she longed to be able to find such comfort any time she wanted it. But she couldn't abandon her family. She must explain the turn of affairs to Louisa before she could accept his offer of marriage.

Judd shifted so her cheek lay in the hollow of his shoulder. "I think we've both forgotten a very important fact—God is in control. He will provide an answer. It surprises me we should forget when we've both experienced His help in just the past few hours. Madge, my sweetheart, I am going to pray and trust God to give us a solution because—" He turned her to search her face.

She thrilled at the warmth of his love, clearly visible in every line and feature.

"Because I don't want to waste one moment of being together and loving you."

Hope and trust grew as she met his look. "I, too, will pray."

"God will provide a way."

She nodded. Judd's complete assurance left no room for a shadow of doubt.

He kissed her again and then took her through the house, showing her the things he had done. Besides dusting and cleaning and removing curled and cracked linoleum, he had repaired broken window frames and rehung a sagging screen door.

"Everything looks so good." She longed for the day she could share it with him as his wife. Although she couldn't imagine how it would be possible with her family needing her, but she would do as Judd advised—trust God.

How sweet to have him tell her those words. Almost as sweet as hearing, "I love you."

One day soon—God willing—she'd hear them every morning when she wakened.

Chapter Fifteen

Five days had passed since Judd's proposal. He'd attended church with them as Judd Kirk. His presence was sweet torture for Madge, as nothing changed to make her feel she could accept his offer of marriage. And how she longed to. Every thought, every breath ached for it. Even as she hung sheets, she thought of the joy she would get hanging sheets of her own.

Judd reminded her to trust and pray. How she laughed at his urging. "Ironic how my words are being quoted back to me."

He grinned. "Just proves how well I listen. I'll make you a very good husband. Always ready to heed your advice."

"If it suits you." She struggled to keep her voice teasing when she really wanted to wail against the need to wait.

Monday morning arrived and with it, laundry to do. Not needing to make a mortgage payment, she'd cut down on her customers. She still owed George and

Grace for the car, and for that she worked two after-noons a week. Even with reduced customers she kept busy. Of course, she stole as much time from her work as possible to run over to the Cotton place.

Sally put some wet sheets through the wringer. "When are you and Judd getting married?"

Thankfully she bent over the washtub so she could keep her face hidden from Sally. Surely if her sister saw her, she would see the longing. Forcing false cheerful-ness into her voice, she answered, "I don't have time."

Sally grew still. "I never thought marriage to be con-sidered an obligation you had to schedule in."

Madge hoped her sister would drop the conversation.

Instead Sally shifted to study Madge more closely. Madge kept her head over the tub, even though she had no more need to. Finally she couldn't bend any-more without ending up sore, and she straightened and made a show of arching her back, pressing her hands to her hips.

Still Sally waited.

"What?" Madge asked.

"Will you ever see me as anything but your little sis-ter, too young to be counted an equal?"

The question caught Madge by surprise, and she stared at Sally. "What are you talking about?"

"You know. And you don't fool me. You think you have to keep doing this job." She pointed toward the washtubs. "Even though you found a way to pay off the mortgage, you can't stop being in charge. You can't be-lieve I could do this job. You—you—"

Madge gaped. She'd never seen her sister so upset.

Sally planted her hands on her hips and drew in a deep breath. "You think you have to stay here and look after us. As if you can take Father's place. As if—" Sally began to build up steam again. "As if I couldn't do my share. Fine." She spun on her heel. "Forget marriage with a fine man like Judd, and stay home and be a martyr if that's what you want." She stomped toward the house and slammed the door after her.

"Sally?" Her little sister had a temper? Who would have guessed it? She turned back to the laundry, then paused and stared at the wringer. Sally thought she could manage? Could she? She'd accused Madge of trying to replace Father. She wanted to deny it, but a sliver of truth caught at her protests and dug in with a vengeance.

She thought of the decision to sell the land and keep the house, the arrangement for a lowered mortgage, even the deal to trade the car for the mortgage. Then there was the sale of the horses and all but a milk cow. Everything had been at her suggestion, with Mother's approval. Madge groaned. She *was* guilty of thinking she had taken Father's place. It gave her a sense of control, as if she could single-handedly keep the depression away from their door. And, too, it made Father feel close. Perhaps she strove for his approval even though he was gone.

Judd had urged her to pray and trust God. She had prayed and thought she trusted. But in this area she felt she must work. She hadn't even considered the family might not need her as much as she thought they did. But even if they could manage without her, there remained the problem of Louisa. How could she face her sister knowing she had taken Judd away?

God, show me the answer in this.

First, she must speak to Mother. She found her in the front room darning stockings. "Mother, Judd has asked me to marry him."

Mother smiled. "I know. He told me."

"You aren't upset that I…" She struggled for a word that didn't make her feel guilty, then gave up. "I stole him from Louisa?"

"You can't steal something that doesn't belong to another person. He never saw her the same way he sees you."

"But Louisa—"

Louisa burst into the room. "I saw how it was between you two. Yes, at first I thought he belonged to me." She colored prettily. "At first he seemed ideal, but then he began to talk of adventure, ranching in the west and all sorts of things I wouldn't have enjoyed. And his eyes blazed whenever Madge entered the room. It was making me miserable to try and keep his attention on me. So…" She ducked her head and spoke very quietly. "I decided to play matchmaker instead."

Madge laughed. "So that's why you sent us to the play."

"You enjoyed it, didn't you?"

"I did." She smiled, her heart full of sweet memories. "You're sure you're not angry?"

"I'm happy for you." She opened her arms, and the girls hugged.

Madge turned back to Mother. "I haven't said yes because I wasn't sure you could manage without me."

Mother rolled away the yarn and stuck the large needle in the ball, then pulled Madge to her side. "Madge, you have been a real help. We couldn't have managed without you. I'm proud of how hard you've worked, and your father would be, too."

Madge nodded and blinked back tears. She needed to hear those words.

"Thanks to you, our home is now secure. And it's time for you to move on with your own life. I had hoped Justin would be suitable as Louisa's husband, but I'm nothing but happy he is suitable as yours. We will be fine without you." She patted Madge's hands. "And you and Judd will be close if we need help."

Peace flowed through Madge.

"What are you waiting for?" Mother asked. "Go to him."

With a burst of happy laughter, Madge sprang to her feet. "I will. I am." She hugged Louisa again, then rushed outside where Sally had returned to the laundry and skidded to halt. She should stay and help. But really, did she need to? "Sally, can you finish here? I want to see someone."

Sally turned, saw the look on Madge's face and laughed. "I can do this with one hand tied behind my back. Now get out of here. Leave me alone." She turned back to the task. "And give Judd a kiss for me."

Sally's laughter followed Madge as she raced across the field. She was out of breath by the time she reached the Cotton place. "Judd?" she yelled.

He bolted from the barn, took one look at her and dropped his hammer to sprint to her. He studied her face.

"I've come to say yes." She smiled welcomingly, then laughed as he swept her off her feet and twirled her around.

Epilogue

Three months later

Madge looked at herself in the mirror in the side room of the church. The pale blue dress Sally had made her emphasized the sparkle in her eyes. Louisa had done her hair, pulling it into an upsweep, then allowing the unruly curls to fall around Madge's face.

Sally's likeness appeared beside Madge's. "You glow." She hugged Madge. "I'm so happy for you."

Louisa's face appeared over her other shoulder. "You deserve every bit of happiness. I pray for nothing but the best for you and Judd."

Madge shifted to meet Louisa's eyes. "You don't hold any resentment that I stole him from you?"

Louisa giggled. "You can't steal something I never owned. He never saw anyone but you. I'll trust God to bring me a man who looks at me the way Judd looks at you."

Mother poked her head through the door. "Girls, it's time."

The three of them peered into the mirror a moment longer, smiling.

"Come on," Louisa urged.

"Yeah, you've kept him waiting long enough," Sally said. "Insisting you had to work at Gratton's."

"I had to pay off the car."

"We know," the girls chorused.

Sally went down the aisle first, then Louisa. Madge followed. She'd promised herself she'd concentrate on everything so the details would be forever branded in her memory, but as soon as she saw Judd, she forgot all else. He wore a black suit and white shirt, but despite them he had a rugged outdoor look. He loved working outside and had managed to locate enough feed for a few head of cows.

"The drought will end, and when it does I'm going to be ready with a herd while others are scrambling to find replacement cows," he'd told her one night as they discussed their future.

Together they had cleaned and polished the house and collected odds and ends of furniture to add to the things left behind by the Cottons.

At the front pew, Mother held out her hand and Madge paused to squeeze it. She turned to take Judd's mother's hand and smiled past the woman, at George.

Mrs. Kirk had come to help with preparations and meet Judd's intended. She'd seen George downtown and broken into tears.

Judd had grown angry. "That man should have left town."

"I'm very glad he didn't," Mrs. Kirk had said, then had dried her eyes and crossed the street to speak to him.

"Seems your mother is ready to forgive him," Madge had murmured.

"She's just asking for more trouble."

But Mrs. Kirk had told Judd she'd had nothing to forgive. "He made a mistake and he feels bad about it. I don't intend to let it form a barrier. Life is too short for pettiness."

Judd had sputtered and protested, but his mother did not relent. Eventually Judd had admitted his mother seemed happy.

"Shouldn't that be what matters?" Madge had asked.

Judd had swept her into his arms and kissed her soundly. "How can I protest when I'm so content with life? I can only hope she is as happy."

Now Madge turned from those in the pews to face Judd, and her heart swelled against her ribs in supreme joy.

"I love you," she mouthed.

"I love you," he mouthed back.

People chuckled. Apparently anyone watching could also read his lips.

She didn't care. She didn't care if the whole world knew of their love.

Judd reached for her, drew her to his side and kept her there until the preacher announced they were man and wife. Then he turned and kissed her before God and these witnesses.

"God is good," she murmured against his lips.

"And we'll prove it over and over in the years to come."

They turned to receive congratulations and good wishes from their friends and neighbors.

Life, Madge knew, would be sweet and precious shared with this wonderful man.

* * * * *

THE COWBOY
COMES HOME

My God will supply all you need
according to his riches in glory by Christ Jesus.
—*Philippians* 4:19

For Sierra.

As my eldest granddaughter you hold a special place in my heart. It has been my joy to watch you grow and see you become a beautiful young woman. I hope we can become closer in the future. My prayer is that you will find true joy and meaning in life through opening your heart to God's love. I love you.

Chapter One

Golden Prairie, Alberta, Canada
Spring 1934

She needed eyes in six places at once to keep track of that child.

"Robbie!" An edge of annoyance worked itself into Sally Morgan's voice. Yes, she understood how a boy who was about to turn six might be upset by so many changes in his life. His mother had passed away just after Christmas. His maternal grandmother had stayed until spring and then Sally started coming during the day. But the child needed to realize life was easier if he didn't fight every person and every rule.

Sally found Carol playing with her doll in the patch of grass next to the big tree at the front of the lot, her plain brown hair as tidy as when she'd left for school. Even her clothes were still neat and clean. The girl was only eight but had adjusted much better than her brother. "Have you seen Robbie?"

Carol didn't even glance up from her play. Simply shook her head.

"Where can he be this time?" As soon as she'd realized he was missing she'd searched the house. She'd looked in the shed in the back of the lot where he often hid. Now she marched toward the barn. The children's father would be home shortly and expecting his meal. She'd left the food cooking on the stove. If she found Robbie soon she could hope to keep supper from burning.

She stepped into the cool, dark interior of the barn, now unused. Mr. Finley didn't own a horse. He drove a fine car instead. "Robbie!" she yelled, then cocked her head to listen. She heard nothing but the echo of her voice, the flap and coo of pigeons disturbed by her noisy presence and the scurry of mice heading for safety.

She left the barn and turned her gaze to the narrow alley separating the fine big yard on the edge of town from the farm on the other side. Would Robbie have ventured into forbidden territory? Most certainly he would if the notion struck.

Sparing a brief glance at the house where the meal needed attention, she headed for the gate, pausing only long enough to call to Carol, "You stay there while I find Robbie."

Her steps firm with determination and mounting frustration, she strode across the dusty track to the sagging wire fence. From where she stood she saw nothing but the board fence around the back of the barn. Sighing loudly, she stuck her foot on the wobbly wire to clamber awkwardly over the fence. She landed safely on the far side and hurried forward. Three steps later she skidded to a halt.

A man leaned against the fence. A man with an I-own-the-world stance, a cowboy hat pushed back to reveal a tangle of dark blond curls, and a wide grin wreathing his face. She spared him a quick study. Faded brown shirt, tied at the neck like a frontier man of years ago. Creased denim trousers. He dressed like he'd very recently come off a working ranch.

Sally's worry about Robbie collided with surprise at seeing a man in Mrs. Shaw's yard. A sight, she added, that made her feel a pinch in the back of her heart. It had to be the way she'd hurried about searching for Robbie that made her lungs struggle for air.

Robbie. She'd almost forgotten she was looking for him. Her gaze lingered on the man two more seconds. Then she forced herself forward another step, following the direction the man looked.

Her heart headed for runaway speed.

Robbie stood within reach of the hooves of a big horse.

She choked back a warning. If anything startled the animal he could trample Robbie, which would certainly reinforce some of the things the boy had been told, like don't go near a horse that doesn't know you. Stay out of people's yards unless invited—but she had no desire to see him learn in such a harsh fashion.

"That's it. No sudden moves."

She didn't need to turn to know the deep voice came from the man leaning against the fence. He sounded every bit as relaxed as he looked. Her gaze darted back to him. Yes. Still angled back as if he didn't have a worry in the world. He was a stranger to her. She knew nothing about him except what she saw, but it was enough to convince her it took a lot to upset his world.

She envied him his serenity.

"His name is Big Red. I just call him Red."

"Can I touch him?" Robbie's childish voice quivered with eagerness.

She shifted her attention back to him. Normally the boy didn't ask permission and if he did, he paid no mind if it was refused, but he stood stock still waiting for the man to answer.

"Sure. He's as tame as a house kitty. But speak to him first. Maybe tell him your name and say his, like you want to be friends."

Sally watched in complete fascination as Robbie obeyed.

"Hi, Big Red. My name is Robbie Finley. Can I be your friend?" Slowly, cautiously, perhaps a bit fearfully, the boy reached out and touched the horse's muzzle. The horse whinnied as if answering the boy.

Robbie laughed out loud.

The horse lifted his head, rolled back his lips and gave an unmistakable horse laugh.

Sally chuckled softly. It was all so calm. Sweet even. Not at all the way Robbie usually behaved.

"I suppose you've come for the boy?" The man peeled himself from the fence and headed in her direction.

Her amusement fled. Feeling exposed and guilty, she glanced about. She was trespassing, along with Robbie.

But that didn't bother her as much as the foolish reaction of her heart and lungs, her thoughts and skin— she'd never known her skin to tingle so that it made her cheeks burn. It was how the man grinned that filled her with a need to run and hide.

"Allow me to introduce myself. Linc McCoy."

She nodded, unable to push a word to her brain let alone her mouth. The name had a familiar ring to it. Or was it only her stupid reaction making her think she'd heard it before?

"Are you Robbie's mother?"

Words jolted from her mouth. "Oh, no." A rush of them followed. "His mother is dead. I'm only the housekeeper. I take care of them. Every day. I make meals and—" Then a blank mind.

"Oh. I don't believe I've had the pleasure."

Pleasure? Yes, it was a word that fit this man. He seemed to embrace life with his smile, his relaxed stance. Even his dark eyes—brown as mink fur—said life was good. Fun. To be enjoyed. Ah. That would explain why Robbie had responded so well to him. Robbie didn't have much use for rules or anything interfering with his idea of fun. She tried to think how unnatural it was in a grown man but instead she smiled back, as bemused as Robbie was with the horse. Suddenly she realized he grinned because she hadn't given her name. When had she ever been so foolish? So slow thinking? "I'm Sally Morgan."

"Looks like we'll be neighbors."

Another burst of words shot from her mouth. "Oh, no. I don't live here. I only come in the daytime. I live out of town." She waved in vaguely the direction of the Morgan home. "Not very far from town. Just a nice walk. I come to take care of the house and the children."

How could she have forgotten her responsibility? "Come along, Robbie. Your father will be home shortly."

Robbie stuck out his lip in an all-too-familiar gesture.

Linc McCoy strode to the boy's side with a rolling gait. "Nice meeting you, Robbie. Red says so, too, don't you, Boy?"

The horse whinnied and nodded his head.

"See. He agrees."

Robbie giggled, but when he turned back to Sally his look overflowed with rebellion. He had the same coloring as his sister, brown hair, brown eyes. On Carol it was sweet. Not a word she would use to describe Robbie.

Mr. McCoy planted a hand on Robbie's shoulder and turned him toward Sally. "You run along now. Perhaps you can visit again."

"Only with permission," Sally warned.

"That's right. You have to ask before you come over. Wouldn't want to worry Miss Morgan, would you?" He shifted his warm, steady gaze to Sally, and her breath stuck halfway up her windpipe. "It is Miss, isn't it?"

She nodded. It was an innocent enough question. It was only her befuddled brain making her think it brimmed with interest. "Yes." If she didn't get back in a matter of minutes, not only would supper be ruined but she was bound to say something really and truly stupid.

Robbie didn't protest when she grabbed his hand

and hustled him to the fence. He scampered over, but she hesitated. There was no graceful way to climb over and land on her feet.

Mr. McCoy followed her. "Allow me." He pushed the wire down with his foot and extended his hand to help her over.

What a predicament. Place her hand in his and most certainly stumble over her tongue, or climb over on her own and most certainly stumble to the ground.

She chose dignity over wisdom, placed her fingers in his cool firm palm and wobbled her way over the swaying wire. "Thank you," she murmured, managing to make her thick tongue say the two syllables without tangling them.

Abe's car pulled into the narrow driveway.

Oh, no. She couldn't possibly make it back before he discovered her absence. "Run, Robbie." She grabbed his hand and fled for the back door.

They burst into the house. Sally choked on the burnt smell. Abe held a smoking pot in his tea-towel-protected hand.

"I'm sorry," Sally gasped and rushed to take the pot. The potatoes were ruined. She dumped the pot in the sink and quickly checked the rest of the meal. The green beans she'd shoved to the back of the stove looked a little limp but were edible. The meat simmered in now glutinous gravy, but it could be salvaged with the addition of hot water. "Everything will be ready in a minute or two. I'll call Carol." But when she turned to do so, Abe blocked her way.

"Where were you? I come home expecting supper

and discover my daughter home alone, you and my son missing. Did you let him run away again?"

Her tongue seemed to stick to the roof of her mouth. She sucked saliva to moisten it. Why did he blame her when Robbie was so difficult?

"I need someone who can handle my home and children."

She nodded miserably. She had always considered herself efficient until she started work here. And her future depended on proving it. Everyone knew Abe Finley was in need of a new wife and mother for his children. He was a man with a good home and a government job that offered stability. Too bad he couldn't smile with as much pleasure as Mr. McCoy did. She dismissed the thought before it had a chance to roost.

"It won't happen again." Not if she had to chain Robbie to the stove.

"I'm glad to hear that." He turned on his heel. "Call me when you have things properly organized."

She was organized. She did watch his children with due care. A thousand protests sprang to her mind but were quickly squelched as she turned back to the stove. Abe wasn't unkind. He simply liked things done properly, neatly. It wasn't too much to expect. Especially if she wanted him to offer marriage to make the arrangement permanent.

Too bad he couldn't enjoy life as much as Linc McCoy appeared to.

Sally slammed a pot lid on the cupboard with more force than necessary. Why was she thinking about a stranger when her future lay in this house? If she proved herself acceptable—and she vowed she would. And who was Linc McCoy to be hanging about Mrs. Shaw's place like he owned it?

She managed to present a passable meal, substituting slabs of bread for the potatoes. Her father had always said there was nothing quite as good as bread and gravy, but she could tell Abe didn't share the opinion. However, he ate without complaint and pushed from the table a little later, having eaten enough to satisfy most any appetite.

"You did fine despite your mistakes. Thank you."

"You're welcome." She met his gaze for a moment but as always felt awkward and darted her glance past him to the dirty dishes. "I'll wash up before I head home."

"I appreciate that."

Yet somehow she wondered if he did, or if he expected it. Immediately she scolded herself for her wicked thoughts. Why was she suddenly so keen to criticize him? She had no right. She was here to do a job. With the unspoken agreement that it could lead to more.

A window stood over the sink and as she washed dishes, she glanced out frequently. She faced the back of the yard, toward Mrs. Shaw's place. A gate near the barn swung back and Linc, astride Big Red, rode out. He sat on the horse like the two were one, his hat pulled low to shield his eyes from the slanting rays of the sun. Red raced down the alley between the two properties. Linc and Red flowed like fast-moving water down the fence line. At the corner, the horse reared.

Sally's heart clamored up her throat. He was going to be thrown.

But instead, he let out a loud whoop that reached her through the open window. Then he laughed and rode back.

He saw her staring at him and waved his hat, grinning so widely and freely it tugged at some remote part of her heart. Oh, to feel so free and full of enjoyment.

With another whoop, he guided the horse past the barn and out of sight.

She didn't know who he was, but he certainly seemed to think life was a lark. She forced her attention back to the stack of dirty dishes and hoped he would ride fast and far, out of her thoughts.

Linc galloped two miles down the road before he turned and allowed Red to keep a sedate pace on the way back to his grandparents' farm—now Grandmama's farm. Grandpa had died two years ago and ever since, Grandmama had been begging Linc to come back and help her.

He might never have come, except for the way things had worked out.

He settled back in the saddle and thought of the afternoon. Little Robbie had ventured into the corral, unaware Linc watched. The little boy wore nice clothes but an unhappy expression. He wondered what brought such a look to a child's face until Sally said the boy's mother had died. Linc understood how that felt. His own mother had died when he was but fifteen. Much older than Robbie, but still too young to be motherless. Mothers kept the family together, provided a moral compass. Without a mother…well, his family had certainly gone downhill. Not that he intended to dwell on it or try to find someone or something to pin the blame on.

His mood shifted and he grinned as he thought of Sally. He didn't remember her from before, so the Morgans must have moved in after they left when he was sixteen. Otherwise he would have certainly remembered her. Even then he liked a good-looking woman. And Sally was certainly that, with wavy brown hair falling to her shoulders, capturing the sun's rays like miser's gold in each wave. Eyes the color of olive-green water, like he'd seen in the mountains to the west. Eyes that widened in surprise at seeing him, narrowed with caution before taking his hand. He rubbed his hand against the warm denim on his leg. He had only meant to be helpful, but her cool flesh against his had felt like a hot iron, searing her brand on his palm. He pressed his fist to his chest, feeling marked inside as well and ignored the urge to thump himself on the forehead at such silly ideas. He dropped his hand back to his leg.

Obviously a proper young woman.

Even if she didn't know the McCoy reputation, she would soon enough hear it. Not that it mattered what people said. He'd tried to tell his pa and older brother so six years ago. Stay and prove the rumors false, he'd said. But he was only sixteen and they weren't about to listen to him.

Now he was back and determined to do what he'd wanted back then—prove the McCoys were not sticky-fingered scoundrels.

And of course, care for his injured father.

Time to get back to the task.

Despite the duties calling him, he took his time un-saddling Red, then spent a leisurely thirty minutes grooming him and tidying up the barn before he headed for the house. He paused inside the door and breathed in the homey scents of yeasty bread and cinnamon. No matter where he'd gone in the past six years, he'd missed this place.

Grandmama sat in her favorite spot—a rocking chair by the window—doing needlework. "I 'spect you're missing your freedom."

He understood what she didn't say. That she feared he would leave again as soon as Pa—

Memories of a pretty face flashed through his brain. Even if he had planned to leave, getting to know Miss Sally better was enough to make him reconsider. "I never wanted to go in the first place."

Grandmama glanced up then. "You should have stayed. You could stay now and run this place."

He wondered if anyone else would hope he'd remain. "I had to go with Pa and Harris." Though he couldn't exactly say why. Guess the same loyalty that brought him back with Pa. "How is he?"

"Haven't heard from him."

Which meant he was sleeping. The painkiller the doctor provided was doing its job. Once it wore off, Pa would start hollering and cussing. Poor Grandmama—having to listen to Pa in one of his rages. Yet when Linc showed up on the doorstep dragging his injured father, she had calmly opened the door and welcomed them.

And she'd cried when Linc said Harris had died in the mining accident that injured Pa.

"He was my oldest grandson. Despite his rebellious ways I have never stopped loving him and praying for him." She'd hugged Linc long and hard. "Are you still walking in your faith?" she asked when her tears were spent.

He'd had his struggles, his ups and downs and times of doubt, but he was happy to be able to give her the answer she longed for. "I hold fast to my faith and God's love."

"I don't suppose Harris or your Pa ever made that choice?"

"Not Pa. I don't know about Harris. You know how he always tried so hard to please Pa." Even if Harris believed in God, he might well hide it from Pa so as to not incur his displeasure.

"Then this is why God sent you home. To allow Jonah another chance to change his ways. My Mary would want her husband to become a Christian."

Linc permitted himself a moment of aching emptiness at the mention of his mother's name, then pulled his thoughts back to the present. "I'll check on him." He strode to the bedroom off the front room where Grandmama had made up a bed for Pa. Pa murmured in his sleep. Doc said the drugs made him restless, but for the moment he seemed comfortable. The bruises on his face had faded to yellow and the swelling had subsided. His leg was bound and splinted. Doc changed the dressings on it every day. But it was the injuries to his chest that had done the most damage. Doc said he couldn't tell how badly Pa's internal organs had been damaged. His chances were slim, Doc had been honest enough to say. "About all we can do is keep him comfortable."

Which meant giving him pain medication.

Linc shook the bottle of medicine. It was almost empty. As were his pockets. It had taken a whack out of his savings to bury Harris and the rest to get himself, Red and his father home. He'd have to find himself some sort of work in order to keep the bottle full.

Satisfied his Pa didn't need anything for the moment, he returned to the kitchen and sat at the table, turning his chair to face Grandmama.

"I met a young lady today. Sally Morgan. Do you know her?"

Grandmama carefully put away the yarn and folded the piece of fabric she worked on before setting it on the little table beside her chair. "I know the Morgans. Mr. Morgan died a few years back. The two older girls have married recently. Louisa, the eldest, married a widower with a little girl. They adopted one of the orphan girls before they headed west where he has a ranch. Madge and her husband now own the Cotton farm. They're a hard-working young couple."

"Uh-huh." He wasn't so interested in the family as in Sally.

"Miss Sally is working for our neighbor, Abe Finley." He knew that, too.

"He's a widower with two young children."

"I met Robbie. He came to visit me and my horse."

"Young Robbie has been a bit of a…" She hesitated. "A concern since his mother died."

Linc smiled. "You couldn't come right out and say he's a defiant child?" He'd seen the way he'd glowered at Sally when she said he had to go home.

Grandmama sniffed. "I don't believe in speaking ill of others."

"Too bad others don't share your view." If they did, Linc and his father and brother wouldn't have felt they had to leave town six years ago. And maybe Harris would still be alive. He missed his brother. A blast of sorrow hit Linc and he looked out the window, waiting for it to pass.

He saw the corrals out the window and remembered he was asking about Sally. "So what do you know about Miss Sally?"

Grandmama gave him her best warning expression. "Everyone expects she and Abe will decide to marry. So you stay away from her, you hear?"

"This understanding that everyone has, is it official?"

Grandmama's eyes narrowed. "There's been no announcement, if that's what you mean. But you listen to me, Lincoln McCoy—"

Uh-oh. When she used his full name, he knew she was deadly serious.

"Abe Finley is a fine match for Sally. Don't you go interfering with it."

And he wasn't suitable? Is that what she meant?

"You hear me?"

Linc sighed. He wouldn't argue with her. After all, she had given shelter to Pa and she didn't even like him much. Just as she'd welcomed the four of them when they returned eight years ago, when Ma was filled with cancer and dying. And perhaps she was right. He was a McCoy, after all, and even if he convinced everyone they hadn't stolen the things they'd been accused of, he would still be a McCoy—and who were they but wanderers? Pa never stayed long in one place. In fact, come to think of it, the two years they'd spent on this farm made the longest he could remember being in one place.

Grandmama nudged his leg. "You hear me?"

"I hear ya." What he heard was there was no formal agreement between Sally and Abe.

Chapter Two

Sally pulled a tray of cookies from the familiar oven of home and scooped them to a rack to cool. Ginger cookies perfectly rounded, nicely browned with a sprinkling of sugar. She was a good cook. Yet she experienced so many failures at the Finley place. She must be trying too hard. She sucked in spicy air and pushed her frustration to the bottom of her stomach. She needed to remember she was a child of God, and as such had His approval. "I'll take these over to the Johanssons as soon as they cool," she said to her mother. "I'm sorry to hear the mother is still not feeling well." Mrs. Johansson hadn't regained her strength after the birth of daughter number five. "The children will appreciate fresh cookies."

"How did your day go at the Finleys'?" Mother glanced up from sewing a button on a sweater.

Sally didn't want to trouble her mother with tales of her struggles with Robbie and news of a ruined meal. "There was a man at Mrs. Shaw's."

"Really? How do you know that?"

"I saw him out in the corrals. He showed Robbie his horse. Big Red, he's called."

Mother studied her with watchful eyes.

Fearing her expression would reveal more than she wanted, Sally shaped more cookies.

"So you met this man?"

Sally nodded. "When I went to bring Robbie back. His name is Linc McCoy. I thought I'd heard the name before but can't place it."

"The McCoys are back?" Mother sounded as if a murderer had escaped into their presence.

"I only saw the one. Are there more?"

Mother pushed to her feet and strode to the window. "I don't suppose you know the story. It was fresh when we first moved but died down shortly after."

Sally stared at her mother's back. "What did they do?"

Mother faced her and sighed. "Mrs. Ogilvy kept some expensive jewelry in her home."

Sally waited for more. Everyone knew Mrs. Ogilvy to be the richest lady in town. She lived in a big house at the opposite end of the street from where Mr. Finley lived. She lived alone except for a woman who came in to help care for the house. Mrs. Ogilvy had once ruled Golden Prairie society but had been ill for the past couple years. She was on the mend now and again dominating social activities. Why, at Christmas she'd instigated a town party for everyone, including hobos from their shelter down by the tracks. Sally had even heard Mrs. Ogilvy allowed some of them to live in the old coach house she no longer used. Sally liked the woman who used her worldly goods to help others.

Mother sighed and continued with her story. "Mrs. Ogilvy's jewels went missing. It was never proven, but all the evidence pointed toward the McCoys. They were known as the kind of people who—" Mother stopped. "I don't like to speak ill of others, but from what I understand they had sticky fingers."

"The McCoys?" This news didn't fit with the relaxed, smiling man she'd met. "How many were there?"

"A father and two sons—the younger several years younger than the older."

"What do they have to do with Mrs. Shaw?"

"Mrs. McCoy was Mrs. Shaw's daughter. Her only child. She came home to die of cancer." Mother shook her head sadly. "I can't imagine how she must feel to lose her daughter, then have her grandsons and son-in-law branded criminals."

"But you said they were never convicted."

"No, they weren't, but people believed it was only because of poor police work. They left town to avoid the censure of the community."

Sally pulled out another tray of baked cookies and put them to cool, then slipped a tray of unbaked ones into the oven, welcoming the chance to contemplate all her mother said.

"You say you met Linc McCoy? I'm not certain but I think he was the youngest son. From what I recall, about fifteen or sixteen when they left town."

"They might be innocent. You know what gossip is like."

Mother crossed to Sally's side. "Where there's smoke, there's fire. I don't want you feeling sorry for this man. It would not serve your purpose to get involved with him. Whether or not they've stolen the jewels, their name carries trouble."

Sally met her mother's eyes without flinching. She understood what Mother meant. People would likely feel the same way about the McCoys now as they had back then. She shifted her gaze. The lowering sun shone through the west window, highlighting the ever present dust in the air. Through the window, she studied the struggling garden. "I need to take water to the garden." She'd saved the dishwashing water. "I'll feed the chickens as soon as I finish the cookies."

Mother returned to her sewing, knowing they were in agreement. Sally would do nothing to besmirch her reputation or put her security at risk. She'd avoid Linc McCoy, which shouldn't be hard.

Mother paused. "I wonder what brought them back."

Sally wondered if all of them had returned. She'd seen only Linc—the man who seemed to think life was for enjoyment.

Well, so did she, only she liked to enjoy it on her terms. She recalled one of her memory verses. *A good name is rather to be chosen than great riches, and loving favour rather than silver and gold.*

She could well say, rather than Mrs. Ogilvy's jewels.

She wanted nothing more to do with Linc McCoy and the shady doings associated with his family.

Sally slipped into the Finley kitchen and began breakfast preparations. Overhead, she heard the family rising. They would soon descend—Carol ready for school, Abe dressed and groomed for his job and Robbie with his eyes silently challenging her.

She sighed. She and Robbie would become friends sooner or later. She just wished it would be sooner.

A short while later, the children descended, Abe's hand firmly on Robbie's stubborn shoulder. Carol was dressed for school, not a seam out of place. From the beginning she insisted she could manage her hair on her own and did a fine job. Robbie wore wrinkled overalls with threadbare knees. If she didn't miss her guess, his shirt was buttoned crookedly, but she would ignore it unless Abe insisted it be corrected. Abe was even neater than Carol, as if he'd pressed his suit while on his body so not a crease was out of place. Freshly shaven, smelling of bay rum with his dark brown hair brushed back. One thing about Abe: he knew how to make the most of his looks, and there was no denying he was a good-looking man and well respected—a good Christian, a devout churchgoer, a man of honor.

Sally recited his attributes as she dished up porridge and poured Abe a cup of coffee. She hated the stuff, preferring a pot of well-steeped tea, but had learned to make a brew to satisfy his requirements. She'd eaten with Mother before leaving home but sat with the family and drank tea as they ate.

Abe left as soon as he finished. He spared them all a hurried goodbye.

Sally found it easier to smile once he'd gone, even though she still found his rushed exits strange. Her father had hugged each of the girls and kissed Mother when he left the house. He always had a kind word for them. She'd told herself several times it wasn't fair to any man to compare him to Father, and yet she wished Abe would at least read a chapter from the Bible and pray with the children before he left for the day.

At first, she'd debated with herself as to whether she should take on the responsibility. The deciding factor had been that she should begin as she expected to go on, and if she were to become a permanent part of this home, Bible reading and prayer were what she wanted.

But rather than read from the family Bible, she brought a series of Bible stories on cards with pictures on one side and text on the other that she'd collected in her Sunday school days. She chose the next in the stack to read.

Carol listened intently. Robbie fidgeted, wanting to leave but knowing Sally would insist he stay. They'd fought that battle the first day and Sally had won, knowing she must.

She made her prayer short, asking for the children and their father to be safe. In her heart, she prayed she could live up to expectations and not let foolish thoughts distract her. And why the thought shaped into a grinning man in a cowboy hat, she wouldn't let herself consider.

Carol departed a short time later then Sally turned to Robbie. "Play out back where I can see you."

She washed dishes and put together soup for dinner when both Abe and Carol would come home. Every few minutes she glanced out the window to check on Robbie. He'd dug a hole in the end of the garden and used the dirt to construct a barrier, no doubt hoping to build a place where he could hide from his troublesome world.

Sally grinned. After Father died she'd done the same, only she'd had the loft of the barn where she used loose hay to encircle a little patch where she took her books and an old school notebook, in which she wrote copious amounts of purple prose full of emotionally charged words like hopelessness, emptiness and loneliness. She had felt safe and secure in that little place.

Forbidden, her gaze sought the area across the alley. Quickly, telling herself she was only allowing her eyes a chance to look into the distance, she glanced to the corrals, past them to the bit of yard within her view. Maybe he had left again. No reason such a thought should make her sad. She snorted as several of the words she'd used in her loft hiding place resurrected.

The soup simmered on the stove. She mixed up baking powder biscuits to go with it.

Another glance out the window showed the Shaw yard still empty and Robbie struggling to build his dirt walls higher. The soil was so dry it sifted into a slack pile.

Remembering her own efforts to create a safe place, she ached for the little boy. Hoping he wouldn't be angry at her interruption, she hurried outside. "I can show you how to build higher walls if you like."

He didn't move for a full three seconds.

She knew he warred with a desire to dismiss her and frustration over dealing with the piles of dirt.

"How?" He made certain to sound as if he was doing her a favor.

"I saw some scraps of lumber in the shed. I think you could use them to provide support. Come. I'll show you."

He followed her to the shed and allowed her to fill his arms with bits of lumber.

Back in the garden, she drove the thinner pieces into the ground as uprights and showed him how to place the wider pieces against them and hold them in place with the dirt. As they worked, she told him about the place she'd made in the loft.

She heard a horse trot down the alley and kept her gaze averted to the count of five before she glanced up. Linc on Big Red rode toward the center of town.

He nodded at them, grinning. "Playing in the dirt, I see."

She tossed her hair out of her eyes. "We're building."

"What are you building?"

"I'm not sure. Robbie, what are we building?"

"A fort." He didn't pause from scooping dirt against the walls.

Linc looked from Robbie to Sally, paused a moment then returned to Robbie. "What sort of fort?"

"To keep out the bad guys."

For a moment Linc didn't move, didn't say anything and his grin seemed narrower. "Guess we all need a safe place." He touched the brim of his hat. "Perhaps I'll see you later."

Sally waited until he rode out of sight then pushed to her feet. "I have to check on dinner. Call me if you need any help."

Robbie kept shoveling dirt.

We all need a safe place. Exactly her sentiments. She paused outside the door and studied the house. A good solid house. A safe place? She glanced over her shoulder. Safer than a man on horseback who dropped in from who-knows-where and would likely drop back out as quickly and silently.

She hurried indoors and put the biscuits in the oven to bake.

The meal was ready when Abe stepped into the house. The table was set neatly. She'd put the soup in a pretty tureen in the middle of the table and arranged the biscuits on a nice platter. She'd even found a glass dish for the butter.

Robbie had come in without arguing. He'd dusted his clothes and washed his face and hands. Hardly any evidence remained of his morning spent playing in the dirt.

Sally was satisfied the meal looked as good as it smelled. Everything was done to perfection. As she'd taken care of the many details of creating this meal, she'd taken care of one other thing—sorting out her thoughts. She needed a safe place and this was it. Nothing could be allowed to take that away from her. Especially not a man on a horse.

They all took their places and without any warning, Abe bowed and said grace.

It still startled Sally the way he did it. Father had always said, "Let us pray." And waited for them all to fold their hands and bow their heads.

Abe did things differently. Nothing wrong with that.

He ate in silence for a few minutes, then, as he broke open another biscuit and drenched it in butter and jam, he said, "I hired a man to work on the barn. I want it converted to a proper garage. The yard could do with some cleaning up, too, so I gave him instructions to fix the fence out back, prune the apple trees and generally take care of the chores."

"I see." Abe was one of a handful of people who could afford to pay someone to do repair work for them.

"I don't have time to show him around so perhaps you would do so. Give him access to the tools in the shed. Make him feel welcome. Perhaps offer him coffee in the middle of the afternoon. That sort of thing."

"Will he be taking meals with us?"

"I shouldn't think so. He lives close by."

She quickly did a mental inventory on the neighbors, wondering which one had been so favored by Abe.

"I think he's down on his luck. As a Christian man I feel it my duty to give him a helping hand."

That tidbit didn't help her. Most of the families in town were having trouble making ends meet.

He pushed back and reached for his hat. "He said he'd come over after lunch. It would please me if you helped him in any way you can."

Sally waited, expecting a name, but Abe headed for the door. "Wait. You didn't say who was coming."

"Oh, didn't I? Sorry. It's Linc McCoy. He's staying at his grandmother's just next door." He pointed toward the farm.

Sally's heart quivered. Linc was coming here to work? Abe expected her to help him? The man did strange things to her equilibrium. Things she didn't like or welcome.

Abe must have read her hesitation. "There have been cruel rumors about him in the past. This morning I saw Linc in the store asking after a job and overheard some not-so-kind-hearted women saying no one in town would hire the likes of him. Not a very Christian attitude in my opinion. I believe our church should do what it can to dispel such unkindness. As a deacon I intend to take the lead. I hope I have your support."

"Of course." Thankfully her voice didn't reveal her confusion. "It's very noble of you to give this man a chance."

Her praise brought a pleased smile to Abe's lips.

Sally vowed she would do what she could to help Abe's cause.

Linc considered this job an answer to prayer—an opportunity to earn money to buy more medicine for Pa, but even more, the chance to prove a McCoy could be trusted. Grandmama seemed troubled by the job offer and warned Linc that Sally's association with him, even indirectly, could harm her reputation. He understood her warning and was prepared to stay as far away from Sally as the large yard allowed. But Abe had told him to go to the house for instructions on where to find tools.

He first toured the yard, noting all the things needing attention. Abe wanted the barn converted to a garage for his car. Linc went inside to study what it needed.

"What are you doing here?" Robbie asked from the dark interior.

"Looking."

"At what?"

"The barn."

"You never seen a barn before?"

"Oh, yeah. Lots of them. I could tell you all sorts of stories about barns."

"Nothing special about barns."

"Nope. Guess not. Seems a shame to take the stalls out though."

Robbie emerged from the shadows. "Why you going to do that?"

"So your father can park his car in here."

Robbie made a rumbling noise with his lips. "I'd sooner have a horse."

"Me, too, little guy."

They stood side by side in shared sorrow at the way horses were being replaced with automobiles and tractors.

Linc moved first. "I need to ask Miss Sally to show me the tools. Want to come along?"

"Yep."

Linc wasn't sure who needed the other the most. He, to keep his thoughts in order when he spoke to Sally, or Robbie, who seemed to crave attention, but together they marched to the back door. Robbie stood by his side as Linc knocked.

Sally opened the door. "Mr. Finley said to expect you. He said I should show you what needs doing."

Linc backed up two steps. Robbie followed suit, though not likely for the same reason. Linc did it to gain a safety zone. Even so, he felt her in every muscle. She smelled like home cooking and fresh laundry, the most appealing scent he'd ever experienced.

She slipped through the doorway. "I'll show you around."

I've already looked about. The words were in his brain but refused to budge. Instead he nodded, and he and Robbie fell in at her side.

She led him to the back corner of the yard. "Mr. Finley said the crab apple trees should be pruned."

Robbie climbed one of the trees and sat in a fork, pretending he had a spyglass as he looked out across the yard.

Linc and Sally stood under the scraggly trees that were shedding the last of their blossoms and trying to bud, finding it difficult because of the lack of moisture. He examined the three trees. "Lots of dead branches that need to come out."

She nodded. "I figure they must be tough as an old cowhide to survive the drought and wind and grasshoppers. Especially the grasshoppers. The little pests have gnawed most of the trees to death around here."

"Then I guess they deserve lots of care."

He turned from examining the branches. She stood under a flowering bough. Their gazes collided. Her eyes were wide and watchful. Wary even. No doubt she had heard about the McCoys by now. "You know I'm Beatrice Shaw's grandson?"

She nodded. "My mother told me."

"Did she tell you about the McCoys?"

Sally's gaze never faltered. "She said your mother had died and you have a father and older brother."

"My brother is dead, too. In a mining accident."

"I'm sorry." She brushed his arm with her cool fingers then jerked back, as if she was also aware of the tension between them.

"Pa was injured, too. That's why I'm here. To let him rest and recover." He clung to the hope Pa would get better.

"How is he?"

"Not good."

"Again, I'm sorry. If there is anything I can do to help…."

He stood stock-still, letting her concern filter through him. Not many around here knew of the accident. No reason to hide the fact but no reason to tell it either. He didn't want or expect sympathy—just a fair chance to prove the McCoys were an okay bunch. Yet the way her eyes filled with regret and concern made him realize how much he wanted to share his sorrow.

He leaned against a tree. "I was working on a ranch when I got word about the accident. Harris—that's my brother—was killed outright. Pa was in terrible shape. I made arrangements to bury Harris." He told her details of the funeral. "It was ten days before Pa was able to travel. The doctor out there said to take him home so he could die in his own surroundings. Grandmama's place is the only home we've ever had so I brought him here."

She listened to his whole story without uttering a word, but murmuring comforting sounds.

He fell silent, feeling a hundred pounds lighter having told her. Suddenly he jerked upright. "Sorry. I didn't mean to tell you the story of my life."

She laughed softly. "I expect there's more to your life than that and I didn't mind. Helps me understand."

He didn't ask what it helped her understand, and she didn't explain. Perhaps they both knew the answer without speaking it—his tale helped her understand him, just as sharing it helped him understand how kind and sympathetic she was. He had never before felt so comfortable with another human. Sure, he had unburdened himself to the occasional horse—Red heard lots of his woes—but never before to another person, and most certainly not to a woman.

Grandmama warned him she was a genuinely gentle person. Now he understood what she meant.

Guilt flared through his blood, searing his nerve endings. He glanced over his shoulder as if Grandmama watched.

Chapter Three

"Abe said you would show me where the tools are." Linc's words jerked Sally back to her responsibilities. "Of course." She didn't offer to show him the barn but marched toward the shed at the back of the yard. She paused as they reached the garden. Robbie followed at their heels and veered toward the hole he'd been digging this morning.

She watched him and spoke her thoughts. "I'd like to plant a garden."

"I'll dig the ground for you."

She thought of arguing. Would she look as if she couldn't manage? On the other hand, his help would certainly make the work go faster. Still undecided about how she should handle his offer, she opened the door and stepped aside as he entered. But two feet of distance did not protect her from acute awareness of the warmth of his body as he passed, nor the scent of leather and freshly cut hay. And something more she could not identify, nor did she intend to try. But whatever it was made her feel as if a weight pressed against her chest, making her lungs reluctant to work.

He took his time looking about, then emerged with a round-nosed shovel and a rake.

She had thought long and hard about planting a garden. Well, actually she'd only thought of it this morning and decided growing a garden would prove to Abe she was efficient and capable. Her plan had been to dig the soil on her own, but suddenly accepting Linc's offer to help seemed the wisest thing in the world. It would enable her to get the garden in sooner, which was good.

When he told her about his father and brother, she sensed a man who valued his family above people's opinions. She respected him for that.

He strode to the edge of the garden and began turning over the soil.

Robbie stood before the hole he'd dug. "You can't touch my fort." His expression dared anyone to do so. Sally knew he would fly into a rage if they did.

Linc leaned on the shovel, his expression serious, and pushed his hat back to reveal a white forehead. Brown dirt dusted the rest of his face, and a thin layer wrapped about his pant.

Sally smiled gently. The man could look as handsome in work-soiled clothes as in a polished and pressed suit.

He nodded toward Robbie. "I respect a man who defends his property."

Robbie's expression revealed confusion. "What's that mean?"

Linc scratched his hairline and seemed to consider

his answer with due seriousness. "It means I think it's a good thing you want to protect what you've made."

"It is?" Robbie suddenly stood up straighter. "I sure 'nough plan to do that." He picked up a stick and brandished it like a weapon.

Linc held up a hand. "Now hang on a minute. Did I threaten your fort? Did I say I was going to mow it down? No. I listened to your words. No need to get physical when your words work."

Robbie dropped his weapon.

Linc returned to digging, his back muscles rippling beneath the fabric of his faded brown shirt.

Sally stared. The McCoys had a reputation for taking things. What no one had said, perhaps had not noticed, was this McCoy had a way of giving things. He'd given Robbie the assurance his words could convey his desires. He'd given Sally a feeling of safety.

Now why had she thought such a foolish thing?

She spun around and stared at the house, as if it provided the answer to her question. Just because Linc knew what to say to Robbie to defuse his anger did not mean he offered safety. Safety meant a house. Assurance of staying in one place. Steady employment. Enough to eat.

Her heart burned within her at a rush of other unnamed, unidentifiable things that safety and security meant. She grabbed the rake and smoothed the garden soil behind Linc.

He turned. "I can do that." His voice rang with amusement and so much more.

She stopped and considered him. Did he think she needed protecting?

No one had thought so since Father died, and a lump lodged in the back of her throat. She swallowed hard. "Is there something wrong with the way I'm doing it?" Confusion made her words sharp.

He studied her, a grin slowly wreathing his face. "Can't say as I ever considered there might be a right or wrong way to rake." He leaned on the shovel and contemplated the idea. "I suppose if you had the tines upward. Or tried to use the handle—"

Her tension disappeared and she laughed. "You're teasing."

"Seems like a good idea if it makes you laugh. You should laugh more often, don't you think?" Without waiting for her to say anything, he turned back to digging.

She stared at his back. Didn't she laugh often enough? Or was he saying he liked hearing the sound of her amusement? Perhaps liked making her happy? As she bent to resume raking, she tried to think how she felt about the idea. No one else seemed to care if she laughed or enjoyed life. Abe certainly didn't. Seems all he cared about was if she kept his life orderly.

There she was again, comparing Abe to another. It didn't escape her troubled thoughts that this time it wasn't her father but a man hired to do chores.

She banged a clump of dirt with the rake, taking out her annoyance on the soil. She knew what she wanted and how to get it. And it wasn't by comparing poor, unsuspecting Abe to every man she knew or met.

Linc worked steadily up the length of the garden, turning over clumps of dry hard dirt. She followed, smoothing the soil for planting. Without rain she would have to baby the plants along with rationed bits of water, the same as she did at home.

Neither spoke as they worked. Crows flapped overhead, cawing. The wind sighed through the grass and moaned around the buildings. Robbie yelled some sort of challenge to an unseen intruder. Sally paused to watch the boy.

Linc had stopped, too, and grinned at Robbie's play. Then turned his smile toward Sally, capturing her in a shiny moment.

The amusement they shared made her eyes watery, and she turned away. The feeling was more than amusement but she refused to acknowledge it. She riveted her attention to Robbie.

He leaped out of his dirt fort and charged at the invisible foe, brandishing the same stick he had waved at Linc. He turned, saw them watching and lowered his weapon. Then determination filled his eyes and he marched toward Sally, his stick held like a sword. "You are my captive. I will take you to my fort. You will stay with me until someone rescues you." He shot Linc a narrow-eyed look.

Sally backed away, uncertain how to respond.

Linc straightened and grew serious. "Never fear, fair maiden. I will rescue you from your wild captor."

She giggled and allowed Robbie to shepherd her into his fort. The hole might be the right size for a five-year-old but barely accommodated her legs, so she stood awkwardly while Robbie guarded her from the solid ground of the garden. They were on eye level with each other, close enough that she saw the mixture of excitement and worry in his eyes. She understood how badly he wanted to play, yet couldn't believe any adult would play with him. When had she ever seen Abe play with the boy? Never. When did she play with him? Almost never. Sure, she read to him. Gave him crayons and coloring books. Even helped him do jigsaw puzzles, but she had never romped with him. Why not? Father had played with her and her sisters. She could remember games of tag and hide-and-seek. He'd even taught them to play ball and croquet.

Her thoughts stalled as Linc crouched low and worked his way cautiously to the edge of the garden. "Someone has captured my fair maiden," he murmured. "I must rescue her before she is harmed."

Robbie pressed a hand to his mouth to silence his excitement and wriggled with delight.

Linc pretended to search behind a clump of grass. "Where can they have taken her?" Keeping low, he ran to the shed and opened the door. "Maybe they will capture me, too. I should hide." He darted inside and pulled the door shut.

Silence followed his disappearance.

Robbie stood stock-still, seemed to consider his next move then yelled out in his fiercest voice. "Mister, I got your lady over here."

The door cracked open. Linc peeked out, and seemed surprised to see Robbie and Sally. "The fair maiden. I will come to her rescue." He emerged, brandishing a length of wood matching Robbie's. He planted one hand on his hip and danced forward in some kind of fancy step while waving his wooden sword. "I challenge you to a duel. Come out and face me like a man."

Sally chuckled softly, but her enjoyment ran much deeper than amusement. Linc made a mighty impressive swashbuckler.

Robbie, holding his sword high, stepped forward, meeting Linc at the edge of the garden. *Crack. Whack.* The swords crashed against each other.

Sally sat on the edge of the hole, grinning at the pair. One thing about Linc—he seemed to know how to have fun. He also knew how to talk to Robbie in such a way as to bring out the best in him. Guess she'd have to give him credit for being loyal to his family, as well. It couldn't have been easy to bring his father back to a place where he knew he'd face censure. But he'd returned so his father could recover…die…in comfort. Her eyes stung with unshed tears.

Linc fell to the ground, and Sally jolted to her feet. "Are you hurt?"

He pressed his hands to his chest. "Mortally wounded, fair maiden. Mortally wounded."

Instinct brought her out of the hole, but Robbie waved his sword and ordered her back. "You must stay until you are rescued."

She shook her head as she realized it was all play acting and sat down again on the edge of the dirt hole.

Linc groaned, rolled on his side and heaved a deep sigh. Then he was quiet. So quiet and still that Robbie tiptoed over. Linc waited until he bent over him to check if he was okay, then grabbed Robbie's sword and held it to the boy's chest. "You are my captive. Set the fair maiden free or prepare to die."

Robbie backed toward the dirt fort. He signaled Sally. "You have been rescued. Go and never bother me again."

Linc reached out and helped Sally from the hole in the ground. He pulled her to his side.

All pretend, she assured herself. Her silly feelings of being protected were not real.

Linc laid Robbie's wooden sword on the ground and edged away, keeping Sally pressed close behind him. "We will meet again, you scoundrel. Next time you won't be so lucky." He turned, grabbed Sally's hand and raced around the shed and out of sight to lean against the warm, rough wall. He laughed, long and hard.

Sally giggled, as delighted with his merriment as she was by his sense of play.

Finally he sobered enough to speak. "Harris and I used to play war games."

"Who was your fair maiden?"

"Usually some poor unsuspecting neighbor girl." He laughed again. "It got so the girls ran indoors when we approached."

She chuckled, enjoying the mental picture of girls running away screaming. Suddenly her amusement died. She doubted the girls ran from him still. Not that it mattered to her if they did or not.

Robbie tiptoed around the edge of the building. "What are you doing?"

"Is it safe to go back to digging the garden?" Linc asked.

Sally sprang into action. "I have to get to work. No more play." She hurried back to her raking. What had she been thinking? She had responsibilities.

Behind her Linc spoke to Robbie. "She didn't mean it. There will always be time to play."

Sally snorted. Showed what he knew. "Play is for children."

"Do you really mean that?" Linc picked up the shovel and resumed digging.

"I guess there is a time and place for play. And people who can take the time." She spoke the words firmly, as much to convince herself as him.

"I gather you don't count yourself one of them."

"Not when I have responsibilities."

He worked steadily. "There will always be responsibilities."

"True."

He reached the end of digging and stopped to wipe his brow on his shirt sleeve. "So you don't play? Grandmama says you have two sisters. Surely you played with them."

"I used to. When I was young and carefree." Why did she feel she had to defend herself? She expected him to ask why she wasn't any longer carefree, but instead he asked, "What games did you and your sisters play?"

"Dress up. Plays. Tea parties." She didn't want to mention the games she'd played with Father.

Linc placed the stake in one end of the garden and stretched a length of twine to the far end, marking a row for Sally. As he worked, he was acutely aware of her studying his question, though her fingers sorted through a small tin bucket full of seed packets.

She'd been a good sport joining in Robbie's game. The boy seemed almost afraid to play. Or rather, to engage adults in his play.

Linc tried to remember a time his father had played with him, but couldn't. Harris, five years older, had been the one who roughhoused with Linc, threw a ball endlessly while he learned how to connect with the bat, and involved him in long complicated games of cops and robbers.

"My father died almost five years ago," Sally finally said. "Just before the crash. Mother says it was a mercy. That it would have broken his heart to see how his family had to struggle."

Linc sat back on his heels and watched her. She had forgotten about the pail of seeds and stared into the past. Her eyes darkened to a deep pine color. A splotch of dirt on her cheek made him want to reach out and brush it away, but he didn't want to distract her. He guessed she would stop talking if he did, and he longed to hear who she was, who she had been.

A shudder raced across her shoulders. "I can't believe how things have changed."

He didn't know if she meant from her father's passing or the depression that followed the stock market crash. Likely both. "It's been tough." It was both a question and a statement. So many unemployed men, many of them in relief camps in the north. The idea behind the camps was to give the unemployed single men a place to live, food to eat and meaningful work to do.

Linc thought the reason was more likely a way to get the desperate-looking men out of the way so people weren't reminded of the suffering of others. He had seen women with pinched faces, aching from hunger and something far deeper—a pain exceeding all else—as they helplessly listened to their children cry for food. The drought and grasshopper plague took what little was left after the stockmarket crash. Things were bad all over, but he wanted to know the specifics of how her life had changed. He wanted to know how she'd survived.

"The whole world—my whole world—went from safe to shattered in a matter of days."

"Losing a parent can do that to you."

She blinked, and her gaze returned to the present. Her eyes, holding a mixture of sorrow and sympathy, connected with his. "I guess you understand."

Something in the way she said it, as if finding for the first time someone who truly understood her feelings, made him ache to touch her in a physical way, to offer comfort. And keep her safe. Only the distance between them stopped him from opening his arms. "Your sisters would, too."

She averted her gaze, but not before he caught a glimpse of regret. "Of course they do, but they coped in their own way. Madge, she's a year older than me, did her best to take Father's place. She guided Mother in making decisions about the farm, and because of her efforts our house is safe and secure." She brought her gaze back to his and smiled, as if to prove everything was well in her world. "Louisa is two years older and spent so much of her time sick and forced to rest that she lived in her books. Father's death hit her hard." This time she seemed to expect the shudder and stiffened to contain it to a mere shiver. She brightened.

He discovered he'd been holding his breath and released it with a whoosh.

"I didn't mean to get all sentimental. I mentioned my father because you asked about games. He taught us to play softball."

"Ball, hmm." He pushed his hat far back on his head and stared away into the distance, imagining a father and three little girls laughing and giggling. "Did you like the game? Were you good at it?" His question seemed to surprise her.

"I tried really hard because I wanted to please my father, but I preferred a game of tag. Father knew a hundred different ways to play the game—frozen tag, stone tag, shadow tag—" She giggled nervously. "I guess that's more information than you expected."

It wasn't. In fact, he wanted more details. "Why did you like tag better than ball?"

She shuffled through the seeds and waited a moment to answer. "Because—" Her voice had grown soft, almost a whisper. "It's just for fun. No one can be disappointed because you couldn't hit the ball." She again turned to the bucket of seeds. "Now I must get this garden planted. And I've kept you from your work long enough."

Her words hung in his ears. She seemed to care so much what her father thought. But then, didn't everyone? His father made it clear he thought Linc didn't measure up to Harris. Although he didn't want to be the sort of man his brother had been—rowdy and hard living, caring little for laws or who got hurt in his schemes—Linc did wish his father viewed him as more than a mother's boy. Too soft for real life. Of course, his father's version of real life hadn't exactly worked out well for either him or Harris.

But Sally was right. Work called. He'd promised a day's work for a day's pay, and he intended to provide it. He went into the shed, found a ladder and saw and carried them out. Sally bent over a row, dropping seeds into a little trench. He paused, thoughts buzzing in his head like flies disturbed from a sunny windowsill. Noisy but nameless. His heart strained with wanting to say something to her that would—what? He could offer nothing. She came from a good family, and he? He was a McCoy.

Until today it hadn't mattered so much.

He hurried across to the struggling crab apple trees. Every step emphasized the truth. He was here to take care of his injured father. She had aspirations to marry Abe Finley.

But as he tackled his job, he stole glances at her. She worked steadily, seeming unmindful of the searing sun and the endless wind whipping dirt into her face as she bent over the soil. At that moment the wind caught the branch he had cut off and practically tore him from his perch on the ladder. He struggled to keep his balance, and had to drop the branch. It lodged in the heart of the tree. He jerked to free it, and managed to kick the ladder out from under him. He clung to a solid branch with his feet dangling. The branch cracked ominously, and he stopped trying to pull himself upward.

How inglorious. Hanging like a kitten gone too far out on a limb. "Sally. Could you give me a hand?"

He couldn't turn to see her, but he knew the second she realized his predicament.

She gasped. "Oh, my word. Hang on. I'm on my way."

"Hang on?" he sputtered. "I fully intend to."

She giggled a little as she trotted across the yard. The ladder was heavy and awkward and she struggled to place it in a spot that would enable him to use it. "Try that."

He swung his feet, found the rungs and eased his weight to them. His body angled awkwardly between his hands and his feet. The limb cracked as he shifted. "Step back in case this breaks."

"Hurry up and get down."

He had to let go of the relative safety of the branch and fling himself toward the ladder. He sucked in air, tensed his muscle and made his move. The ladder shuddered but stayed in place. He looked down. Sally steadied it. His heart clawed up his throat. If the branch had broken…if he'd fallen… "I told you to step back." He sounded angry.

She blinked and looked confused, as if trying to decide if she should obey, then her eyes cleared. "I will once your feet are on the ground."

He caught two rungs on the ladder on his descent. His feet barely touched the ground before he swung around to face her and planted his hands on her shoulders. He wanted to shake her hard but resisted and gave her only a little twitch. "You could have been hurt if that branch gave way or if I fell. Next time listen to me when I tell you to get out of the way."

Suddenly, as if obeying his words, she retreated a step, leaving him to let his hands fall to his side.

"If you had fallen and hurt yourself, how would I explain to Abe—Mr. Finley? He gave me instructions to see you had what you needed and offer you coffee. You do drink coffee, don't you?" Her eyes alternated between worry and interest in his reply.

"Yes, I like coffee just fine." His anger fled, replaced by something he had no name for. The dark churning feeling in the pit of his stomach made coffee sound bitter.

Her only concern was pleasing Abe, meeting his expectations.

"Fine." She turned toward the house, called over her shoulder. "I'll holler when coffee is ready."

"Fine. I'll get this tree done."

Her steps slowed to a crawl and she slowly turned. "Make sure the ladder is secure before you go back up."

"I don't aim to break any limbs, except the damaged ones on the tree." He didn't even try to keep the tightness from his voice. After all, how could he care for his father and earn enough money for pain medication if he broke an arm or leg?

No sir. He had his priorities straight.

Chapter Four

Sally ground the coffee beans with a great deal of vigor. She had helped him and ended up getting scolded. She should have let the man fall on his head. Might teach him a lesson.

The coffee grinding forgotten, she stared at the far wall of the kitchen. He might have killed himself. Or done serious physical harm. The stupid man. Did he think himself invincible? She shivered as her mind filled with a vision of his battered body beneath the tree.

She sprang to the window to make sure he wasn't sprawled motionless on the ground. Her breath thundered from her lungs as she saw him astraddle a branch.

She sucked in air, finding her ribs strangely stiff, then turned back to the task of making coffee. She didn't want him hurt on her watch. Abe would surely think she'd neglected her duties if he was. There was no other reason. But her lungs stiffened again as she thought of looking up in anticipation as he called her name and how her heart jolted when she saw him dangling in midair. The remnant of a panicked feeling lingered behind her breastbone, and she forced it away with determined deep breaths.

She poured the ground coffee into the pot and set it to boil. Carol would soon return from school, and Sally always prepared a snack for the child. Carol was way too thin and barely ate enough to keep a mouse alive. Sally ached for the child, understanding that she mourned her mother's death. Much as Sally had done for her father.

Linc would have to wait for coffee until Carol got home. She ignored the reason for her decision—there was safety in having both children to hide behind.

How ridiculous. He was only here to do odd jobs for Abe. And she was here to establish how well she could cope. Having focused her goal clearly in her mind, she gave herself a good study. Her skirt carried a liberal amount of dust from working in the garden, and her shoes needed cleaning. Moving toward the plate glass mirror over the couch in the front room, she saw blotches of dust on her face, her unruly curls frosted with the ever invasive brown soil filling the air. "Sally, you look like a homeless tramp. Go clean up," she said.

A few minutes later, shoes cleaned, skirts dusted, face washed and hair brushed until it gleamed, she paused again in front of the mirror and smiled at herself. Now she'd pass inspection. And just in time, as Carol slipped through the back door. Only because Sally knew enough to listen for her did she even notice her entrance. "Hi, Carol. How was your day?"

"Okay." She sank into her customary chair at the kitchen table and let her head droop.

"Anything special happen?"

"No." The word seemed to require a great deal of effort.

Sally studied the child a moment longer, wishing she could offer comfort, but Carol would shrink back if Sally tried to hug her. What she needed was her mother, but her mother was gone. Sally touched the top of Carol's head. "We have company for snack time."

Carol perked up. "Who?"

"Why don't I let you see for yourself?" Sally went to the door and called. "Coffee's ready. Come and get it."

Linc dropped to the ground and gave her a wave to acknowledge he'd heard.

Robbie straightened, glanced toward Linc and when he saw the man wave, he turned to Sally and did the same. When Linc dusted off his pants, so did Robbie. Only in Robbie's case, the result was a brownish cloud.

Sally watched another moment, smiling as Robbie imitated everything Linc did. She wondered if Linc noticed.

The distance prevented her from seeing his eyes, but he flashed a grin at her that made her gasp and duck back inside. She pressed her hand to her chest and instructed her heart to beat calmly. She did not understand this out-of-control reaction. She, Sally Morgan, twenty years of age, was a cautious young woman who did not do foolish things. Nor was she about to change because someone had a wide smile that made her think of wildflowers and open spaces.

Having set her mind back on a corrected course,

she put out a coffee cup for Linc, poured milk for the children and placed a selection of cookies on a plate.

Linc and Robbie came through the door together.

"I got a real good fort built," Robbie said. "I think I'll put a fence around it."

"Good fort needs a good fence." Linc sounded as if it was the most important thing he could discuss.

"You seen any forts?" Robbie asked.

"Only in museums. I'm grateful we don't need them to protect us anymore." He glanced about. "Is there a place I can wash up?"

Sally indicated the sink in the back room that served as pantry and laundry room.

Robbie followed Linc and washed his hands without being told. If only the boy could be so cooperative all the time. She poured coffee into the cup she'd set out for Linc and waited for the pair to return.

Robbie scampered to his chair and downed his glass of milk in loud gulps. "Can I have more?"

"Whoa. Slow down," Linc said. "You wouldn't want to drown yourself, now would you?"

Robbie giggled and planted himself more squarely in his chair, apparently intending to wait patiently.

"And who is this pretty young gal?" Linc indicated Carol.

His words jarred Sally into action. "This is Carol Finley." She told the girl who Linc was, saying he visited his grandmother across the alley, leaving out all the vicious rumors.

"Pleased to meet you." Linc reached for Carol's hand and bent over slightly as he shook it.

Carol flushed a dull red, pulled her hand to her lap and ducked her head.

Guess he had the same disconcerting effect on both young and grown girls. The thought comforted Sally, but she experienced a twinge of sympathy for Carol's confusion.

Linc shifted his attention to the table, nodded toward the cup of steaming coffee. "For me?"

Sally jerked herself out of her thoughts. "Yes. And please, sit down and help yourself to cookies."

He sat and tasted his coffee. "Yum. Hard to beat fresh coffee."

Sally refilled Robbie's glass and passed the plate.

Carol lifted her face as she took a cookie. Her eyes darted toward Linc and she ducked away again.

Smitten, Sally thought. *And as embarrassed about her reaction, as I am about mine.*

"Did you bake these?" Linc lifted a ginger cookie to indicate what he meant.

"Yes." Sally prayed her cheeks wouldn't darken in echo of Carol's reaction. She was, after all, a grown, self-controlled woman. "My father's favorite cookie."

"They're good." He sighed. "Not at all like the hard tack and beans a cowboy gets used to eating."

Robbie nearly squirmed right off his chair. "You a real cowboy?"

Linc held out his arm. "Feel."

Robbie pressed his hand to Linc's forearm.

"I feel real to you?"

Robbie giggled.

Carol watched the pair. "He didn't mean real in that

way. He meant do you live out on the hills, camping with cows and herding them?"

Sally almost dropped her cookie. It was the most she'd heard Carol speak at one time since she'd started caring for them a month ago. She tore her attention from Carol back to Linc, as curious over his answer as either of the children.

Linc leaned back, a faraway look in his eyes. "I spent many nights sleeping on the ground with a herd of cows bawling in my ear. Lots of fun but hard work, too. And like I said, often the food wasn't that great."

He might not appreciate the food, but there was no mistaking how much he liked his sort of life. A shudder crossed Sally's shoulders. She could imagine nothing appealing about such an unsettled existence.

"You cook your own food?" Robbie asked, his eyes and mouth as round as the top of his glass.

"Depends on whether I was alone or with a crew. If I was alone, I didn't have much choice. Either cook or starve to death. But when we had a roundup the ranch provided a cook wagon. That was great." He sighed and patted his stomach. "Some of those old cooks worked magic with flour and water and fresh beef."

Carol had slid forward on her chair, mesmerized by the way Linc talked. "Did you sing to the cows?" She lowered her gaze a brief moment. "I heard that cowboys sing to calm them. Our teacher taught us 'The Old Chisholm Trail.' She said the cowboys like to sing that song."

"Come a ti-yi-yi-yippy-yippy-ah." Linc half sang, half spoke the words.

Carol's eyes glistened. "That's it."

Linc chuckled. "We had one old cowboy by the name of Skinner. He always brought along his fiddle and played it after supper, just as the moon cast a glow on the trees, making them look like pale white soldiers. I tell you, there's nothing more mournful than a fiddle playing "Oh Bury Me Not on the Lone Prairie." He shivered but his face belied his words. He looked as if it was the best part of life.

Sally didn't take her eyes off his glowing face. Without looking, she knew both children were equally as mesmerized. She blinked and forced her attention to other things. Her responsibilities. "Children, finish up. Do your chores and then you can play until suppertime."

They downed their cookies and milk and raced away—Robbie to take away the pail of coal ashes Sally had scraped out of the stove earlier in the day. He often made a big deal of the chore, when all he had to do was carry the pail to the ash heap at the far corner of the yard and bring the empty pail back. This time he didn't utter one word of complaint. Carol's chore was to sweep the front step and sidewalk. She grabbed the broom and hurried outside.

Linc drained his coffee and pushed back from the table. "I thank you." He grabbed his hat off the back of the chair and headed for the door where he paused. "You coming out again?"

Why did her heart pick up pace at his innocent question? She half convinced herself he spoke out of politeness, not out of any real desire for her to join him. With the portion of her brain that remained sensible, she brought out the right words. "I can't. I have to make supper and…" At a loss to think what else she needed to do, she let her words trail off.

"Of course." He pushed his hat to his head and stepped outside. "Thanks again." He strode away, his long legs quickly creating distance.

She stared after him as he returned to the crab apple trees and gathered the branches he'd removed. His arms full, he headed for the garbage barrel by the ash pile and broke the branches to stuff them into the barrel. What did she hear? She lifted the window sash and listened.

"Oh, do you remember sweet Betsy from Pike?"

He was singing.

She listened in fascination. He didn't have a particularly fine singing voice. In fact, it was gravelly, as if he sang past a mouthful of marbles, and he missed a few of the notes. But what he lacked in talent, he more than made up for in enjoyment. The notes fairly danced through the air and frolicked into her heart, where they skipped and whirled until they were well embedded.

The front door slammed. Carol skidded into the kitchen and stored the broom. She headed for the back door. "He's singing." She left again so fast, Sally didn't even have time to close the window and pretend she hadn't been listening as eagerly as young Carol.

Carol trotted to the garden to stand by Robbie. Shoulder to shoulder they watched and listened to Linc, who continued to break branches, oblivious to his adoring audience.

Sally studied the two children. Both were under his spell. She slammed the window shut. They were children, prone to hero worship. She, on the other hand, was a grown woman who knew better than to chase after… after what? She didn't even know what she thought she'd been chasing. Certainly not stability or sensibility. She turned and studied the kitchen. Very modern, with an electric refrigerator Abe had shipped all the way from Toronto. A gas range stood in the corner to be used in hot weather. He'd shown her how to light the pilot and how to set the controls on the oven, but Sally had never used a gas stove and wondered if she would ever be comfortable doing so. She preferred to use the coal cookstove.

Abe was very proud of the modern fixtures, especially the stove. "It's a Canadian invention," he said with enough pride that Sally thought he would like to take credit for the innovation.

She shifted her gaze, itemizing the benefits of the house. Two stories. Four bedrooms and an indoor bathroom upstairs. All the bedrooms had generous closets.

Downstairs, besides the kitchen and back room, there was a formal dining room, complete with a china cabinet holding a fancy twelve-place dishware collection. Sally thought the plain white dishes with gold trim rather unnoteworthy. Her choice of pattern would have been something with a little color in the form of a flower. There were so many lovely rose patterns.

"I like to entertain here," Abe had said, indicating the formal dining room and the array of dishes. "Dinner parties for my business associates." He eyed the dark wood paneled room with windows covered by heavy forest-green drapes shutting out most of the light. Obviously it was his favorite room in the house.

Sally had nodded, her smile wooden. She could cook a meal for twelve with no problem. But a dinner party? Business associates? It sounded stiff and dull.

She gave herself a little shake. Of course she could do a dinner party. No need to be nervous because she didn't know Abe's business associates and had never given a formal dinner. How hard could it be? Cooking was cooking.

And if she didn't get to her meal preparations this minute, she would be hard-pressed to have supper ready when Abe came through the door.

She hurried to the back room and found potatoes. As she peeled them, she enjoyed a view of the backyard. Robbie played in his fort. Carol sat cross-legged nearby, scratching in the dirt. She paused often to glance up, a dreamy look on her face. Sally didn't need to follow the direction of her gaze to know the reason. Linc had returned to pruning the crab apple trees. From what she could see, he removed a great number of branches. The trees looked downright sparse. *I hope he knows what he's doing.* Abe would be very upset if Linc killed the trees.

Linc stepped back and surveyed the damage, then hoisted the ladder to his shoulder and went to the little shed. After stowing the ladder, he headed for the house. His gaze flicked to the window and he smiled.

Sally developed a sudden interest in the task of peeling potatoes and hoped he didn't think she'd been staring.

He knocked.

She dried her hands on a towel, smoothed her apron and walked slowly to the door just to prove she had other things holding her attention. "Yes?"

"I'm headed home to check on my pa. Tell Abe I'm done with the trees and will start working on the barn tomorrow, unless he prefers I do something else."

"I'll let him know." Abe no doubt would have specific ideas of what he wanted done and in what order.

"I'm off then." He took a step toward the back gate.

"I hope your pa is okay. Say hello to your grandmother for me."

He touched the brim of his hat. "I'll do that." His mouth pulled to one side. He seemed to consider saying something more, then nodded without voicing his thought. "See you tomorrow." And he swung away, passing the garden. He echoed a goodbye to the children before he vaulted over the fence, not bothering with the gate.

Sally stared after him until he disappeared from view behind the board fence. Even then she continued to stare. What was it about this man that pulled at her so hard? Like a promise. Of what? The man was a cowboy. By his own confession, he slept on the cold, hard ground, often with nothing but cows for company. It should have turned him into a recluse or at least a man with poor social skills. Linc might not fit into everyone's idea of a refined gentleman, yet there was something about him. Something she couldn't put her finger on, but she also couldn't deny its existence, even though she wanted to.

"Is he coming back tomorrow?"

Sally's gaze lingered one more heartbeat, her mind indulged in one more puzzled thought, then she turned to Carol who stood before her, her face a mixture of hope and fear. "Your father has hired him to do yard work. I should think he'll have enough to keep him busy for a week or two. Perhaps even a month." She utterly failed to keep a note of joy out of her words.

"Good." Carol marched past her, into the house and up the stairs. The words of a song trailed after her. "Oh, do you remember sweet Betsy from Pike?"

An echo sounded from the garden in a low, monotone singsongy voice.

Sally stared. Robbie was singing? Come to think of it, he'd been pleasantly occupied all day building his fort. She watched, her eyes narrowed in concentration. In her experience, Robbie being content was foreign. The few times it happened had led to a major explosion. Maybe he'd wait until she left to shift into defiance. Except…how would Abe deal with it? He had little patience with Robbie acting out. "Losing his mother will not be tolerated as an excuse," Abe insisted. Yes, she understood Robbie must find a better way to express his displeasure but—

Lord, these children are hurt and frightened by their loss. Help me help them. Help them find joy in life and be able to believe they can again be safe.

She thought of how she'd found the feeling of safety after her father died, through helping her mother and sisters keep things organized and in control, doing what she thought her father would approve of. How could she help these children find the same sense of safety?

"Robbie, come wash up for supper."

He jerked as if she'd struck him, and his chin jutted out. "Leave me alone."

"Your father will soon be here, and he expects you washed and ready to sit down."

Robbie gave her his fiercest glower.

"Robbie, I think your mother would want you to do your best to please your father."

His scowl deepened. "She won't know what I do."

"Maybe not. But you will. You know what would please her. You can honor her by doing it."

He turned his back to her and continued moving a pile of dirt. It seemed he did his best to make sure most of it fell on him.

"Robbie, please come to the house." She kept her tone firm and soft.

"You ain't my mother."

"I know that." She didn't expect she could replace their mother if she married Abe—when she married Abe, she corrected. "No one can replace your mother." She let the words sink in.

"I betcha Linc didn't wash his hands when he camped out with cows."

"I have no idea if he did or didn't, but I noticed how well he cleaned up before coffee." She'd noticed far too well, taking in how his face shone from the scrubbing and how his hair, bleached almost blond on the ends but darker where it had been hidden from the sun, had been plastered back in an attempt to tame the curls. How they slowly returned to their own wayward tangle.

She'd had to refrain from checking her hair to see

if her curls were doing likewise. "He cleaned up really well." Her words had a difficult time squeezing past the tightness in her throat.

Robbie studied her reply for a moment, then bolted to his feet to race across the yard. He didn't slow down as he passed her, nor did he glance toward her. His whole attitude clearly said he would wash up because a man like Linc, a man he admired, had done so. He would not do it to please Sally. No siree.

She sighed and followed him inside. Would she and Robbie ever have anything but an uneasy truce? She didn't have time to think about that at the moment with dessert to finish, potatoes to mash and the meat to check. She took dishes from the top shelf—the best everyday dishes—found a red checkered tablecloth and set the table as nicely as she could. Too bad she didn't have flowers to put in a vase in the middle of the table.

This meal would be flawless. Abe would see that she could run his home as well as any woman.

Robbie came from the back room, water dripping from his ears. He'd combed his hair back.

"You look very spiffy."

He jerked to a halt and gave her a look fit to fry her skin. "I do not."

Instantly she realized she'd offended him. Actually, it was pretty hard to miss. She knew exactly what she'd done wrong. She'd made him sound like a sissy. "You're right. You look like a frontier man. Maybe even a cowboy. Ready to get out and ride."

He held her gaze a moment then tipped his chin in

barely there acknowledgment before he crossed to the table with a faintly familiar swagger.

She didn't have to think hard to know where she'd seen it before. Robbie had done his best to imitate Linc's rolling gait.

No, she definitely wasn't the only one in this house to be affected by his presence. She stiffened her spine and held her chin high. Only she wasn't a child. She was an adult who knew exactly what she wanted. A stable life, a nice home. No way she'd ever consider camping out on the prairie to be something romantic.

The strains of "Oh, bury me not on the lone prairie," echoed through her head. She meant every word of the song.

Chapter Five

Linc crossed toward his grandmother's house, singing that silly song he couldn't get out of his head. Several times he'd discovered he sang it aloud and stopped instantly. He ought to have more consideration for his surroundings. It wasn't like he was with a bunch of cows or even some cynical, fun-making cowboys who would josh him good-naturedly, or otherwise, depending on their personal objectives in life.

Once he heard Robbie singing along in a voice lacking both strength and musical ability. Not that Linc thought he had the latter. Lots of people had felt free to point that out to him. He countered with the same words every time. "Mostly I sing because I'm happy. Sorry if it has the opposite effect on you." Mostly he continued to sing, unless it seemed likely to start a fight.

But when he heard Robbie, he figured now was not the time to have second thoughts about raising his voice in song. Seems the boy had little enough to be happy about in this life. Sure he had lots of good things—a warm home, a father with a steady job and the hope of gaining Sally for a stepmother. Momentarily the thought made the song die on his lips. He sure hoped that Robbie, Carol and their father would appreciate Sally the way she deserved. But that thought aside, Robbie didn't realize how good he had it because right now likely all he considered was what he'd lost. His mother. Linc knew how sorrow could make all other thought impossible.

He'd mostly gotten over his own loss, though there were times when missing his mother seemed like having a pile of hay lodged in his stomach. It just wouldn't go away. Now he had the fresh pain of losing Harris. And the dreadful specter of his father's possible death.

But the day had been pleasant. Seeing Sally's smile, playing with Robbie, watching Carol light up when he sang a cowboy song. As he hit the back step of Grandmama's house, his happiness dissolved into reality. He flung the door open. "How is Pa?"

"Same, my boy. I gave him more medicine an hour ago. He's been resting since then." She turned from arranging slices of yeasty-smelling bread on a platter. "I heard you singing as you crossed the yard." Her smile was gentle. Not at all reproving.

But Linc felt as if he stood before ten pointing fingers. How callous to be happy with his brother buried in the mountains and his father likely dying a slow, painful death. Yet for a few hours this afternoon he'd shoved the knowledge to the back of his brain and enjoyed himself. Yes, he'd had fun.

He didn't realize he smiled so openly until his grandmother straightened. "What have you been up to, Lincoln McCoy?"

He sobered so quickly his lips almost knotted. "Grandmama, I was working all afternoon." Playing with Robbie and Sally most surely qualified as work. He was amusing the boss's son, after all. "Did you know the Finleys have a tiny grove of crab apple trees? I pruned them. Hopefully they will become stronger and more productive now. And I turned over the garden soil."

Grandmama sniffed. "Those trees have been there longer than the Finleys." She studied him a full thirty seconds. "First time I ever saw someone so pleased about a little yard work."

His sigh was long and purposely exaggerated. "Would you feel better if I dragged through the door, my chin bobbing on the floor and moaned and groaned about how hard life is?"

Her sigh was equally long and exaggerated. "Of course not."

He started to smile, but she held up a warning hand.

"But I'd feel a lot better if you told me Sally Morgan was away for the afternoon."

He narrowed his eyes, vowing he would not let her guess how glad he was that she wasn't gone. "Now why would that make any difference to you?"

She matched his narrowed eyes. Not for the first time in his life he realized how alike they were in their gestures, and often in their speech. "Because I fear it means a lot to you."

He wanted to protest. Say it didn't make a speck of difference. Assure her he never once looked at Sally.

Never even noticed her. But he couldn't lie. If he tried, she would know immediately. The trouble with two people having the same mannerisms was she would see his attempt at lying as clearly as if she had lied. Instead he shifted directions. "Didn't you say she was unofficially promised to Abe Finley? Practically engaged to be married." He hoped his silent emphasis on *unofficially* and *practically* didn't come across in his words.

"I said it. Did you hear?"

"I must have, since I repeated it to you."

Grandmama took three steps toward him, stopped with her very sturdy shoes toe-to-toe with his dusty cowboy boots. "I mean, did you hear it here?" She tapped his forehead. "Or is it stuck somewhere between there?" She touched his right ear. "And here?" She flicked his left ear.

"Ow." He jerked away and grabbed at his ear, pretending a great injury. "Why'd you do that?"

"You don't need to think you're too big for me to handle, young man. If you don't behave yourself I'll hear, and if I hear, I'll deal with you."

"Ho, ho." He bounced away a few feet. "You might find it hard to put me over your knee and smack my bottom."

"Your size doesn't intimidate me."

He stalked right up to her and leaned over to meet her eyes. Never once did she falter. Not that he expected her to, any more than he expected she would consider trying to carry out some form of corporal punishment. "I'm a big boy now. Maybe you should be afraid of me." To prove his point, he wrapped his arms around her waist and lifted her off the floor.

She squealed. "Put me down, you naughty boy."

He spun around the room, accompanied by her choked laughter. "Not until you tell me what a good boy I am."

"Never."

He swung around the room again.

"Put me down. I'm getting dizzy."

"Am I the best boy in the world?"

"You're the best grandson this old woman will ever have."

"Good enough for me." He set her down and steadied her as she regained her balance. "Hey, wait a minute. I'm your only grandson."

She chuckled and gave him a fond look, liberally laced with teasing. "Now do you want supper first or you want to check on your father first?"

He laughed. "Still good enough for me." He glanced toward the bedroom. "I'll check on Pa first."

"Good idea. Call me if you need anything."

He headed for the doorway and paused before he stepped into the room. It always shocked him to see Pa like this—all busted up, his color almost as bad as Harris's had been.

He scrubbed his hands over his eyes and pushed away his morbid thoughts. To neutralize them, he allowed one mental picture of Sally. He had many to choose from—her laughing as they escaped Robbie's kidnapping, her concern when he faked a mortal injury, her anger when he almost fell from the tree, her shyness over coffee, the way she watched him out the kitchen window, all the time pretending she wasn't.

He chose the way she shied away from him at the table. If he needed any further proof she was aware of him, that was it.

He smiled, let the thought smooth his tension. Yes, he understood she and Abe were meant to be, but he promised himself he would deal with reality after he was through caring for his father. He stepped into the room. "Pa?"

His father stirred, managed to drag one eyelid open. "Linc. Where am I?"

Doc had warned Linc that Pa's mind would become more and more confused. "We're in Golden Prairie, at Grandmama's house."

"Harris is dead, isn't he?"

"Yeah, Pa. We buried him back at Coal Camp."

"He had a nice putting away?"

"Best possible. All the miners came out. They even shut the mine down for the funeral. There were lots of flowers. Harris's friend, Sam, sang 'Amazing Grace.' It was very nice." He would never hear the song again without choking up with sorrow.

"Good." Pa groaned again. "I'm in terrible pain." His words were tight.

Linc poured out a spoonful of the medicine and held it to his pa's lips, then pulled a wooden chair close to the bed and sat by his father, talking softly, his voice providing comfort until the medicine took effect.

He wet the facecloth in the basin of water and wiped his face gently. "Pa, I wish I could make you feel better."

"Me, too." His father's voice cracked.

"You want a drink?"

"You got anything stronger than water?"

Linc's lopsided grin quivered. "Coffee?"

Pa snorted. At least, he attempted to. "Ain't what I meant."

"You know Grandmama would sooner swallow tacks than have the devil's drink in her house."

"I sort of recall." Pa's voice faded. Talking consumed all the energy he could muster.

Linc held a cup of water to his lips and supported his head as he drank.

Pa fell back, exhausted. He would sleep until the medicine wore off, then Linc would be there to give him more.

But oh, it hurt to see his powerful, stubborn Pa like this.

Again, he found solace in picturing Sally. This time he chose the mental picture of her planting the garden. How she straightened and met his gaze across the yard. Even that far away, he enjoyed the way her eyes watched him. He couldn't see the color across the distance, but he didn't need to. He supposed officially they were hazel, which seemed a flat word when describing her eyes. Golden brown with flecks of green. He'd been fascinated to watch the color shift from almost green to gold when she turned toward the light. It had been all he could do not to stare.

His mind smoothed as he let his thoughts drift along the pleasant trail. Pa moaned and Linc sighed. Try as he might, he could not ignore his father's plight. He wished there was some way to help him. All he could do was pray. Not only for God to ease his pain, but also for his father to realize eternity waited—and he needed to choose where to spend it.

He touched his father's arm. "I'll be back later." He returned to the kitchen where Grandmama waited to serve supper.

She sighed. "I wish I could spare you this. Spare both of you."

His face must have revealed his pain. He made no attempt to disguise it. "I wish it, too." He rubbed his eyes, suddenly so weary he could think of nothing he'd rather do than sleep for the next three days.

"Sit and eat."

Food held no appeal, but his grandmother had spent the afternoon cooking. The least he could do was show some appreciation. He waited for her to sit across from him and reached for her hands before he bowed and said grace.

Soon enough he discovered he could eat heartily, even though he ached inside. His energy returned with eating. He dried dishes for Grandmama then returned to the bedroom. Already Pa was growing restless as the pain medication wore off. He reckoned it was safe to give another dose and waited for the medicine to ease Pa's discomfort.

Pa began to breathe easier as the medicine did its work.

Linc rose, planning to slip away and let his father rest.

"Don't go," Pa gasped.

Linc sat back, his legs rubbery. Was this the last breath his father would draw?

"It gets mighty lonely in here." Pa's voice was reedy.

"I'll stay with you until you fall asleep."

Pa opened his eyes long enough to give Linc a grateful look.

Glad he could do something that earned Pa's approval, Linc eased himself into a more comfortable position.

"I miss your ma," Pa whispered.

"Me, too."

"She used to read to me."

"I remember." Pa could write his name, decipher enough to buy something in the store, but not much else. "Do you want me to read to you?"

Pa's eyes flew open, filled with a combination of pain and hope. "It might give me something else to set my thoughts on."

Linc gained his feet.

"Not the Bible."

"Okay, Pa." He didn't bother to keep the disappointment from his voice. In the front room stood a huge cupboard, the lower shelves crammed with books. He searched the titles. *Pilgrim's Progress.* Perfect. He pulled it out, returned to the bedroom and began reading. "'As I walked through the wilderness of this world, I lighted on a certain place where was a den, and laid me down in that place to sleep; and as I slept, I dreamed a dream.'"

Pa made no protest, though the message was almost

as clear and pointed as any scripture. Indeed, he lay quietly, breathing slowly.

Linc paused, wondering if he'd fallen asleep.

"Continue," Pa said.

Linc read for an hour until his voice was hoarse. Quietly he closed the book, waiting to see if Pa would protest.

His father cracked one eye open. "More tomorrow?"

"Of course."

He remained until he was certain Pa slept, then tiptoed away, his insides knotted in dreadful anticipation of the fact that his father wasn't getting better.

Only one thing eased his mind—remembering Sally. According to what she said, she only stayed long enough to serve supper to the family. She'd be gone by now. Too bad. He might have slipped over to speak to her. The walls of the house seemed to press in on him. "Grandmama." She sat at the kitchen table doing some fancy handiwork. "I'm going for a ride."

"I expect you need to get away for a bit."

He paused at the outside door. "Where did you say the Morgans live?"

Grandmama dropped her handiwork and gave Linc a look fit to bleach his skin pure white. "I didn't say. And best you stay away."

Linc grew still. He barely breathed. "Even my own grandmother thinks I'm not fit to associate with decent people," he muttered.

Grandmama had the grace to look uncomfortable. "I didn't mean it like that. It's just—" She shook her head, unable to finish what she started to say.

"Just what? She shouldn't associate with the likes of me? Shouldn't even be seen in my company?" He spun on his heel. "I'll try and keep it in mind." He strode toward the barn as if chased by an angry posse and quickly saddled Big Red. He rode from town at a moderate pace, but once he reached the open road, he urged Red into a full-blown gallop.

He rode until the wind cleared his brain, then turned and rode back at a more leisurely pace. Rather than go directly back home, he rode up and down familiar streets. He'd been back in Golden Prairie for days, but his movements had been restricted to his grandmother's place, the Finley place and a few businesses in the heart of town as he looked for work. Now he was curious. How much had the place changed in the years he'd been away?

He passed the redbrick two-story school. The same dusty yard. The same worn playground equipment— a slide, a pole swing and two teeter-totters. The same flagpole directly in front of the main doors with parallel sidewalks where girls lined up on one, boys on the other to march inside. His time in this building had been mostly pleasant.

With a flick of the reins, he moved on. Houses on either side of the street had faded, their yards threadbare. Everywhere he saw evidence of the drought. He recalled the names of people who had lived in the houses. The Stewarts—a middle-age childless couple. The pair sat on matching rockers on the veranda, watching him with all the interest of a small town resident seeing a stranger in the midst of their lives.

Next to them, the Rowans lived with a houseful of young ones who would be mostly grown by now. Charity Rowan had been in his grade. She'd always been friendly. Wonder what became of her? He paused before the house and considered going to the door to ask after her and the other children.

Mr. Stewart rocked to his feet and moved to the top step. "Hey, there."

Linc turned toward the man. Although the greeting wasn't unusual, the tone of the voice was far from friendly, and Linc's shoulders tensed. "Hello, Mr. Stewart. How are you?" Far as he knew there was no reason for rancor between him and this man.

"You're that McCoy boy, aren't you?"

"I'm Lincoln McCoy." He didn't normally give his full name, but somehow he wanted the man to know he bore a noble name, though he doubted Mr. Stewart or anyone would think Abraham Lincoln in the same thought as Lincoln McCoy.

"Heard you lot were back in town."

Linc half expected the man to spit. His wife sat behind him, her arms crossed firmly over her thin chest.

"Came to see my grandmother. Help her out a bit."

"Likely help yourself to anything else you can get your hands on. No one has forgotten how Mrs. Ogilvy's jewels disappeared. Maybe they couldn't find evidence, but none of us have ever believed you innocent."

Linc tried to think how to answer. He had nothing to hide. No shame to disguise. He hoped coming back would prove his innocence to the townsfolk. But only if they gave him a chance.

His hopes had risen when Abe offered him a job. Linc was more than grateful after he'd spent the morning going from business to business and being flatly turned down. He knew it had more to do with his name than the depressed economic atmosphere. If he'd had any doubt, the clucking of tongues by a group of gossipy women in the store where he'd gone to ask for a job made it clear. That's when Abe had stepped in, taken in the situation and said he needed a man for yard chores. Abe had given him a chance to prove himself.

Not that Linc was foolish enough to believe Abe was anything more than an exception to what most people thought, but he owed the man for offering him a job. He directed his attention back to Mr. Stewart. "I have my eyes on nothing that isn't my own." Guilt stung him. Could he honestly say those words in regard to Sally? But that wasn't what Mr. Stewart meant, any more than Linc did.

Knowing his interest in Sally ran against his gratitude to Abe sent a twist of guilt through Linc's thoughts.

Mr. Stewart made a noise ripe with disbelief.

Stung by the man's unwillingness to accept the facts, Linc didn't bother to moderate his words. "Seems to me a man who refuses to abide by what a court of law decided—namely, that the McCoys are innocent—is as guilty of dishonoring the law as a man who steals."

Mr. Stewart gave Linc a hard look. "You might have fooled the law, but you didn't fool me."

Linc kept his words low but let each one carry a weight of protest. "Sounds to me like you've appointed yourself judge and jury." He wondered if the man had heard of Harris's death and their father's injuries. But it was unlikely such knowledge would influence the man's attitude. He seemed pretty set on seeing the Mc-Coys as undesirables.

"Just consider yourself warned. We'll be watching you. Don't think you can pull a repeat performance." Mr. Stewart returned to his rocker, crossed his arms and glared, he and his wife a matched set of disapproval.

Linc studied them a full thirty seconds. His insides protested. He ached for a way to prove his family's innocence. The McCoys were restless, sometimes aimless. His brother and father had chased after adventure and the next big chance. None of those things made them bad people. The theft of Mrs. Ogilvy's jewels had been conveniently laid on the McCoys. Likely someone passing through had seen an easy mark and lifted them. But no one ever considered that. Not with the McCoys handy.

But the harsh look on Mr. Stewart's face and the equally forbidding one his wife wore informed Linc there was no point in further argument with this pair. He prayed they didn't represent the attitude of the majority of Golden Prairie residents.

All he wanted was a chance to prove the McCoys were good people.

He reined away and headed straight for his grandmother's home. At least she had never accused him. A suspicion burned the edges of his brain. Did she suspect Linc's father and simply not say so to spare Linc's feelings? Did she have doubts about Linc? Hadn't she said he should stay away from Sally? As if in her heart she didn't believe he was good enough to be in the same circle of friends as a Morgan girl?

He allowed Red to slow his pace.

Did anyone in this town believe a McCoy was capable of being a decent person? Did his own grandmother?

How long before Sally heard everyone's opinion of him? How long before she looked at him with the same guardedness or outright suspicion?

Not that it mattered. She intended to marry Abe Finley. He wondered if the two of them had discussed it already, or if it was merely an unspoken understanding.

Never mind. He was in town to ease his pa's dying hours and perhaps help his grandmother. He wouldn't let the opinion of a few…or many…drive him away.

He rode into the yard, took Red to the barn and brushed him down before he headed for the house. His palms were sweaty, and he scrubbed them on the side of his trousers. One thing he intended to get straight right here and now—what did Grandmama think?

The door crashed open.

Grandmama looked up, startled by his noisy entrance. "Linc, is something wrong?"

He jerked out a chair and dropped into it. "I saw Mr. Stewart." He tried to tame his thoughts lest they burst out in unfair accusations. "He made it clear I am under suspicion as a McCoy and not welcome in this perfect little town."

Grandmama's short laugh was mirthless. "The town is far from perfect, and I'm sure Mr. Stewart doesn't speak for everyone. At least, I've never heard that anyone voted him official spokesman."

Linc gave her a direct, demanding look. "Does he speak for you?"

His grandmother looked shocked. "You have always been welcome here."

"Do you think the McCoys stole those jewels?" He deliberately aligned himself with his father and brother.

She shook her head. "I don't want to think so, but after your mother died.... Well, your father was pretty upset and didn't much care what he did."

"So you think he might have taken them?"

She considered his question for the briefest moment. "I prefer to believe a person is innocent until proven guilty. And in this case, there was no evidence against your father. That's good enough for me. It should be good enough for you and for all those people out there, too."

Satisfied, he nodded and went to check on his pa.

He appreciated his grandmother's attitude, but it wasn't shared by everyone.

He wondered what opinion Sally held.

Or perhaps he didn't want to know.

Chapter Six

Sally watched from the window for Linc's appearance the next morning. Abe left instructions for her to tell Linc to paint the front fence before he started converting the barn into a garage.

Abe had left for work early. Carol had already departed for school.

It had been a good morning. Robbie came to the breakfast table on the first call, dressed neatly and ready for the day.

She and Abe looked at one another in surprise. As they studied each other, she saw in his expression something she'd never seen before—approval. But even more. Something that made her want to fidget.

Sally lowered her eyes first. She wished she could take credit for Robbie's compliant behavior, but knew it was Linc's doing. The boy was eager to see him again.

She tried to make herself believe she didn't share the anticipation.

"Nice to see you here on time," Abe said to Robbie.

"I got work to do," Robbie said with utmost sincerity.

Again Sally sent Abe a look of surprise and amusement.

Abe shifted away first this time to study his son.

"Really? What are you doing?" He sounded every bit as doubtful as surprised.

"Building a fort."

"Ah. Of course. Well, eat up and do your chores first."

Sally had smiled at Robbie's eager obedience as he ran to obey and then dashed outside. She looked out the window. Robbie had found a bunch of twigs and began to construct a fence around his hole. She realized with a start these twigs were from Linc's pruning yesterday. He must have broken them to the right length for Robbie to use. Her heart felt bathed in warm honey to think he would do this little extra for the boy.

Robbie looked up and waved to someone she couldn't see, then bounded to his feet and raced toward the barn.

Yesterday Linc came to the door upon his arrival. Today it seemed he didn't intend to, which meant she would have to leave the security of the house in order to relay Abe's instructions.

She removed her apron and draped it over the back of the chair. Then she changed her mind and again tied it around her waist. This was not a social call. He was here to work, and she had her own chores to take care of.

Ignoring the mirror in the back room, she went directly out the door. Robbie had disappeared, hopefully into the barn. The big doors stood open and a murmur of voices came from inside.

She paused at the gaping doorway and stared into the gloomy interior. "Hello?"

"We're over here." Linc's voice came from a distant corner.

She hesitated, not wanting to join him in the shadows. Afraid of revealing too much of her confusion in the low light. "I need to talk to you."

Muffled footsteps brought Linc to the bright patch of sunshine, Robbie at his side. "What can I do for you?"

A thousand things flooded her mind. Fun things. Picnics in the sun. Walks at dusk. Star watching—she jerked her thoughts into submission. "Abe said to ask you to paint the front fence first. He says there is paint in the last stall of the barn."

"Sure. Not a problem." His eyes flashed with humor, as if he'd read her wayward thoughts.

She lowered her gaze to Robbie. "Don't get in Mr. McCoy's way."

Robbie stuck out his bottom lip. He hung between wanting to impress Linc with his good behavior and wanting to inform Sally what he thought of her order. Normally he would have exploded into a rage, but after a moment of struggle, he crossed his arms over his chest. "I ain't bothering Linc, am I?" He appealed to the man at his side.

Linc ruffled the boy's hair. "I have no complaints."

Sally considered her options. Forcing Robbie to leave Linc alone would surely precipitate a scene, and she didn't feel up to dealing with one of his tantrums. "What about your fort? I saw you building a fence."

"Yup." But no indication the boy meant to move.

Deciding it was up to Linc to tell the boy to leave if he didn't want him hanging about, she retreated into the sunlight and turned toward the house. "I'll be back to check on you."

"Okay," Linc and Robbie said in unison.

She stopped and slowly turned. "I meant Robbie."

Linc grinned unrepentantly. "You're welcome to check on me, too."

Their gazes locked and went deep. Her heart stirred with a feeling unfamiliar, unsettling and equally unwelcome. "I'm sure you don't need it." She fled for safety behind the kitchen door.

She would avoid returning to the pair, but she worried Robbie would get into trouble. She could imagine him doing a number of things she would regret. But they moved outside to start painting the fence, which allowed her to glance out the side window in the back room to see them. Of course, she couldn't help it if doing various chores made it impossible to avoid the room and just as impossible to avoid the window. So she told herself, even as guilt heated her cheeks. She had no business admiring the way a man's muscles rippled as he applied long smooth strokes of paint.

Enough. She spun from the window and did not return for fifteen determined minutes. She glanced out and saw Linc still at work, but she saw nothing of Robbie.

The boy could be anywhere. She rushed from the house and looked around. No Robbie. She called his name.

Linc straightened. "He's in the barn."

She lengthened her stride as she hurried for the building. "Robbie?"

"What?" he answered from the corner.

She edged closer and saw he'd found some cans and lengths of leather and was constructing something. If she had to guess, she'd say the cans were horses, and he'd hitched them to a piece of wood that might be meant to be a plow or some sort of equipment. The boy was a farmer at heart. Too bad his father was a town man. Too bad Abe didn't see the value of hard physical work.

Sally's mind wandered, forbidden, to Linc and the way he made work look easy, even seemed to enjoy it.

Her thoughts were particularly wayward this morning. She made up her mind to do something about it. "I have to go to the store. Clean up and come with me."

Robbie threw himself to the ground and kicked his heels. "Don't want to. You can't make me." His voice was tight.

Sally already knew defiance was his middle name. Nothing short of a lightning bolt would force the boy to change his mind. She stuck her hand in her pocket and pulled out two pennies. "I have a hankering for one of those candy sticks. I thought you might want one, too. I guess if you don't want to come, I'll buy myself two." She paused a beat. "Unless…" She waited.

He stopped kicking but lay still a minute, making sure she understood he didn't give in easy. "Guess I'll go," he muttered, as if he did her a great favor.

"Fine. Cinnamon is my favorite flavor. What's yours?" She reached for his grubby hand. Today she would not insist he wash up. Hopefully they would not encounter his father, who would surely disapprove of taking his son out in such a dusty state.

"I like 'em all, but maybe I'll get a licorice one." He took her hand and accompanied her peacefully.

They went out the gate and had to pass Linc on their way to the store. He stopped painting and watched them approach.

"I'm going to the store," she said quite needlessly, as if it mattered to him.

"Have fun." He waited for them to pass.

She continued onward, vowing not to look back, but as they turned the corner she glanced his direction. He still watched. Knowing he'd seen her looking, she jerked her attention to the sidewalk in front of them.

A few blocks later, she and Robbie entered Sharp's store. A gaggle of women turned as they stepped inside.

Sally's heart stalled. Why did they all stare at her? She handed Robbie a penny. "Go buy a candy stick for yourself."

He needed no second asking.

Sally turned to Mr. Sharp. "Can I get some canned peaches?" She planned to make peach cobbler for supper. "Two dozen eggs and…" She felt the women crowd close as she completed her order.

How long could she ignore them? She bent over an ad for Dodd's Kidney Pills tacked to the countertop and pretended a great deal of interest in the product.

Her pointed disinterest didn't deter the women one bit. Not that she really expected it would.

"I hear the McCoys are back in town." The words were accented by a loud sniff.

"Maybe they think Mrs. Ogilvy has more valuables to steal."

Sally straightened but kept her back to the women, not wanting them to get any satisfaction out of her reaction. No doubt the protests flooding from her mind would be evident in her expression, but how dare they accuse Linc of such despicable motivations when he'd come because of his dying father?

"Don't suppose they'll do the noble thing and confess."

Several jeers greeted the remark.

Sally turned to face them. She knew each of the women. Mrs. Brennan was a known gossip, as were her three grown daughters standing at her side. Miss Carter, a bitter spinster who liked to imagine the worst of everyone. But seeing Bessy Johnson and Granny Smith with them surprised Sally. She faced that pair. "I would think you'd give a man the benefit of doubt." She spread her glance across the others. "And how cruel to think of such things when Harris McCoy is barely cold in his grave, and Mr. McCoy is not likely to recover from his injuries."

The women stared at her.

"Why Sally Morgan," Bessy Johnson protested. "Are you defending the likes of the McCoys? Surely you haven't fallen under their spell somehow."

As one, the group shook their heads and made tsking noises.

Sally's cheeks burned. She shouldn't have spoken

out so harshly. So rashly. "I'm sorry. I know nothing about what happened before we came." All she knew was what she had seen and felt the past few days.

"I suppose that explains a lot." Miss Carter patted her arm, as if to say only Sally's innocence allowed her to speak out on behalf of the McCoys. "You didn't see the three of them always eyeing up things and ducking down abandoned alleys when a decent person came along."

"Maybe they understood the decent people of Golden Prairie meant to shun them and didn't plan to give them a chance."

As a group, the women sighed.

"You are far too innocent and trusting for your own good," Mrs. Brennan said. "But I warn you, Sally Morgan, watch yourself around that young McCoy."

Granny Smith leaned closer, favoring Sally with more than a hint of peppermint. "I hear Abe has hired the younger boy to do odd jobs. Is that true?"

Sally nodded mutely.

"How odd." Granny Smith turned to the others. "Doesn't it seem strange to you?"

They murmured agreement.

She returned her snapping gaze to Sally. "Why would he do such a thing?"

Relief eased the tension in Sally's lungs. She could answer this truthfully and freely. "He told me the man was innocent and deserved to be treated fairly. Said it was his duty as a leader in the church to show a good example."

The women drew back, practically creating a vacuum around Sally.

Mrs. Brennan was the first to recover. "He thinks he's being fair? Sounds like he's judging the rest of us. Well, I declare." She drew in a long-suffering gasp. "He'll live to regret his decision." She pinned Sally with her unflinching gaze. "I hope you are wise enough to give that young man a wide berth."

Sally tried to keep her expression blank, revealing none of her guilt and wariness, though she wondered if she succeeded when Mrs. Brennan's eyes narrowed.

"You must be careful around such men. They have a way of turning a person's thoughts into turmoil so what you always knew to be right and good suddenly doesn't seem enough." She turned her attention to her three gaping daughters. "Never let a man—any man—divert you from the straight and narrow path."

"Yes, Mama," they murmured in unison, then flashed looks ripe with accusation at Sally.

Is that what they thought? All of them? Sally went round the circle, looking at each woman and the variety of expressions. Some harsh and accusing, like the Brennans. Others leaned more toward resignation, as if feeling sorry for Sally. For something they had already decided she'd done. Miss Carter alone managed to reveal a touch of compassion.

Their silent accusations were unfounded. Their compassion unnecessary. She knew right from wrong. Even more, she knew what she wanted from life, and that was a home and security such as she'd known when Father was alive. Which Abe could give her. She drew herself up as tall as she could. Her voice rang with pride. "You judge me to be a silly young woman. I should think you would know better. You all know me well enough to know I always do what is right."

Mr. Sharp handed her the basket of things she'd ordered. She took it and faced the women again.

"I not only do what is right, as you all know, I do what is wise. Come along, Robbie." Her head high, she marched from the store, thankful that Robbie followed without making a fuss.

The women waited until the screen door slapped shut, then they all began to speak at once.

Sally couldn't make out what they said, but she heard the surprise in the collective chatter.

"What did they mean?" Robbie asked.

She'd hoped he hadn't heard or hadn't listened. "About what?"

"They said bad things about Linc, didn't they? He's not a bad man. He's a nice man."

"They were talking about a different time." But not about different people. She would do well to keep it in mind.

But who was Linc? She tended to side with Robbie. He seemed like a good, kind man. He'd returned to make sure his father was comfortable in his final days, even though he likely knew the kind of reception he would receive.

Or was she being naive? Choosing to see only what she wanted to see?

They were almost back. Linc continued to paint the fence. As they drew near, he stood and wiped his hands on a rag. "I'll take that." He grabbed the basket and carried it to the kitchen table.

"They were talking about you," Robbie said.

Linc shot Sally a look ripe with regret. "Looks like a great candy stick."

Sally realized she'd forgotten to buy herself one.

"Yup." Robbie sucked on it. "Why did they say bad things?"

"Did they?"

Robbie took the candy from his mouth. "I couldn't understand what they said, but they did this." He puckered his mouth and looked cross. "I know what that means."

Linc chuckled. "I guess you probably do. But seeing as I didn't do anything naughty, you must have heard them wrong."

Robbie studied him a moment longer then, seemingly satisfied, wandered out to the fort under construction.

Sally watched him cross the yard, all the time aware of Linc studying her.

"So the opinion of the good folk of Golden Prairie hasn't changed?" His words were low, as if resigned to the inevitable.

She didn't answer. Didn't pull her gaze from watching out the window.

"What do you think?"

His question, so direct, so void of emotion, jarred her from trying to maintain disinterest. She jerked her gaze to him and saw something in his eyes that said he wasn't as uncaring as he tried to portray.

She swallowed hard. "I think…" Her heart opened

up and dumped out a tangle of emotions—things she couldn't identify and didn't want to own. One thought followed another before she could see the first clearly. Others came on the tail of each until they seemed to pull her in a hundred different directions. She lifted her words from that tangle and focused on the only solid thing she could grasp at the moment—Abe. She knew who he was, what he stood for and who and what he would be into the future. "I think Abe is right. You deserve a chance."

His expression faltered. He shifted on his feet. For a moment she thought he meant to walk away. Then he nodded. "Does that mean we can be friends?"

She smiled softly. "It looks like we already are."

"Good to know." His words were brisk and he left the house without a backward look, his shoulders squared as if defying the world.

Had she disappointed him? She watched until he disappeared from sight. Friends was good, wasn't it? She could offer nothing more. Likely he didn't want more, either. It was enough.

Strange how it felt totally unsatisfactory. As if she'd fallen short of gaining a prize.

Now she was getting downright fanciful, and she had no patience with such sentimental nonsense. She turned her attention to the groceries and put them away, leaving out the can of peaches to use for dessert.

All she needed to do in order to soothe her thoughts was keep her mind on her work, and she turned her attention to lunch, preparing pretty sandwiches and arranging cookies on a special plate.

Lunch came and went. Carol returned to school. Abe thanked her for a well-done job and left for work. Robbie went out to join Linc.

Sally looked around the empty house. It practically echoed with her thoughts…which she tried to avoid. Friendship was all she could offer.

The dishes needed washing. The floor needed scrubbing. The windows could do with a polishing. She immersed herself in a flurry of activity, yet the afternoon trudged by on slow-moving legs.

She glanced at the clock. Still an hour before Carol would be home from school. Enough time to bake fresh cookies for the afternoon break. Linc had liked the ginger cookies. What would he think of snickerdoodles? Perhaps she could soothe her own disappointment by showing Linc—and ultimately herself—how nice friendship could be.

Carol slipped in almost unnoticed.

"As soon as you're changed, would you go tell Linc and Robbie that tea is ready?"

"Okay." Carol clattered up the stairs.

Chuckling at her uncharacteristic eagerness, Sally stared after her.

Carol raced back down and out the door.

The coffee boiled, and Sally grabbed it before it sputtered over on the stove. She would not admit an eagerness matching Carol's. It was only an after-school snack.

But when she heard him approaching, the children chattering at his side, she had to admit this was no ordinary snack time. She didn't mean just the way the children acted. Her heart did unusual things, too. As if controlled by a spirited puppet master who laughed and sang with joy.

He stepped into the room. She felt his presence, from the soles of her feet to the roots of her hair. And although she tried to ignore him, her gaze was drawn unerringly to his face. His eyes were dark and guarded. She gave a tentative smile. "I hope you like snickerdoodles."

His lips curled slowly, and as they did the ice in her veins she'd been unaware of melted. When his eyes flashed warmth, she started to breathe normally.

They could surely enjoy friendship.

"I love snickerdoodles. And fresh coffee. And—" He didn't finish, and she wouldn't allow herself to fill in the blank he'd left. "I'll wash up."

As he ducked into the back room with Robbie at his heels, Sally smiled in satisfaction. They were friends, and it felt good.

As they sat around the table eating warm cookies, she felt at peace. Abe would expect her to treat Linc well.

"How was school today, little Miss Carol?" he asked.

Sally expected the usual murmured one-word answer, but Carol put her cookie down and glanced at Sally and then Linc.

"The big girls told me a bad story."

Linc shot Sally a look full of regret. She realized with a start he expected it to be about him. She prayed it wouldn't be. Didn't the man deserve to be treated fairly and without prejudice? Was Abe the only one willing to do so? It proved what a good man Abe was. "Do you want to tell us about it?" Linc's voice was soft, inviting.

Carol studied her half eaten cookie. "They said you were a bad man. That you stole from Mrs. Ogilvy." Her bottom lip quivered.

Linc allowed Sally a glimpse of his sorrow and regret then turned his attention to Carol. He caught her chin and pulled her face toward him. "Carol, I assure you I am not a bad man. But you must choose what to believe. Everyone must." He let his glance rest on Robbie a moment, and then on Sally.

She felt his silent pleading. Oh, if only she could tell him all she felt—that he was good and noble and very brave to return to a town ready to judge him so harshly. But fearing speaking from her heart would unleash things she didn't understand and knowing they would interfere with her plans, she hoped her smile said enough. Then she turned to Carol. "Honey, do you think your father would hire Linc to work here if he thought he was a bad man?"

Carol shook her head.

"So who do you think is right? Your father or some girls at school?"

"Father, of course. He is always right."

"There you go."

Carol let out a hefty sigh. "I knew it anyway."

Sally shifted her gaze to Linc and looked deep into his eyes. "So did I."

Linc's grin threatened to split his face. "Ladies, I can't thank you enough for your confidence in me."

Sally had smiled at him long enough, but she couldn't

pull her gaze away. The air between them shimmered with something far beyond friendship, but she couldn't—wouldn't—name it.

Robbie pushed his chair back. "Time to go back to work."

The moment ended, and Sally scrambled to her feet and hurriedly started to gather up the dishes.

Linc rose more slowly, as if aware of her confused feelings. "You're right, Robbie. Let's go paint the fence."

Carol trailed after them.

It wasn't until the door closed behind them that Sally sank into a chair and buried her head in her hands. What was there about Linc that left her so fractured inside? Unable to remember who she was and what she wanted?

Or perhaps Linc wasn't to blame.

She could hold no one else accountable for her behavior, and she stuffed all her errant, confused thoughts behind a solid door.

She knew exactly who she was and what she wanted. Not for even a moment would she forget. At least not again.

Her mind full of determination, she turned her attention to the task of cleaning up the snack and preparing the evening meal.

Chapter Seven

Linc finished painting the fence, cleaned the paint supplies, scrubbed his hands and turned toward his grandmother's.

Friends, Sally said. Her eyes flashing with golden light as she said the word and smiled at him. A friend in this town was good news. But it felt like so much more than friends. The way her gaze captured his, probing, yearning. The way she defended him. She said she believed he was a good man. It seemed as if Heaven opened and showered her words down on him. A blessing beyond imagination.

He paused at the back fence of the Finley yard and waved at Robbie. "See you later."

Robbie glanced up. "You'll be back tomorrow, won't you?"

Linc nodded. "Got that barn to fix up. You want to help?"

Robbie grinned. "Can I?"

"Ask your father tonight, and if he agrees, I'd be glad

of your help." The boy needed to feel useful. And Linc needed to believe he had something to offer besides—

Friendship?

He could no longer deny himself a glance toward the house. Yes, she stood at the window, watching. When she saw him looking at her, she tipped her head down as if whatever she did was vastly more interesting than him.

And why should he care? Friends didn't look for signs of interest, did they?

He almost convinced himself he wasn't the least bit disappointed when she looked up again and gave a little wave.

Maybe it didn't signify anything, but his heart felt years lighter as he sketched back a salute. He sang as he crossed to the other yard and marched up the steps into the house.

As always, when he crossed the threshold, the reason for being at Grandmama's hit him like being bucked off a horse, face-first into the dirt. His happiness at Sally's wave warred with the pain of his father's lingering death. Seemed neither of the emotions was about to win or lose. He simply had to contend with the inner turmoil. "How's Pa?"

Grandmama stirred a pot. The air filled with the delicious smell of butterscotch pudding. "I checked on him a few minutes ago and he appeared to be sound asleep, but see for yourself."

Linc paused as he passed the stove and took a deep breath. "Sure smells good." He hugged his grandmother around the waist. "You always did make the best puddings."

She smiled at him. "I guess I figure you only deserve the best."

He grinned. "Maybe don't deserve it, but sure do enjoy it."

"You're a good boy." She patted his cheek. "Don't ever forget it."

"I'll try not to." His grandmother's approval did a lot toward making him believe his worth, but didn't hold a candle to Sally's friendship. Though the word *friend* somehow grated across his thoughts, leaving them tender.

Friendship was good, he firmly informed his brain.

But was it enough?

Grandmama studied him. Afraid she would read his mind—knowing if she did, she would point out yet again how Abe Finley could offer Sally all the things she needed and deserved, things he, Linc McCoy, could not—he stepped back.

Grandmama had one of those looks that said she read him like a book. Then she sighed. "Go see your father. I'm afraid supper will be a while yet. Some of the ladies got together to piece a quilt, and I just got home."

Grateful she refrained from saying all the things she thought, Linc nodded and went to the bedroom. So Grandmama had been out all afternoon. He didn't like to think of Pa being alone, but really, there was little anyone could do apart from giving him a little water if he'd take it and handing out the pain medication.

Pa lay spread eagle under the covers, his breathing

catching every so often, which indicated the level of his pain, the doctor said. "Pa," he called softly. But Pa didn't stir, and Linc didn't try to disturb him. Let him sleep while he could. He studied the man a few minutes as pain and regret raced through him like raging flood waters. *Oh, Pa, I hate to see you laid so low.* Even more, he despised the way Pa had been treated in this town. At least his present circumstances spared him from hearing the comments of the townsfolk.

He returned to the kitchen where his grandmother labored over a pile of vegetables. "I think I'll go for a ride."

"Fine. Fine. Don't worry about rushing back. Everything will keep."

He went outside and threw a bridle over Big Red's neck. "I need to get some fresh air. How about you?"

Big Red was far more interested in a bit of green grass he'd discovered in the far corner of the yard.

"It'll be here when we get back," Linc assured him as he led the animal to the barn and saddled him. "A little exercise will do you good." He patted the horse's side. "Wouldn't want you to get fat and lazy."

He headed out of town, purposely in the same direction as last time, for no particular reason other than to avoid going the opposite way which, unless he chose an indirect route, would lead him past Mrs. Ogilvy's house. He was innocent. His father and brother were innocent, yet he felt branded. The idea of riding past her house made his skin tighten.

He rode into plenty of open space this way. In the distance he saw the boxlike orphanage atop a hill, as if whoever built it wanted it to always be visible. Perhaps so the people of the surrounding area wouldn't forget those in need of help and kindness. Letting his pain edge his thoughts, he wondered how often the orphans received those things. If the way Pa was treated indicated anything, likely not often.

Ahead of him on the trail he saw a woman walking.

Sally.

He'd know the way she walked—quickly and purposefully—anywhere. Just as he'd recognize the way her curls bounced with every step, catching sunshine in each curve of hair.

His frustration and anger dissolved.

She turned as she heard his approach and waited at the side of the road for him to pass.

He reined in and jumped to the ground. "You're on your way home?"

"All done for the day."

"I'd think Abe would give you a ride." If he was Abe, he'd never allow her to walk home unescorted.

"He's offered many times, but the children are happy at home. I don't like to drag them out for no reason. Besides, I love the quiet."

He drew to a halt. Did he detect a hint of regret in her voice? "Would you prefer to be alone?"

She stopped walking, too, and her eyes widened in shock. "Oh, no. I didn't mean that."

"Good." The smile curving her mouth crowded into the corners of his heart. She plainly didn't mind his company. "Then I'll walk you home."

They fell into step, Red plodding along after them.

At first neither of them spoke, then they both tried to say something at the same time.

Linc chuckled. "You go ahead."

"I was only going to ask where you've been the past six years and what you've done. What were you going to say?"

"That maybe the drought will end this year. Maybe this will be the year prices recover." It was but a drop of all the things running through his thoughts to be said. He wanted to know so much. All about her. How she managed. What she did, liked, wanted.

She looked about. "If it doesn't, how will some of these people continue?"

Her question brought him back from his flight of errant thoughts. "It's tough to hang on."

"All that keeps many of them going, me included, is knowing whatever happens won't separate us from God's love."

"I believe in God's love and care, but love doesn't fill a child's stomach."

She slowed and looked toward the orphanage. "My sister, Madge, would argue. She says God will provide our needs." She gave a soft chuckle. "And He does." She told him how her sister prayed for a way to save their home and how she'd been offered a job that unexpectedly provided just the right answer. "In a way none of us could have predicted."

"So you are well taken care of now?" If she lacked anything, he'd do his best to supply it. Never mind that his limited resources barely allowed him to buy Pa's pain medicine.

"We live frugally, as everyone does, but we never go hungry."

His insides shifted from worry to a bubbling sensation of relief. "It sounds like this sister of yours is a real fighter."

Sally laughed out loud, drawing a smile to Linc's mouth. He liked her laugh. "She has a faith that moves mountains." Sally sobered. "I wish I had that kind of faith."

Their steps lagged so much that Big Red nudged Linc between the shoulders. Linc pushed him away. He was in no hurry. "What kind of faith do you have?"

She looked startled. Then seemed to consider her answer. "I've never tried to name it, but I guess I have a needy faith."

How intriguing. What did she need? Again, if he could in any way supply what she lacked, he'd do anything he could to do it. "Can you explain?"

"I need things from God, like security, safety, the assurance my needs will be met." She shrugged. "I don't expect you understand what I mean."

"Do you mean your faith believes God will provide all that He's promised? Or you'll believe it when you see it?"

"Ouch." She stopped and faced him. "That sounds like doubt, not faith. But maybe you're right. I want things to be in place." She considered him a moment, her gaze delving deep into his soul, seeking answers, perhaps wondering if he condemned her for her sort of faith.

"I didn't mean to sound critical." He'd only wanted

her to realize God was bigger than her needs. He wanted her to feel secure in His love and care. He let her search his thoughts, hoping she would find something to make her feel safe.

How foolish. Wasn't it God she needed to depend on? But, he silently argued, it would be nice to help God in this matter.

"What kind of faith do you have?"

His grin felt lopsided. "I've never thought of it, either." He contemplated his answer. "I guess I have a surviving faith."

They moseyed onward.

"Explain what you mean."

"Okay." Again he sifted through his thoughts to bring some sense to them. "I've survived. My faith has survived through tough times and doubts."

"What sort of doubts?"

She was peeling back the layers of what he truly believed and how he'd arrived at that point. He'd never considered his journey too deeply, but now found he wanted to—and more, he wanted to share it with Sally. Wanted her to glimpse the workings of his inner being. "My mother tried to teach me about God, but I guess it didn't ring true. I knew she'd run off with my father, who had a terrible reputation. When I think of it now I realize how it must have hurt my grandmother."

She touched his elbow. "But she opened her home to them when they asked."

Her fingers on his arm carried a thousand unspoken messages. Likely they were only in his head, and she didn't have any idea of where his thoughts went—along a trail of a deep, intense…well, he'd settle for calling it friendship, seeing it was all that was available to him. "And she's done it again. Despite whatever she thinks of my father, she welcomed us without reservation. Her charitable attitude impressed me from the start. I wondered how she could be so kind even when she didn't approve. She offered unconditional love, so I could believe it when she said God loved me unconditionally. I chose to become a Christian because of Grandmama."

"What a wonderful heritage she's given you."

He agreed completely. "Tell me how you became a Christian."

Her gentle smile widened her lips and filled her eyes. And settled into his heart like a homing pigeon returned from a long journey. "My father led all of us to the Lord. I knelt at his knees when I was eight and prayed the sinner's prayer. I don't remember the words, but I know what I meant and felt. It was a special time."

"Your father was a special man."

"He was indeed, and I miss him." A break came in her speech, and then she continued. "I think of him so much, but most of all at bedtime. He made each of us promise to read a chapter from the Bible every night before we go to bed. I've missed very few evenings. I've found such strength and comfort in my daily reading."

Her words created a hunger in his heart.

"Do you read the Bible daily?"

"I haven't made it a habit, but maybe I need to."

"Now were you going to tell me what you've done, where you've been since you left here?"

"Nothing very exciting, I'm afraid. I went with

Pa and Harris for the first few years, but they never stayed long in one place. They hunted gold in the mountains, worked on the railroad, drove freight for a few months, then they started working in the coal mines in the Crowsnest Pass. For some reason they seemed to enjoy that. I hated it. I didn't even make it through a full shift before I staggered out to the light and vowed I'd never go into the pit again."

She sent him a look so full of sympathy he had to stop and draw in air to clear his thoughts.

"I don't suppose you've ever seen the Frank Slide?"

She shook her head.

"Boulders the size of houses came crashing down on the town. Seventy-six people were buried alive." Words poured from him, words stored up for so many years, things he'd never been able to openly say to his father and brother. "The rocks became their grave markers. The Indians called the mountain the mountain that walks. They knew it was unstable, but no one listened because there was a rich vein of coal beneath the mountain, and coal is worth a lot of money. It isn't worth a man's life, or the life of his wife and children though." He slowed his words and then went on. "I decided I preferred sky and grass to coal, and from then on I worked on a ranch."

"And then you lost your brother in a mine accident. How terrible."

"At least he didn't suffer."

"Unlike your pa. I'm sorry. How is he?"

"Not getting any stronger." He told how he had started reading *Pilgrim's Progress* to him. "I pray it will speak to my father and he will become a Christian before he dies."

"I will pray for it, as well."

He took her hand and squeezed it. "Thank you." So this is what it felt like to have a good friend? Except he wanted more. He wanted to be free to wrap his arms around her and hold her close, finding comfort in that. He ached to offer her what she needed.

Security and safety.

"This is where I turn off." They had come to a long driveway. He saw a solid two-story house and a small but adequate barn.

"I'll walk you the rest of the way."

She stepped back, shock filling her wide eyes, darkening them to deepest green. "I couldn't let you do that."

He didn't need a blaring announcement to understand she didn't want him to. "Of course not." His voice cracked with disappointment. Up until this moment, he thought they were enjoying each other's company. Being friends. Isn't that what she wanted?

She shook her head and her gaze darted away to his left, to his right, always avoiding meeting his eyes. "Mother wouldn't understand."

Her words struck him so hard he stepped backward and bumped into patient Red.

Red. Escape.

Exactly what he needed. He flipped the reins over the horse's head and swung into the saddle. "I understand." He nudged Red and trotted toward town.

He understood all right. Way too well. He could be her friend, but not in public. Being seen with a

McCoy—even by her mother—threatened the very things she needed—the things he allowed himself to briefly think he could offer. Safety and security.

The sky had darkened. He glanced upward. The sun still shone as brightly. It had simply lost its warmth. He was a McCoy. Not for the first time, he thought of changing his name to Smith or Jones or even Black. Yes, Black would suit just fine. But he didn't want to be someone else. He wanted to be seen as a good man with the name McCoy. Was that too much to ask? Seems it was.

Well, he had gotten along without friends most of his life. That was nothing new. But all his excuse-making and reason-seeking did not ease the darkness in his soul.

He valued Sally's friendship. Obviously more than she valued his.

He reached the yard and took Red to the barn and cared for him.

As he stepped into the kitchen, the aroma of stew and pudding greeted him, as did his grandmother's smile, and he pushed his disappointment to the background.

Supper was good. He ate a good-size portion and hoped his grandmother wouldn't notice a certain lack of enthusiasm. Afterward, he dried the dishes for her then went to Pa's bedside.

"Where you been, boy?" His father sounded lonesome, not demanding.

"I went for a ride. You remember, I work at Mr. Finley's during the day."

"What'd you do today?"

"I painted the front fence. Mr. Finley likes things to

look nice." Abe cared what people thought. He'd hired
Linc because Abe did what was right and noble—out
of duty. He stood for safety. Security. Just what Sally
wanted. Thought she needed. But it sounded false, shallow and rigid at the same time.

"This man live alone?"

Linc told him of the two motherless children. "They
have a housekeeper now who will likely become their
stepmother." Saying the words out loud felt like bringing up bitter acid.

"She nice to them?"

He could gladly say she was. "She'll make a fine
mother to them." But the idea of her living according
to Abe's expectation of duty twisted his insides. She
needed to know life was to enjoy. God's world was to
enjoy, His salvation was to enjoy.

But if he took a good look at himself, did he really
believe that? If he did, he wouldn't let gossip and spite-
fulness, nor even rejection from a friend rob him of
enjoying all God had given. *Lord, help me see beyond
these hurts to Your everlasting love.* He let peace fill
him. "Would you like me to read to you again?"

He read another hour to his father, then slipped away
and went to his room.

Sally read the scriptures every night because of a
promise to her father. She asked if he read the Bible.
He had never made a practice of it before, but now he
found his copy of the Good Book and opened it at the
beginning of the New Testament and began to read. As
he did, all but a remnant of his bitterness disappeared.
Somehow reading in his room and knowing Sally read

in hers made him feel close to her and restored the feeling of companionship.

Perhaps it was all he could expect. Could it be enough?

It had to be.

Chapter Eight

Next morning at the Finley house, Sally glanced around the table. Carol waited for her father to say grace. Robbie had a hand on either side of his bowl, and eyed the steaming porridge hungrily. Sally slowly brought her gaze to Abe. As usual, he wore his dark blond hair slicked back. His black suit was immaculate. He was a good, decent man; handsome in a gentle way.

He bowed his head and prayed, catching her off guard. By the time she bowed her head, he was done.

"Robbie will be six in two weeks' time," Abe said after he'd tasted his coffee and enjoyed a few spoonfuls of his porridge.

Robbie didn't stop eating, but he slid a look at his father—a rather hopeful look, Sally thought.

"Their mother thought the children should have a special party when they turned six and were grown up enough to start school. Do you suppose you could plan something?"

"What do you have in mind?" *What did your wife do? Can I do, as well?*

"Whatever you think Robbie would enjoy. Within reason."

She nodded, hoping he would give a clue as to what he meant by "within reason." But he didn't offer any details.

"I've prepared a list of guests." He pulled a piece of paper from his pocket and passed it to Sally.

She glanced over it. Six little boys from either business or church connections. Four little girls from Carol's class. At least he'd thought to include Carol in the celebration.

"Can you manage that?"

"I'm certain I can." She had no idea what he wanted, but she'd make sure it exceeded any expectations. She'd prove to everyone she was worthy of this job…even more, the role of Abe's wife.

Carol and Robbie watched her guardedly, perhaps afraid to get their hopes up for fear of being disappointed. Right then and there Sally decided she wanted to bring them pleasure, even more than she wanted to please Abe. Hopefully she could do both.

Abe finished and pushed back from the table. "And get rid of that pile of junk at the end of the garden before the party."

An instant pall covered the table. Robbie dropped his spoon and bunched his hands into fists. Sally stared at Abe. How could he order the destruction of Robbie's fort? Didn't he realize how important it was to the boy? Perhaps he didn't. After all, he only saw the boy in the evening. How was he to know Robbie spent most of his waking time playing there? She must explain its importance.

She rose. "I'll be right back," she said to the children and followed Abe through the dining room to the front door, where he prepared to leave for the day.

"Abe, may I speak to you a moment?"

"Of course. I hope you feel free to talk to me whenever you want."

She paused. Was he inviting her to share confidences? But this wasn't the time. Not that she could think of anything she wanted to tell him, apart from this one thing. "About Robbie's fort—"

He raised his eyebrows. "His fort?"

"Yes. That pile of junk in the garden. It's his fort. He spends a great deal of time playing there. It seems to give him a lot of pleasure. Would you reconsider having it destroyed?"

He looked at her so intently she wanted to squirm. "Do you think it's important?"

"I do."

"You feel I should leave it be?"

"It's important to Robbie."

"Very well. If you think it's best, I'll bow to your wishes." He headed back to the kitchen, Sally at his heels.

"Robbie, Sally says that—" he made a vague wave toward the fort visible from the window "—your fort is important to you. Is that right?"

Robbie nodded, his lips set in an angry frown.

"If it's important to you, then it may stay." Abe waited.

At first, Sally wasn't sure what he expected. Then it seemed plain. "Robbie," she whispered. "Thank your father."

Robbie looked ready to explode, unable to shed his anger so quickly. But he managed a muttered, "Thank you."

Satisfied, Abe left.

Sally and the children didn't move, even after they heard the front door close. Time was slipping away, and she read the children their Bible story then sent Carol off to school.

She turned her attention to cleaning up the meal as Robbie headed out to his fort. Smiling her satisfaction that she had succeeded in saving it for him, she watched out the window as he got a spade from the shed.

He carried it to the tangle of dirt and twigs that kept him happily amused for so many days. Perhaps he meant to make the walls higher but—

She gasped.

He banged away on the walls, destroying them inch by inch.

Sally threw aside the cloth and rushed outside. "Robbie, what on earth are you doing?" She grabbed the shovel. "You don't have to destroy it."

"He only let me keep it 'cause you said something. Give me the shovel." He lunged for it, but she jerked away.

"Does it matter why he let you keep it? After all your hard work you deserve to enjoy it."

But all Robbie seemed to care about was getting his hands on the shovel, and it took all Sally's concentrated dodging away to keep it from him.

"Hey, hey. What's going on?" Linc vaulted the fence and swept Robbie into his arms. "What are you trying to do?"

Breathless, Sally leaned on the handle of the shovel.

Linc lowered Robbie to the ground, but kept a firm grip on him. He squatted to eye level. "Care to tell me what this is all about?"

"It isn't a pile of junk."

Linc gave Sally a look of confusion.

"His father called his fort junk. Said it had to go." She turned to the boy struggling to escape Linc's hold. "He didn't know. Once I told him how important it was to you, he understood. He said you could keep it. Remember?"

Linc turned back to the boy. "I don't see why you were fighting with Sally. Seems she spoke up for you. Don't you think that calls for a little gratitude?"

The fight slowly drained from Robbie, and he sank to the ground. Linc released him, but stood ready to intervene if the boy exploded again. Robbie hung his head.

Linc glanced toward Sally, his eyes asking for an explanation, but she was at a loss as to what to do or say and indicated it with a shrug. Linc stared into the distance for two beats then sat down beside Robbie. "I guess you were pretty upset when you thought you were going to lose your fort. After all, a man likes to hang on to the things he's worked hard for. I understand that. But a man also has to learn to aim his anger and frustration in the right direction so he doesn't hurt the ones who care about him. Or destroy the things he wants to protect. Do you understand?"

Robbie gave no indication one way or the other, except to scuff his heels in the dirt.

Sally waited, not knowing what to expect and realizing how inept she was at dealing with the crises in Robbie's life—of which there seemed to be many.

"Sometimes I don't know who I'm mad at," Robbie said.

Linc sat beside Robbie. "That happens to me, too." He sounded as morose as the boy, and Sally almost smiled at the disconsolate pair sitting side by side in the dirt. They both wore such similar expressions. Except it wasn't a laughing matter. No one's pain was amusing, no matter how big or small. Being the youngest, she'd often wondered if anyone cared about her concerns. After all, it was old news to her older sisters and likely her parents. Everything that happened to her had previously been experienced and dealt with. Once her father had asked what bothered her. It was something small— so small she couldn't even remember what it had been. But she still remembered his words.

She spoke them aloud now, hoping they would encourage Robbie and Linc as much as they had her. "My father once told me anger only fuels pain. It misdirects our energies."

Two pairs of eyes turned to her, waiting for more, perhaps hoping she had an answer to how to deal with frustrating anger and disappointment. "He said the best way to deal with anger was to do something positive like help someone, make something, go somewhere. I guess that's why I like to help people. It makes me feel like life isn't out of control. I suppose that's why Linc rides his horse. It's a way to direct his feelings into action."

Robbie sighed. "I can't do anything."

She studied his fort. "Maybe you can."

Linc got to his feet and stood beside her, also studying the fort. "I think you could."

Robbie sprang to his feet. "What? What can I do?"

"Well, if your father thinks this looks like junk, maybe you need to make it look better. Finish the fence. Tidy up the dirt around it." Sally could see how doing so would improve the view from the window.

"There was a bit of paint left in the can. I could thin it, and you could paint these boards." Linc tilted his head from side to side. "How would it be if I showed you how to build a gate for your fence? Then it would look really great."

Robbie grabbed a twig and drove it into the ground next to the others forming the fence. "I'm going to finish the fence first."

Linc smiled at Sally and gave a subtle thumbs up. She grinned back. They had averted a crisis with the boy and given him a way to sidetrack his anger. Maybe it would help him in the future.

Her smile faltered when she remembered how she'd hurt Linc yesterday, when she refused to let him accompany her to the house. She hadn't meant to, but how would she explain to Mother, who feared any friendship between Sally and Linc would ruin her chances of marriage to Abe? Mother would never understand the friendship Sally had with Linc. In her room last night, she had worked it all through. She and Linc were forced to spend time together as coworkers. She admired his way with the children and the way he cared about his family. But she knew where her duty lay. She'd fought the word duty. What kind of relationship was based on duty? There was more to it than that. There was— she'd plumbed her heart for what she felt toward Abe… Safety, security—the very things she'd told Linc she needed. Yet she appreciated Linc's company. She felt comfortable opening her heart to him and talking about her faith, her family, her fears.

They turned and headed for their own tasks—he to the barn and she to the house. They reached the place where their paths must diverge.

"You're good with him," Sally said, wanting to express how much she appreciated him, even though she wouldn't let him walk her to the door.

"So are you."

They nodded mutual respect.

Linc adjusted his hat and seemed to want to say more. She hoped he didn't want to discuss last night. It took him a moment to form his words. "I wish I could say it was because I'm all grown up and speak from wisdom, but honestly, I feel like Robbie and I are on equal footing. I look at my pa and want to be mad at someone, but I don't know who it would be. It's a helpless, frustrated feeling."

"I think it's something we all struggle with. Remember how I have a needy faith? That's part of it. Standing back and knowing I'm helpless is a terrible feeling. I need security. You asked if I trusted God or needed to see before I believed."

"I wasn't questioning your faith."

"Well, I honestly don't know which it is. I know God is my rock and salvation. I know He holds my future, and that's a comfort. But I'm not sure I believe it's enough. I watch families move away with all their possessions piled in the back of a truck. They have nothing left. How do they go on?"

"There is always hope."

"Hope is a pretty little balloon that won't last until morning."

He chuckled. "I guess if it's full of hot air, that would be true. What if it's full of something permanent, like God's promises? It wouldn't collapse or blow away then."

She stared into the blue distance as a bubble of something looking clearly like hope but feeling more solid landed in her soul. A verse her father had her memorize many years ago came to mind. "'Blessed is the man that trusteth in the Lord, whose hope the Lord is. For he shall be as a tree planted by the waters.'"

"Exactly. It's not a balloon, but a solid tree."

"I like that. It feels secure."

"I better get to work." He touched the brim of his hat.

"Me, too." It wasn't until she was back in the house that she recalled Abe's request for a birthday party for Robbie. What would a six-year-old boy want? She had only sisters, and they had loved dress up and tea parties. Robbie would obviously not like such things.

As she finished the breakfast dishes and tidied the house, she tried to come up with a plan. She wanted this party to be remarkable. She wanted to prove to Abe that she could manage anything he and his family required. But by midmorning she was no closer to a solution.

She watched out the window as Linc showed Robbie how to hang a gate. A smile tipped her lips and cheered her heart. Linc had once been a little boy. He would know what boys liked for a party. She waited until he headed back to the barn, leaving Robbie with some thinned paint and a brush, then went to talk to him.

She paused in the doorway and waited for her eyes to adjust to the gloomy interior. The squeal of spikes being pulled from old wood indicated his location. "Linc?"

"I'm over here."

She could see him now. "You used to be a little boy."

His grin gently mocked her. "I think that's pretty obvious."

"I guess I didn't need to point it out. I only meant to say I have never been nor known any little boys really well, and now Abe wants me to plan a special birthday party for Robbie, and I have no idea what he'd like."

Linc's arm fell to his side, the hammer dangling at his knee. "You're asking me for help?"

He needn't act so surprised. "Advice, at least. What would he like?"

Linc leaned against the stall and grinned. "I know exactly what he'd like." He glanced around like a coconspirator, leaned close and whispered, "A pony to ride."

"Oh, perfect! But I don't know anyone with ponies. Most people can't afford to feed pets like that."

His grin deepened, making her thoughts feel as if they had boarded balloons and were trying to soar or escape or—she punctured the balloons. She could not allow such nonsense.

"I know someone. Leave the pony to me." He must have seen the lingering doubt in her eyes. "Okay?"

Would Abe consider it suitable, safe for his son? "I better check with Abe first and get his permission." She turned her steps toward the house, then stopped. "I hope he agrees. Robbie would be thrilled."

Later, after supper was over and the kitchen cleaned she would normally hurry away, but Sally needed to talk to Abe. Alone. He'd said he hoped she would talk to him whenever she wanted, but she struggled to find the words to make this simple request. What was wrong with her that she turned into a tongue-tied child at the thought? Shouldn't she be able to speak her thoughts and wishes to him freely? After all, if they were to marry, she couldn't continue to feel so immature around him, but something about Abe made her anxious and uncertain of herself. She sucked in a deep breath. She must overcome this shyness.

He sat in his chair reading some documents. He preferred the children play quietly after their meal, so Robbie moved a little car across the floor and Carol colored a picture.

All she had to do was ask him to come to the kitchen. Or even go outside and walk around the yard. Instead, she wiped the table again and rehearsed her words.

"You're still here?" He stood in the doorway. "I thought you'd be gone."

Why should he think so? She always said goodbye before she left, and she hadn't done so. But his presence in the room gave her an opportunity to voice her question. "I wanted to speak to you before I leave."

"Go ahead." He filled a glass of water.

She lowered her voice. "I thought of having a Western-themed party for Robbie's birthday."

"Sounds fine."

"I'd like to have a live pony for the children to ride."

The glass of water, halfway to his mouth, stalled and he slowly lowered it. "Do you have a pony?"

She shook her head.

"Are you familiar with how to control one?"

"No, but Mr. McCoy offered to bring a pony and he knows about horses." She waited as Abe studied her, silently exploring her expression.

"Linc McCoy?"

She nodded.

He turned away as if he needed time to consider his answer. Then slowly faced her again. "I wanted to give McCoy a chance. I just didn't think it would involve my children."

A hundred defenses sprang to her mind. Wisely, she held them back, except for one. "It isn't like he'd be alone with the children." Though what difference that made, she couldn't say. Linc posed no threat to anyone, least of all a dozen children. But her answer seemed to satisfy Abe.

"Very well, but I want the pony to be under adult control at all times." He drained his glass and set it down. "I would not want any harm to come to my children—any of the children."

"I assure you they will all be safe." She washed his glass and returned it to the cupboard. "I'm leaving now." She called a goodbye to the children.

Would Linc ride down the road again? She could hardly wait to tell him Abe had given permission to proceed with the party. But she reached the turnoff to her house without seeing him. She paused and looked down the road, hoping to spot an approaching rider.

The road was as empty as the rain barrel at the side of the house.

It didn't matter. She'd see him tomorrow. But try as she did, she couldn't deny how her heart practically burst with a need to talk to him, tell about her day, discuss ideas for the party.

Angry at herself for such foolishness, she stuffed the idea into a corner in the far reaches of her mind and resolutely turned her steps toward home.

Linc glanced out the window. From where he sat at his pa's bedside, he saw only the bright blue sky. He'd hoped to take Red out for a run. The horse needed to stretch his legs. Linc barely acknowledged the fact that if he was out there at this moment, he would likely overtake Sally on her way home. But Pa was restless today and Linc couldn't, in good conscience, leave him.

"What did you do today, boy?"

He told how he'd begun removing the stalls at one end of the barn in order to make room for Mr. Finley's car. "I told you about the children. Well, seems Rob-

bie is about to turn six and his father says it calls for a
birthday party. Sally didn't know what a boy would like,
so I suggested a pony for the kids to ride."

"Sally? That the name of the woman who is going
to be the new stepmother?"

Abe had a big solid house, a good job. He could provide security. Everything Sally wanted and needed. A
needy faith, she'd said, and her words made him understand so much more. Sally wasn't one to take risks. Still,
hearing his own father talk as if Sally was already Abe's
wife made his throat spasm. Aware his pa watched him,
he tried for a grin and missed. "Yeah, that's her." His
voice betrayed him, sounding regretful rather than the
nonchalant tone he aimed for.

"Uh-huh. Tell me about her."

"She seems like a good woman." It wasn't enough for
Pa, so Linc provided details of Sally's family.

"Sounds like a good family," Pa said.

"I expect they are." Which about said it all. The Morgans were a good family, and the McCoys would never
achieve a similar status. Good thing Sally planned to
marry Abe. Now there was a good, upstanding man.
After all, he'd even considered it his duty to give Linc
a chance.

Not that Linc wasn't grateful. He glanced at the medicine bottle he could now refill. Yes, he was very grateful.

Though at the moment, he felt like Robbie. He
wanted to find a shovel and whack something.

"You're a good boy, Linc," his father murmured.
"Don't let anyone make you think differently."

Linc nodded. He could hardly point out that others thought differently, mostly thanks to the way Pa had acted after Ma died. But as he thought of Sally marrying Abe simply for security, he thought he understood a little better why Pa had gone a little crazy. Not that Linc would do so, but he couldn't abide the notion that Sally would settle for anything less than love and happiness simply for the sake of feeling safe.

It was almost dark before Pa settled and Linc felt free to ride Red away from town. He always took the same direction. Only now it wasn't simply to avoid passing Mrs. Ogilvy's house. Now it was because it took him the direction of the Morgan house. He rode to the turnoff, slowed enough to give the place a good study and was rewarded by the sight of Sally leaving a small fenced area he assumed was a garden spot. He watched until she stepped into the house, then he reined around and returned home.

He only wanted to assure himself she was safe and sound at home. He was only slightly disappointed to miss a visit with her. Or so he tried to convince himself, without much success.

The next morning, Sally hurried from the house before he made it halfway across the yard to the barn. "Abe says we can have a pony. He thought it was a fine idea. Isn't that great?" Her eyes sparkled like a precious gemstone. "He only says someone has to lead the pony at all times." She sobered a fraction. "Can you really get a pony?"

If only her pleasure was because they would be

working together, not because Abe approved the party plans. "I know a man who'll lend me one. And I can certainly be in charge of it during the party, if that's acceptable." Perhaps Sally, or Abe, would object to a McCoy associating with the fine children of the Golden Prairie residents.

"Knowing you were in charge would give me utmost confidence." She clasped her hands and looked excited. "I know Robbie is going to be so happy." She paused. "Do you think we should keep it a secret?"

We? She put the two of them in the same thought? He tried not to let the idea fill him with sweet pleasure but failed miserably. Yes, it was only for Robbie's party. It was only so Sally could please Abe, but nevertheless, the words rang with all sorts of possibilities.

She looked puzzled as she tried to decide what was best. "What would please Robbie more? To know ahead of time or have the pony as a surprise?"

Back to the subject at hand. "I think it would be hard for him to wait patiently. Why not keep it a secret?"

"Right." She tipped her head and her smile deepened, sending bright green shards through her irises. "There's so much to think about when raising children."

"It's likely easier if you've known them from birth."

Her smile faded slowly. "I wonder if I'll make a good stepmother."

He wanted to tell her to forget about being a step-mother, think about being—

He wouldn't allow himself to finish the thought, even though he knew he meant to say, *Think about being my wife. The mother of my children.* He knew he could never give her the solid acceptance Abe could. But again the troubling thought of last night surfaced—was security enough for a good marriage? But the worry lines creasing her forehead made him want to give her assurance. "You sincerely care about the children. I think that's important."

She nodded. "I hope so."

Linc noticed she hadn't said she loved them. Did she love Abe? He tried to convince himself he hoped she did because he didn't want to think of her in a loveless marriage. Would she choose such an arrangement simply to get the things she needed? Or thought she needed? He pushed away all disobedient, wayward feelings.

Yet errant thoughts flitted about like wild birds. She honored and valued a good name. He could not offer that, though given time, perhaps the McCoy name would stand for something besides suspicion.

He shifted his gaze to the big house. He thought of Abe's position in town and forced himself to acknowledge he had nothing to offer her. He had to remember it.

In the meantime he would help her make Robbie's birthday party a roaring success. If it enabled her to achieve her goal of becoming Abe's wife, he must console himself with the knowledge it was what Sally wanted. And he wanted what was best for her.

If only he could convince himself Abe Finley was better than a McCoy. Others would have no difficulty telling Sally it was so, but Linc believed he was equal to Abe in matters of honor and trust.

Did his friendship give him the right to ask Sally what she thought?

Chapter Nine

She was going to do this in a spectacular fashion. Sally spent hours creating invitations for each child in the shape of a cowboy hat. Besides date and time, the invitation instructed the children to wear clothing suitable for a cowboy party. Mothers of little girls in frilly dresses wouldn't want their darlings riding a pony. Nor would they want their little boys to get horse hair all over their Sunday best pants.

The day of the party arrived. Guests weren't due until after lunch, but she wondered if Robbie would last until then.

"What's the surprise?" he asked for the umpteenth time.

Sally smiled patiently, enjoying his excitement. "If I told you, it wouldn't be a surprise and I'd ruin it for you."

"I don't mind."

It was Saturday, so Abe was home. He spoke to his son. "Robbie, you have to wait. Is your room clean?"

He didn't need to ask Carol. She kept hers spotless, as if afraid to have anything out of place. Sally understood it for what it was—an attempt to be in command of her life. Like Sally, she'd learned the value of being in charge of those things she could manage. Life had too many things she had no control over.

Robbie wolfed down his lunch and bolted from the table. "Is it time to start?" Robbie stared at the big grandfather clock in the front room. "Is the clock running okay?"

"See for yourself." The huge pendulum swung back and forth with patient regularity.

He sighed and moved to stare out the window. "Maybe I better get ready in case someone comes early."

Abe looked at Sally and shrugged as if to say he was fine with the idea.

"You might be right. Run up and change." She had helped him create a real Western outfit, complete with a cowboy hat Linc had located, a vest on which she'd sewn fringes and trousers with a fringe down each leg.

He was halfway up the stairs before she finished speaking. Carol followed at a sedate pace. Sally had added a fringe to a dark skirt she found in Carol's closet and decorated a matching vest for her. Linc had donated a cowboy hat that was once his mother's.

The children returned a few a minutes later. They looked great. Abe had not seen the outfits, and blinked at first glance.

Sally's throat clamped tight. Had she made a mistake in letting the kids dress up? Was he expecting Sunday outfits? "It's a Western-themed party," she murmured, although he knew.

"Of course." He shifted his gaze to the children, allowing Sally to draw in a steadying breath. "You look like..." His pause was noticeably long. "Little cowboys."

A knock signaled their first guest. With relief, she took in the cowboy outfit the boy wore. One by one the children arrived, and all were dressed appropriately for the day's activities.

With Linc's help, Sally had set up Western-themed games—a sawhorse with a saddle for the kids to play on, another sawhorse with a piece of wood to resemble a cow's head and a lariat so the kids could practice roping it. She'd drawn the heads of several animals—a sheep, a cow, a horse, a dog—on a sheet of wood, and Linc had cut holes where the mouths were, so it became a beanbag throw game.

With Linc's help she soon had all the children involved in the games. After a bit, when things seemed under control, Linc slipped away. They'd worked it out that he would bring the pony from the front of the yard so the kids wouldn't see it until it was right there.

Sally grinned. Things were going extremely well.

Mrs. Anthony, mother of one of the little boys, must have thought the same. "This is a lovely party, Abe." She sounded genuinely pleased. "Sally has done a good job."

Only a few feet away, Sally heard every word, though she wondered if the woman was aware of the fact.

Mrs. Anthony continued. "It appears the McCoy man has helped her."

Sally stole a look at Abe for his reaction.

Abe glanced around the yard. "He's made the place fairly gleam."

"You did right giving him a chance to prove himself." Mrs. Anthony nodded approval as she followed Abe's gaze to the newly painted fence and the other improvements, courtesy of Linc.

Plump Mrs. Tipple sidled close to the pair. She darted a glance toward Sally and leaned in close. "You allow that man a lot of free rein in your yard. Aren't you the least bit concerned?"

Abe drew himself rigid in righteous indignation, although Mrs. Tipple seemed oblivious to it.

"He has done nothing to give me cause for concern. In fact, he is partially responsible for the games and the surprise yet to come."

Mrs. Tipple tried to appear regretful. "I admire your charity, Abe, but a con man is known to be charming. You must be cautious. After all, you have two young children and need I point out…an impressionable young woman?"

Abe shot Sally a startled look, which she pretended not to see as she developed a sudden interest in the way one of the children held the lariat. Would the unkind comments cause Abe to reconsider hiring Linc? The panic catching at her stomach made it difficult to straighten from her task. Her concern was only on Linc's behalf. He'd told her he needed the money he earned here to pay for his father's pain medication.

Abe shifted his gaze away, but Sally didn't relax. She couldn't, not knowing Linc's fate.

"I appreciate your concern." Abe spoke slowly. "But I'm sure you feel as I do. That a man should be judged fairly. No evidence. No crime. God warns us, 'Judge not, that ye be not judged. For with what judgment ye judge, ye shall be judged.' I'm sure none of us wishes to be condemned without evidence."

Sally's breath whooshed out. Abe was truly a good and righteous man.

Mrs. Anthony and the others murmured agreement, and Mrs. Tipple wisely withdrew, though Sally guessed from her expression she hadn't changed her mind.

At that moment, Robbie screamed. "A pony! You brought a pony! Can I ride it?"

Everyone's attention turned toward Linc as he marched across the yard leading a black and white pony. The children raced toward him. The adults drew in a collective gasp of surprise.

Abe grinned satisfaction at Sally. She flashed him a shy smile then turned her attention to Linc and the children. "Everyone line up and you can take turns riding. Mr. McCoy will lead him around for you. The birthday boy can go first."

Robbie needed no nudging. If only he would obey every suggestion so eagerly.

The other games instantly forgotten, the children lined up and waited for their turn. As soon as Linc lifted one off the pony's back, that child hurried back to the end of the line for another ride.

The sun dropped toward the west and still the children wanted to ride the pony, but Sally had sandwiches and cake to serve. The mothers had begun to grow restless. They had family obligations at home, and being a Saturday, baths to supervise and Sunday clothes to put out.

Sally clapped her hands. "Children, the pony is getting tired. He needs to rest. Why don't you come indoors for sandwiches and cake?"

They would have refused, but Linc held up his hands to signal the end of riding the animal. "Our pony needs something to eat and drink, and so do you. Run along now."

Amid a flurry of disgruntled murmurs, Linc led the pony out the back gate into the McCoy yard. Reluctantly, the children trooped inside, washed up and gathered around the table. But hunger had its place, and they wolfed down sandwiches and cake.

Sally passed Robbie his gifts. He received an assortment of crayons, coloring books, storybooks and balls. Sally had chosen two metal trucks for him. Abe presented him with a Meccano set. Robbie looked at the perforated metal strips and nuts and bolts as if the toy was broken.

"It's a building set," Abe explained. "I'll show you how to use it later."

"Thanks. Thanks everyone," Robbie said. "This is the best birthday ever."

The children cheered their agreement. Sally knew a moment of sweet victory.

Shortly afterward the guests departed amid a flurry of more "thank yous." As soon as the door closed behind the last one, Robbie headed for the back door.

"Where are you going?" Abe asked.

"To help Linc with the pony."

"He's gone home. I think you better stay here."

Robbie skidded to a halt. "Aw." He seemed about ready to defy his father.

Sally leaned over and spoke softly. "The pony needs his rest."

Robbie nodded, not eager to accept the inevitable.

"Come, Robbie," Abe said. "I'll show you how to use the Meccano set."

Robbie's expression said he didn't expect to have any fun, but he and Abe were soon creating something.

Sally cleaned up the kitchen. "I'm headed for home now," she said when the last dishes were put away.

Abe glanced up. "Thank you for the party."

Robbie bounced to his feet and ran to her. He threw his arms about her and hugged hard. "Thank you for the best party ever."

Her eyes glassed over with moisture as she hugged him back. "I'm glad you had fun." She couldn't look at Abe, embarrassed by her emotions, and simply called goodbye to them all, then slipped out the back door.

Instead of heading directly home, she went out the gate toward the McCoy place. Linc had made this all possible, and she meant to thank him.

She followed the sound of his singing into the barn where he watched the pair of horses. The pony had been brushed until his coat gleamed. Big Red allowed the smaller animal to share the hay in the manger.

Linc turned at her approach. "Party over?" He lounged against the corner of the pen, completely at ease.

She envied his ability to relax even when life was rather messy for him. It made her feel she lacked something. But she couldn't think what it could be and dismissed the thought. "Everyone is gone home, and the debris is cleaned up." She stopped at his side. Close enough to feel the heat from his body, but not touching. She knew something in her connected to him in a way she had never before experienced. The intensity of the unnamed, unacknowledged emotion frightened her. It must be denied. So she kept a space between them while allowing herself to stand close enough to feel him with every twitching nerve. "It was a great party. Thank you for making it possible."

"It was fun." He uncrossed his leg and planted both feet firmly on the floor. "Are you headed home now?"

"Yes. It's been a long day."

"I'll walk you home."

It wasn't a question, so Sally didn't answer. If she were honest with herself, she would admit she welcomed his company. Only, she excused herself, because she wanted to discuss the party. Share her sense of success.

He unwound himself from the post and they headed into the bright sun of the late afternoon.

She told him about Robbie's expression of appreciation.

"You're pleased with how it turned out?"

"Yes." Abe seemed pleased, too, but she didn't say so.

Their feet created little brown clouds of dust as they walked along the dry road. There had been only a hint

of rain this spring. The hopeful farmers put their carefully hoarded bit of grain in the ground, but nothing had
come up. Nothing would until rain came.

"The children certainly enjoyed the pony," Linc said
after a few minutes of pleasant quiet. "They seemed to
have fun with the games, too."

"It was a great day all around." She lifted her head.
The orphanage windows flashed the reflection of the
slanting rays of the sun. She slowed her steps. Linc realized she had fallen behind and stopped, turned, his
expression concerned.

"What's wrong?"

"It's not wrong. It's right." She stared at the orphanage. "That was a great party. According to Robbie and
his friends, the best ever. Seems a shame not to share
it with some other children."

He followed the direction of her gaze. "You mean—"

"Yes. The children at the orphanage. Wouldn't that
be a great surprise for them?"

Linc chuckled softly, a sound like a gentle breeze
through trees. It brought her gaze to him. His eyes were
warm as the sunshine, silently admiring her. She felt
heat steal up her neck and pool in her cheeks at the way
he looked at her, but she couldn't pull her gaze away.

"I think they would enjoy it immensely. Who do we
get permission from to do this?"

He'd fallen in with her suggestion without one word
of dissent, assuming they would do it together. It was
like having someone read her heart. Her insides warmed
to match her cheeks. "I'll ask the matron, but she won't

object. She'll be pleased as can be that the children will have this opportunity."

Linc stood at her side, shoulder to shoulder as they looked toward the orphanage. She felt his eagerness match her own. "How many children are there?"

"Twelve."

"There's a lot more room out there, so I'll borrow more ponies and we'll make games the same as Robbie's party."

"I'll make a big cake."

"I wish I could buy them each a gift."

Sally's pleasure at the generous idea filled her heart. "I don't think they will mind not having gifts."

"But—"

How her heart grew at his concern for these children. "Maybe we could think of something simple. Something we could make." She tried to think of something, but was distracted by the studious consideration on his face.

"Something small so they could each have one." He crossed his arms and studied the problem. Suddenly he brightened and faced her. "I could make little cars and trucks for the boys."

"I could make dolls for the girls."

His expression brightened with another idea. "Could you make tiny dolls?"

"I guess so. Why?"

"If Abe will let me use the leftover scraps of lumber in the shed, I could build a dollhouse."

She beamed at him. "Perfect. Just perfect."

They moved on, brimming with ways to make the party even better than Robbie's. Her turnoff was only a few yards away. She didn't want this time to end, nor did she want her enjoyment ruined by Mother's comments. "Will you attend church tomorrow?"

"I'll be there with my grandmother if Pa is resting so we can leave."

She stopped. This was where they must part ways. If only it didn't have to be. She stifled the thought before it could take root in her brain. But her thoughts proved to be stubborn today. When she was with Linc, something inside her broke free. There were many things she wanted to tell him, hopes and dreams to share.

Linc looked down at her, his eyes full of hope and promise and— "I better get back to town and take care of Pa." He touched the brim of his hat in a goodbye salute.

Regret. She saw it as clearly as she felt it, an echo of her own heart. Despite her resolve to keep her thoughts reined in, her insides suddenly flooded with secret joy that he didn't want this to end any more than she did.

"I'll see you tomorrow, if all goes well." He stepped back but didn't turn toward town.

She realized he waited for her to take the first step that would send them on different journeys. She inched backward. "See you tomorrow."

He nodded. "Tomorrow."

A promise pouring joy into her heart.

She spun around, lest he see the evidence in her face. Only once did she glance back. He sketched a salute as he headed toward town.

Tomorrow seemed a long way off.

She didn't realize how much her expression gave

away until she stepped into the house. Mother stood in the kitchen doorway, her eyes steady and observant.

"That man walked you home again."

"Yes." Guilt clawed into her heart, ruthlessly destroying her happiness.

"Does Abe know how much time you spend with that man?"

"'That man' has a name. Linc McCoy. And we were doing nothing to give Abe concern. In fact, we were discussing—"

Mother cut her off. "You better take a good look at what you are doing. Are you willing to risk Abe's displeasure for the company of this man?"

She wouldn't even speak his name. As if it was soiled. Sally knew better. Linc was a good man. Ready to help orphans. Willing to take care of his injured father. Concerned about his grandmother. But Mother saw none of the facts, nor would she welcome the words from Sally's mouth. "It was perfectly innocent."

Mother studied her solemnly, but Sally refused to squirm under her examination. They had done nothing wrong. Forbidden thoughts and wishes didn't count unless they were acted upon, and Sally didn't intend they should be.

Mother finally relented. "Very well. Just be a little more circumspect."

Sally went to the table and picked up a sock to darn. "I don't know what you mean." And she didn't. She and Linc had done nothing wrong. And what they did was in the open for everyone to see. And judge.

How would Abe judge them if he'd walked behind them?

Her cheeks stung with heat, and she bent her head so Mother wouldn't see. If he could read her thoughts he would have cause to wonder if she would make a suitable wife, but it wasn't like she hadn't done her best to control her thoughts. In the future she must do a better job.

"Robbie said it was the best birthday party ever. All the children seemed to have fun. Abe said I did a good job. He was pleased." He'd defended Linc against sly accusations.

The tension across her shoulders eased. Abe would understand and approve of Sally offering Linc friendship and acceptance. "Abe believes we shouldn't judge people without evidence. He almost scolded Mrs. Tipple for saying things that cast suspicion on Linc's reputation."

Mother joined her at the table and took up another stocking to darn. "Abe is a good man."

"Yes, he is."

"I hope you won't forget it."

"Mother." She puffed out her cheeks. "I don't intend to forget it." But Linc was a good man, too. She felt connected to him more than Abe. But then, what did she expect? She and Linc had worked together on a project that gave them both pleasure. Once she and Abe married and they spent more time together, things between them would change. They'd find things they were both keen about, like the children. She would not allow the thought demanding to know what else they had in common.

Abe was a good man with a solid reputation. He could give her what she needed. The safety and security she'd lost when her father died. She recognized a flaw in her reasoning, but would not examine what it was or what it meant.

Linc strode back to town. He found a small stone and kicked it ahead of him for several steps until it rolled into the ditch.

He'd almost asked her if he might accompany her to church. But he'd bitten back the request. She couldn't sit with him. She was more than half promised to Abe. They could only share the common goal of giving the orphanage children a special day. A smile curved his lips and eased through his insides. They had to build games, make toys. He would cut out the trucks and cars and small wooden dolls to fit in a dollhouse. She'd paint them and dress the dolls. Of necessity, they must work together to coordinate this party.

The idea settled into his thoughts like sweet tea.

The next morning Pa took his pain medication and slept. He seemed more comfortable these past few days. Linc wanted to believe it meant he was healing inside and would recover, even though the doctor offered no such hope.

He and his grandmother went to church together. Grandmama sat fifth row back on the right side, just as she had when he'd accompanied her six years ago. He sat beside her and glanced around.

Heads turned his way. Some people nodded a greeting. Just as many jerked away or gave him a hard warning stare as if to say, "We're watching you. You don't need to think you'll get away with anything this time." Grandmama, as aware as he of the murmur of disapproval rippling through the crowd, took his hand and squeezed it.

"God sees the heart," she murmured.

It should be enough. It had to be. But he felt like he'd been branded on the forehead with the giant letter *G*, for guilty. Though he'd done nothing. Nor had his father and brother. Seems not everyone was ready to believe his innocence.

Abe came in with Carol and Robbie, scrubbed and in their best. They sat two rows from the front on the left, allowing Linc a good view of them. Abe looked neither to the right nor the left. He faced ahead and his children did likewise, though Robbie squirmed until Abe quieted him with a hand on his shoulder.

Abe had given Linc a job despite the rumbles of disapproval from the sainted men and women of the church. Linc owed him for the welcome he'd offered. He was a good man. The sort who could give Sally the things she needed. Things unavailable to a man who carried an undeserved but unrelenting bad reputation.

He shifted his gaze to the cross carved into the front of the pulpit. God accepted him. God knew his heart. But a part of him longed for more. Acceptance. Not by those squirming in the pews around him. But acceptance that made him able to think of marriage, a home and a family.

He'd never find it here with the cloud hanging over his family name. Things were different to the west in the ranching country. As soon as his pa was well, he'd return to that area. This time he'd find a place of his own, and a sweet woman to court.

The idea didn't ease his mind. In fact, it sat cold and lonely in his thoughts.

Sally wasn't in the church. He didn't have to turn around to know. The most obvious clue was that she didn't sit at Abe's side. But even without that information, he knew because of the emptiness he felt.

Suddenly the emptiness flooded with light. He smiled and glanced over his shoulder. She came down the aisle behind him and sat with an older woman, one row back and across from where he sat with Grandmama. He could almost reach out and touch her. He settled for a smile and nod of greeting.

The older woman's look was less than welcoming. It must be Sally's mother. Perhaps his glance had been more revealing than he meant. He quickly faced forward again. He gaze fell on Abe. Linc sat up straighter. Why hadn't Sally and Abe sat together? His spine softened.

They probably didn't think it appropriate until they made a formal announcement.

But if he'd been in Abe's shoes, he would have no regard for what people might say or think or how they would judge. He would sit proudly by her side, cherishing each moment of her company.

He wouldn't care about others. The truth of what that meant ached through him. More proof of how Abe was the perfect man for Sally.

And Linc McCoy didn't belong in the same league.

Thankfully the pastor rose and opened the service before Linc felt sorrier for himself.

The text for the sermon was Jeremiah chapter thirty-two, verse seventeen. The pastor read it in a strong deep voice. "'Ah, Lord God! Behold thou hast made the Heaven and the earth by thy great power and stretched out arm, and there is nothing too hard for thee.'" The scripture verse and the pastor's wise words were exactly what Linc needed for the day. For the week. Perhaps for many weeks and months and years. Whatever he must do, God would provide the strength he needed.

When the service ended, he took his time exiting the pew. Perhaps by delaying, he could avoid Sally and especially her mother's demanding look. He offered his arm to his grandmother and guided her down the aisle.

Sally and her mother were gone, but his chest refused to relax and allow him to breathe easy.

Many people greeted Grandmama. Some included him. Others avoided them. Linc clamped his teeth tight at how obvious they were. Grandmama would be hurt by their behavior. He wanted to rush her home, pack his pa across a horse and ride away rather than see his grandmother treated so poorly. But of course, escape wasn't possible. Not as long as Pa was mending. Or dying. He hated to admit the latter.

They stepped into the sunshine. The pastor waited at the door to shake their hands. At least he didn't shun them.

Linc's intention was to leave as fast as he could. Get

back to his grandmother's home and his pa—his only reason for being here.

But Sally stood in the yard, surrounded by a knot of people. They all watched him. Were they waiting for him? He hesitated. Were they about to run him out of town?

Well, they could try, but he didn't intend to go anywhere until he was good and ready.

He descended the steps, Grandmama at his side.

Sally waited for them to draw near then called him. "Linc, come and meet my sister and her husband. And Mother." She introduced them. "Mother, Judd and Madge." One by one they greeted him. "I spoke to Matron about our idea of a party. She loves it."

"It's a wonderful gesture on your part," Judd said. "I understand you want to make some little toys. I have extra lumber you can use, and my barn is available if you need a place to work."

Linc allowed himself the briefest glance at Sally. Her eyes glowed with eagerness. Was it because her family supported their idea? Or was she anticipating time together, as was he? Aware of Mrs. Morgan's watchful eye, he kept his expression as bland as he could. "That sounds like a great idea. When can I have a look?"

"No time like the present," Judd said.

"Why don't you join us for lunch?" Madge added.

Linc tried to fathom if they meant Sally, too. Did they mean to encourage his wayward thoughts? "I have to take care of my pa, but perhaps later this afternoon if that's convenient?"

"That would be great. We'll see you later then." Judd and Madge moved on.

That left him and Grandmama alone with Sally and Mrs. Morgan.

Thankfully, Grandmama took Mrs. Morgan's arm. "Shall we visit the cemetery?" Grandpa was buried there. 'Peared Mr. Morgan was, as well.

Mrs. Morgan's glance at her daughter was unmistakably warning.

Linc waited until the two older women moved away before he spoke. "Does your mother disapprove of me?"

Pink stained Sally's cheeks, and she shifted so he couldn't see her expression. "She worries."

About what? But he couldn't voice the question. Didn't want the answer because she no doubt worried that Linc's reputation—the reputation hung on him by his last name—would somehow dirty her daughter. "No need. Assure her we are only concerned with giving the orphanage kids a fun party." He hoped Sally believed him.

He certainly didn't. In fact, it was time he analyzed his feelings. He'd like to ask Sally about hers as well, but wondered if the time for that would ever come.

Chapter Ten

Linc spent two hours with Pa and then headed for the farm where Judd and Madge lived. He was familiar with the Cotton farm and knew it was close to the Morgan place. When he reached the driveway, he paused to look toward Sally's house. Would she come over? She hadn't said anything after church. Would she realize they needed to discuss plans for the toys? But he understood why she might stay away. He was a McCoy, and even if he'd been someone else, she made her intentions clear—to marry Abe Finley and enjoy the sort of life he could promise.

Sighing reluctant acceptance, he reined Big Red toward the house.

Judd stepped out as he approached the house. "You like to ride?" He silently admired Linc's horse.

"Prefer it to a motor vehicle." He saw the shiny car by the house. "No criticism meant."

"None taken. I like a good mount, as well. Trouble is it's hard to find decent feed. Hard to pay for gas, too.

So mostly we walk, unless we've got a distance to go. Swing down. There's some sprouts of grass over there your horse can nibble at." He waved toward the corner of the yard.

Linc dismounted in the indicated spot and let the reins dangle to the ground. Red would graze contentedly until Linc called.

Judd followed him. "It's really a fine idea to help the orphanage out this way, you know. Anything I can do?"

"You've offered your barn and the needed wood."

"I'd like to do more if it's possible."

Linc grinned. "You want to lead a little pony around?"

Judd grimaced. "A spoiled pony?"

"Yup." His smile widened at the look on Judd's face. "They don't bite…often."

"Thanks for the reassurance. Sure, I'll help."

"Great. I thought of getting at least four ponies, maybe more. The man I know has a dozen, but we won't need that many. However, I need someone to lead each pony so I guess the number I get depends on the amount of help I get."

"Madge would help."

Linc swallowed back a protest. He'd thought of men to do the job.

Judd read his thoughts. "Don't underestimate Madge. She's pretty strong." He chuckled. "And please don't hint that you don't think she could do the job because she isn't a man. I would have to spend the next five years listening to her grouse about it."

"My lips are sealed." Linc raised a hand, as if vowing in a court of law. "You're sure she'd do it?"

"Ask her yourself." They headed toward the house—a sturdy home built to last. The barn was a solid structure, too. He remembered when the former owners, the Cottons, had built it. Although now weathered from the elements, with the paint sanded away by the continual battering of the dusty air, the place was full of promise and possibility.

He turned his gaze from studying the surroundings to the house and almost stumbled. Sally stood beside Madge, her expression a little guarded, a little wary and—he let himself believe—a touch hopeful. He swallowed hard, but it did nothing to push away the lump forming in his throat. The sun peeked around the corner of the house and highlighted her features. She was beautiful. She was lovely.

And she was spoken for.

He tried again to swallow back the thickness, and again failed.

"Sally came for dinner. She thought she should stay and help you pick out pieces of wood for the dolls. She said something about a dollhouse, too." Judd rambled on about the wood he had and suggestions as to what they should use.

Linc heard his voice, but his words were lost in the tangle of his thoughts. He hoped she'd be here but hadn't expected it. Her presence caught him off guard. He fought for control. Sanity. Reason. They were both here for only one reason—build toys for the orphanage. Nothing more. Nothing at all. Though he regretted it with an ache that yawned past the horizon and out of sight.

Slowly his thoughts righted themselves. By the time they were close enough to speak, he hoped he could do so without revealing any of his confusion.

Judd pulled Madge to his side. "Linc needs people to lead the ponies around for the party. You want to help, Madge?"

"I'd love to."

"Thanks," Linc said. His voice sounded calm and steady. "The more help we have, the more ponies I can bring."

"I could take care of a pony, too," Sally offered.

Linc hesitated. "Someone needs to supervise the games and keep the children in order. Like you did at Robbie's party." Mentioning the boy—Abe's son—was a needed reminder to himself of where Sally belonged and where Linc fit into this scheme—the provider of ponies, the builder of toys. His mind said it was okay.

Too bad his heart didn't believe it.

"Let's have a look in the barn." Judd pulled Madge's arm through his and smiled down at her as he led them away.

Linc waited for Sally and fell in at her side, keeping a discreet and safe six inches between them.

The barn smelled of sweet hay, musky mushroom, dank animal droppings—the scent of a barn used often for the purpose intended.

Judd directed them toward the far corner and a neat stack of lumber. "The previous owners left it. Most of it is too small to be of use, but will be suitable for toys."

He shoved a square tub toward Linc. "You should find something in here for the dolls and cars." He pushed aside some other pieces. "Give me a hand here."

Linc sprang forward and helped lift out some larger pieces.

"These will be great for the dollhouse."

They leaned the pieces against the opposite wall, and he stepped back to study the wood. Sally edged forward at the same time, and they bumped into each other.

He jerked forward, almost planting a foot in the tub of wood and making a spectacle of himself. He caught his balance, ignored the pain in his shin from his encounter with the metal tub and crossed his arms over his chest, hoping to signify to everyone he was completely in charge of both his body and his emotions.

Sally seemed not to notice and bent to sort through the pieces of wood.

He shuffled back, but the wall crowded him. Judd and Madge blocked the alleyway. The air in the corner was hot, depleted of oxygen, and he began to sweat.

Sally pulled out several pieces of wood, lined them up on the ground and sat back on her heels to study them. "Why don't we make them in different sizes, just like the children? Let's make a mother and father, too."

Madge knelt beside her. "Sally, you always have the best ideas."

Judd joined the girls. Linc stayed apart, arms still across his chest.

Sally glanced up at him. "What do you think, Linc?"

He shifted his gaze to the pieces of wood. He folded his tight knees and crouched beside Sally, the only place there was room. He tried to keep his distance but she reached into the tub, her elbow brushing his arm. His thoughts stalled. He couldn't breathe. It was much too hot and closed in. But when he told himself to get up and leave, his muscles refused to move.

Sally lined up the assorted pieces before him, each time her arm brushing his. "What do you think? Can we make a family of dolls from this?"

The words zinged through his mind, demanding an answer. He fished around until he could solidify a thought. "No reason why not."

"Feel free to work here," Judd said. "It'll save you hauling stuff back and forth."

They spent several minutes examining wood, choosing some for cars and trucks, some more for the dollhouse. Everyone contributed suggestions. They moved away from the lumber and moseyed toward the door, giving Linc breathing space.

"I'm going to make tea. Come along when you want a break." Madge headed for the house.

"I'll help." Judd jogged after her.

Sally remained, leaning against one side of the door, smiling as she studied the horizon. "This is going to be so much fun."

Linc pressed his shoulder to the opposite side of the doorway, the warm wood scratching through his shirt. He would have a mark on his skin, but he welcomed the pressure and the pain. Did she mean fun to work with him? Or simply fun to make toys for the children? The latter, of course. He knew that was it, but he could not persuade his mind to think along the same lines.

She shifted, favored him with a questioning look that sucked the air from his lungs. "You're certain your grandmother won't mind us using her paint?"

He'd offered to bring half-used cans from Grandmama's basement. "I'm sure." His voice grated. He cleared his throat and tried again. "It's leftover stuff. Likely most of it will be useless, but we'll find enough to paint the toys."

Her eyes gleamed with what he took for excitement. "Are you looking forward to doing this?"

"Like you said, it's going to be fun." He didn't mean only because they were doing something for the kids. To stall his thoughts before they went any further, he casually mentioned something that had been forming in his mind over the past hour or two. "I think I'll tear down Grandmama's old corrals. She's been after me to do so. With half a dozen ponies to take care of, I need something better. I figure I can salvage enough from the old ones to build something smaller and more solid." He knew he rambled. But talk was his biggest defense. Talk and distance, which right now he didn't seem capable of finding.

"How's your pa?"

"The same. Sometimes I think he's improving. Doc says not to get my hopes up."

"I'm sorry." She touched his forearm with her long, slender fingers. How did she remain so cool when his skin fairly beaded with sweat?

"Is there anything I can do to help?"

Her question, her concern sliced through his defenses, laid his heart open and vulnerable. For one sweet flicker of time he let himself think of taking comfort in her arms, pressing her head against his neck, leaning his chin against her hair.

It could not be, and he fought for reason. Slowly it returned, full of acid regret that Abe could offer her the things she wanted and he, Linc McCoy, could not. "Not much anyone can do, but thanks for offering."

She withdrew her hand, leaving him suddenly cold, his sweat icy on his skin.

"I was surprised you didn't sit with Abe at church."

Her shoulders twitched. When she faced him, her eyes had lost their happy sparkle. He had effectively reminded her of who they were and what the future held, even as she had by asking him about Pa, reminding him of who he was. "Why?"

"Isn't that where you belong?"

She lowered her gaze. "Not yet."

Did he detect regret? He half reached for her, wanting to tip her chin up so he could see her eyes, gauge her emotions.

"Come on, you two. Tea is ready and waiting." Judd's invitation jerked them both toward the house.

Linc was grateful Judd called before he did or said anything foolish. At the same time, he wondered why the man couldn't have waited a few more minutes.

Sally hugged her arms about her and smiled up into the crystal clear sky as she walked across the field the next evening. It was still full daylight out, and she was grateful for a few more hours of sunlight.

She likely should be scowling at the empty sky. The

country desperately needed rain. But she couldn't bring herself to worry about drought and hardship at the moment.

The sun poured gold into the colorless grass left over from winter. The strong light gave the budding trees a green shimmer. Spring filled the world with hope and joy. And in no place more so than her heart.

She and Linc had agreed to meet after supper and work for a few hours on toys, and Sally skipped toward Madge and Judd's place, rejoicing in the beauty of the season and all the good things in her life. Now she was about to share them with the children at the orphanage.

Her steps slowed, and she faced her thoughts honestly.

It wasn't the children filling her mind with such anticipation, but rather, the idea of an hour or two with Linc.

She stopped walking and forced her emotions under control. This was about a party for the orphans. She and Linc only shared the task of preparing for it.

Her thoughts firmly reined in, she resumed her journey, but by the time she reached the boundary of Madge's yard, her joy and her spritely step matched the sun for intensity as she headed directly for the barn.

The interior was dim and still, heat wafting from the corners.

"Hi, there," Linc called from the back. "Glad to see you made it."

"Was it ever in question?"

He didn't answer, and she made her way to the stack of lumber. He sat back on his heels watching her, his expression a combination of welcome and wariness. As if he wondered if she would suddenly realize how dangerous it was for her to agree to work with him, and might change her mind.

She wished she could erase his doubts. He was a good man and he needed to believe it, even if no one else did.

She did. But she dare not tell him. "I said I'd come and here I am." It was all she could offer.

"Great." He jumped to his feet. "Let's take this lot outside." He indicated the pieces of wood she had lined up yesterday. "I'll cut out the shapes."

"I'll sand them. Did you bring paint?"

He pointed toward an odd assortment of cans, and she squatted to examine them. From the drips on the dusty cans she saw there were several colors—green, black, pink and mauve.

"This should do nicely."

"Yep. I thought I would paint the cars and trucks that very girly pink."

His dry tone drew her eyes to his face. Slowly she pushed to her feet and grinned at his mock sorrow. Found she couldn't escape his dark eyes, didn't want to as the look went on and on. With a guilty jolt she realized she had lost all sense of time, space and decency, and lowered her gaze. Had she imagined the moment? She stole another look. No. She had not. His eyes brimmed with a warmth she couldn't deny.

Any more than she could acknowledge.

She cast about for something to otherwise occupy her

thoughts, and spied the pieces of wood laid out. "You want them outside?"

He stepped back. "It will be less stifling outside, don't you think?"

"Certainly." Though it was her thoughts crowding her lungs, not the stale hot air of the barn interior. But more space would surely help her keep her wayward mind under control, and she scooped up a handful of pieces and went out to a grassy spot.

Linc followed, carrying more wood and a jigsaw. He studied the selection of wood, chose a piece and started to cut. Within a few minutes, he had fashioned the shape of a little girl. He handed it to Sally along with a sanding block. She settled on the ground and began work as Linc sawed another shape.

He paused to consider his progress. "I feel sorry for those kids in the orphanage. It's bad enough losing one parent when you're young. But to lose both and not have any family to take you in—" He ended on a shrug.

She shuddered. "I know. I can't imagine not having family or a home. Though some do have family, but for one reason or another they can't take in another child or two. One of the girls has an older brother who works on a nearby farm, but he isn't old enough to make a home for them. Another has an old uncle." She chuckled as she thought of the man.

Linc watched her, a bemused expression on his face. "The authorities wouldn't let her live with him?"

She laughed again. "I don't think most of them would care, but he's a recluse. I don't suppose he would welcome a little girl." She held Linc's steady gaze, her thoughts traveling along the road on their own journey while she stayed caught in the warmth and interest in his eyes. "Though now that I think about it, little Janie might be the best thing that could happen to her uncle. She's a spirited young thing. I think she might force him out of his shell."

"Maybe it could be arranged."

"Maybe. But no one seems interested in confronting the recluse. Live and let live."

"Sometimes a person has to be willing to change things."

She tried to blink. Tried to tear her gaze from his. Tried and failed. It felt like he meant something more than Janie and her uncle.

He continued to speak softly. "Someone needs to tell this uncle that a little girl would benefit by having a real home. If he would welcome her, two people would benefit. Him and Janie."

She continued to stare, seeing a man who wanted things to work out in a kindly fashion. Who cared about others. Perhaps identified with their situation because of the way his life had turned out—judged without cause, shut out unfairly.

"'Course, it takes courage to confront such matters. To admit that accepting things the way they are, without examining other options, is to miss out on something better." He blinked. A shutter seemed to close over the view she'd had of his heart, and he resumed work on the piece of wood.

She couldn't move. Couldn't remember what she'd been about to say. Couldn't even think what she should be doing. She shifted, saw the doll shape in her hands and resumed smoothing the edges. He meant something besides the little girl at the orphanage and all the children there. She suspected he meant something far closer to home, but she couldn't…wouldn't let herself think he meant her…them.

She worked in silence, but between them hung a constraint like a wooden wall. She didn't like it and attacked it with words. "My sisters and I go to the orphanage on occasion. Sometimes we take cookies up to them. Or help with the garden. We play music for them or read to them. But this will be the first party we've done. It should be lots of fun. Not only for them but us, too." She couldn't seem to stem the rush of words. They poured from her mouth like a raging river. "I feel sorry for the children without parents, but they are a pretty happy lot and every time I visit I realize a person chooses how they will face life. Whether they'll wallow in misery or enjoy the good things available to them." The torrent stopped as fast as it started, and she bit her bottom lip. What had possessed her to rattle away like that?

Only one thing. Linc's suggestion that courage was required to change things.

"It takes courage to accept things," she murmured.

"True." But he sounded sad at the thought.

She had nothing more to say on the subject, and they worked in blessed silence for a few minutes.

Linc held out another shape, this one of a boy. "What do you think?"

She studied it. It resembled a figure from a chain of

paper cutouts. "With a face and clothes painted on, it will do nicely. Will it stand up?"

"I hope so." He perched it on a slab of wood, and it balanced rather crookedly. He laughed. "Looks like he's about to fall over."

"Or being a boy, maybe he's running after something."

He slanted his attention toward her. "I like your version better." His gaze was open to her.

Again she felt as if he opened his heart and soul and invited her to explore. *My, but aren't I getting fanciful? Wouldn't Madge laugh at my silliness?* She forced her attention back to her task.

And he to his. "I'll check the level more carefully on the rest of these."

The air shimmered between them, full of things she couldn't explain. They caught at bits of her heart, pulling them taut as violin strings attached from some invisible source. All it required to start a melody was someone to caress the strings.

Why did the idea fill her with both dread and excitement?

Linc held out another doll figure and laughed. "I'm trying to think what my cowboy friends back at the ranch would say if they could see me now."

She thought of several things they should say about him. Like he was thoughtful, caring, more concerned with what a child needed than what an acquaintance might say. Her lungs spasmed as she realized he had learned through harsh experience not to let what others said or thought change who he was. He could easily have become rebellious, angry. Instead, he grew patient, kind and perhaps even tolerant. "What would they say?"

He took off his hat and ran a hand through his hair, unaware he set the golden curls into a frenzied dance and left bits of sawdust behind.

"Most of them would jeer, but they'd also grab a saw and help me."

"Sounds like they're a good bunch." She stared at the flecks in his hair.

He concentrated on sawing another shape. "Don't misunderstand me. Some are scoundrels of the worst sort. Others are softies." He favored her with a wide grin. "Though they'd likely threaten to beat me into submission if they heard me say so."

Their gazes connected and clinched. She felt the sun on her shoulder, saw the way it slanted through his eyes, making it impossible for her to escape.

"You have a smudge on your cheek." He brushed it away with a fingertip, sending little sparks through her veins to pool into a sunlit puddle in the bottom of her heart.

She swallowed hard, tried to control her heartbeat, which threatened to hit runaway speed. "You have sawdust in your hair." Not giving herself time to consider her actions, she leaned closer and picked the flecks from his curls, surprised at the coarse texture of his hair. She was even more surprised by the way her heart thundered against her rib cage.

He caught her wrist and lowered her hand, resting it against his arm.

"Sally."

Her name sounded so sweet and inviting on his lips that she was caught in a web of wanting, yearning, wishing, hoping—foolish impossible thoughts all tangled into one long ache.

"Sally." His voice deepened, and he searched her gaze.

Linc held her hand against his arm. It was so small. The touch of her fingers on his head had started a stampede of emotions he feared would get out of control if she continued. He still couldn't suck in air enough to relieve the pounding of his pulse.

Yes, he knew she had plans to marry Abe. Yes, he knew her mother didn't approve of him. Why, if she knew how he felt about her precious, sweet daughter at this moment, she'd likely run him out of town on a rail.

He did not want Sally to marry Abe.

He fought for the return of reason. He could not offer her the things she wanted. Not here. Not with the judgment of local residents hanging over his head like a conviction. Maybe some other place....

He allowed himself to stroke the back of her hand. To explore the tender flesh of each fingertip before he released her and took up the saw again. "Sally." Her name tripped over his tongue like honey fresh from the comb. "Have you ever considered living anywhere but here?"

She jerked as if shocked at his words. "Never. My family is here. My home is here."

He nodded, slowly released her hand and returned to the task of sawing human shapes from scraps of wood. Her security was here. Her memories, too. Leaving and forging a life to the west obviously wasn't an option.

He paused and considered slapping himself across the side of the head. As if she would consider going anywhere with him. He had nothing to offer her.

But his heart.

Not enough.

He forced his thoughts back to creating toys for the children. Soon he had a row of little wooden boys and girls and two larger figures to represent a mother and father. He bolted to his feet. "I think I better start on the dollhouse."

He dragged out large pieces of wood, and a little later had a shell constructed. While he worked, Sally watched and continued to sand the little figures.

He stood back to study the house. "Now what?"

Sally stood beside him. "Rooms, I suppose. Maybe a window or two. Right here."

She reached for the spot at the same time as Linc, and their arms brushed.

Such a jolt ran up his nerves, she might as well have plugged him into a light socket. But he didn't jerk back. It was like their skin had been melded together by the heat. She turned her face to him, her eyes wide with shocked awareness.

He held his breath, wondering if she would acknowledge the emotions sparking in the air between them.

It seemed she had forgotten to breathe.

"Sally," he whispered.

Pink stained her cheeks. She blinked. Moved away. Turned her attention back to the dollhouse. "We need a kitchen, a front room, some bedrooms." She rattled on and on about what the dollhouse needed.

He jammed his hands into his pockets. Too bad she wouldn't admit what she needed.

Trouble was, she had, but he didn't like it because she didn't need him.

For half a minute he considered abandoning this project in order to avoid her. But he knew he wouldn't. Knew he would allow himself to savor every moment they shared.

Above all, he wanted to avoid thinking of the inevitability of it coming to an end. But it would, unless he did something. He jerked his hands from his pockets and turned to face Sally, grasping her shoulders in his palms, feeling her slenderness and wanting to pull her into his arms and protect her from every unhappiness. "Sally, I like being your friend. It means a lot to me." He wasn't saying what he felt and tried again. "But is it possible for us to be more?"

Her eyes flashed sunshine, and her lips parted.

He'd surprised her—that was plain. He wanted to say how much he cared, but he was afraid to lose what they had. If she refused even friendship…he couldn't begin to think how he'd deal with it.

She ducked her head, hiding her expression. When she lifted her face again, he dropped his hands and stepped back. Even before she spoke, he knew her answer. "I like being your friend, too." Her words were soft, pleading.

He nodded, understanding what she didn't say. It was all she could offer.

Because he did not have the stability, the reputation,

the security Abe had to offer, and she couldn't accept anything else.

"Friends it is." At the uncertainty in her eyes, he forced a gentle smile to his lips. "Friends who trust God to care for them." Would she hear his words as a challenge to trust her future to the Good Lord rather than Abe? *Please God, help her see this truth.*

Until she did, Linc would never have the place in her heart he ached for.

Chapter Eleven

Sally pretended she didn't know what Linc had suggested—something more than friendship—and succeeded in ignoring it until bedtime as she opened her Bible and prepared to read a chapter.

Overwhelming emotions tore at her heart, making it impossible to think.

Oh, Father. I miss you still. I suppose I always will.

She looked at the passage she was about to read, but the words blurred before her and she simply stared at the page, trying to sort out what she felt. Sorrow and sadness at her father's absence. Confusion over her feelings for Linc.

Yes, she had feelings for him. As a friend?

Her conscience begged her to be honest. Did she care for him more than she should? As more than a friend?

She groaned. How could she? She wasn't fickle, working for one man's approval while enjoying offers from another man. Nor was she one to run after romance and adventure. It was too risky. And that's what

Linc signified. Not stability and security. Caring about him beyond friendship made her quiver with fear, made her want to run to the little corner in the loft and build walls of hay about her.

Oh, God, help me know the right way.

Blinking away the sting of tears, she focused on the Bible in her lap. The pages fluttered in a breeze coming through the window and stopped at a place where she hadn't planned to read. The Psalms. She chose chapter sixty-eight, and at verse six read, "God setteth the solitary in families." She need not read further. God had directed an answer to her confusion. Families for the solitary. This was a sign for her. She wasn't totally alone, though she sometimes felt it. She belonged in a family, and Abe could offer her that.

Closing the Bible, she stared through the window. In the darkness a light flickered at Madge and Judd's, bringing back a rush of memories of Linc and their time together. He was a good man, even though so few were prepared to believe it.

What he offered was frightening. Like flying. People weren't made for flight. Flying was for the birds.

With determination she stuffed back every remnant of confusion. She would not falter in doing what was right for her.

The next morning she watched for Linc, wondering if he would be different after asking for more than friendship. He crossed the yard toward the barn, glanced at the house and saw her. A smile wreathed his face, and he waved.

She waved back, a weight of worry dropping from her heart. He seemed happy enough to continue being friends. She returned to her work. A few hours later, she realized she sang under her breath…one of the songs Linc so often belted out, as if his heart couldn't contain his joy.

It wasn't until Carol came home from school and they gathered for coffee that Sally and Linc had a chance to talk, though with the children present they could not speak of anything personal. She couldn't say if she was more relieved or disappointed that it was so as she handed him coffee and offered cookies from a lard pail. Her heart twisted with apprehension. Would he somehow punish her for her decision?

He accepted the coffee, chose three cookies then looked up at her and smiled. "Thanks. I've been looking forward to this all afternoon."

Dare she think he meant more than cookies and coffee? Her smile curved her lips and filled her heart as she sat beside Carol and enjoyed a cookie.

But by evening, when it was time to go to Madge and Judd's to work on toys, her doubts returned. Would he still be happy to see her?

He saw her crossing the field. "Hi, Sally." He waved and jogged out to meet her.

Her heart took flight at the way his smile welcomed her. She should have known he wouldn't let her decision affect their friendship.

"Grandmama found some bits of wallpaper she said we might like to use for the dollhouse. What do you think?" He held out a bundle of rolled paper.

She unrolled it to see several different patterns. "This is perfect. Look, I can put this in the living room." She indicated a swatch with big red cabbage roses. "This will be lovely in a bedroom." The piece had tiny pink medallions on a pale green background. "Maybe there's something for a boys' room." She flipped the pieces until she discovered a green foiled pattern. "What do you think of this?" She looked at Linc for his opinion.

His eyes were warm as fresh coffee. "I like it." His gaze did not drop to the piece of wallpaper she meant, but held hers in an endless look that seemed to hold her close.

She could not tear her gaze away. Perhaps because she did not try, though it entered her mind she should do so.

Linc let out a deep sigh and turned away, leaving her dizzy. With relief, she explained to herself. Though it felt a lot more like disappointment.

"I got here early and cut out trucks and cars." Together they walked to the hillside by the barn, where Linc had laid out the toys under construction.

They settled down to work. Sally, content to be here, sharing this project, thought Linc seemed equally at ease.

"Look." He drew her attention to Madge's cat, stalking a magpie. "He doesn't stand a chance at catching that bird."

"Macat is pretty determined. The bird harasses her constantly. She can't cross the yard without the bird diving at her."

"So it's revenge she wants?" Linc parked himself beside Sally to watch the cat.

With a great deal of effort, Sally kept her emotions under control. No reason she should be so aware of how close he sat or how his arm brushed hers.

Macat inched forward. The magpie danced away, pulling a bit of meat with her.

"The bird has stolen her dinner. Poor Macat." Why did her tongue feel so thick? Was it something she ate? She knew it wasn't.

Macat pressed to the ground and didn't move, but her gaze never left the bird who squawked as it pulled at the meat. Sally was about to give up waiting to see what would happen when Macat sprang. She leaped into the air even before the bird took flight and managed to catch the bird in her claws. But the magpie wasn't about to be caught, and flapped his wings in Macat's face. With a yowl of protest, Macat released the bird. The magpie flew to a nearby branch and scolded loudly as Macat stalked off.

Linc roared with laughter. "Poor bird," he managed to say.

"Poor Macat. She almost had him. Now the bird will make her life even more miserable."

He patted her shoulder. "The bird has the advantage. He can fly."

Fly. The word reminded her of her thoughts of last night. "Being able to fly is good." One foot seemed poised to leave the ground.

He patted her shoulder again. "For the most part, I prefer to have my feet solidly on the ground."

"Me, too." She pulled her thoughts back from the edge.

Four more delightful evenings Sally worked at Linc's side. The dollhouse was coming together well, with the dolls and trucks progressing nicely.

Her conscience was at ease about spending time with him. She was doing good work, and they had plenty of supervision, though Judd and Madge only wandered out to offer a few words then disappeared to tend to their own concerns. Most of all, she had made it clear she wanted only friendship from him, and he seemed content with her decision.

But more and more, the word friendship sounded and felt empty.

Not that she could contemplate the idea of losing his friendship. Seeing him, working with him and talking to him strengthened her for each day's work. The idea didn't seem quite right, but she didn't bother to examine it more closely. Doing so made her uneasy. Her plan to marry Abe was sound. He offered what she needed. Unbidden, not really welcome, Linc's words flashed through her mind. *Friends who trust God to take care of them.*

What did he mean? Did he refer to his own situation?

She reached the door to her home. Tonight, as every night, Mother waited for Sally as she returned from Madge's, but this time her displeasure could not be ignored. "If you weren't with Madge and Judd I would forbid this." When Sally started to protest she was doing the work for the children, Mother raised a hand to stop her. "I know you think it's only a good deed, but Sally, you need to bear in mind the dangers of spending so much time with Lincoln McCoy."

"Dangers? Do you think he would harm me?"

Mother grew very serious and insisted Sally sit down. "He could very well harm your reputation. Abe is a church leader. He is an upright man. A good man, but don't presume to take advantage of his good nature. I doubt he would overlook indiscretion on the part of the woman he is considering for his wife and the mother of his children."

Sally drew up tall and straight. "I assure you I am not being indiscreet, nor do I intend to be." She'd made it clear to Linc they could only be friends. What more could she do?

Mother sighed deeply. "I'm sure you are sincere, but sometimes, my dear, your emotions cloud your judgment."

Guilt stung her cheeks. Yes, her thoughts were not as innocent as they should be. But what could she do? She couldn't back out of this commitment to the orphans. But the truth was, she couldn't imagine walking away from what she and Linc were doing. Silently she informed her brain that what they were doing was planning a party for the children.

She would guard her thoughts and actions. She had tried her best to do so.

From now on she would strive even harder.

Every day Sally continued to work at Abe's house, caring for his children and his home and doing her best to live up to his expectations. And her own.

The afternoon after Mother had spoken to her, while she finished cleaning the kitchen she watched out the window as Robbie played in the yard. He spent less time at his fort since the birthday party, when he'd become the owner of a horse made from a wooden sawhorse with a blanket pad for a saddle and the make-believe cow he tried constantly to rope. Linc had given the boy a few lessons on roping, and Robbie could almost get a loop over the wooden cow head.

She laughed as he gave up swinging the lariat and sauntered over to drop the loop over the cow, and then backed away holding the rope and acting as proud as if he'd successfully lassoed it.

The children at the orphanage would enjoy the games and pony rides as much as Robbie. When the party was over, the children would be the proud owners of the same games Robbie now enjoyed, plus a fairly large dollhouse, various-size wooden dolls and enough cars and trucks for each boy to own one. She and Linc managed to spend an hour or two most evenings working on the project. The matron suggested they have the party the last weekend in May, lending a sense of urgency to get everything ready.

At the same time, Sally often found herself taking far longer to paint on a face, or smooth out the edges of a piece of wood than it required. The hours spent working with Linc held a special sweetness.

Perhaps Mother was right. She walked a dangerously thin line between right and wrong. However, she was determined to stay on the right side of that line.

Even while allowing herself to enjoy preparations for the party.

As Sally watched Robbie play, she told herself she was doing nothing wrong. It wasn't as if Abe had asked her to marry him, even though the understanding had been clear when she started working for him. He had told Mother what he had in mind. Sally knew and had agreed in principle. In fact, she promised herself she'd prove she could pass inspection, be a good mother, run the home efficiently. She and Linc were working together on a project, one Abe approved of, one that was good for the community and one that displayed Christian virtues. After all, didn't the scriptures command them to visit the fatherless and widows in their affliction? That's exactly what they were doing. No one could fault her on that issue.

Carol would be home from school soon, and they had begun taking the after-school snack outside. From the first, Abe had instructed her to give Linc coffee, so she did.

Not that it was a hardship. It was, if she were honest, another highlight of the day. She liked the way Linc talked with the children and told them stories about ranching in the west country.

She put the cups of sweet iced tea on a tray along with a plate of cookies as Carol clattered into the house and raced upstairs to change her clothes.

Sally waited for the girl to join her, then they went outside. Linc had built a crude bench on the north side of the house, out of the blazing sun and somewhat sheltered from the wind.

Robbie saw them and dropped his lariat to run over.

"Go call Linc," Sally said.

"I'm on my way." Linc strode from the barn, his head bare, his hair frosted with dust and wood shavings. "The barn will soon be a garage."

Then he'd be done. Abe had no more jobs for him. What would he do? Would he stay? Leave? Doubtlessly it depended on his father. Was he improving as Linc hoped and prayed he might, or fulfilling the doctor's dire prediction?

She waited to ask until they lounged against the wall of the house, indolent in the heat. "How's your father?"

Linc dangled his hands between his knees, the glass of tea empty in his grasp. "He's noticeably weaker."

"Is he going to die?" Carol asked.

Linc turned the glass round and round. "I don't know. Maybe."

"You'll be an orphan if he does."

"Hadn't thought about it, but I guess so."

"Did your mama die a long time ago?" Both children seemed keenly interested in Linc's situation.

He put his glass on the bench beside him and grasped each child by a shoulder. "My mama is in Heaven. I miss her, but I know I will see her again. If I knew the same about my pa, it wouldn't be so hard."

Robbie pressed to Linc's knee. "Mama made me promise to never forget about Heaven. She said Daddy would tell me how I could go there when I was big enough. Do you think I'm big enough now?"

Linc shared a happy smile with Sally. "Indeed I do. You talk to your father tonight."

"Do you want my father to talk to your pa, too? Tell him how to be ready to go to Heaven?"

Linc looked across the yard toward the place where his father lay. "I wish that would do it."

Carol leaned her head against Linc's shoulder. "I miss my mama. Sometimes I wish I could forget her so I wouldn't miss her so much."

Linc bent his head to rest it on Carol's forehead. "You don't ever want to forget her, even though remembering sometimes makes you ache inside. After all, she gave you life. She'd want you to be okay. To enjoy your life."

Carol nodded. "I guess so." She sprang to her feet. "I'll try my best. Come on, Robbie. I'll play cowboy with you." Robbie always wanted his sister to join him, but normally she chose to play by herself.

The pair scampered away.

Sally pressed her lips together to hold back the rush of emotion. She missed her father but would never forget him. "You're so good with them."

"I suppose it's because I know how they feel. But then, so do you." He pushed to his feet. "I better get back to my task. Will you come to work on the toys tonight?"

"I'll be there." And if she intended to be an efficient homemaker, she needed to finish supper preparations.

She spared no effort in creating a particularly nice supper. She'd purchased a roast on Abe's credit. Rich aroma wafted from the oven where it cooked. Because of the heat she'd even forced herself to use the gas stove. Abe would no doubt be impressed. She mashed potatoes to creamy perfection. The succulent gravy was without a single lump. She'd resorted to tinned vegetables, but made a white sauce for the peas and added a few tiny white onions from another can. For dessert she'd made a raisin pie. Pie baking wasn't one of her best skills, but this one turned out rather well. A white cloth covered the kitchen table and the better dishes sparkled in the late summer light.

Abe stepped into the house. "It smells great in here." He looked at the table. "Is this a special occasion?"

"No." Suddenly her efforts felt like a child trying too hard to get attention. "I just wanted to do this." Did he appreciate it? Had she done a good job, or would his wife have done better?

Why did she feel like she was on trial? Probably because she knew she was. He'd said to Mother, "If Sally proves to be adequate…" Sally had listened shamelessly beyond the door as the two of them talked. Mother had said, "She will be more than adequate." Yet she was never certain she measured up to Abe's invisible mark. A contrast to the way she felt as she painted dolls and trucks in Judd's barn. She didn't have to measure up for Linc.

Perhaps it was guilt over such thinking that compelled her to make this meal better than ordinary.

"It looks very nice. I'm impressed."

"Thank you." The children had washed until they shone, and at their father's signal sat at the table, Abe at one end, Sally at the other. She watched for him to bow his head. This time she wouldn't be caught off guard.

Without so much as a glance at the others, Abe lowered his head and said grace.

The meal was well received, the pie tasty and the children well behaved. Sally silently congratulated herself on a job well done.

Abe pushed his dessert plate away and leaned back. "Very nice, Sally. Children, you may be excused."

They pushed their chairs back and glanced longingly out the window. Sally understood they wanted to go out and play in the warm evening, but their father preferred they play indoors after supper so they went to the front room to find inside toys.

Sally rose, gathered up dishes and carried them to the sink.

Abe, for some reason, did not immediately leave the table. "Sally, sit down please. I'd like to talk to you."

Her fingers gripped the stack of plates so firmly she couldn't release them. Was he about to fire her? Or—her fingers tightened even more—ask her to marry him? She forced her hands to relax, set the dishes on the counter and returned to her chair, schooling her face to reveal nothing. "Yes?"

His smile seemed stiff. "You've worked hard. I want to show my appreciation by taking you out for dinner."

A myriad of emotions rushed to her mind—embarrassment at his praise, pleasure that he cared to show appreciation, hope his approval meant something more, fear it did. The thoughts tangled and twisted like autumn leaves caught in a tiny whirlwind. "That…that would be nice," she managed to stammer.

"Can we make it tomorrow—Friday? I've asked Mrs. Anthony to watch the children."

It would be just the two of them? Her heart banged

against her ribs. She'd never been alone with him. What would they talk about? She realized he waited for her to speak. Had he asked a question? Oh, yes, tomorrow. "That would be fine."

"I'll pick you up at your place about seven. That should give you enough time to clean up before we go out."

She looked down at what she wore. If she removed her apron would it not be good enough? Or was he referring to her hair? Only by squeezing her fingers together did she stop herself from running her hands over her mop. No doubt it was as untidy and unruly as ever. Somehow she must find a way to control it before they went out. "That will be fine." She squeezed her words from a tight throat.

"Good." He rose and left the room.

She stared at the table. Her insides felt empty, swept clean by a harsh wind. She couldn't think. Couldn't push to her feet. Suddenly a flood of urgency swept through her, sending nervous energy to her limbs. She must hurry home and find suitable clothes. Experiment with combs to tame her hair. She sprang into action, cleaned up the kitchen in record time, called a breathless goodbye to the Finleys in the other room and rushed out the back door.

By the time she drew abreast of the turnoff to Madge and Judd's place, her heart raced from her haste and she stopped to stare. She'd promised to help Linc tonight. Her gaze shifted to her home in the distance. She needed to prepare. Her eyes returned to the nearby barn. The party was planned for Saturday, and the toys needed to be finished. Linc needed her assistance.

The moments ticked past as she studied the situation, feeling as if her heart was being torn in two directions. In the end, wisdom won over emotion and she decided to hurry home. But first she needed to explain her absence to Linc. She turned her feet toward Madge's house, determined she would not change her mind.

Linc didn't go to Judd's place Friday evening. The toys were finished—the last coat of paint drying. The party was to be on Saturday. Sure, there was last-minute stuff to do, but last night Sally had said she wouldn't be there.

"Something else to do," she'd murmured, avoiding his gaze. She offered no explanation but left shortly afterward. Usually they worked at least two hours. Sometimes they joined Madge and Judd for tea and cookies. Often they set aside the work to sit in the shelter of the barn, watching the sunset. He meant to make the most of their "friendship." Every night he prayed Sally would allow more. Last night she had rushed away before he could enjoy any of those pleasures.

"Are you done reading?" Pa asked, his voice weak.

"No, Pa." He brought his thoughts back to the present and read more of the story.

After a few moments, Pa touched Linc's knee. Linc lowered the book to see what he wanted. "Why aren't you making toys tonight?"

"We're finished." Every day he'd given Pa a description of what they'd done. "The games and toys are ready to take over. We just have to wrap the smaller things and load them for transport."

"Is Sally wrapping the presents alone?"

"No. Sally had other plans tonight. Madge will look after doing it."

"Oh. That explains it."

It explained nothing. He could have gone out to Judd's if he wanted. He returned to reading so Pa couldn't ask any more questions or voice any more assumptions.

After a bit Pa grew tired and Linc closed the book. "I'm going to check on the ponies." He had brought them in that morning.

Pa nodded. "I'd like to meet Sally. Do you think she'd be willing to visit me?"

"I'll ask her." Linc could no longer deny that his father grew steadily weaker. His face had a pasty color. He ate nothing and drank very little. He'd be pleased if Pa met Sally while he was well enough to appreciate her fine qualities. Oh, but how he hated to admit his father was dying. Needing to find release in physical work, he hurried outside. He had completed one pen to hold the ponies, but an old section near the corner of the barn still needed to be rebuilt.

As he lifted heavy posts and nailed salvaged planks, he prayed for his pa. *Lord, please don't let him die before he chooses to prepare for Heaven. Give him enough days. Please.*

He'd taken down most of the old corrals, allowing a clear view from Grandmama's kitchen window into the Finley backyard. Soon that was all he'd have—a view. He'd about finished converting the barn for Abe. He was grateful for the work the man had provided. But what next?

He didn't know. He felt as if his life had stopped. Except for the time he spent in Sally's company, when he felt more alive than he could remember. He stopped hammering nails and stared at the Finley yard. He'd tried to tell her how he felt, but she'd stopped him. Did Sally consider herself duty-bound to proceed with the agreement with Abe? Was it really what she wanted? Would she consider something else? Maybe something not as solid as what Abe offered, not as secure, but safe in that his love would never be conditional.

The way his smile stretched his mouth, he was glad no one could see him standing there grinning up into the sky. He loved her and freely admitted it. Seemed until she and Abe made formal promises to each other, it was fair to let her know. But every time he came close to saying something, she shied away as if knowing the words on his tongue and not wanting to hear them. Yet he couldn't miss the way her eyes sought his, her expression tentative until he gave her a smile as full of assurance as he could manage. He let himself believe she needed his approval, his acceptance…his love… although she wasn't ready to admit it.

Given time, she'd realize love was more important than anything else she had her heart set on. He saw no reason to hurry. One of these days she would be willing to trade security for love.

He went back to building the fences, hope exploding through him until he wanted to shout. Instead, he settled for singing loudly, not caring who heard or what they might think.

Mother had helped Sally alter a dress. They'd removed the soiled collar and given it a plain neckline. It wasn't the latest fashion, but Sally thought the dark blue satin suited her. Four combs half subdued her curls. She would have to slip out to the ladies' room partway through the evening and do it over.

"Here he is." Mother tried to sound nonchalant as Abe drove up in his big car, but she missed doing so. "He's coming to the door."

Nervousness set in with the grip of a winter storm. "Mother, do I look okay?"

"You look fine. Really fine." She hadn't said so, but Sally knew she hoped this evening would produce a firm offer of marriage from Abe. Mother would not be happy until she made sure all three of the girls found good men to marry. She was satisfied with Judd and Emmet as mates for the older girls. And only Abe would do for Sally. Linc's face flickered across her thoughts. Mother didn't approve of him. She'd even gone so far as to list her reasons. No home. A shady family history. A bit too brash for her comfort.

Abe knocked.

"Goodbye, Mother," she murmured as she went to the door.

Abe stepped in at her invitation. "I'll have her home in good time, Mrs. Morgan."

His assurances might have pleased Mother, but they made Sally feel about as old and responsible as Carol.

However, he held the door for Sally and complimented her on her dress, so she pushed aside any resentment.

"I thought the hotel dining room would be nice."

She hadn't thought to ask where they would eat. The dining room at the hotel was the fanciest place in town, where visiting dignitaries ate, where travelers on the railroad ate. Or at least they had before the Depression hit. Not many people visited anymore.

But the dining room still operated, still gleamed with a polished wooden floor, tables covered in white linen set with sparkling china, silverware and glasses.

Young Alice, wearing a black dress and a little white apron, hurried forward as Sally and Abe stepped into the quiet room.

"Hi, Alice," Sally greeted the girl.

"Welcome. Please let me show you to a table."

She'd known Alice since the Morgans moved to Golden Prairie. The girl had been three years behind her in school. If even Alice felt it necessary to be formal in this place, it must be reserved for serious business only. Sally's nerves returned.

She sat when Abe held the chair. She took the black clad menu when Alice practically placed it in her hands. The menu offered a four-course meal with little in the way of options, and she gladly let Abe order for them both.

They received steaming bowls of beef noodle soup, and she gratefully turned her attention to it.

The soup bowl was empty far too soon. The air around them drowned in quiet. Only two other parties dined. A pair of businessmen poring over documents and a very stern man with a younger woman across from him. They had little to say to each other.

Sally stole another peek at them. They might have been herself and Abe.

Abe leaned back as they waited for the next course. "When is this party you are doing for the orphans?"

"Tomorrow."

"So soon?"

"Yes." She couldn't remember the last time she'd been so tongue-tied and unable to add anything to a conversation.

"Are you ready?"

"Apart from a few last-minute details."

"Good. It's a very nice thing to do." He cleared his throat and continued. "I'm pleased you are concerned with the less fortunate in the community."

"Thank you." She barely met his gaze, but even so, her eyes stung with embarrassment.

Thankfully Alice served a salad. They scarcely finished before she put the roast beef meal before them.

The pair of men shuffled their papers and sat back as if done with their business. The man and woman lingered over tea, neither of them speaking. Sally wondered if Abe was aware they were equally silent.

The plates were whisked away, and Alice brought chocolate mousse served in very pretty glass bowls. Sally tasted it, sweet and rich. It clogged her throat and she set aside her spoon.

"Is there a problem?" Abe asked. "We could send it back. Get something else."

"No, it's fine. I'm full." She wondered if she could swallow anything…more from tension than eating too much, however.

Abe ate his dessert and sat back. When Alice appeared at his side, he asked to have the table cleared and tea brought.

The tension in Sally's nerves increased with every passing moment. Alice set a pot before her and asked if she wanted to pour.

Sally shook her head. "You do it." She wondered if she could lift a cup to her mouth, let alone pour from a full pot.

Then they were alone. The businessmen departed. At some point the other couple had silently stolen away.

"Sally." Abe's voice startled her. "I brought you here for a special reason."

She nodded.

"I'm very pleased with how you manage my home and how the children have settled down."

Her gaze crept to him.

"I think it is time to make our arrangement formal. Sally, would you become my wife, a mother to my children?"

She stared at him unblinkingly. Was that all there was? No word of love or affection or promise of forever? Of course, the latter was understood.

"You will be free to run the home as you see fit, so long as you maintain the standard you have shown yourself capable of. I will see you have a reasonable allowance for household expenses and your own needs. You will be well taken care of."

He offered security, safety. Her tension eased. It was what she wanted. What she'd prayed for. If a tiny rebellious part of her wondered if there could be more, she pointedly ignored it. Abe meant all the things that had disappeared when Father died. Words from Linc's mouth reverberated through her head. *Friends who trust God to take care of them.* Surely this was God's way of taking care of Sally. She tried to fill her lungs, but they seemed to be made of wood.

"I accept."

Abe's smile was genuine. "Very good. I'm pleased. Come." He got to his feet and eased her chair back. "We're done here."

She waited as he took care of the bill and then let him lead her back to the car. He settled her inside and closed the door firmly. The click of the latch echoed in her head.

He turned the car back toward home, but stopped at the bottom of the driveway and turned to her. "I didn't buy you a ring. We can wait until we get married. But I'd like to seal our agreement in the time-honored way."

She had no idea what he meant.

"With a kiss. If I may?"

"Oh. Of course."

He leaned toward her. She leaned toward him. Her hands remained demurely in her lap. One of his hands rested on the steering wheel, the other on the back on the seat, bare inches from her shoulder. They met halfway. His lips were firm and cool as they touched hers for one second. Another. She didn't know if she was expected to pull back first or if he should be the one.

He sat up.

She straightened.

"I need to get back to the children."

"Of course."

"Do you want me to inform your mother?"

"No. I'll tell her if that meets with your approval."

"That's fine. I could make an announcement at church on Sunday."

"Do you mind waiting a few days so I can tell my sisters before they hear it from some other source?" She'd have to write Louisa.

"Of course. I should have considered that."

They reached the house. Abe jumped from the car, and she waited for him to open the door for her. He held out his hand and helped her alight. Apart from the kiss, it was the first time he'd touched her.

But it wouldn't be the last.

She better get used to the idea. "Thank you for the nice evening."

"My pleasure." He walked her to the door, bowed formally and stepped back.

She hurried inside and pressed her back to the closed door, listening for him to drive away. As the sound of the car faded in the distance, she turned to the kitchen where Mother awaited.

As she crossed the floor, her legs began to vibrate so hard she barely made it to the nearest chair.

Mother looked up, her expression one of anticipation. As soon as Sally sat down, Mother reached across the table and took her hands. "Oh, my, your hands are like ice."

Sally nodded. The coldness went clear through to the marrow of her bones and the deepest depths of her heart.

"Did you have a nice evening?" Mother leaned forward, anxious to hear all the details.

Sally could recall nothing of the evening save for one thing, which she blurted out. "Abe asked me to marry him and I accepted."

"Thanks be to God. I've prayed daily for each of my girls to find a good, solid man."

Abe was that all right, but shouldn't she feel something besides admiration? "Mother, am I doing the right thing?"

Mother gave their clasped hands a shake. "Of course you are. Why do you ask?"

"I'm not sure."

Mother tsked. "I saw this coming. You've spent too much time with that McCoy man. You've let his charm sidetrack you. Sally, charm is deceptive and for the most part, self serving."

Linc wasn't self serving. But Sally knew if she tried to defend him she would never hear the end of it. "Shouldn't I feel something...well, special?"

"For Abe? Certainly you should. But love isn't simply an emotion. It's a decision, as well. Choose your love wisely, and it will grow to maturity."

"Did you choose Father wisely, or did you feel something in your heart that couldn't be explained or dismissed?"

Mother smiled. "Your Father was a good man. I loved him deeply. But—" Her expression hardened. "It was the fact he was a good man that allowed our love to grow."

Sally wanted the kind of love her parents had. Was it built on choosing wisely or loving deeply? Must she choose between the two? Could they not be found in the same person? She vibrated with a chill.

"Sally, you are young and impressionable. But there are certain things you simply can't ignore and hope to be happy in the future. You thrive best in an organized, safe and secure world. Abe can offer you what you need. You thought so when you went to work for him. What has changed since then?"

Safe, organized? These concepts were supposed to make her feel secure. Yet they also seemed constricting. As if her wings had been clipped, and she'd meekly allowed herself to be placed in a gilded cage. "Nothing's changed." Tears clogged her throat, but she would not weep and let Mother guess at how confused she was. In Mother's mind, there was nothing to be uncertain about. Abe was simply the best choice for Sally. No questions allowed.

"Then I believe you have chosen the right path in accepting Abe's offer of marriage."

Sally nodded, mute with emotions she couldn't name.

"Sally, your father would be very proud and happy at this moment. Don't you recall how he often said, 'A good name is rather to be chosen than great riches'? He would approve of Abe as a husband for you."

"He would, wouldn't he?" She sucked in air until her

insides had room for nothing more. No more doubts. No more confusion. No more comparison between Abe and Linc. She had chosen the man most suitable to her needs. One her mother approved of. She'd soon enough get comfortable with the idea.

Chapter Twelve

Linc arrived at Judd and Madge's place at noon, as he and Sally had agreed. Judd and Madge were climbing into their car as he swung off Red. "We have to leave right away," Judd explained. "We promised to help organize the children. We'll see you at the orphanage in a few minutes." They drove away, leaving him alone.

He hadn't realized how dusty and dry the yard was until they departed. The wind had a lonely sound to it as it whined around the corner of the barn.

Shaking his head to clear away such thoughts, he turned his mind to anticipation of the afternoon and chuckled for no good reason other than he and Sally would be working together. His grin widened as he went to the barn to wait for her.

The party was going to be barrels of fun. He'd already secured the ponies a quarter of a mile from the orphanage to produce an hour into the party. He let himself picture the children jumping with excitement when he led the ponies to the orphanage. Doing something for these parentless children filled him with joy.

Sally drove in and parked the old rattletrap of a car at the barn door. The wind's whine turned to a hum. The yard no longer seemed dry and empty. He leaned against the door jamb as she climbed from the car. She wore a flowery cotton dress in shades of blue that brought to mind endless summer. Her brown curls danced in the wind. The sun flashed across her face, turning her eyes pine tree green. Her skin glowed like the pretty china Grandmama kept in her cupboard. Taking the party to the orphanage with Sally at his side was going to be better than any Christmas he could remember.

She closed the door and turned, suddenly noticing him. Her hand remained poised midair. Her smile of greeting turned to a look of surprise. "Linc?"

He knew he didn't imagine the tentative eagerness in her voice. He didn't care that she'd read his thoughts and was uncertain what to do. There was no uncertainty in his mind. He wanted to pull her into his arms and speak the words of love crowding his brain. He half reached for her, then changed his mind and crossed his arms over his chest. If he kissed her at this moment, admitted his love and received hers, they might well forget the task ahead of them. Now was not the time or place.

Except perhaps it was. They were alone, and how likely was that to happen again today? Somehow he would make certain it happened. He'd manage to find a time when they were by themselves and free from outside obligations so they could enjoy sweet confessions of their feelings. "My pa would like to meet you."

"He asked?"

"Why is that so surprising?" His words were slow and lazy. He wondered she didn't read his love simply from his tone of voice.

"He doesn't know me."

Linc chuckled. "Which is why he wants to meet you. He likes to hear about my day. You're part of that."

She studied the flat dry landscape. The seconds ticked by. He thought he heard a clock marking time then realized it was his heart. Was she reluctant because of his father's reputation? "My father did not steal those jewels."

Her head came round. "I didn't suggest he did."

"You haven't agreed to see him."

Her eyes didn't quite meet his. "Of course I'll meet him. Why wouldn't I?"

Because people might consider it foolish. But he wouldn't say the words aloud. She'd agreed. That was enough. Once she met Pa, once she'd heard Linc's confession of love, she would change her mind about Abe and grow comfortable visiting in Grandmama's house. "This afternoon after we're done with the party?"

"If it works out." She shifted her attention to the stack of toys. "We better get this stuff loaded. The children will be waiting."

"Let's get to it." He'd wait for a time and place when she wasn't distracted by other things to tell her how he felt.

Madge had wrapped the smaller gifts and labeled them for each child. They stowed the games in the back. Sally draped a sheet over the dollhouse, and they managed to cram it in, as well. Then Linc crawled into the passenger side, edging himself in between the saw horse that would become the body of a cow and the piece of wood shaped like a cow's head for the kids to rope.

They drove up the hill. Madge and Judd, plus two young ladies who accompanied the children to church each Sunday, had the children lined up on the step awaiting Sally and Linc's arrival. The children knew there was to be a surprise, and they looked ready to explode in twelve different directions as they waited.

Sally grinned at Linc. "Have you ever had such an eager welcoming party? I know I haven't."

"Must confess I haven't, either." Though he had allowed himself to dream of being welcomed by a hazel-eyed, curly-headed woman. And perhaps, in time, a few children. He pushed those thoughts to a corner of his mind to wait. For now he must think of these children and give them a fun party they'd never forget. He knew what it was like to lose his mother. Soon he'd know what it was like to lose his father. He also knew what it felt like to be on the fringes of society—tolerated more than accepted. Today he would focus on proving to the children that people cared about them and wanted them to have fun. His private concerns would have to wait.

The children strained forward. Linc and Sally remained in the car. He turned to her and grinned in anticipation of the next few hours. He grabbed the wooden cow head and the saw horse. "Are you ready?"

She lifted the beanbag board and nodded. In unison they stepped out. Together they set up the two games.

All the adults yelled "Surprise!" Then the helpers released the children, who swarmed Linc and Sally.

"It's a party," Sally shouted over the melee. "Games and cake."

The kids were soon enjoying the games. Linc shot Sally a look of pure pleasure, underscored with admiration and love.

She grinned back, then, seeing what his eyes said, her mouth sobered. She turned to little Johnny at her side.

But he'd seen something in her eyes, too. A guarded awareness. A promise of more. He clamped his teeth together to stop a shout of joy from escaping.

Soon it was time to bring the ponies up the hill. Linc slipped away, welcoming the chance to think. Having admitted to himself he loved Sally, he discovered his heart was capable of so much more than he had known. Even though his attention was on the children, he heard her voice, felt it surround his heart like a hug. Even without looking, he was aware of every move she made, almost as if something invisible—but tough as the strongest lariat—stretched between them. As he led the ponies he rehearsed what he would say to her.

Billy, the rowdiest of the kids, spotted Linc. "He brung us horses!" With a whoop echoing for miles, Billy headed directly for the ponies. Only the fact that the animals spent most of their lives in a circus, carrying rambunctious children on their backs day in and day out, kept them from reacting.

"Slow down, Billy," Linc called. "You'll scare them."

The boy took one more step, then seemed to consider the consequences if he continued his headlong rush. "Can I help lead them?"

"Sure. Here. Take this rope." He let Billy lead the second pony, knowing nothing short of a tornado would persuade it to leave the others.

The rest of the children waited noisily.

Sally organized the children, and Linc handed a pony off to each of his helpers. Little eight-year-old Sharon's older brother, Andy, took one. Judd and Madge each took a pony, leaving Linc with the last.

"We'll start with the oldest children." Besides getting noisy Billy on one, Linc figured it would give the more nervous younger kids a chance to see how safe riding the ponies really was.

A little later, he looked at the kids lining up for a second ride. But by his count, only ten had ridden the ponies. He glanced around to find the missing two. A tiny girl sat under the lone tree in the yard, two fingers in her mouth. Her big blue eyes studied him across the space separating them.

Linc turned to Sally, who tried to persuade some of the children to return to the games. "Is that Emmy?"

Sally nodded. "She's a fearful child. I don't think she'll get within shouting distance of these animals."

The fear in the child practically scorched him from across the dusty grass. She pressed back, as shy as a fawn. "Here." He handed the rope of his pony to Sally. "I'm going to talk to her." He strode over and sat beside Emmy, his legs sticking out several feet in front of them. Sort of made him feel awkward and protective at the same time.

"Hi, Emmy."

"Hi," she mumbled around her fingers.

He put the child at about four or five. Awfully young to be without either mother or father. It took two hard swallows to get rid of the lump choking him. "You ever had a pet?"

The fingers came out of her mouth and she studied him, her eyes wide and hungry, making his throat tighten until he could barely breathe.

"Once I had a kitty. Miss Dolly. Before Mama and Papa and baby May died." Tears pooled in her eyes and threatened to overflow.

If she cried, he would be sorely tempted to join her. Instead, he forced his voice to work. "Kitties are nice. Soft and cuddly." He tore his gaze from the child's and looked toward the ponies. Sally watched, her smile a little uncertain, and in that moment he knew they felt the same regret, the same sadness over the plight of little Emmy. Again it seemed something reached from his heart to hers, binding them together. He knew it was love. Two hearts beating as one. Two souls feeling as one.

"I miss Miss Dolly," Emmy whispered on a shudder.

He guessed Miss Dolly was not the only thing she missed, and his heart twisted so tight he wondered it could still beat. "One of those ponies over there is hoping a little girl named Emmy will choose to be his friend."

She shifted her attention. "They're awfully big."

"Nah. They're not that much bigger than a full-grown kitty."

Emmy laughed, a sweet tinkling sound. "Kitty that big would sure scare away the mice."

Linc let out a roar of laughter. The little one had a sense of humor hidden behind her fear. Who'd have guessed it?

Sally's eyebrows came up, as if asking to share the joke.

Linc bounced to his feet and held out his hand to Emmy. "Come on. I'll show you what nice pets they are."

Emmy considered the ponies, considered his hand then stared into his eyes.

He let her see that he meant her no harm...that he liked her and wanted to help her, wanted to be friends.

Holding his gaze in trust, she took his hand and walked to the ponies. Allowing Sally to continue holding the lead rope, he picked up Emmy, amazed at how little she weighed. "Now this here is Pat the pony. He likes being petted."

Pat hung his head and never so much as twitched a muscle as Linc rubbed his hide and scratched behind his ears.

"See. Just like a big cat."

Emmy giggled and reached out one tiny hand, but quickly drew it back and buried her head against Linc's neck.

He had never known anything half so sweet as the feel of the little girl in his arms. He met Sally's gaze and knew from the look in her eyes that she guessed his reaction, and he wondered if it would make it easier for her to accept his confession of love. Perhaps in the future he would hold a tiny girl like this with a mop of curly hair and big hazel eyes like Sally's.

He pushed back a rush of emotions and turned his attention back to sweet little Emmy, who gave him blue-eyed consideration. They studied each other for several seconds, then she smiled. He smiled back. Mighty good thing she couldn't read his mind, because if she could, she'd know she could have asked him for the moon at that moment, and he would have tried to rope it and give it to her.

"Why don't you sit on old Pat's back for a moment? He'll think you don't like him if you refuse."

Emmy considered Pat's sad appearance which, in Pat's case, was a permanent state. "Okay. But you have to keep hold of me."

"I will. I promise." He perched her on Pat's wide back, his hands around her waist.

She clutched his arms.

He lifted his gaze to Sally's across the horse. Let her see how much he enjoyed holding Emmy and protecting her. Let her see all that his heart held…hope for a future full of love and little children. Shared with her.

Her eyes widened and turned pine green. Her cheeks blossomed pink roses. She opened her mouth. Closed it again and jerked away to stare across the yard.

Emmy squeezed his arm hard. "'Nough."

He turned his attention back to the child and lifted her from the horse. She clung to him, her feathery hair tickling his nose.

But one more child had still not ridden a pony. "There's someone missing," he told Sally.

She glanced about. "Claude Knowles. He was here earlier playing beanbag toss. I wonder where he's gone."

Billy overheard them. "Claude's a big crybaby. He's probably hiding inside 'cause someone laughed when he missed every single hole in the game." He made a sound of derision. "He should have been a little girl."

Linc handed Emmy to Sally and squatted down to Billy's eye level. "Son, it pains me something awful to hear you made a younger child unhappy." Billy's expression grew hard. If Linc didn't miss his guess, the boy meant to make someone pay for Linc's reprimand. He didn't want to be responsible for that happening. "I had a big brother. Harris was his name. He spent hours teaching me how to bat a ball. He taught me how to skate and showed me how to pretend sword fight."

Billy's eyes lit up at the mention of sword fights.

Linc knew he had to do more damage control. "We only used little bits of wood and never ever hurt anyone. My point is, my brother helped me learn to do stuff I didn't know how. Probably would have never learnt if not for him."

Billy considered him curiously. "So where is your brother now?"

"Billy, I buried him a few weeks ago. He was killed in a mining accident." He wiped his hand across his face. "He was a good big brother. I will always miss him."

Nodding sympathy, Billy turned away.

Linc could only hope and pray Billy would choose to help the younger ones in the home rather than mocking them.

"I'm going to see if I can find Claude." He let himself enjoy Sally's wide approving smile, then turned away to search for the boy.

Matron assured him Claude was not in the house, so he circled the yard and found the boy nearly invisible as he pressed to a wooden box in a corner near the road, where he could observe the activities from a very safe distance.

He sat beside the boy. "Claude. You gonna join the others?"

"No."

"Miss Sally and I sure would like it if you did. And there's a pony waiting to give you a ride."

"I prefer not to ride a pony, thank you."

"Okay. But maybe you can tell me why not."

"Don't care to."

Linc considered the statement, but discovered he didn't believe it. "Fine, but everyone gets a turn."

"I don't want a turn. Thank you, anyway."

Linc got to his feet, walked up the little hill, took the pony from Sally and led him to Claude. He sat beside Claude again with the pony's lead rope in his fist. "Everyone gets a turn. It's up to you how you use it. You can ride or not."

Claude didn't answer, though Linc felt his careful, guarded study of himself and then the pony.

In a few minutes, Linc got to his feet. "Time for everyone to get a second turn." He hoped Claude would realize Linc included him.

Sally waited until he had one of the children on Pat's back to whisper, "What was that all about?"

"He's ready for adventure but needs a little encouraging."

He gave all the children another ride, let Emmy sit on Pat's back with Linc's hands holding her, then took the pony down to Claude again. Still Claude didn't move.

Another round of rides. This time Emmy allowed Sally to lead the pony a few steps, so long as Linc remained at her side.

As soon as Emmy was done, Linc took the lead rope and went to Claude. Before he got there Claude bolted to his feet. "I'll ride."

"Up you go then." He lifted the boy, pleased at the look of triumph on the child's face. His gaze connected with Sally's, and a bolt of joy shot up his spine at her blatant approval. Then she glanced away, as if aware of how much she'd silently communicated.

He hoped she wasn't wishing she could take it back, and pressed tight to his heart the sweet knowledge of how she felt.

They spent the next two hours giving the children rides. Several times he caught Sally watching him. As soon as she saw that he saw, she looked away, pretending to be terribly busy with something else. But not so fast that he didn't see a flash in her gaze that made him wonder what she was thinking and when she would tell him. He almost laughed aloud at the sweet assurance that she seemed more aware of him than she might be willing to admit.

Later, she'd meet his pa. He hadn't realized how much he wanted it until now. He didn't want to be an outsider anymore. He wanted to be accepted by the community as an equal. A person to be respected. He wanted to be accepted by Sally, her friends and family.

Sadly, he guessed, unless he achieved such acceptance, Sally would continue to have doubts about him. Security was so important to her and meant more than a permanent address. It included things such as safety, a solid job and a secure position in society.

And yet, what more could he do than what he was doing? Live an honorable life. Attend church. Help others. *Lord God, help people to see that I am a good man.* God accepted him. So did his grandmother. But it was no longer enough.

The ponies were tiring. "Time to let them rest."

"Aw. One more ride," Billy begged. The others anxiously but silently added their request.

"'Fraid not. But why don't you see what Sally has in the car for you?"

As they turned her direction, she laughed and raced them to the car, arriving seconds ahead of the older children. She stood, her back to the car, and waited for the younger ones to catch up and for the adults to join them. Her face glowed with joy and her curls bounced around her head.

Linc handed the ponies off to the others, who were to take them back to the shelter and feed and water them. Then he jogged over to help Sally. He edged past the children and stood shoulder to shoulder with her at the side of the car. For a moment, he let himself swim in the pleasure of her nearness, her warm skin against his, her wildflower and cinnamon scent filling his senses.

The children pressed closer, reminding him of where

his thoughts belonged. "Okay, you lot. Back up two steps and sit in a semi-circle."

They tripped over each other as they obeyed.

Linc took Sally's hand, telling himself it was necessary in order to pull her to one side. He didn't believe it, but perhaps the others did. He opened the door and handed her the wrapped dolls to distribute to the girls. He took the wrapped trucks and passed them to the boys. Then he and Sally leaned against the warm side of the car, their shoulders again touching, and watched the children unwrap presents.

He loved the expressions of joy on each face. "They really like the gifts."

"Not often they get something for no reason."

"Then I'm glad they learned there doesn't have to be a reason to do things for people we care about." He wasn't sure what he was talking about, except it wasn't only about the children. Did she hear the way his voice caught in his throat as he mentally put her on top of the list of people he cared about? Could she tell he meant to do everything in his power to make her happy?

The children were about to move away to play with their toys. "Hang on a minute."

Sally grinned at him—sending his heart into full gallop—as they pulled the dollhouse from the car, hidden under a draped sheet. "Katie, do you want to take off the cover?"

The tiny girl with a tangle of blond hair shyly came forward. She pulled off the sheet and stared at the dollhouse. It was the oldest girl, Maddie, who said, "It's a dollhouse."

The girls oohed and aahed as they gathered round to examine it. Soon they were putting their dolls in various rooms.

The boys looked disappointed. "Who wants an old dollhouse?" Johnny muttered.

Linc chuckled. "It's a new dollhouse. But you boys get to keep the wooden horse and cow and the bean bag game. You can practice riding and roping and tossing beanbags." Whooping their joy, they raced back to play.

Linc sighed. It felt so good to bring joy to these children.

Sally moved to his side. "It's great to see them enjoy themselves."

"It is indeed." He readily admitted he got as much pleasure out of sharing the day with her as in seeing the children have such fun.

Judd had slipped away a few minutes ago and now returned, Mrs. Morgan beside him in his car.

"Here's Mother with the cake." Sally hurried to help her.

Linc's heart dropped to the soles of his feet. Mrs. Morgan made no secret of her disapproval of him. She nodded a sober-faced greeting to him and favored the others with a wide smile. The children called, "Hello, Mrs. Morgan."

"I wonder if they'll be able to tear themselves away from the toys to eat cake," Madge said.

The matron laughed. "I doubt we'll have to call them twice."

A table had been carried outdoors. Sally placed the cake on it and called, "Who wants cake?"

Linc laughed when the children left their toys immediately.

Sally laughed, too, and he allowed himself to glance at her. Their gazes caught, full of shared warmth and something more. Something he hoped went far deeper than pleasure over the children. Something that would meet the deepest needs of his heart and allow her to admit her love for him because, more and more, he was convinced she loved him even if she didn't yet acknowledge it.

Mrs. Morgan nudged Sally and she jerked away, suddenly very interested in adjusting the cake so it was precisely in the middle of the table.

Linc shifted his gaze to meet Mrs. Morgan's warning stare. He held steady for a heartbeat, silently informing her he would not be intimidated, and then he turned to watch the children who each ate two pieces of cake then dashed back to their play. The adults lingered over their thinner slices, served with tea.

"This was a great party," the matron said. "Thanks to Sally and Linc for their hard work."

The assembled adults clapped.

Linc grinned at Sally, not caring if his look was tender, telling. Let Mrs. Morgan think what she wanted. Let the others speculate. "We're now old hands at this, so if anyone wants to reserve our services for a future party…" Sally's eyes darkened, warning him not to go too far. "Well, I'm sorry to say we won't be available."

Judd clapped him on the back. "How long are you hanging around?"

The question, innocent enough, reminded Linc they

all saw him as transient. Perhaps hoped for it. "I've no plans."

Mrs. Morgan didn't sniff. Yet her expression said as much as if she had. *A man with no future.*

He didn't mean it that way. "I can't make plans until I see how my father does."

Judd murmured sympathy. "Sally says he isn't doing well."

"I hope and pray he will get better, but the doctor doesn't offer any encouragement."

Sally turned to him, her eyes awash in understanding. "I can't imagine how difficult it is for you. I remember when my father died. It was hard to watch him go downhill, but at least he didn't linger for ages in pain. I guess, in hindsight, I should be grateful."

Her concern touched him in a spot deep inside that he had not been aware of until this very moment—a tender spot that welcomed the balm of her sympathy.

The others remained quiet, as if lost in their own sorrow.

Madge broke the silence with a long sigh. "I miss him a lot."

They drew together to hug each other, Mrs. Morgan in their midst.

Linc stood outside the circle. He was tired of being on the outside looking in. He wanted more—to be accepted, to belong, to matter. To be part of a family.

Mrs. Morgan straightened. "We all miss him, but he would want us to get on with our lives. I want you to come to dinner tomorrow after church."

Linc understood she meant her family. Sally knew, too, but at least she managed to look a little regretful.

The sisters gathered up the remnants of the tea and carried them to the house. Judd watched one of the boys trying to throw the lariat and hurried over to help him. The littlest child fussed, and Matron picked him up and headed for the house.

Linc's nerves twitched as he realized he was alone with Mrs. Morgan. He glanced about for something to take him elsewhere, but before he chose a direction, she began to speak.

"My oldest daughter married a young rancher. They're doing well for themselves and their two daughters."

Linc nodded without comment.

"Judd bought the Cotton farm, and they have a good solid home. He will no doubt do well once this drought ends."

"Which will be soon," he murmured. "God willing."

"Amen to that."

He could think of nothing more to say. He didn't need an advanced university degree to understand why Mrs. Morgan had told him these things. She meant for him to understand her daughters married men she approved of. Not men like Linc, with a tainted past and an uncertain future.

He wasn't good enough for her daughter.

But he wasn't about to let her make his choices. He felt something special for Sally. Had seen the depths of emotion in Sally's gaze often enough to think she might have similar thoughts. He'd let Sally decide what she

wanted. A man of substance and reputation like Abe—
or a man with a heart that belonged to her.

Sally stepped from the orphanage, and her footsteps
faltered. Mother and Linc talked together. Her heart did
a funny little flip-flop. Were they talking about her?
Then she remembered the one thing she'd tried to avoid
thinking of all day long. She'd agreed to marry Abe. Her
heart lurched to her throat. Surely Mother wouldn't tell
him. They'd agreed to make a formal announcement at
Sunday dinner with the family there, along with Abe
and his children.

She hurried closer.

"I need to get back to Pa," Linc said.

Sally's air whooshed from overanxious lungs. They'd
been talking of his father. "I'll give you a ride."

Mother gave her a look that normally would have
Sally apologizing and changing her behavior. But this
time, she only smiled sweetly.

"It will get him home sooner. In case his pa needs
him."

Mother's expression did not lose its disapproval, but
neither did Sally change her mind.

"You take him home," Judd said, blissfully unaware
of Mother's concern. "I'll see Mother Morgan home."

The others joined them. Amidst a flurry of thank-
yous and goodbyes, Sally and Linc climbed into the car.

She finally persuaded herself to relax when they
were almost back to Golden Prairie. But for the life of
her, she couldn't think of anything to say to Linc. Her
thoughts seemed stuck in a knot.

He sighed expansively. "Another party done. What do you think? Should we do this for a living?"

His teasing eased her mind. "Yeah. Sure. Let's take it on the road."

His laughter danced across her mind and she grinned, pleased at making him laugh.

"I can imagine how much you'd enjoy living in temporary quarters. Say a circus tent. Moving from place to place like some kind of kid-size Wild West show."

She wrinkled her nose. "I don't think I'd like it much."

They reached town and she eased the car toward the barn, where the ponies would by now be happily munching their feed.

"Come with me to check the ponies?"

His eyes said so much more than his words, begging for her company. She wasn't ready to go home and face her mother's disapproval and demanding questions, so she murmured agreement.

He took her hand as she stepped from the car and retained it as he led her into the barn. They checked each animal and came to Big Red's pen. The horse nickered a greeting. Only then did Linc drop her hand to toss some hay at his horse. He leaned against the pen and considered Sally, his gaze steady.

She didn't move away. Didn't shift her gaze. Something about the way he studied her gave her a feeling of being blessed. The look went on and on until she felt as if he'd read every secret longing, every hidden wish. Not only read them, but promised to fulfill them.

He grinned. "It was a good party, wasn't it?"

Was that all they had to talk about? "I thought so." She could hardly find her voice.

He reached out and plucked a bit of straw from her hair, his knuckles brushing her cheek, sending a wave of warmth up her skin. "Do you want to meet Pa now?"

Sally's thoughts went crazy. *Did you think he meant to kiss you? And if he had, were you going to stand there and let him? No, of course not.* She had promised to marry Abe. She would never do something so dishonorable. She'd been raised better than that. "Now is as good a time as any."

"Good." Again he took her hand as he guided her from the barn. As if she needed guidance. The alleyway was wide and clear. She had only to head for the door. But she didn't pull away.

He dropped her hand as they stepped into the sunlight. "Sometimes Pa is too groggy to talk."

"That's fine." She clasped her hands together at her waist. She did not miss his touch, she told herself several times as they crossed the yard and stepped into a big kitchen warm with evening heat and welcoming smells of cooking and home.

Mrs. Shaw sat in a small wooden rocker, eyeglasses perched on her nose as she bent over needlework. She glanced up at Linc's entrance and blinked twice when she saw Sally at his side.

"Pa wants to meet Sally," Linc said.

"Hello, Mrs. Shaw." Sally knew the woman from church and community events. "I hope I'm not intruding."

"Oh my, no. You are most welcome. Come in. Linc, check on your father first."

He signaled for Sally to wait while he hurried from the room.

"How did the party go?" Mrs. Shaw asked.

"Very well."

"Linc was so pleased to be able to…you know, do something for the community."

Sally nodded. Mrs. Shaw sounded like Linc didn't expect anyone would let him be involved. "The children love him. What are you making?" She bent over the handiwork. "Why, it's beautiful." Deep red roses with a touch of pink on an emerald green background.

"It will be a cushion pad for my little wing chair in the front room."

Sally stared, drawn by the colors and the carefully executed flowers. "I've never done counted stitch work."

"It's time-consuming but very rewarding. Take a peek in the other room." Sally moved to the doorway. "See the picture over the desk?" It was a big scene of an English countryside.

"It's wonderful."

"It took me three winters to complete."

"But what a masterpiece."

"Why thank you, dear. If you want to learn how to do it, I can teach you."

"I might take you up on your offer. Winters are long."

Linc stepped from a doorway across the living room and saw her looking at the picture. A smile flashed across his face, as if pleased to see her there. "I see Grandmama is showing off her skills."

His grandmother snorted. "I am not showing off.

Sally admired my roses so I thought she might like to see that picture. She called it a masterpiece."

Linc jostled Sally with his elbow. "You've earned yourself a special spot in her heart with that comment." He kept his voice low, but his grandmother still heard.

"If you keep it up you might find yourself cooking your own meals."

Linc pressed his hand to his heart. "Oh, please. Not that. I'll be good. I promise."

His grandmother laughed. "Go away with you."

Sally chuckled. It was good to see the affection between them. She liked a man who got along equally well with his elders and children. The thought stung her brain with accusation, which she ignored. But then she instantly excused herself. Of course it was okay to like Linc. Wasn't she supposed to show kindness to everyone?

Linc squeezed his grandmother's hands, then turned back to Sally. "Pa's awake. He's anxious to meet you."

She knew the man was bedridden. Had been since his accident. But suddenly she realized she'd agreed to step into a man's bedroom.

Linc watched her closely and read her hesitation. "It's okay." Linc held out his hand and she took it, finding strength and reassurance in his touch. He pulled her to his side. "He's weak but likes to hear what's going on around him. I said we'd tell him about the party."

They stepped into the room. A shrunken man lay against a pillow, his skin almost as white as the cotton cover. Yet his brown eyes—so much like Linc's—regarded her with unblinking curiosity. Linc pulled her forward. "Sally, this is my father, Jonah McCoy."

"I'm pleased to meet you." Sally held out her hand, then realized he didn't have the strength to lift his arm. Instead she reached down and squeezed his hand where it lay on the bedcovers. His skin was cool.

"So you're the young lady who has been keeping Linc occupied."

She shot a glance at Linc. What had he said? But Linc regarded his father, a look of sadness on his face. Sally swallowed back the tightness closing off her throat. She couldn't imagine watching her father suffer his way to death. "He helped put on a very successful party for the orphans."

"Tell me about it."

Linc pushed a chair toward her, and she sat at Mr. McCoy's bedside. "He taught a little boy how to throw a lariat. You should have seen the look on young Johnny's face when the loop actually landed over the wooden cow head. Johnny always pretends to be tough, but I thought he was going to hug Linc when he succeeded." She told of the games. How Maddie, the oldest girl, organized the others for the beanbag throw. How she managed to get Linc to take part in the game and how Maddie had blushed and giggled when Linc lost to her and congratulated her on her strong right arm.

Linc leaned against the head of his father's bed and seemed as keen on the stories as his father, so she continued, dredging up each and every detail. How young Claude Knowles—

"Wait. I used to know a man named Claude Knowles. A widower who lived over to the west."

"That would be young Claude's grandfather. He and Claude's parents died a year ago."

"And the boy has no other relatives?"

"Not that I'm aware of. Or perhaps they couldn't afford to take him."

"Sad. Everyone should have family and a home. Son," he spoke to Linc, "I'm sorry I didn't give you that." He drew in a breath that caught partway. He coughed and grimaced with pain.

Linc grabbed a bottle. "Pa, here's more medicine."

But Mr. McCoy waved away the offer. "Not just yet." His voice was thin with his pain. "I want to hear the rest of Sally's story."

So Sally continued. How Linc had picked up little Emmy and the girl had clung to him. Her heart squeezed tight as she recalled his gentleness with Emmy and how the girl adored him. This fearful, shy child trusted Linc instinctively. That said a lot about a man, as far as she was concerned.

She told Mr. McCoy how Linc had gone to Claude's side and given him the time and space he needed to choose to take a pony ride. Linc seemed to understand that sometimes a person needed time to get his head around an idea. She related how Claude sat in the grass and ate his cake so neatly that not a crumb fell, while the older boys, Johnny and Billy, had wolfed down two pieces each with no regard for what ended up on their face and clothing. How the little ones chased after each other and rolled in the dusty grass simply for the joy of playing. "Of course, the ponies were a big hit. I guess the children will remember it for a long time." She went on to describe the children receiving the toys. "Linc is responsible for all of them. He cut them out. He made the dollhouse."

"It wasn't just me," he protested. "You finished everything."

She couldn't tear her gaze from Linc's, feeling a deep connection as she shared this time with his father.

Mr. McCoy coughed again. "I believe I'll take some medicine now."

Linc measured it out. "We'll let you rest now, Pa."

"Thank you, Sally, for visiting a weak old man." He could barely manage a whisper.

"It was my pleasure." She squeezed his hand again.

Linc led her from the room, gripping her hand as if he feared to let go. She held on tight, understanding how difficult it must be to see this every day. She wanted to assure him his father would get better, but one look at the man and she knew it wasn't going to happen.

Linc led her through the kitchen, still holding her hand. "We're going to check on the ponies," he told his grandmother.

At his expression of sorrow, the older woman pressed her lips together and her eyes glistened with tears. The look she gave Sally seemed to beg her to help Linc as best she could.

Linc strode from the house, Sally in his wake. He didn't slow his steps until he reached the spot beside Big Red's pen where they had stood previously. He let out a long, shuddering breath.

With her free hand, she touched his shoulder. "I'm sorry. This must be very difficult for you."

He pulled her into his arms and held her tight. She let him, wrapping her arms around him, offering comfort the best way she could. He shuddered, clung to her. After a bit, his breathing eased and he pressed his cheek to her hair. "Sally."

The thickness of his voice, ringing with emotion, strummed something inside her. The way he said her name filled her with longing she couldn't explain.

He eased back, caught her chin with his finger and tipped her head so he could look in her eyes. "Sally."

His gaze dipped deep into hers.

A tiny nudge in the back of her brain tried to get her attention, tried to tell her something. She ignored it.

He studied her lips so longingly, she forgot to breathe. He shifted his gaze, ran it slowly across her cheeks until he meet her eyes. "Sally," he said a third time, his voice so deep it rumbled in her heart.

She was mesmerized by the look in his eyes, the ache in his voice. Her heart seemed to stretch, widen, maybe even open.

He lowered his head, paused and sent her a questioning glance.

She couldn't move. Couldn't think.

He touched his lips to hers. Warm, gentle, tentative.

Her arms wound around Linc's waist, her palms pressed to his back. Her heart pounded against her chest. This was how a kiss should make her feel. Not cool and distant like Abe's had.

Abe. The man she'd promised to marry. She jerked

away, pressed her arms to her side and stepped back, forcing herself from his embrace.

"No," she groaned. "I can't." Her words came in hard bullets. "Abe asked me to marry him last night, and I said yes."

She panted as if she'd run a mile.

Chapter Thirteen

Linc clamped his lips together and let her words blast through his brain before he spoke. "You what?"

"Abe and I are getting married."

"Why?" It didn't make sense. She'd kissed him as much as he'd kissed her, and not unwillingly. In fact, she had sighed softly and leaned into his embrace as if she'd found home. He reached for his hat to shove it forward, then remembered it hung on a hook in the house and settled for rubbing his hair. "Why?" he asked again.

She rocked her head back and forth. "It wasn't unexpected. Both of us know that's why I'm there. He's happy with how I run his home and the way I care for his children."

"It sounds like a business agreement. You do the housework and he'll provide you with a house."

She lifted her chin but couldn't quite meet his eyes. "He's a good man."

"Granted." He could tell her Grandmama wanted Linc to take over the farm, and he had about decided to do so, but he didn't want her to choose him in order to get a roof over her head.

"I'm not marrying to get a house."

"Do you love him?" It hurt to even say the words.

She sighed as if dealing with a rebellious child. "You don't understand."

His knees almost buckled. She hadn't said she loved Abe—the one argument that would make Linc walk away. Her omission gave him hope. "I do understand. But you can't marry a man to replace your father. You can't marry him for security alone. Sally." He took a step toward her, but she held up protesting hands and he drew back, not wanting to scare her off. "Sally, you talk about faith. Said your faith required security, safety. No person on this earth can promise you that completely. Nor should you expect it. Only God holds the future. There will come a time when you will have to trust Him because there is nothing else left. Why not do it now? Don't marry Abe for security. Trust God for it. Marry me for love. Choose me. I can't promise circumstances won't change or bad things won't come into our lives. But I can promise to love you and cherish you every day of my life." His words struggled past the tightness in his throat. "Sally, choose me."

She continued to rock her head back and forth, her eyes clouded with uncertainty.

Again he tried to close the distance between them, but she held up her hands once more.

"I can't. Mother would never understand. She'd not forgive me. The dinner tomorrow is to announce to the family my engagement." She pressed her fingers to her mouth, and with a little cry, dashed away.

He didn't follow. She'd made her choice clear. She would not, could not, go against family expectations. She would never give up the security of someone like Abe for a man like Linc, with a history of wandering, a hint of scandal attached to his name and nothing to offer but his love.

The sound of a motor mocked him as Sally drove away. All he could do was pray. And he poured out his heart and longing to God in a way he had never before done. *Oh, God. You know I love her. I could live with this mind-shattering ache if she loved Abe. If I thought Abe loved her—but I think he only wants someone who will do his bidding and run his house well. She wants something she can only find in trusting You fully. I have lots to learn about faith, too. We could learn and grow together if she would let it happen. God, please make her see love is what matters in the long run.*

Darkness had fallen by the time he left the barn. He tiptoed into the house, turned off the light Grandmama had left on in the kitchen, paused to make sure Pa was comfortable. When he saw his father slept, he trudged upstairs to his bedroom and fell, fully clothed, on the bed.

The next morning, Linc woke with a pounding headache and headed down the stairs for a cup of coffee. Grandmama was up and the coffee perked on the stove.

Grandmama looked at him and her eyes widened. "My word, what happened to you?"

"Fell asleep in my clothes," he murmured as he filled a cup and took several swallows, not caring that the hot liquid burned his tongue.

"Why?"

"Don't ask." He didn't mean to be curt, but he had no desire to discuss how he'd made a fool of himself kissing Sally and then begging her to choose him. Yet he'd make a fool of himself again if he thought it would convince her to change her mind.

Grandmama shook her head. She opened her mouth as if to say something, but at Linc's warning glare, thought better of it.

The coffee did little to ease his bad mood. He didn't expect it would. "I'll check on Pa." He strode away, ignoring Grandmama's questioning look. He couldn't explain his mood to her.

Pa twisted restlessly, moaning. Linc thought he was asleep, but his eyelids rose halfway at Linc's entrance. Linc sprang forward. "You need your pain medication. You should have called. I would have given it to you earlier."

"Thought I could hold off."

"Well, don't try it again." His words were soft with concern. He administered the medicine then sat beside Pa, singing softly until the medicine did its work. He knew from the lines gouging Pa's thin face that the relief was minimal. He hated to disturb him, but Pa needed cleaning up so he got a basin of water and washed him all over, as gently as he'd wash a newborn baby. He carefully rolled his father from side to side as he replaced the soiled sheets with clean ones. He took the sheets to the back porch and put them to soak.

Grandmama waited in her Sunday best when Linc returned to the kitchen.

He'd forgotten about church. "You go ahead without me. I'll stay with Pa. He's having a bad day."

"I can stay if you need me."

"We'll be fine."

Grandmama touched Linc's cheek in a loving gesture. "He's fortunate to have such a loyal and caring son. I will be praying for you both. He doesn't have much time left to make a decision."

Linc hurried back to Pa's room, afraid to speak. If Pa had to die, all Linc wanted was for him to choose Heaven before he did. He picked up *Pilgrim's Progress* and started to read.

Pa interrupted him. "I like Sally."

"Good."

"Seems you do, too."

"Pa, she's agreed to marry Abe Finley."

"I'm sorry to hear it."

Not near as sorry as Linc. He was grateful for an excuse to miss church, to miss seeing her sit at Abe's side or seeing Abe sit up front, knowing Sally would soon join him. Not that he was glad for Pa to be suffering.

"Son, you're a good man. Never got into trouble like Harris."

Linc didn't bother pointing out how Pa and Harris got into trouble as a pair. Neither of them would be doing so again. The future looked lonely to Linc.

"There's something I need to tell you." Pa took a

deep breath that brought on a bout of coughing. "It's not something I'm proud of." More coughing cut off his words.

"Pa, rest."

Pa nodded. "You're a good man. You deserve someone like your ma to share your life."

Linc wondered what else his pa meant to say. But he didn't seem inclined to try again, and Linc didn't want to tire him. "Do you want me to read?"

Pa nodded, and Linc read for an hour. Pa's discomfort increased. "Let's see if you're more comfortable on your side." He rolled his father and placed two pillows at his back. "Does that help?"

"Some."

Linc rubbed the exposed shoulder gently. Pa sighed, finding comfort in the motion so Linc continued until his father relaxed. Then he slipped from the room, praying Pa would rest for an hour or two.

He wandered the house, but it felt crowded and he strode out to the barn. He needed to do something. Something physical. He didn't care to dishonor God by working on Sunday, but he had to do something to relieve the aching of his bones. He grabbed a shovel. A big old post at the corner of the barn had broken off and needed to be dug out. He drove the shovel in the ground and stomped on it. Over and over he lifted dirt from a growing hole. The post must be buried halfway to China. Whoever put it in the ground had meant for it to stay.

Two feet down, his shovel hit something hard with a clang. He tried several different spots, but each time hit the obstruction. Likely a rock. He welcomed the challenge of digging it out. Soon he could tell the object had a flat top. Then he saw the corners were square. He dropped to his knees and leaned over to scrape away the dirt by hand.

What he found was a metal box. He pulled it from the hole and stared at it. What was a container doing here? Had it been buried by accident? Something someone had lost? Or hidden? The lid was bent, and it stuck so he couldn't open it. He went into the barn, found a screwdriver and pried the lid up.

"No. It can't be." He sank to the floor and stared at the contents of the box.

Sally glanced about the table. Abe sat at her left, in the place where Father would have sat, Carol on her right. Robbie sat on the other side of his father, Madge and Judd next to him. Mother sat at the far end of the table facing Abe. Everyone was there except Louisa and Emmet and their girls. Yet it wasn't their absence she felt. Only one person's absence blared across her senses, even though he'd never been in the Morgan home and likely never would be. Still, he seemed to hover like an invisible guest.

Linc hadn't been in church, either. Mrs. Shaw had stopped to speak to her and explained Linc's father wasn't up to being left alone. Sally wished she could tell Linc how much she cared about his father's sufferings. But last night when she'd tried to comfort him, it had ended up in a kiss.

Her cheeks stung, and she suddenly found it necessary to adjust the napkin in her lap.

Mother stood at her place at the other end of the table. "Dinner is ready, but before we eat, Abe and Sally have an announcement. Abe?"

Abe stood and cleared his throat. "Sally and I are going to get married."

Sally held her head high and faced her sister and brother-in-law. They would never have reason to suspect she had stolen a forbidden kiss in the secrecy of the Shaw barn.

Madge's look lingered on Sally, full of unspoken questions.

Sally smiled.

"About time," Judd said. "You've got a prize in Sally."

Moisture pooled in Sally's eyes, but she widened them. She would not cry.

"I'm aware of that." Abe squeezed her shoulder. "She's proven herself very capable."

He appreciated her. Valued her. She wanted nothing more. Not promises of love to last a lifetime. Love was cold comfort without a roof over one's head. Not that she was marrying Abe solely for that reason. He was a good man. A solid citizen. And what, a demanding voice asked, is Linc? Is he not a good man? A solid citizen? Of course. But he had no roots. As far as she knew, he planned to return to cowboying, and she'd listened to enough of his stories to know what kind of life that was. Following a herd of cows. Living on the range for much of the year. Where did that leave a wife?

Abe sat down, and Mother asked him to say the blessing.

Sally knew enough to bow her head immediately. At Abe's amen, she realized she was only being foolish when her heart should be overflowing with gratitude. This was what she wanted. Had wanted for a long time—a man with stability. A man who would—

Abe handed her the bowl of potatoes, and she took them with wooden hands.

She'd been about to say, a man who would make her feel as her father had. But what did that mean? Her father had cherished her, protected her, guided her. Is that what she expected from Abe? Would she get it? Would he love her like Linc did? Oh, how her wicked thoughts tortured her. She pushed them aside and turned to assist Carol.

Carol ignored the offer of potatoes and studied Sally's face. "Does this mean you are going to be my new mother?"

Sally nodded. "But I don't expect to take your mother's place. No one ever should. Is that okay?" She would have preferred to discuss this with the children in private, but Abe insisted they hear the announcement along with everyone else.

"I guess so." She took potatoes and passed them to Mother.

Sally turned to find Robbie glaring at her.

"I don't want a new mother. I don't need one. You can be the housekeeper. That's all."

Abe's expression grew stern. "Robbie, you will apologize. Sally is to be your mother and you will behave."

Robbie glared from Abe to Sally and said not a word.

"Robert Abraham Finley." Abe's warning tone was unmistakable.

Sally knew how explosive Robbie could be. "Let it go for now," Sally whispered, and received a look from Abe to match the one he gave Robbie. She instantly wished she could pull her words back.

"He is my son and he will obey me." Although he kept his voice low, everyone at the table heard him.

Sally longed to melt into the floorboards. "Please, Robbie," she whispered.

Robbie must have felt sympathy for her discomfort. "I'm sorry."

"Sorry, who?" Abe prompted.

"I'm sorry, Sally." No mistaking the slight emphasis on Sally's name, stubbornly informing one and all she would never be anything else.

For a moment, Sally feared Abe would correct the boy further, but he let it go.

"That's fine." He faced the others. "Sorry for the disruption."

There was a sudden rush of passing food and comments about the meal. Slowly the tension drained from the room, and Sally thought it might be possible to swallow a mouthful of potatoes and gravy.

"Abe, you should have come to the party at the orphanage. Sally and Linc did an excellent job." Judd didn't seem to think it odd to link Sally's name with Linc's, but Sally's potatoes stuck partway down her throat and would go no farther.

"I saw their work at Robbie's party and was impressed." Abe smiled at Sally. "As I told her, I'm pleased she is involved in community efforts."

"Sally has always been the one to help others," Madge said. "Remember how she took soup and covered dishes to the Anderson family for three months when the parents were so sick?"

"I just like to help others."

"It's your way of keeping things safe."

Madge's words stung. As if she meant Sally helped others for selfish reasons. As if Sally had a need to control life. She didn't. No matter what Madge or any of them thought. No matter what Linc said.

"Maybe I help just because it needs to be done. Because God says true religion is to help widows and orphans. To share with others."

Mother cleared her throat, subtly letting them know they were not to argue.

Thankfully the subject was dropped, but Judd and Madge returned to talking about the party at the orphanage, which did nothing to help Sally forget Linc. Heat stung her cheeks at the memory of that kiss. She hoped if anyone noticed, they would put it down to excitement over her engagement.

The meal seemed to go on and on. Would it never end? Would they ever leave her in peace?

Finally Abe pushed away from the table. "An excellent meal, Mrs. Morgan. Thank you."

Mother nodded. "I hope it's the first of many, now that you are to be my son-in-law."

Sally wondered if maybe the roast had been a little

off, though no one else seemed to be bothered in the slightest.

"Children, thank your hostess."

Carol and Robbie dutifully thanked Sally's mother.

"It's time I took this pair home."

Even Carol looked unimpressed with the idea of leaving. Sally understood they would have to play quietly in the front room for the rest of the day. Would Abe allow her to change any of his rules when they married? She guessed he would resist the idea. She, too, could look forward to Sunday afternoons confined to the house, reading or perhaps writing letters. Maybe she'd find a distant pen pal and write long, chatty letters once a week. Someplace exotic, like Africa or South America.

Abe and the children said goodbye to everyone. Robbie made certain to give Sally a most fearsome scowl when he thought no one else was looking. Then they were gone.

She grabbed the dishes still on the table, carried them to the worktable and poured hot water in the basin. Madge came to her side. "I suppose I should offer congratulations."

Mother joined them. "Indeed. This is a wonderful opportunity for Sally. Father would be well pleased."

Madge sighed as if she didn't agree, but she kept her thoughts to herself, for which Sally was grateful. She wasn't sure she could deal with any more doubts or questions at the moment, and kept her attention on washing dishes.

Finally the kitchen was clean. Judd and Madge departed for home.

Mother patted back a yawn. "I think I'll have my Sunday afternoon nap."

A few minutes later, Sally was thankfully, peacefully alone. She glanced around the room where the family spent so many enjoyable hours, and realized she'd never felt more alone or lonely in her life. Of course she would miss the home she'd known with her parents and sisters. A certain amount of sadness was to be expected.

The walls felt too close…the heat oppressive. She fled outdoors, her racing feet carrying her to the barn. Panting far harder than the short run should cause her to, she scrambled up the ladder. Her foot slipped on a rung, and she cried out. But she was safe and scrambled to the wooden floor, then made her way to the far corner. Every bit of hay had been fed to the cow, so she couldn't build walls about her. All she could do was pull her knees to her chest and press her face to her arms, still out of breath and overheated from her run. She waited for her heartbeat to return to normal, then lifted her head.

The loft door was closed, leaving the interior in gloom. A musty smell permeated the air. Pigeons cooed on the roof overhead. Sally tried to concentrate on every detail in a vain attempt to still the raging emotions inside her chest. Emotions she couldn't understand or even name, but they roiled and twisted until she thought she couldn't bear it.

"Oh, God," she moaned. "Help me."

But her turmoil did not ease. Was it guilt? "Forgive me for kissing Linc. That was wrong."

No relief came with her confession. Had she omitted doing something God expected?

But what did God expect?

To trust Him to take care of her.

But she did so, to the best of her ability. She sucked in dusty air and coughed. She must work this out, straighten out her confusion. But the more she flung about trying to sort her troubling thoughts into order, the more tangled they grew.

A rustling below drew her attention, then she heard someone on the ladder. She drew back into the corner, hoping she would be invisible.

Madge's head popped through the opening. She scanned the loft. "There you are. I thought I might find you here." Not waiting for, nor likely expecting, an invitation, Madge climbed up and slid across the floor toward Sally. "We used to have a lot of fun playing up here." She sank down to sit beside Sally. "Seems a long time ago."

Sally made a noncommittal sound, not wanting to relive the earlier, happier times.

"Things have to change as we grow older." Madge grew quiet and still. Neither of them spoke. But Sally knew it wouldn't last. She could sit and keep her thoughts to herself all day long, but Madge never could. It was only a matter of minutes before she'd say what was on her mind, what had brought her here on a Sunday afternoon when she could be with Judd.

"Sally."

Yes, here it came. Not that it mattered. Nothing

Madge could say would erase Sally's confusion. Maybe there was no solution for it.

"Sally, why did you agree to marry Abe?"

"What?" The question startled a response from Sally. "It was the reason I went to work for him. You knew that from the beginning."

"But I've seen you with Linc." Madge wiggled her eyebrows, as if to suggest she'd seen more than the two of them working on toys.

Sally hoped the dim lighting hid the way her cheeks burned. "So what?"

"Come on, Sal. You can't be so dense you don't feel the sparks between the two of you."

"Guess maybe I am." The sparks meant nothing. They couldn't. "What kind of a girl would I be if I agreed to marry one man while I harbored feelings for another? Father would certainly have had something to say about that."

Madge gave Sally a long hard study. "Do you think Father would approve of your engagement to Abe?"

Sally nodded. "He's a good man."

Madge shook Sally's arm. "You can't marry a man simply because he's well respected. Nor because you think Father would approve. Sally, this is your life. Until death do you part. You have to listen to your heart in matters like this."

Easy for Madge to say. She always knew what she wanted and went after it. Likely she'd never entertain contrary feelings. But Sally felt as if her heart was in a tug-of-war. She simply couldn't sort out the confusion. The only way was to choose the wisest thing and forget everything else. "I have to do what I think is best, and that's marrying Abe."

Madge crossed her arms over her chest and sighed heavily. "I will, of course, support whatever decision you make."

Sally smiled for the first time all afternoon. "Even if it kills you to do so. Right?"

Madge chuckled, then suddenly sobered. "It's not me who will have to live with the decision. It's you. So please—" She flung about to face Sally. "Please, dear little sister, make sure it's the right one."

"I'm trying to."

Madge looked about ready to say more, then pressed her lips together and wrapped her arms about Sally.

Sally leaned her head against Madge's firm shoulder. Not everyone could be as strong and sure of things as Madge. People like Sally simply had to push ahead, trusting God to guide them even when they couldn't see where their path led.

She must listen to her head more than her heart, and like Linc said, trust God to take care of her.

Next morning, Sally's resolve had deepened. She knew Abe was the man God had put in her life to provide for her needy faith. As she made her way to the Finley home, she wondered how she would endure Linc's presence as he finished the barn. Seeing him, knowing how he felt would make it difficult to stick to her decision. She hated to hurt anyone. But breakfast was over and the kitchen cleaned, and still he had not appeared.

She stared toward the Shaw backyard, the new corral fences allowing her a good view.

Was it just two days ago that she and Linc had shared such a wonderful day? The party at the orphanage. The visit to his father. The forbidden kiss in the barn. Her insides flooded with guilty heat. She must never think of it again.

But like rebellious children, her thoughts returned to reliving events of that afternoon. They'd fed and petted the ponies.

The ponies. Of course. He'd taken them back today.

It was as if the sun broke through the clouds in her mind. She glanced at the sky. Strange, no clouds interrupted the blue. She sang one of Linc's silly songs as she carried the dishwater to the garden.

Robbie crouched in his fort. "Where's Linc?"

"Taking the ponies back."

"Oh." The answer seemed to satisfy him, and he returned to his play.

Sally hurried to work once more on Tuesday. Life was good. And it had absolutely nothing to do with the possibility of seeing Linc today. So what if the thought cheered her unreasonably? What was wrong with being friends with the man? After all, Abe didn't seem to object. But then, he didn't know about the kiss.

No reason he should.

But the morning passed without Linc showing up. She didn't get so much as a glimpse of him, even though she spent a great deal of time staring at the yard across the alley.

Robbie stomped to the doorway and glowered at her. "Where is he?"

"Maybe his father is too sick to leave."

"It's your fault. You're going to marry my father, so Linc won't come anymore."

Sally had not let herself consider the idea, but it hovered at the edges of her brain. Had he left town? Was he avoiding her?

She gave herself a mental shaking. Best she get used to the idea. Being Abe's wife would make it impossible to continue as she was with Linc.

No more kisses. But couldn't they be friends?

Only if Linc welcomed it.

And if she kept her thoughts in proper submission.

Chapter Fourteen

Linc had prayed for something to change, but this was not what he had in mind. Not by a long shot.

He had dusted the metal box off and carried it inside. "Pa, what's this?"

Pa grunted awake.

Linc put the box on the chair and opened the lid to reveal several necklaces and brooches and two rings with enormous stones. "These are Mrs. Ogilvy's missing jewels, aren't they?"

"I hoped you wouldn't find it."

"You stole it? And all this time I have defended you. Held my head high, telling myself and everyone who would listen that the McCoys were innocent."

"I tried to tell you but then decided no one need ever know. How did you find it?"

"I dug out an old post."

"At the corner of the barn."

"That's right."

"It was the worst decision I ever made. What can a

man do with jewels? Once the Mountie sent a description of them across the country, I could never cash them in. So I buried them and moved on."

"Now what?"

Pa coughed weakly. "I guess it's up to you."

"Thanks, Pa. Thanks a lot."

"I'll go to my grave with this over my head."

Linc's anger and resentment melted. "Pa, you can go to your grave forgiven and ready for Heaven if you choose."

"God ain't likely to forgive a man like me."

"God says in His word, 'If we confess our sins, He is faithful and just to forgive us our sins, and to cleanse us from all unrighteousness.'"

"I guess that applies to ordinary sins."

"When the Roman soldiers crucified Jesus, he prayed they might be forgiven. Doesn't seem to me there is anything much worse than killing God's son."

"I suppose it is worse than stealing and lying."

"I'd say so. Pa, you can have your sins forgiven and be ready to enter Heaven. Please, won't you choose it?" Silently he prayed God would crack open his father's stubborn heart.

"I'll think about it. Now what are you going to do with that stuff?"

"The jewels? I'll have to think about that, too."

He had to return the ponies to their owner on Monday and welcomed the opportunity the trip provided for him to think about what he should do. If he turned the jewels over to the Mountie, his pa would be arrested. If he held them until after Pa's passing, he would be as guilty as Pa of hiding the truth. But oh, how he wished he didn't have to face the fact that the McCoys were guilty.

The faint hope he had that Sally might reconsider her plans to marry Abe and choose Linc instead died a painful death. He would never be worthy of such a woman. She would never consider linking her name with that of a McCoy. Everything people said about the McCoys was true.

He prayed as he took the ponies back. He prayed as he returned to Golden Prairie. He sought something besides the only answer he could find. But nothing more came. He must do what was right, even though it was hard. Harder than anyone would ever know.

His pa was dying, and Linc was about to turn him over to the law.

Tuesday morning, he spared a brief glance at the Finleys' backyard and caught a glimpse of Sally watering the garden.

Setting his mind to do what he must, he walked away from the view, stuck the metal box, now covered with a blanket, under his arm and marched down the street toward the Mountie's office.

He set the box in front of the lawman and began his explanation. "My pa and brother stole the jewels and buried them in this box behind the barn. I discovered it while fixing the corrals. Only thing I ask is you let my pa die in peace."

"Sorry, son. I must question your father and get the truth. I will be mindful of his condition, however."

Linc had to console himself with that assurance. "I

want to return them to Mrs. Oglivy and apologize as best I can."

"By rights this should be kept as evidence, but I suppose we can take pictures of the contents. First, I need you to give me a written statement." He pushed paper, pen and ink to Linc.

Linc wrote the facts out as precisely as possible, then he and the Mountie marched down the street. There wasn't much call for a photographer, so the business was combined with undertaker. Linc stalled on the doorstep. He'd soon enough be visiting this man for the latter.

The photographer asked no questions, but Linc could practically hear the cogs in his head working at high speed. No doubt he had figured out what he took pictures of. Although the Mountie had reminded him this was official business and was to be kept under wraps, Linc wondered how long it would be before the whole town knew the McCoys had Mrs. Ogilvy's jewels in their possession all this time. Over six years. Six years of living a lie, believing a lie.

Mrs. Ogilvy looked surprised when she saw the Mountie and Linc on her doorstep. She noticed the metal box but said nothing.

"Can we come in?" the Mountie asked.

"By all means." She stepped aside. "Forgive my lack of manners. Come and sit." They trooped into a big living room with a large number of red items—red cushions, red drapes, red pictures. The walls were practically covered with pictures. What didn't have a picture held a china cupboard or shelf loaded with knickknacks. He guessed many of the contents of the room were valuable. He sat stiffly on the red couch.

The Mountie sat beside him. "Linc has something to say."

So he repeated the story as the Mountie handed her the box of jewels.

She waited until he finished then slowly, tenderly lifted each item from the box. "Everything is here. The necklace and rings my grandmother brought from Russia. The pearls Grandfather gave to her on their wedding day. This necklace, my own dear Harold gave me on our wedding day. These are like children to me. Each one reminds me of a loved one and their life." She reached for Linc's hand and squeezed it. "Thank you for returning them to me."

It was all Linc could do not to bolt to his feet. He had done nothing worthy of thanks. Shame stung his thoughts. Shame that his family was as bad as people said.

"Now, young man, tell me again where you found this."

He told her about fixing the corrals and digging out the broken post.

"You say you weren't involved?"

"For the past six years I've believed the McCoys were falsely accused." No doubt his bitterness and disappointment dripped from every syllable, but he didn't care.

"Where were you that day six years ago?"

"I was helping my grandfather cut some hay in a slough. You know, the one west of town. He owns that land." He'd been blissfully content for the first time since his mother died. He liked working the farm. Grandfather had suggested Linc buy a few head of cows and start his own herd. His grandfather had already paid him wages in the way of a sorrel gelding that he rode every chance he got.

Mrs. Ogilvy nodded. "He used to get a good stock of hay off that slough." She directed her attention back to Linc's story. "Where have you been and what have you been doing since you left here?"

He told her everything.

"You like working on the ranch, it seems."

"I do."

"Will you go back there when you're done here?"

He wondered at her line of questioning, but considering what the McCoys had done to her, he willingly answered. "I don't know what I'll do. Grandmama needs help but—" He shrugged. "Might be best for her if I leave."

"I understand your father is not well."

"He's dying."

She gasped. "Oh, how dreadful. I understand he was in an accident. Tell me about it."

Linc did not want to think about the accident, the death of his brother, the impending death of his father and now the guilt of the McCoys. He wished he could run away from all this, but he knew no matter how far he went, his past would accompany him. In short, precise words, he told of the mining accident, burying Harris and then transporting Pa home. "I hoped he'd recover, but I accept now that he won't."

Mrs. Ogilvy patted the back of his hand. "You've been through a lot, young man." She turned to the Mountie. "What happens now?"

"I must investigate," the Mountie said.

Mrs. Ogilvy shook her head and turned to Linc. "I'm sorry this has to happen while your father is dying."

They left a few minutes later. "If your story proves correct, I won't be arresting your father, though I will lay charges."

"If it proves correct? Do you think I'd turn in my father falsely?"

The Mountie gave him a hard look. "It's mighty convenient to have your brother dead, your father soon to be joining him from what I hear, and you as innocent as a baby, if one believes your story."

"Then get busy and find your proof." He stormed away. How had things gotten so complicated?

"I'll be over in an hour to question your father. Don't go anywhere."

Linc spun around. "I think if I planned to leave town, I would have buried the jewels again and not said a thing." He told Grandmama to expect the Mountie then retreated to the barn. But he found no peace there, only the sense of dread hanging over his head. Even memories of Sally and the one kiss they'd shared failed to ease his mind.

He forced himself to remain in the barn, telling Big Red how mixed up life had become until it was time for the Mountie to come, then he returned to the house. Grandmama hovered at the stove and jerked about when Linc banged the door.

"My, you startled me. I'm as nervous as a young bride. Last time I had the police in my house...well, they were accusing your father of stealing from Mrs. Ogilvy. I never believed it possible. Still don't."

"Pa regrets it, if that's any consolation."

"Can't say it is, with a Mountie about to march into my house. I expect all the neighbors will have their noses pressed to their windows."

Linc tried to sound caring but failed. "There is no such thing as a secret in a small town." He went to Pa's room to prepare him for the visit.

Pa twitched. "Is he going to arrest me?"

"No. He's just coming to discover the truth."

"I'll tell him. You can count on it."

"Yeah, Pa."

Linc sat with Pa as the Mountie questioned him. After Pa finished, the Mountie asked, "You're saying Linc had nothing to do with this? No knowledge of it?"

"That's correct. He was just a boy."

"He was sixteen. About the same age as when Billy the Kid started his life of crime."

The hair on the back of Linc's neck stood up at being compared to such a notorious criminal. "My father says I'm innocent and I am."

"I guess if I was about to die, I'd do what I could to clear my son's name, too."

Linc bolted to his feet. "Sounds like you're calling both me and my pa liars."

The officer's expression remained impassive. "I'm saying you'll need more proof than your father's word." He didn't wait for Linc to show him out.

Linc ignored his pa's call. He ignored Grandmama's plea to cool down. Instead, he raced to the barn, threw a saddle on Red and rode away from town as fast as he could.

How did he prove his innocence? Grandfather was the only one who could vouch for where he was, and he was gone.

His mad ride took him by Judd and Madge's farm. He would not think of all the good times he'd enjoyed there with Sally. Then he passed the Morgan place. He'd never be welcome there now. Not with guilt hanging over his head.

He rode farther then, finally, out of consideration for his horse, slowed. Still he rode on. If only he could ride until he reached a place where no one knew him. He'd change his name and never have to face the shame of being a McCoy. But eventually his anger cooled. His pa was dying. And Linc would not abandon him to die alone, or leave Grandmama to care for him. So he turned Red about and headed back to town, his heart feeling cold and heavy in his chest.

Sally had seen the Mountie stride into Mrs. Shaw's house and wondered what was wrong. He left half an hour later without a backward look. And then Linc raced to the barn, and a few minutes afterward rode Red away at a furious pace. Sally longed to know the cause of all this commotion. She considered going to the house and asking Mrs. Shaw.

But she cleaned the kitchen and prepared a dessert as she considered it. Would Mrs. Shaw find her concern unwelcome? Finally, she could stand it no longer. She must find out what was wrong, but before she could put action to her thought, a knock came on the front door and she went to answer it.

"Madge, what are you doing here?"

Madge stepped in and hurriedly closed the door behind her. "Have you heard?"

"What?" It wasn't like Madge to be so mysterious.

Madge pulled her to the kitchen and insisted she sit.

"What is this all about?"

Madge sat beside her and took her hands. "The McCoys have suddenly found Mrs. Ogilvy's jewels and turned them in. The Mountie questioned both Linc and his father. Everyone is talking. Apparently Mr. McCoy claims to be solely responsible and says Linc is completely innocent."

"How do you know all this?"

"People have seen the Mountie and Linc going to Mrs. Ogilvy's with a metal box. No doubt the missing jewels, and someone overheard the Mountie talking about the McCoys' explanation."

"Lots of someones involved."

Madge never even took note of Sally's sarcasm. "Of course, everyone speculates they've figured it all out so Linc would get off the hook, and his father will not live to go to trial. Mighty convenient, people are saying. You were right. It was wise to choose Abe."

Sally jerked her hands away. She hadn't chosen Abe because she suspected Linc of being involved in anything shady. "Is that what you think? That Linc is guilty and seeking to escape judgment this way?"

Madge didn't answer, but her eyes revealed her doubt.

"You saw him at the party. How he loves kids." Sally felt a storm of words building and did nothing to stop it. "He came back so his pa could die at home. Why would he do that? Why not stay away rather than face what people are saying? And why would he turn in the jewels at all? Why not keep them hidden? Didn't I hear you saying what a nice man he was just two days ago?" She jerked to her feet. "Nice men don't steal and lie. Furthermore…" She lowered her head to within a few inches of Madge's face and favored her with a glower. "Nice people don't make such accusations."

Madge sank back, her expression stubborn. "Perhaps you're right. But we'll never know the truth."

Sally let out an explosive sound. "I know the truth. He would not steal. Nor would he take advantage of his father's illness to clear his own name. None of this makes sense. Where did he find the jewels?"

Madge shrugged. "Guess he knew where they were. How else would he find them?"

"You are wrong. Everyone is wrong."

"Right. Everyone is wrong but you. I suggest you consider why you need to believe he is innocent." She pushed to her feet and stuck her face close to Sally's. "Perhaps you better consider what Abe will think of such rabid defense of another man." She stalked from the room, heading for the door, then stopped and returned. "Sally, I know you feel you have to defend the underdog, but in this case there is more to consider."

She again left the room, and the outer door clicked shut behind her.

Sally sank to the closest chair. How could Madge have done such an about-face, going from defending Linc, even so far as to tell Sally to follow her heart, to believing his guilt? Linc was innocent, even if no one believed it. She knew it with all her heart.

She pushed her way through the rest of her chores and made an adequate supper for Abe and the children, though she had no appetite.

Abe waited until they'd finished and the children left the room to speak to her. Of course he'd heard the rumors and must address the situation. "Did you hear that Linc found the Ogilvy jewels?"

"Madge came by and mentioned it."

"Seems he isn't the upright citizen I believed he was. I don't want you or the children to associate with him any further. I'll tell the children right away." He left the room, taking for granted Sally's agreement.

She studied the fourth finger on her left hand. Abe would one day, and probably soon, put a ring on that finger. He had the right to expect her to agree with his decisions. She rubbed a fingertip around the spot where the ring would be. Wasn't this what she wanted? To be safe and secure in a house with a man who would always take care of her, always believe he knew what was best for his family? It held a certain protective quality. She wouldn't have to deal with hard things. Abe would see to that.

Just as her father had done his best to protect her. When he died she'd felt so vulnerable. All sorts of bad things had happened. The drought and Depression had hit. Men were swept away to relief camps. People went broke and moved away, as broken as their bank accounts. The Morgans had lost most of their land and almost lost their house. She did not have the strength to face such adversity anymore. Abe would take care of her.

In the other room, Robbie yelled at his father. He obviously did not like Abe's instruction to stay away from Linc.

A little later Sally left and walked home. The road seemed longer than usual, the heat more oppressive, the dust harsher.

Mother waited at the kitchen table. "You're late."

"The heat slowed my feet."

Mother studied her long and hard before she spoke. "Madge told me about the McCoys. I trust you have had nothing further to do with that man."

That man. "I suppose you mean Linc?"

"You know I do. I was right to tell you to avoid him."

Sally tried to control the words rushing to her tongue. She succeeded only in controlling the anger accompanying them. "Mother, I can't believe you judge Linc without evidence. In fact, against evidence. He found the jewels and turned them over to the police. I understand they were returned to Mrs. Ogilvy. What would you have him do? Why not continue to hide them to protect himself and his father? I think he did the only noble thing he could do, and it must have taken a great deal of courage. Though I expect he thought he would be heard without prejudice and judgment. I suppose that was his mistake. To trust people to treat him fairly."

Mother stared at Sally like she'd announced she intended to shave her head. "Are you planning to defend him against all others?"

"What would be the point? People will believe whatever they want." A weariness like nothing she'd ever known tugged at her bones. She wanted to go to her room and sink into her bed.

"Sally, you are engaged to Abe. I hope you will conduct yourself in a manner that honors that."

Her mother needn't have bothered with her warning. Linc had made no effort to see her or speak to her in two days. She didn't expect he would do so in the future. After all, he knew she was planning to marry Abe. He would respect that.

The next few days proved the accuracy of her thoughts. She glimpsed Linc once or twice, but he didn't even glance in her direction. The Mountie returned once that she saw. He might well have been there other times.

Sally wanted to go over and ask how Linc's father was. She wanted to tell Linc she didn't believe what everyone was saying, but Linc needed nothing from her and Abe had been clear about not speaking to him.

She looked around for Robbie. Twenty seconds ago he was playing in his fort, but now he was missing. Again. Since Linc no longer spent time with the boy, Robbie had returned to his practice of disappearing, disobeying and generally letting one and all know how unhappy he was.

Stepping outside, she called his name. No response, of course. She trudged to the barn and again called his name. A faint rustle alerted her to his location, and she went to where he huddled in the far corner. She sank down beside him.

"He's not a bad man," Robbie mumbled.

She knew he meant Linc. "I know that."

"Then why can't I see him?"

"You have to obey your father."

"But he's wrong."

Sally didn't reply. She agreed with Robbie, but it would be wrong to speak against his father.

"Do you think he'll leave?"

The question scraped her heart hollow. Who would blame him if he rode away and never returned? "I expect he will stay with his father." It was likely the only reason he remained. Sally had not given him any other reason. Nor could she. She had promised to marry Abe.

She waited for a sense of peace and security to ease through her.

But she waited in vain.

Chapter Fifteen

Linc sat at his pa's bedside, watching the covers over his chest to make sure they continued to rise and fall. Pa barely roused from his uneasy rest anymore.

Doc stepped into the room and shook his head. "It won't be long now. Call me if you need anything, though there is little I can do at this point. I'm sorry."

Linc nodded without taking his gaze off Pa. Seemed there was little anyone could do to solve any of Linc's problems. He simply had to accept life would not be what he had allowed himself to dream.

The Mountie had returned a day ago and said Linc's name was cleared. The statement left by the only eye-witness was vague, but the Mountie had been able to locate the man and he was certain there were only two men, and Linc wasn't one of them.

He'd said charges wouldn't be laid against Pa because of his weak condition.

Not that it made any difference. People would believe what they chose to believe. There was no point in expecting them to change and suddenly decide Linc McCoy would be welcome in their midst—accepted as a noble, honest man.

He'd return west, join up on a ranch and hope he could forget this time in his life. But his heart refused to find peace with his plan. He wanted to stay. He wanted to live here in Grandmama's house, raise a family with Sally. Be part of the community.

But the community would never accept him.

Sally would not be part of his dream. Moreover, she didn't deserve to have her name associated with his. Far better to be Mrs. Abe Finley, an accepted and respected member of the community.

Grandmama hugged him when he told her he would not be staying permanently. "I'm sorry, Linc. I hoped and prayed things would turn out differently. I will continue to pray for things to change. I need you." She drew back to look into his face, studying him so hard he had to force himself not to break eye contact. Her eyes clouded with tears. "I think you need things you can only find here."

His only reply was to hug her back. What he needed and wanted were not choices he had. He returned to Pa's bedside, afraid to leave him alone.

Pa stirred and opened his eyes, clouded with pain and confusion. He tried to pull in a deep breath and coughed, pain spasming through him.

Linc knelt at the side of his bed. "Pa, just rest."

Pa shook his head. "Call your grandmother."

Linc hesitated. Was this the last? He sniffed back a rush of tears and went to the doorway. "Grandmama?"

His voice was low, but he couldn't have made it louder if he tried. His throat seemed to have closed off.

Grandmama hurried from the kitchen. "Is it...?"

"Pa asked for you." He waited for her to join him and led her to the chair close to Pa's head.

She took his hand. "Oh, Jonah. I hate to see you like this."

"Mother Shaw, you have been a true Christian woman."

Both Linc and Grandmama leaned close to hear what Pa said. Linc took Pa's other hand. He couldn't speak past his pain, but no matter how much it hurt to watch, he would stay with Pa until the end.

Pa turned his gaze to Linc. "You have been a good son. Always. I'm glad your name is cleared." He fell silent. His eyes drifted shut. His breathing was so shallow Linc feared it had stopped. "Oh, Pa. Don't die without making things right with God."

Pa's eyes flew open.

Linc couldn't believe the flare of life in them. Maybe the doctor was wrong. Maybe Pa would fight back and live.

"I wanted you both here so I could tell you. I made my peace with God. He took away my sins. My burden and guilt are gone." His smile was the sweetest thing Linc had ever seen. "I only wish I hadn't been stubborn so long."

Tears streamed from Grandmama's eyes as she leaned over and kissed Pa's cheek. "Jonah, my prayers have been answered." Her voice broke, and she couldn't go on for a moment. "Be sure and say hello to Mary for me."

Linc pressed a kiss to Pa's cheek then. He thought Pa was crying, then realized the moisture on his cheek came from his own tears. He hadn't even realized he cried.

"Go to sleep now, Pa. I'll see you in Heaven." His heart cracked. He wanted to share life with Pa as a Christian, but it would never happen.

He and Grandmama continued to hold Pa's hands. Linc stroked Pa's forehead and tried to sing the words to the old song, "In the sweet by and by, we shall meet on that beautiful shore." His throat grew tight but he forced the words out, not caring that the melody was lost in the cracking of his voice. Any more than he cared about the tears flowing freely down his face and dripping to the bedcovers.

"He's gone," Grandmama whispered. "Gone to Heaven." She choked back a sob.

But neither of them moved. Finally Linc closed Pa's eyes, crossed his hands over his chest and stood at the side of the bed. He pulled his grandmother to her feet to stand beside him. "I will miss him more than anyone will ever know."

Grandmama turned into Linc's arms and sobbed.

He led her into the kitchen and eased her to a chair, then made them tea.

Grandmama sniffed and dried her tears. "Mary is gone. Harris is gone. Now your pa. And you'll soon be gone, too." She let out a shuddering breath. "I will be alone again."

Linc squeezed her hands. "I will be here long enough to make arrangements for Pa's burial. I wish I could stay longer."

Grandmama gave him a fierce look. "There's no reason you can't stay. You're a good man. You know it and I know it. Why not give the people around here a chance to discover it?"

"I thought I had. Seems they are only waiting for a chance to see me as anything but good."

"If you want something badly enough, you will fight for it."

Did she mean his reputation or Sally? He didn't care enough about the first to remain. He cared too much about Sally to stay and watch her marry Abe.

Grandmama patted his hand. "I guess you say how much you care by what you do."

This time he knew she meant Sally. He pushed to his feet. "I need to call the doctor and the undertaker."

Sally saw the doctor and undertaker both go into Mrs. Shaw's house as she crossed the yard after taking the lunchtime dishwater to the garden. She dropped the pail and pressed her hands to her mouth. Linc's father had died. And she hadn't been there to comfort him.

It was not her right. In fact, she was forbidden to speak to him.

Choking back a cry, she grabbed the pail and dashed for the house. She sank to the nearest chair and buried her head in her hands. Weeping for his loss. Weeping for her loss.

Her loss? She jerked her head upright. She had chosen what she wanted. A secure life. A solid home. A man who had a steady job.

But the words echoed in her empty heart.

What would her father say? Mother was certain he'd approve of Abe. Her father was a solid, steady man who provided a secure home. Even when they moved from Edmonton she had not worried, although they'd lived in a tiny sod shanty while the big house was built. Even there she'd felt safe and secure.

Because her father was taking care of her.

Because she trusted his love.

A fleeting truth fluttered through her head. Something important that she couldn't quite capture and identify.

She retraced her thoughts. Her father took care of her. She trusted his love. Trusted his love. She heard his voice helping her memorize Psalm chapter ninety-one. "Sally, my dear little daughter, whatever happens, remember God loves you and will always be with you. He will cover you with His wings. You need not fear the terror of the night or anything that comes against you. God is your refuge. He will guard you in all your ways."

She missed her father. His steady presence. His care and love. But she didn't want someone to replace him. He would be disappointed if he thought she needed someone to provide the protection he'd taught her to find in God.

God was her Heavenly Father. He would care for her.

Not seeing anything before her, she stared long and hard. What did it mean? What was she to do?

By suppertime she was a bundle of confusion. "I

can't stay. Just leave the dishes and I'll do them in the morning."

Abe's look demanded an explanation.

She couldn't provide him one and gave a vague shrug, as if to insinuate it was something she couldn't discuss. He nodded as if he understood. Probably thought it was a woman thing. Her cheeks burned with embarrassment, but let him think what he wanted. She had to get home.

Mother was in the garden when Sally approached the house, but she managed to slip by unnoticed. She hurried to her room, picked up her Bible and found Psalm ninety-one. She read it over and over, feeling as if the answer was in front of her face. Yet she couldn't put her finger on it.

Oh, God. I feel like something is missing. Show me what I need.

Trust in the Lord. Trust His love and care.

Linc's words came to her as clearly as if he stood before her. *Friends who trust God to take care of them.* Was her confusion because she had put her trust in what marrying a man like Abe could give her…security and a nice home?

She looked closely at the idea. How could she expect a man to do that for her? Shouldn't her trust be in God?

Thoughts swirled through her head as she assessed the choices before her. Trust God, or trust Abe to give her what she needed?

The words of a hymn flooded her mind. "Be not dismayed whate'er betide. God will take care of you." Softly, she sang all four verses. It was the answer she sought. God was her refuge and shelter. Her anchor. Not a house. Not a man. Not trusting in things of this earth that proved so fleeting and insecure. It was God who would take care of her. It wasn't even fair to expect Abe to take on such an onerous role.

She fell to her knees beside the bed. "Thank you, Father God."

She rose from the floor and laughed. She'd been looking for security in the wrong places.

Her heart flying free, her feet light, she descended the stairs.

And came face to face with Mother.

Her mood dipped, and then she stiffened her shoulders.

"Mother, we need to talk."

"When did you get home?"

"A few minutes ago. I slipped by you because I needed time to think and pray." She led her mother to the kitchen and indicated she should sit down.

She sat across from her and considered how to break the news. Gently as possible. "Mother, I have been seeking a replacement for Father. I wanted a man who could guarantee to make me feel as safe and secure as he did."

Mother smiled. "He was a good father."

"Yes, he was. And if he knew how I've been thinking, I feel he would be disappointed with me."

Mother looked startled. "Why?"

"Didn't he teach me to put my trust in God, not man, not possessions, not circumstances or belongings?"

Mother hesitated. "Yes. But I don't see—"

"Both you and I thought Abe could do for me what

Father did. You know, provide security, safety." She didn't say love because that had not entered the agreement. "Father's job was to guide me from childhood to adulthood by teaching me not to seek all those things in a person, but in God, and he did his job well."

"I'm sure Abe can provide as well as your father did."

"But Mother, I can't marry a man and expect him to do what only God can. Only God can promise to take care of me. To guard and guide me. It's what Father taught us all."

"Yes, but—"

"Mother, I can't marry a man I don't love. Do you think Father would want me to?" It was a loaded question and not entirely fair, but Mother had used the same argument to persuade Sally and now needed to understand she couldn't do it.

"I suppose you think love will keep you warm. Give you a roof over your head?"

"That's the whole point. I need to trust God to take care of me. He is my Heavenly Father. Doesn't the scripture say, 'If God so clothe the grass, which is today in the field, and tomorrow is cast into the oven, how much more will he clothe you, O ye of little faith'?"

Mother shook her head. "Maybe I'm of little faith. I want to see you married to a man who can take care of you."

"I thought I wanted that, too. But it isn't enough. And it's putting my faith in the wrong place."

"Are you—?" Mother swallowed hard. "Are you thinking of marrying Linc?"

The question burned through her like a fire-tipped

arrow. "I'm not sure that's a possibility." She'd abandoned him. She'd dismissed him. Why would he give her another chance? "His father died today. I saw the doctor and undertaker go into the house."

"I am sorry."

Sally heard a "but" in her voice and got to her feet before Mother could put it in words. "I'll tell Abe tomorrow I can't marry him, and I'll offer to continue as his housekeeper until he finds a replacement."

"I'm sure he won't have any problem finding someone else."

"Exactly." And if she could so easily be replaced, then he should do it. She wanted a relationship where a man thought she was irreplaceable.

The next morning she took a cake and a covered dish with her when she went to the Finleys'. She would take them across the alley as soon as she got a chance.

Abe stepped into the kitchen, looking as fine and polished as ever.

She faced him bravely. "Don't call the children yet. There is something I must tell you."

His look was impatient. But he didn't ask what was so important that it couldn't wait until a more convenient time. More convenient for him. He crossed his arms over his chest and waited.

"Abe, I've changed my mind. I'm afraid I can't marry you." She rushed on, ignoring the disbelief in his eyes. "It wouldn't be fair. I love your children." It was the one thing that gave her pause. "I admire you. But I would be marrying you for all the wrong reasons."

"I can offer you a good home."

"I know. And there was a time when that and your position in the church and community were enough. Or at least I thought they were. I will continue to look after the children until you find a replacement. If that suits you."

"Fine." He plunked down, then remembered he hadn't called the children and got up again to go to the bottom of the stairs and call them. He returned and stood behind his chair. "A cousin of my late wife's has offered to come. I'll let her know I accept her offer." He sat.

It was over as easy as that. No regrets.

Except for the children. She waited until Abe left to tell them.

"You going to marry Linc?" Carol demanded.

"I don't know. I think he will be leaving."

"You could go with him. I would."

Robbie was far more practical. "Who's going to look after us?"

"Your father said he had someone in mind."

"Good." But she caught a glimpse of hurt in his face before he scowled at her.

"Robbie, I hope we can still be friends. Maybe you can come out to visit, and I'll take you to the loft where I used to build a fort. Remember me telling you that?"

He managed a nod but his expression remained as defiant as he could make it, as if afraid he would cry if he didn't make himself angry.

She understood his hurt. The boy longed for safety and security as much as she did. Knowing they needed to learn the same lesson she'd been so slow to learn, she sorted through the Bible story cards until she found the one about Abraham and read it. "Abraham trusted God, and God took care of him. Your mama trusted God. She wanted you to, as well." She looked from one child to the other. "I'm learning that same thing."

Carol nodded. "I'll try to remember what Mama taught. And you."

Robbie looked thoughtful, though he tried to hide it.

Carol hugged her before she left for school. "I wanted you for a mother, but you love Linc and should be with him."

Sally laughed. "How is it everyone but me saw what I needed?"

Carol gave a shy smile. "Linc loves you, too. I saw that."

"You are a very astute little girl." She hugged Carol one more time, loath to let her go. She'd miss these children more than anyone would guess possible.

Later, she took the food over to the house across the alley. Mrs. Shaw opened the door. "Why thank you, my dear."

Sally glanced past her.

"I'm afraid Linc is not here. He had to see to the grave digging. We're burying Jonah tomorrow."

"I'm sorry. Please relay my condolences to Linc."

"Of course."

Sally left. Restless, she took Robbie to the store to pick up supplies for supper. A gaggle of women watched her as she entered the store.

Mrs. Brennan poked her head forward like a curious turkey. "I understand you were friends with that McCoy man."

Sally smiled and nodded. She was not going to give these gossips anything to titter about.

Miss Carter nudged Mrs. Brennan. "Don't expect there will be many folks at the funeral. Good riddance to bad rubbish, I say."

"How charitable of you," Sally murmured.

"I hope that young McCoy plans to leave. Our town doesn't need the likes of him around. The Mountie says he is satisfied the boy had nothing to do with stealing from Mrs. Ogilvy, but it's not easy to pull the wool over my eyes."

Sally felt like she'd had a sheet over her eyes for years, and now it was gone and she could see clearly for the first time. "I'll be at the funeral."

At least three of the ladies gasped, as if the idea was beyond comprehension.

"You have claimed to be Mrs. Shaw's friend for years. Shouldn't you be there to show her support, if nothing else?"

The women gaped at her. Quiet, compliant Sally, they seemed to say, speaking out like this?

"I'll be there, too."

Sally spun about to face Mrs. Ogilvy, who smiled at Sally then steamed by to confront the other women. "I'm convinced Linc McCoy is innocent of any wrongdoing. He's done his utmost to make things right. He's endured the scorn of this town to stay at his father's side until he died. In my view, that makes Linc McCoy an honorable man. I'm proud to know him."

The women looked uncomfortable. A couple of them would have sidled away, but Mrs. Ogilvy stopped them in their tracks.

"I'm not done. I will remind you of something our Lord said. 'He who is without sin among you, let him cast the first stone.'" Then she regally sailed past and ordered her supplies.

The women were suddenly in a great hurry to leave.

Sally went to the counter to conduct her business. Mrs. Ogilvy turned to her. "You're the young woman who is planning to marry Abe Finley, aren't you?"

"I was. I've since reconsidered it. Our engagement is off."

"I see."

The way she continued to study Sally made Sally wonder what she saw. Something more than the announcement that she wasn't marrying Abe.

"Is there a particular reason? Or perhaps another man you find you care for more?"

"I realized my reasons for such a marriage were all wrong. Seeking security. Afraid of love."

Mrs. Ogilvy chuckled as she patted Sally's hand. "My dear, never be afraid of love. Any more than you would any great adventure."

Sally recalled Linc's words about Claude. How he was ready for adventure but a little fearful, or something to that effect. It perfectly described Sally. But no more. If love was an adventure, she was ready for it.

She only hoped she hadn't waited too long.

That evening, after supper—which was strained with vibrant disapproval from Abe—she broached the subject of the funeral. "I'm going. I wondered if you would allow the children to attend. It might be nice for them to let Linc know they care about his loss."

Abe looked ready to refuse permission.

Carol had tiptoed into the doorway and overheard Sally's request. "I'd really like to go. I remember how good it felt to see how others cared when Mommy died."

Abe studied his young daughter. "Robbie, are you there?"

Robbie popped around the corner, and Sally knew he'd listened to the whole conversation.

"What do you want to do?" Abe asked his son.

Robbie hung his head and mumbled, "I might like to go and say goodbye."

"Very well then. You may take them. But don't linger about afterward."

Sally thanked Abe, but her gaze returned to Robbie. Who did he want to say goodbye to? He'd never met Linc's father. He must want to say goodbye to Linc.

And she wanted to say hello.

She prayed she would get a chance.

The next day she dressed the children in their Sunday best, changed into a black dress she seldom wore because it reminded her of her father's death, and they went to the church.

The gossips in the store were right. Very few people attended the funeral. Linc and his grandmother were in the front row. Farther back sat several older ladies, friends of Mrs. Shaw's. Mrs. Ogilvy marched in and went to the pew directly behind Mrs. Shaw.

Linc's grandmother turned, saw the other woman and nodded her appreciation.

Linc turned, too. Sally saw his start of surprise and his mouthed, "Thank you." Then his gaze continued on to Sally and the children. He let his gaze slide past her.

The pain slicing her heart had less to do with Linc's loss than her own disappointment at the way he ignored her. But then, what did she expect? He didn't know she'd broken it off with Abe and, honorable man that he was, he would never allow himself to seek comfort from a woman engaged to another, even in this dark hour of his loss.

The service was short. Then they followed the casket to the cemetery. Only Linc and his grandmother stood close to the grave. Out of respect, the others remained a few feet away.

The casket was lowered into the ground, then the few who weren't family members marched by and squeezed Linc's hand and his grandmother's.

Suddenly Sally was face to face with Linc. "I'm so sorry," she murmured.

His expression was hard as granite. "Thank you."

She had planned to ask if they could talk later, but his sternness robbed her of all thought.

He turned to the children, effectively dismissing her, and hugged each of them. "Thank you for coming."

Carol clung to him, sobbing. "Are you going to leave now?"

"Soon." He straightened and avoided looking at Sally.

She hugged Mrs. Shaw, offered her condolences and

hurried home. The children seemed relieved to have seen Linc and spoken to him.

Only Sally struggled to hold back tears.

He was leaving soon. Would he give her a chance to tell him she no longer planned to marry Abe?

Would it matter to him any longer?

Chapter Sixteen

Numb from head to toe, Linc led his grandmother home. It was over. He tried to find relief in knowing his father's suffering had ended. He tried to console himself with the knowledge Pa had gone to Heaven.

But he simply felt empty.

Grandmama sank to a chair and sighed, a sound so heavy it seemed to scrape the floor. "I could use some tea."

Linc, welcoming a reason to do something, filled the kettle and put it on to boil. Then he sat down and stared at the tabletop.

"What now?" Grandmama asked.

"I don't know."

"I realize you haven't had time to deal with your father's death, but are you planning to leave soon?"

"I figure I can join up with some ranch."

"Pardon me if I say you don't sound enthusiastic."

"I don't feel anything." The kettle boiled. He made the tea, waited for it to steep and poured a cup.

"Aren't you having any?"

Linc shook his head. "I think I'll go for a ride and clear my head."

"Linc, there is something I want to say. Now is probably not the best time, but I want you to think about it. I've already made it clear I want you to stay and take over this place. But it's more than that. Linc, I'm getting old. I don't want to be alone. I need you here."

She'd said it before, but never so clearly expressing both her want and her need for him to stay. "Grandmama, I don't know if I can stay." The idea of seeing Sally married to the man across the alley was more than he could deal with right now. Perhaps he'd never be able to deal with it.

"Linc, I wish you'd reconsider. If not for me, then for that Morgan girl."

"She's going to marry Abe."

"Does she love him?"

Linc shrugged. What did it matter? She was willing to sacrifice love for her idea of security. Maybe he couldn't blame her. There were times he longed for the things she wanted. The difference was, he didn't see any chance of getting them here. He looked about the room, realizing how much he loved this place. Too bad it was tainted with the misdeeds of the McCoys.

"Like I said before and will say again in the hopes of persuading you to reconsider leaving, you could stay and prove the McCoys are good people."

"I'm not sure anyone would ever believe it."

"Eventually they would. Just promise me you'll think about it."

"Okay." He left then and rode Red long and hard.

He passed Judd and Madge's place without sparing it a glance. He approached the Morgan farm. Steeled himself to keep his face forward and look neither to the left nor the right.

Soon the orphanage was ahead of him. He heard the laughter of one of the children, but rode on. Every place he passed was full of memories of Sally and the times they'd enjoyed together

Six years ago he'd said goodbye to this place, even though he'd wanted Pa to stay and prove their innocence. Small wonder he didn't agree to. Hard to prove a lie.

Now Linc was leaving again.

Running away again.

Now where did that come from? He wasn't running from anything.

Except people's judgment. And Sally. Acknowledging he would be running from Sally made him lean over the saddlehorn and groan.

He pulled Red to a halt and led him up a small hill, where he sat and stared at the drought-ravaged countryside.

The drought would eventually end. Those who managed to hang on would be glad they had stayed through the tough times. They would have their land and homes still.

The thought tangled with something Grandmama had said about staying. Stay and prove the McCoys were good people. Stay and fight for Sally.

Like those who stayed and fought for their land through the present trials.

Of course, they had no assurance when the drought would end. Could they even know for certain it would? Could he have any hope his circumstances would change? Did it matter? Or was faith enough?

He'd taken to reading his Bible every night, feeling a connection to Sally as he did so, but also something deeper, more secure, more necessary—a connection to God. Out of curiosity about what those books at the end of the Old Testament with the funny names were about, he'd read several. Some of the verses were like songs of faith.

They listed a number of disasters—drought and failed crops—then concluded by saying, "Yet I will rejoice in the Lord, I will joy in the God of my salvation. The Lord God is my strength, and He will make my feet like hinds' feet, and He will make me to walk upon mine high places."

The verses filled him with fresh hope and strength.

Should he stay and fight for his name? For Sally? What if he stayed and nothing changed? What if people still accused him of stealing? And Sally married Abe?

If it didn't turn out the way he wanted, it wouldn't change God's love for him. Nor God's promise to give him the strength to go forward.

And at least he would have tried.

He bowed his head and prayed, asking God for wisdom and strength to do what he should, asking for God to intervene so things would turn out the way Linc wanted, but if they didn't, he asked for faith and trust to go on without bitterness.

Peace colored his thoughts, and he remained on the hillside for a long time, simply breathing in contentment.

Dusk had spread its skirts across the sky when he made his way back to town. Grandmama burst out crying as he strode into the house, and he rushed to her side. "What's wrong?"

"I thought you might have gone without saying goodbye."

"I'm not going."

She stopped crying immediately and wiped her eyes. "Did I hear you correctly?"

He told her what he'd decided and why. Before he finished, she squeezed his hands and smiled widely.

"Good for you."

The next morning Linc wakened and bolted to his feet. Then he remembered he didn't have to check on Pa and sank to the edge of the bed. It would take time to accept that his father was gone. Not that he wished him back. But he missed Pa and Harris. He missed his mother.

However, the future beckoned and he again sprang from his bed.

Today he would find a job to tide him over until the farm could be brought back into production.

Finding a job turned out to be a challenge, just as it had before Abe offered him a chance. But after two days he saw a small sign in the window of the hotel. Handyman wanted. He strode inside and said he'd like the job.

The manager looked him up and down. "What do you have to recommend yourself?"

"I'm a hard worker, and I'm hungry."

The man laughed. "I need someone to make repairs on the building, do some painting, wash the windows, keep the floors clean. Can you do that?"

"I can do it so good you'll never have a complaint."

"Pay isn't much."

"Don't expect much. Just enough to keep me and my grandmother fed." And maybe save a little to restock the farm. But he wasn't going to worry about that. He would trust God for the future. Right now he wanted a job for more than the money it would bring. He wanted…needed…to make himself visible. Prove to the good townspeople of Golden Prairie that the McCoys could be trusted.

"You got a name?"

Linc didn't hesitate. "Lincoln McCoy." He held out his hand. "Didn't catch your name."

"Orville Jones. Say, aren't you the young man who found Mrs. Ogilvy's jewels?"

"I am." Linc would not hide from all that meant. "I was also accused of having a part in stealing them. But I didn't do it. Is that going to be a problem?"

Orville studied Linc long and hard. "Why would you return them if you weren't innocent? Besides, didn't the Mountie investigate and decide there was no evidence against you?"

Linc nodded.

"That's good enough for me."

"Thank you. Now point me to the work."

He left later in the afternoon, knowing Orville was satisfied with his work. Now he was ready to speak to Sally.

A trickle of worry trailed through his thoughts. As soon as he recognized it, he reminded himself he had made a choice to trust God.

He hurried home. This was about the time of day Sally left the Finley place to head home. He paused long enough to tell Grandmama about the job and explain he was going for a ride.

"I trust you are going to find Sally."

He chuckled. "Seems a man can't have any secrets around here."

She tweaked his ear. "I'll be praying."

His heart full of gratitude, he hugged her and trotted out to saddle Red.

The dusty road ahead was empty. There was no sign of Sally. Was he too late? Or too early? He looked over his shoulder and saw only the dust raised by Red's hooves.

Drawing near Judd's turnoff, he slowed. Perhaps Sally had stopped to visit her sister. But he didn't turn in. Only one person he wanted to see, and he wanted to see her alone.

He signaled Red to go forward at a walk, all the time scanning the road, the driveways, the landscape for Sally. Nothing. Not so much as a flicker of movement.

He swallowed hard and sank low in the saddle. He'd

practiced what he'd say. Tried to guess how she'd respond. It hadn't crossed his mind he wouldn't see her.

Where is she, God? Sometimes it was hard to trust.

He rode on two more miles, loath to return disappointed. But there seemed no point in going farther, and he finally reined around. "Let's go home, horse." His chin almost rested on his chest as he headed back to town.

Big Red neighed, causing Linc to jerk his head upward.

There she was. At the end of the laneway staring at him. He dropped to the ground and strode toward her. "Where were you?" As if she had to inform him of her whereabouts!

"I went to visit Madge."

"I didn't see you." Did she hear the ache in his voice, or only the demanding note of his question?

"I saw you. I thought—" Her voice cracked. "I wondered if you were leaving the country. Are you?"

He heard in her voice more than her words said. A longing. A wish that he wasn't leaving. And it gave him hope. "Guess you haven't heard."

"What?"

"I got a job at the hotel. Orville seems to think I'm worth taking a chance on."

"You aren't leaving?"

"Nope. I'm taking over Grandmama's farm. She needs me. I need a home." He needed more, but only Sally could give him what he truly needed. He feared to ask her to give him a chance. "How are Abe and the children?"

"Good. I no longer work there."

He couldn't think what she meant. He would not allow himself to hope and dream without reason. "Really?" When had his voice ever before sounded so strained? "Why is that?"

"His wife's cousin is taking my place."

He tried not to look confused, but guessed he failed miserably when she giggled.

"Why? You— She—" He gave up and lifted his hands to beseech her to explain.

"I told Abe I couldn't marry him."

"You did?" Had he swallowed a whistle to make his voice so squeaky? "Why?"

"I realize my security is not based on a house or marriage to a man who can take care of me."

He nodded, silently asking for more.

Her smile was as sweet as the kiss of morning sunshine. "I've chosen to trust God to take care of me and my future."

He grabbed his hat and slapped it against his thigh, whooping so loudly that Red snorted and sidestepped away. "Me, too."

"You, too, what?"

"I decided to trust God even when life doesn't look like a bed of roses. When people are saying my name with twisted expressions on their faces, when the girl I love is saying she plans to marry someone else."

She looked serious, though it appeared to be a strain. "You love someone?"

He tossed his hat to the saddle and faced her, close enough to see the green in her eyes shift through a variety of shades. "I love you, Sally Morgan. With my whole heart. What do you think about that?"

She ducked her head. "It sounds very nice."

He caught her chin with his fingertip and lifted her face upward so he could study her. Her eyes were warm and welcoming, her lips curled softly with pleasure. "Will you marry me?"

His confidence dipped. What if she didn't say yes? He rushed on before she could answer. "I can't promise you we won't have struggles. I can't say life won't be hard. I don't know what the future holds. I only know God holds our future, and He is the only One strong enough for the job. But I can promise you I will love you as long as I live. I will do my best to make you happy and keep you safe and secure." He ran out of words and waited for her reply.

"God will take care of us."

"Us?"

"I can't think of anyone I would sooner share the challenges of life with than a cowboy by the name of Linc McCoy."

"You'll marry me?"

"Yes, I'll marry you. I love you. I choose you."

The words poured through him like molten honey. His heart filled with joy until he thought it would burst. He caught her mouth with his and kissed her soundly and thoroughly, in a way that didn't begin to express the depths of his love for her. He leaned back and smiled at her. "I've come home."

She wrapped her arms around his waist. "You need

to come to my home." She tilted her head toward the house up the lane.

Reality hit with a thud. "Your mother won't be pleased."

"Let's give her a chance." She withdrew her arms enough to take his hand. "Come on."

Sally clung to his side as they strode toward the house. The closer they got, the more tension she felt in his body. A tension that burned along her nerve endings. She'd made it clear to Mother she would only marry for love. No doubt Mother suspected it was Linc she loved, but she still trembled at facing her parent's disapproval.

All her life she had tried so hard to be good, to do what her parents wanted, to be compliant. But she was no longer a child, and she could not live a lie. "It will be okay," she said, as much for herself as Linc. "Mother will understand." *Oh, Lord, make her see I must follow my heart. And that Linc is a good man.*

They hesitated at the door. She turned to look into Linc's face, and love for him flooded her thoughts. Nothing else mattered. "Come on."

They stepped inside. Mother must have seen them coming, for she stood in the kitchen doorway waiting for them. A myriad of emotions crossed her expression—resistance and disapproval—but then she studied each of their faces and acceptance appeared.

"Come in. I'll make tea and you can tell me all about it." She turned back into the kitchen.

Sally grinned up at Linc. "She's giving her approval."

Linc's eyes blazed with joy, and he pulled her into

the hallway and kissed her quickly, then tucked her arm through his. "That's to remind you what's in here." He patted his chest to indicate his heart.

She imitated his gesture. "And what's in here."

Epilogue

May 24, 1935

Sally stood in the midst of the crowd, Linc at her side. It was the official opening of the Ogilvy Central Park. Mrs. Ogilvy had donated funds for a park in the heart of town. The town fathers had discussed what they wanted. But no one took action.

Then Linc had stepped forward with a design.

She leaned over to whisper in his ear. "I think it should have been called the McCoy Park. You did most of the work." He'd drawn up plans and presented them to a town meeting. There were those who wanted to dismiss his ideas because he was a McCoy, but Mrs. Ogilvy had silenced all criticism by announcing to one and all she bore no ill will toward the McCoys, and certainly none toward Linc. "He's an honorable man I consider myself privileged to know." Sally had heard her say those words before, as had a handful of women, but now the whole town heard them and knew Linc had Mrs. Ogilvy's approval.

After that, the majority were happy enough to let Linc volunteer to do the work.

He'd spent so many hours this spring leveling the ground, planting flower beds, putting in trees that Sally had started taking meals to him. Together they had sat in the half-developed park and talked about the future.

"You don't mind Grandmama living with us?" His words brought her back to the present.

"Of course not. Where else would she go?" She and Linc had discussed it extensively before their marriage, but as Sally said, it was her home. They were the intruders. "Besides, she's teaching me to do counted stitch pictures." One was a secret between Sally and Linc's grandmother. They'd used a photograph of Linc's parents taken shortly after their wedding, and Sally was turning it into a picture to give to Linc on their first anniversary.

Linc pulled her to his side, and from the look in his eyes she knew he would have kissed her if they weren't in such a public place. They'd married in late October and had enjoyed a blissful winter of learning more and more about each other.

"This couldn't have happened without the efforts of Linc McCoy," Mr. Reimer, spokesman for the town council, said, drawing both Linc and Sally's attention back to the ceremony. "Thank you, Linc. We consider you an asset to our community." A roar of agreement went up from the crowd.

Sally wrapped an arm about Linc and held tight.

She dare not look at him, knowing this acceptance and approval meant more to him than anyone but herself would ever know. "You deserve it," she whispered, then stood at his side as people filed by, shaking his hand and thanking him.

When the line of well wishers had passed, Linc draped an arm about her shoulders and smiled at her. "Are you happy, my sweet?"

"I'm happy and so proud I could almost burst."

Sally's mother stopped by. "You did us proud, Linc."

He dropped a kiss to her cheek. "Thank you, Mother Morgan. Your approval means a lot."

She lifted her face, a regretful expression pulling at her lips. "I'm sorry I ever misjudged you. I hope you won't hold it against me."

Linc grinned. "I've long since forgotten it. You should, too."

"Thank you." She patted his cheek. "Don't forget we're all getting together at my house for supper."

"We'll be there."

Sally's mother went to speak to Linc's grandmother.

Linc leaned close to whisper in Sally's ear. "We wouldn't miss it."

Their secret warm between them, Sally adored him with her eyes, knowing she could inform him with words and kisses how much she loved him when they were alone.

Later that day they gathered around the table at the Morgan home—Louisa, Emmet and the girls, who had come for a visit, Emmet's aunt, Madge and Judd and

Mother and Linc's grandmother—now as much a part of the family as anyone.

Mother looked around at her family. "I am so blessed. I have prayed for my girls to each find a good man, and God has honored me beyond my expectations."

Emmet cleared his throat. "We would like to make an announcement." He and Louisa looked at each other with such devotion, Sally's eyes stung with unshed tears to watch them. "We are going to adopt a baby. A young woman came to us and asked if we would take her child. The baby is due in September." The two little girls beamed so bright, Sally knew they were thrilled about the news.

Sally and Linc grinned at each other, then joined in congratulating the pair and asking questions.

A minute later, Judd signaled for quiet. "Madge and I have an announcement, too. We are having a baby in October. There'll be two cousins close in age."

Linc laughed. "Make it three. We're having a baby in October, too."

Mother lifted her hands in the air in a gesture of worship. "Three grandbabies at the same time. I am so blessed."

The three sisters echoed her sentiments, and the three cowboys-turned-husbands nodded agreement.

Later, after the dishes were done, the three sisters wandered outside.

"Babies together." Sally laughed, her heart full. Louisa and Madge laughed, too.

Sally studied her eldest sister. "If only you lived closer so the babies could grow up together. Like we did."

"Do you ever miss this place, Louisa?" Madge asked.

Louisa's expression was so serene that Sally knew her answer before she spoke. "I miss Mother and you two, but I wouldn't sacrifice a minute with Emmet. Besides, we'll come often to visit, and you must bring your babies to visit me."

Sally and Madge nodded agreement.

Madge turned to stare at the barn. "Do you think Father would be pleased if he could see us?"

Sally reached out and drew her sisters into a three-cornered hug. "He taught us well. Now it's up to us to live what he taught us and teach it to our children."

Louisa kissed Sally's cheek and grinned across at Madge. "When did our little sister become so wise?"

Madge chuckled. "When she learned to listen to her heart and welcome a cowboy home."

Sally nodded agreement, and then, arms entwined, the girls returned to the house and their loved ones. Sally's heart felt ready to burst with joy, and she guessed from the expressions on her sisters' faces that they shared her happiness.

She could ask for nothing better.

* * * * *

 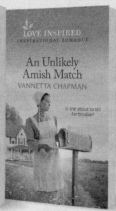

SPECIAL EXCERPT FROM

🌿

LOVE INSPIRED
INSPIRATIONAL ROMANCE

What happens when a beautiful foster mom claims an Oklahoma rancher as her fake fiancé?

Read on for a sneak preview of
The Rancher's Holiday Arrangement
by Brenda Minton.

"I am so sorry," Daisy told Joe as they walked down the sidewalk together.

The sun had come out and it was warm. The kind of day that made her long for spring.

"I don't know that I need an apology," Joe told her. "But an explanation would be a good start."

She shook her head. "I saw you sitting with your family, and I knew how I'd feel. Ambushed."

"I could have handled it. Now I'm engaged." He tossed her a dimpled grin. "What am I supposed to tell them when I don't have a wedding?"

"I got tired of your smug attitude and left you at the altar?" she asked, half teasing. "Where are we walking to?"

"I'm not sure. I guess the park."

"The park it is," she told him.

Daisy smiled down at the stroller. Myra and Miriam belonged with their mother, Lindsey. Daisy got to love them for a short time and hoped that she'd made a difference.

"It'll be hard to let them go," Joe said.

LIEXP1120

"It will be," Daisy admitted. "I think they'll go home after New Year's."

"That's pretty soon."

"It is. We have a court date next week."

"I'm sorry," Joe said, reaching for her hand and giving it a light squeeze.

"None of that has anything to do with what I've done to your life. I've complicated things. I'm sorry. You can tell your parents I lost my mind for a few minutes. Tell them I have a horrible sense of humor and that we aren't even friends. Tell them I wanted to make your life difficult."

"Which one is true?" he asked.

"Maybe a combination," she answered. "I *do* have a horrible sense of humor. I *did* want to mess with you."

"And the part about us not being friends?"

"Honestly, I don't know what we are."

"I'll take friendship," he told her. "Don't worry, Daisy, I'm not holding you to this proposal."

She laughed and so did he.

"Good thing. The last thing I want is a real fiancé."

"I know I'm not the most handsome guy, but I'm a decent catch," he said.

She ignored the comment about his looks. The last thing she wanted to admit was that when he smiled, she forgot herself just a little.

Don't miss
The Rancher's Holiday Arrangement *by Brenda Minton,*
available November 2020 wherever
Love Inspired books and ebooks are sold.

LoveInspired.com

LOVE INSPIRED
INSPIRATIONAL ROMANCE

UPLIFTING STORIES OF FAITH, FORGIVENESS AND HOPE.

Join our social communities to connect with other readers who share your love!

Sign up for the Love Inspired newsletter at **LoveInspired.com** to be the first to find out about upcoming titles, special promotions and exclusive content.

CONNECT WITH US AT:

Facebook.com/LoveInspiredBooks

Twitter.com/LoveInspiredBks

Facebook.com/groups/HarlequinConnection

Get 4 FREE REWARDS!

We'll send you 2 FREE Books plus 2 FREE Mystery Gifts.

Love Inspired books feature uplifting stories where faith helps guide you through life's challenges and discover the promise of a new beginning.

FREE
Value Over
$20